Bardstown

By

Sissy Marlyn

Copyediting by: Robert Ritchie

BEARHEAD PUBLISHING

- BhP -

Louisville, Kentucky
www.bearheadpublishing.com/sissy.html

Bardstown

By Sissy Marlyn

Copyediting by: Robert Ritchie

Cover Design by Bearhead Publishing
First Printing - August 2006
ISBN: 0-9776260-4-0

Disclaimer
This book is a work of fiction. The characters, names, places, and
incidents are used fictitiously and are a product of the author's
imagination. Any resemblance of actual persons, living or dead is entirely
coincidental.

Proudly printed in the United States of America

BARDSTOWN

TAKE

TIME

BHP

1

11/3/07

DATE

DIRECTOR   Sandy

PRODUCED BY   Sissy Marilyn

Enjoy !

Other Novels by Sissy Marlyn:

Her first trilogy – the "I" Series
Intimacies
Illusions
Indecisions

Her first murder mystery – the "Jury Pool" Series
Jury Pool – Summons to Die

To order: www.bearheadpublishing.com/sissy.html

Acknowledgements

Thanks to the following individuals, places, and things that helped to make *Bardstown* become a reality:

Bowling Green, Kentucky – A place I've always loved to visit.

Barren River Lake and State Park – Doesn't everyone love going to the lake? This park is a great place to visit.

Mariah's 1818 – A fine, historical restaurant, with delicious food, right in the heart of Bowling Green, Kentucky's charming downtown area.

MGM – Disney World, Lake Buena Vista, Florida – For planting the seed that became this novel.

Bardstown, Kentucky – A city steeped in rich history and tradition. Another town I love to visit.

1980's Recording Artists and Their Hit Music – Inspired by music I listened to and enjoyed as a teen and young adult.

1980's Film and Television Stars – Inspired by movies/television shows I watched and loved as a teen and young adult.

Mann's Chinese Theatre, Hollywood, California – Visited a few years ago. A great place!

Culver City Soundstage, Culver City, California – Home of the *Bonanza* television series.

Dedication

To Nalla Cat for faithfully getting me up in the morning and leading me to the PC to write. For your purring encouragement of each and every line.

To my ever faithful and continually expanding reader base. You are the reason I continue to write. Your unwavering encouragement touches my heart!

To my Bearhead for tirelessly turning out such wonderful novels and for his love and support. What a lovable 'bear'head he is!

The Cast

Elizabeth Warren (Liz) – Beautiful, talented, young woman who lives to dream. Her dreams: To become a famous actress and to meet, marry and have children with a man she truly love.

Alan Michaels (Alan) – Handsome, responsible, new man in town with a bright future ahead of him. His dreams: To meet, marry, and have children with a woman he truly loves and to some day run his uncle's automobile dealership.

Jameson Thornton (James) – Ruggedly adorable, playboy actor who believes the world owes him everything. His dreams: To stay on top in the acting world and to possess anything, or anyone, that he wants. He will stop at nothing to obtain his goals.

The Plot

The "Bardstown" Triangle – How will Elizabeth's life be affected by these two very distinct men and their exceedingly different dreams? How will she decide which path to take and which dream to follow? Will the choices she makes forever condemn her future? Or will Elizabeth's most important dream come to pass

Chapter 1
Beginnings

*The bible tells us that in the beginning there was man,
and then God created woman to be with man.
One could argue that this means man is not truly complete
without woman in his life, and modern man still appears to
search for the woman who will make his world complete.*

~ Sissy Marlyn ~

T he second of two curtain calls, thundering applause, elevated cheers, and even a few loud whistles radiated from a packed, high school auditorium. A happy, smiling, young cast held hands and bowed to their adoring audience.

As the giant, red velvet curtain closed for the final time, and the auditorium illuminated, the noise in the room continued but transformed. Now, the sounds became people scrambling from their metal chairs, excitedly discussing the play, and swiftly filing out of the theater.

Backstage, Elizabeth Warren's curved lips stretched from ear to ear. She bounced up and down and shared congratulatory hugs with her equally enthusiastic and satisfied cast mates.

"That was wonderful, Elizabeth!" Her drama teacher, a short, chubby woman with outdated, pointy-framed glasses, bragged, giving Elizabeth a warm embrace. "You are truly a natural actress."

"Thank you, Mrs. Hodge," she replied with elation. "We couldn't have done it without you. You're a wonderful director!"

"Elizabeth's totally right. We for sure couldn't have done it without your phenomenal leadership, Mrs. Hodge," her best friend, Kathy Michaels, quickly acquiesced. She threw an arm around Elizabeth's shoulder and pulled her aside.

Having shared the lead with Elizabeth in the play *Grease*, Kathy looked the part of an actress – tall, blond, and curvaceous, with large, ocean-blue eyes. The extra stage makeup they wore brought out the brilliant blue in her eyes all the more.

"Thank you, girls," Mrs. Hodge responded with a wide smile. She spied another group of students approaching her, so she excused herself and scampered away to congratulate these others as well. They had all worked so hard on this play, and their hard work had more than paid off.

"Perfect as always, Liz," Kathy playfully told her friend. She continued to eagerly pull her closer to their makeshift dressing rooms – the girl's restrooms in the hallway. They needed to change out of their costumes. Kathy was dressed seductively in formfitting black leather, and Elizabeth donned a red V-neck blouse and pink shorts in fifties style.

"Why thank you, Katherine," Elizabeth teased, elevating her head and feigning a bad English accent. Regardless of her shorter height, Elizabeth threw a chummy arm around Kathy and fell into perfect stance with her. "I merely did what comes most natural to me."

As they proceeded through the backstage exit door, which connected directly to the bustling, main school hallway, Elizabeth spied her mother and father coming toward her through the crowd.

"Are we all going to get together at *Antonio's*?" she asked Kathy, lightheartedly waving to her parents.

"Of course!" Kathy confirmed with a happy laugh. Spotting her own mother searching for her through the horde of people, Kathy released Elizabeth from her grasp. "See you at *Antonio's*," she added, before impatiently rushing away to greet her mom.

"See ya," Elizabeth replied. She swirled from her friend's fleeing back to greet her own parents.

"Great job, sweetie," Elizabeth's father praised and pulled her against his large chest for several minutes.

When he released her, Elizabeth looked into her mother's icy blue eyes. Her eyes gave Elizabeth a blank, indifferent stare. Her mom's arms crossed, she made no change in her posture. There would be no hug from her mother. Elizabeth's feelings might have been hurt, but she did not expect affection, congratulations or praise from her mother. Her mom pegged acting an enormous waste of time, and she made no bones about this opinion.

However, Elizabeth's mother must have been intimidated by her daughter's and husband's expectant glares, because she did at least utter, "You did good, Elizabeth. I still don't see the purpose in it, but you did a good job pretending to be someone you aren't."

"Thanks," Elizabeth mumbled in reply.

She averted her eyes, so she did not have to look at her mother's disapproving grimace. Instead, Elizabeth focused on her father. Other than the female body and longer hair, Elizabeth looked a great deal like her father. She stood about the same height – five-six – and had light brown hair and green, almond-shaped eyes just like his. Elizabeth looked very little like her mom – bright auburn hair and blue eyes. They also differed vastly in personality. Elizabeth's mom was very uptight, and Elizabeth showcased her dad's laidback nature.

She could not help but notice her dad's reproachful glance at her mom. "I better be going. I need to go and change and get out of here. I'm supposed to join my friends at *Antonio's* for a celebration," she told her parents.

"That sounds nice. You go and have a good time," her dad instructed. He bent and kissed her cheek before affirming, "I'm very proud of you!"

"Thanks, Daddy," Elizabeth said, flashing him a wide, toothy grin. She also gave him another hug. "I'll be home by eleven."

"Have fun," he called.

Elizabeth skipped away through the crowd toward the restrooms.

* * * *

When Elizabeth arrived at *Antonio's*, she breathed in the familiar scent of fresh baked pizza and hurried to a room in the back where she and her friends religiously gathered. Two, long tables, covered by vinyl, red and white checkered tablecloths, resided in this room. Matching, cloth, red and white checkered curtains hung from two windows that looked out on a crowded parking lot. Lights, ornamented with an octagon, Coca-Cola, stained-glass cover, hung from the ceiling on a chain. This lighting made the room bright. A jukebox in one corner played a popular song, Men at Work's *Who Can It Be Now?*. In the other corner a *Ms. Pacman* machine stood. A few boys from school gathered around it, competing to see who would get the higher score.

Many simultaneous conversations brought a roar to the room. The voices seemed to be in direct competition with the jukebox. Elizabeth's eyes made a sweeping survey of those seated at the large tables.

The tables were practically full already. Elizabeth's eyes spied Kathy sitting at one. She also spotted an empty chair beside her friend. *She's saved me a seat*, Elizabeth recognized with gratitude. A man, who Elizabeth had not seen in four years, sat on the other side of Kathy's empty chair – Kathy's cousin, Alan Michaels.

Elizabeth guided her legs toward the empty chair between Kathy and Alan. "Hi, guys," she called in a friendly voice as she approached the table.

She could not help but stare into Alan's handsome, vivid, blue eyes. She noted he also studied her as she approached. Elizabeth allowed her mind to travel back in time to when she was fourteen, and had her first real crush on a cute, eighteen-year-old boy. That boy had been Alan Michaels. The same mesmerizing eyes and luminous, blond hair now belonged to a strikingly handsome man. Forcing her eyes to look away from Alan, Elizabeth slid the chair away from the table, sat down, and propelled her chair back up to the table.

"You were totally rad tonight in the play, Elizabeth," her friend Michelle gushed. She sat across the table.

"Thanks!" Elizabeth replied with a glorious smile.

"For sure! I'll totally second that," her friend Laura chipped in. She sat on the other side of Michelle.

"Don't you just totally feel like a star now?" Kathy kidded with a playful chuckle. "Is that why it took you so long to get here? Were you, like, being fashionably late?"

"For sure! You know it," Elizabeth played along with a giggle.

"Anyway…I'm so glad you finally joined us," Kathy said. Then she added, "My cousin Alan has been waiting to see you again. Do you remember him? He spent about three weeks at my house the summer before we started high school."

Do I remember Alan? To Elizabeth, this was a silly question. However, she had never shared her crush on him with Kathy. They had been too young. It had been her private secret.

"Hi, Alan," she greeted a little shyly with a warm smile. Sitting beside him, his perfect face seemed almost a little too close. The smell of his musk cologne delighted her nostrils. "Where have you been hiding yourself? How come you never visited Kathy again? I remember you sharing her pool with us and pulling my pigtails."

"I remember that too," he reminisced, returning her smile. He had glistening, straight, white teeth.

Elizabeth fondly remembered his mischievous smile as well. Alan had worn it a great majority of the time. He had delighted in teasing Kathy and her. She also recalled him making a perfect, human diving board of himself. She and Kathy had taken turns being expertly hoisted into the air and then playfully plunging head first into the water. Alan's young arms and legs had been strong even then, but they were large and bulky with muscle now.

Of course, why shouldn't they be? After all, Alan is a grown man now, and what a sexy man he has become. Elizabeth looked away from him again. She felt very flustered all at once.

"I see you're not wearing your tempting pigtails any more," Alan spoke again. "Your hair is lighter than what I remember, but it's still certainly long enough for a few fun pigtails to pull." He chuckled then, and he boldly reached to take a few strands of her hair into one of his hands.

"So what brings you to town again after so much time?" She changed the subject. Her spine still tingled from the gentle brush of Alan's hand in her hair.

"I just moved here this week from Lexington," he briefly explained. "So you may be seeing a lot more of me from now on."

I hope, Elizabeth wished. Her heart skipped a beat at the knowledge Alan would be living in Bowling Green now. She had to tell herself to calm down. *Just because Alan is living in town doesn't mean he's interested in seeing me.*

Before she had a chance to reply to Alan's good news, Kathy chimed in, "Alan graduated from U of K last week. He is going to help my dad run the auto dealership. He just got his business degree."

"Awesome!" Elizabeth chirped. *Maybe I should take my car to the service department of that dealership soon for a tune up or something. I could visit with Alan while they are working on my car.*

"And Alan, you'll be pleased to know Elizabeth is going to be a world famous actress," Kathy bragged, giving her friend a rough, though affectionate, shove in the back. The unexpected push propelled Elizabeth's upper body in Alan's direction, bringing her face dangerously close to his.

"I can just about believe that. As your friends said, you were terrific tonight," Alan complimented. His eyes danced in amusement over Kathy's obvious instigation. "I really enjoyed watching your play."

"Thanks," Elizabeth modestly replied and blushed under his admiring gaze. She looked down in embarrassment.

She's cute, Alan thought. *A little young maybe, but still cute.* He debated for only a second before he reached in his back pocket and pulled out his wallet. Opening it, he began searching for something.

Elizabeth raised her head and watched him out of the corner of her eye. *I wonder what he's looking for.*

Alan finally pulled forth a business card from his uncle's auto dealership. Turning it face down, he held it out toward Elizabeth and asked with a mischievous snigger, "Could I have your autograph? Then, one day when you become a big Hollywood star, I can prove I knew you when."

Elizabeth took the business card from his hand. She laid it on the table in front of her. She pulled forth her purse, found a pen, and with a conniving giggle, scribbled her name on the card. Under her autograph, she bravely jotted down her phone number.

"Here's my autograph. I also wrote down my phone number. In case you get lonely in this new place, I could try to show you around," she suggested.

She's flirting with me, he noted. "Hmm...well now...I just might need a lot of showing around," he replied with a slight snicker, taking the card back.

As he slid it from Elizabeth's hand, Alan gazed directly into her eyes. In response, Elizabeth's body inwardly trembled.

"We only have one more week of school, and then Elizabeth is free all summer," Michelle contributed from across the table, glancing at Laura and Kathy with a conspiratorial giggle.

Elizabeth's face grew intensely warm once more, so she broke eye contact with Alan. She had never felt so extremely self-conscious around a guy before. Maybe it had something to do with the fact that she had had a crush on Alan for many years, or more likely the fact that he was drop-dead gorgeous.

Alan smiled. A sure sign of her attraction to him, he liked that Elizabeth was so flustered by him.

The pizzas her friends had ordered before Elizabeth arrived were delivered to their table. "Good! I'm, like, starving," Laura commented, reaching for the pizza closest to her.

Kathy reached for another pizza, between her and Michelle. As everyone filled their plates, they all seemed to concentrate on eating, and the conversation amongst everyone temporarily lulled. Time seemed to fly after that.

Before Elizabeth realized it, the hands on the wall clock pointed to almost eleven. She had not gotten a chance to talk to Alan again, because she had been eating and talking to Laura, Michelle, Kathy and other classmates. Time for her to start for home, Elizabeth told Kathy, Michelle and Laura, "I've got to motor. I told my parents I would be home by eleven,"

She briefly looked over at Alan. Appearing to have a hardy appetite, he finished off his fourth piece of pizza.

"I need to go too," Kathy agreed. They both slid their chairs out and stood.

"I'll see you guys at school tomorrow," Michelle said, waving.

"See ya," Elizabeth and Kathy said almost in unison.

"Bye guys," Laura also said.

Alan looked up at both of them then.

"Thanks for coming and celebrating with us, Alan," Kathy addressed him.

"It was my pleasure, cuz," he said with a radiant smile. He stood and gave Kathy a small hug. "You guys drive safe going home."

"It was awesome seeing you again, Alan. I'm stoked that you came tonight," Elizabeth added. She awkwardly stood beside Alan and Kathy. *I wish he would give me a hug too.*

"It was great seeing you again too, Elizabeth," he said. "You take care."

He's dismissing me, she thought with disappointment. *I should have talked more to him. But maybe he just isn't interested. After all, he just graduated from college, and I'm only finishing high school.* "See ya," she said and scampered away, heading across the room. Kathy quickly fell into pace beside her.

Elizabeth raced from the backroom, through the front of the restaurant, and past tables filled with other customers. She pushed open the front door, and bolted out into the night, with Kathy right behind her. The parking lot was brightly lit by strategically placed security lights.

"What are you trying to do…run a race?" Kathy asked as she drew up beside her friend and scurried toward Elizabeth's car.

"I'm so sure," Elizabeth said with a giggle. "I was just…I need to get home," she lied. *I needed to get away from Alan. From his rejection.*

"You're spazzing on my cousin, aren't you?" Kathy dared to ask, giving her friend another playful shove.

"He's cute, for sure. I noticed that. But I don't think he's into me," Elizabeth shared her discontent, reaching in her purse to retrieve her car keys. They were standing beside her car.

"Why do you think that? He's totally into you. He put the card with your telephone number in his wallet, didn't he? That was a gnarly move by the way. I liked that."

"Thanks," Elizabeth chuckled. "Do you really think Alan will call me?"

"For sure," Kathy assured her. "I kept seeing him glance at you when you weren't looking. I saw you doing the same to him too." She giggled again.

"Well...he isn't hard to look at."

"Neither are you," Kathy stated.

"You don't think the difference in our ages will be a problem?" she asked, fidgeting with her keys. She watched a man and a woman with kids, get into their car across the way.

"I'm so sure. What's four years? You'll be eighteen in a month. You'd think Alan was in his thirties or something to hear you ask that."

"I so hope you are totally right," Elizabeth confided.

"So you do want Alan to call you?" Kathy prodded. She was leaning against Elizabeth's car now.

"For sure! Your cousin is a major hunk!" she confessed her attraction.

"And you've totally been into him forever."

"How did you know that?" Elizabeth questioned.

"I could tell. You looked like you wanted him to pack you in his suitcase when he visited when we were younger. You had a major crush on him. Now, you're both grown. I think the two of you would make a rad couple."

"Well, let's hope Alan thinks the same thing," Elizabeth said. She unlocked her car door. "See ya tomorrow at school. Don't you dare say a word to Alan about any of this."

"I'm so sure I would do that," Kathy rebutted. *But I might find ways to get the two of you together again if he doesn't call you right away.* "I'll see you tomorrow. Don't dream too much of Alan tonight," Kathy teased, starting away toward her own car, which was a few parking spaces down.

"Hey, Kathy. Wait up," Ricky, one of the guys in their class, called. He was walking across the parking lot toward her.

"I might be a little late getting home," Kathy said with a chuckle, winking at Elizabeth.

"For sure," Elizabeth snickered, shaking her head. Kathy enjoyed playing the field. "Bye," Elizabeth said, and got into her car.

She watched as Kathy and Ricky walked off toward Kathy's car. Elizabeth smiled and shook her head again. As she drove off, she thought about Alan once more. *I really do hope he calls me.*

Chapter 2
The Call

A telephone call received from someone we are attracted to —
true bliss!

~ Sissy Marlyn ~

The next day after school, Elizabeth had to force herself to concentrate on her homework. She sat at her desk in her room, pen in hand, attempting to write an essay for an English class. A telephone on her bedside table across the room held her attention. She kept looking longingly at this phone every so often, as if her magical glances could somehow make it ring. Almost dinnertime before Elizabeth finished all her assignments, the telephone rang at last.

Her heart began to race. She sprang with lightning speed from her desk chair, leaving it tottering back and forth. She dashed across the room toward the telephone. She prayed it not be someone calling for her mother. Her friends usually called later, so she doubted it would be one of them. There was only one other person she could think it could be.

"I got it, Mom!" she yelled, snatching the receiver from its cradle in the middle of its second ring. "Hello," she answered in a shaky voice, pressing the phone close to her ear. She waited impatiently for a reply.

"Hello. Is this Elizabeth, the tour guide?" She heard a deep, male voice ask. Her heart leapt for joy as she realized her dream came true – Alan called her!

"A...A...Alan?" She stammered, having a horrible time making her mouth function. Still in shock, part of her had believed Alan would never call. She sat down on the side of her bed.

"Yes, last time I checked that was my name," he teased with a hearty chuckle. Then he added, "I was wondering if you might be available to give me a tour of the town this evening."

Elizabeth wanted to shout the word 'Yes!' in Alan's ear. She could barely contain her brimming excitement. *He really wants to see me again!*

"For sure," she answered at last, tempering her voice so as not to sound overly eager. She did not want to scare him off or sound like an inexperienced kid.

"Great. How does six o'clock sound to you? Maybe we can grab some dinner while we are out," he suggested. "You live down the street from Kathy, don't you?"

"Six sounds awesome," Elizabeth replied in a chipper voice. "I actually live a street over from Kathy. I used to ride my bike to her house. The address is 2422 Skyview. Do you need directions?"

"No. I've passed Skyview on the way to Kathy's, so I think I can find you. I'll see you shortly," he said, bringing their conversation to a close.

"See ya," Elizabeth dreamily agreed. After she hung up the phone, she sat mesmerized for a few more seconds, as if Alan had cast a spell on her. When the entrancement eventually subsided, she sprang to her feet and skipped off toward the living room to tell her parents she had a date tonight. *The most important date of my life*, she thought to herself.

After getting her parent's permission to go out, Elizabeth showered, and changed clothes numerous times. She finally settled on a pair of Jordache jeans, a thin, green, V-neck sweater with shoulder pads and her stylish Duck Shoes. She spent well over an hour fixing her hair, styling it with hot rollers, picking it out to it utmost fullness and making sure it stayed set with a ton of hairspray. She meticulously applied her make-up – foundation, a modest amount of blush, green eye shadow, mascara, and a glossy maroon lipstick. Lastly, she applied some Love's Baby Soft perfume to her wrists.

When she finally emerged, about quarter till six, she still was not certain she was satisfied with the way she looked. Never before had Elizabeth been so unconfident. On the other hand, never had a date been this important to her.

She allowed herself a moment to ponder this date's grand significance. *Is it because Alan is the only guy I've ever dated who isn't still in high school? Or is it because of an age old crush?* She honestly did not know. The only thing Elizabeth knew for certain was she had not been this unsettled about going out with a guy since her first date.

Trying to put her fears aside, she joined her parents in the living room to wait for Alan's arrival. Alan showed up at six sharp. Elizabeth's mother answered the door.

"A gentleman comes inside to pick a lady up for a date," she explained to Elizabeth, making her wait in the living room with her father.

After introducing herself to Alan, Elizabeth's mother brought him into the living room to join Elizabeth and her father. Elizabeth's heart sped as she watched him approach. He looked scrumptious. He was clean-shaven. His short, glistening, blond hair was perfectly combed. He was dressed in tan Dockers and a long-sleeved, light blue dress shirt, which brought out his dazzling blue eyes all the more.

Alan had come directly from work. He would also have been wearing a navy tie, but he had discarded this item in the car. After shaking Elizabeth's dad's hand in greeting, Alan had a seat beside Elizabeth on the large, Old English couch. Elizabeth noted the pleasant smell of his cologne once again.

Elizabeth's mother sat in one of the two, brown, Lazy Boy recliners at a right angle to them. Her dad had a seat in the other recliner. Elizabeth's mom wasted no time beginning her inquisition. "So, Alan, Elizabeth tells us you are Kathy's cousin and you just moved here from Lexington. She also said you recently graduated from U of K, and you are now a manager at Kathy's father's auto dealership."

Elizabeth's insides knotted up. She would be glad when Alan passed her parents' – most especially her mother's – oral exam and they could be on their way. She went through this regime with every new boy that came to the house to date her.

"Yes, ma'am," Alan replied. He kept eye contact with her even though she stared holes through him. Elizabeth's mother would have been pretty – mid-length, shiny, auburn hair and profound blue eyes. But deep frown lines around her mouth made her look tense and unhappy.

"Why'd you move? Weren't there auto dealerships you could have managed in Lexington?" she continued to question, squeezing the arms of the recliner.

Elizabeth cringed. *She makes it sound like Alan is some sort of criminal fleeing Lexington.*

"There are lots of auto dealerships in Lexington," Alan replied, unruffled. "But I would have had to work my way up from the bottom. My uncle is giving me a great opportunity here, so it was worth moving."

"Sounds like a smart move to me," Elizabeth's father agreed. Her father, a tad on the overweight side, had a rounded belly and full face. When he smiled, as he did now, he looked like a big lovable softy.

Score: Alan – 1; Mom – 0, Elizabeth mused, wringing her hands as she awaited her mom's next inane question.

"So there are no special ladies from college pining for you in Lexington?" her mom had the gull to ask.

Interested in the answer to this one, Elizabeth now wondered, *Does he have a girlfriend in Lexington?*

"No, ma'am," Elizabeth heard him answer, relieved. "I dated a lot in college, but there was no one serious."

"There is nothing wrong with that. You are young. You have plenty of time to settle down," Elizabeth's father chimed in again.

Score: Alan – 2; Mom – 0. Way to go, Alan! Keep it up!

Elizabeth's mom pursed her lips at her husband and said to Alan, "I realize you are new in town, Alan, and probably haven't had time to meet any girls your own age. But Elizabeth is still in high school. I know a lot goes on at college, but we won't let our daughter be taken advantage of. I want to make sure this is understood."

Elizabeth felt her face begin to burn. *Oh, my God! I can't believe she said that to him.* Mortified, Elizabeth looked down at her feet, afraid to hear what Alan would say next. *He may just get up and leave. I couldn't really blame him. She made him sound like some sort of pervert. Why does she do this?*

"I have no intention of taking advantage of Elizabeth, Mrs. Warren," Alan assured her. "She offered to show me around town, and I decided to take her up on her offer."

"So this isn't a date?" she pressed.

Open up floor! I want to crawl in. Shut up, mother!

Alan glanced at Elizabeth. Glimpsing her embarrassment and struggle to maintain her composure, he felt sorry for her. But he could respect her mother for trying to protect her. After all, he was twenty-two and Elizabeth was only seventeen. *Am I making a mistake taking her out?* he could not help but wonder. She had been so cute at the restaurant the other night, sneaking her number to him; he had not been able to resist her offer.

"It *is* a date," Elizabeth was glad to hear him profess. "But we are *only* going out to get to know one another a little better, and Elizabeth is going to show me around town. Nothing more," he stressed. He made eye contact with her father now, surprised these questions were not coming from him. But Elizabeth's mother seemed to wear the pants in the household. Alan felt a little sorry for Elizabeth's father as well.

"That sounds good," Elizabeth's father sided with Alan again. "You kids have fun. We would like you to have Elizabeth home by eleven."

"That should not be a problem, sir," Alan assured him. He stood, walked over to Elizabeth's father and shook his hand again. Elizabeth's dad gave him a firm handshake and a friendly, unthreatening smile. *This must be where Elizabeth gets her happy, friendly nature*, Alan conjectured.

Alan walked over and offered his hand to Elizabeth's mother once more as well. Mrs. Warren hesitated a moment and then linked hands with him. She squeezed Alan's hand hard, as if to say, 'You hurt my daughter, and I'll crush you'. Her rigid facial expression relayed the same strong message.

The inquest appeared to be over. Elizabeth breathed a sigh of relief. "Are you ready to go?" she heard Alan ask.

She nodded as she sprang to her feet. She could not wait to get out of this house. Before they left, Alan amazed Elizabeth when he told her parents he enjoyed meeting them. *What? Does he like being tortured?* Elizabeth hated her mother's idiosyncrasies.

Most of the guys she dated seemed extremely uncomfortable enduring her mom's pointed questions. Alan, however, had seemed totally at ease. *Maybe it's because he's older*, Elizabeth contemplated.

Once settled in Alan's car – a year old, 1981 Monte Carlo – he turned to Elizabeth and asked with a smile, "Well, where are we going? What is the first thing in this town you would like for me to see?"

Where are we going? A sudden, slight panic registered in Elizabeth's mind. She had not decided where they would actually go. She had been so excited about them being together again she had not planned any further.

Since Alan genuinely seemed to want her to show him some places around town, she needed to come up with a place rather quickly. Elizabeth thought of the lake, but she wondered if going there would be asking for trouble.

She thought, with distaste, of some of the other boys she had dated that had taken her there without asking. She did not want to give Alan the wrong impression. But Elizabeth wanted to show Alan one of the most beautiful places in the Bowling Green area, and that was the lake. Not to mention, it would be a nice place to be alone with him for awhile.

She decided to ask, glancing rather shyly at him, "Have you ever seen Barren River Lake?"

"No," he answered, attentively studying her face. *She's cute as a button.* "But if you'll give me directions, I would like to."

"Gnarly!" she exclaimed, flashing him an enormous grin. "It's very easy to find. It's about forty miles away though. Is that okay?"

"That should be fine," Alan told her, starting the car and heading out.

After a few moments of silence, Elizabeth decided to make conversation. She asked, "So how do you like helping run your uncle's auto shop?"

"I like it a lot!" Alan admitted. His curved lips and dancing eyes effortlessly melted Elizabeth's insides. Safely focusing his eyes on the road again, he continued, "My uncle and I get along great. So for me, getting paid to help him run his business is just a bonus."

"That's the way I would feel if I ever got paid for acting," Elizabeth shared. "I know it may be lame, but I totally do want to be an actress. I'm going to go to college and get a degree in education, because I know it's virtually impossible to make it as an actress. But I guess I can teach drama if nothing else."

"That doesn't sound silly to me at all," he argued, allowing himself another quick glimpse of her face. "I really meant it last night when I said you did a great job with your play. I think you are really talented, along with being very pretty."

Alan's appreciative compliments and his dreamy eyes caused Elizabeth to blush again. "I'm sorry," Alan apologized, reacting to her obvious discomfiture. "I didn't mean to embarrass you. I figured you were used to being told you were pretty."

Elizabeth could only self-consciously giggle in reply, and the two settled into silence again, each lost in their own thoughts for the moment. *He* is *attracted to me*, she concluded with delight.

A few minutes later, Alan broke the silence asking her about high school and how she liked it. They casually conversed about things in both their lives for the remainder of the drive. When they got to the turnoff for the lake, Elizabeth explained, "This is the road to Barren River Lake. It's a 10,000-acre lake. There are 2,000 acres of hardwood forest and rolling green hills. There's an 18-hole championship golf course, miles of wooded trails, spots for picnicking, a campground, a restaurant, lodge and marina. Folks fish here year-round. At the end of this month, after Memorial Day, there is swimming at the beach and paddleboats, and even horseback riding if you enjoy riding horses."

"It just so happens I like to do just about all of that. I'm not a golfer, but I like to hike, picnic, camp, swim, fish, and ride horses," he confessed. He locked eyes with her and displayed a comfortable smile once more. "How about you? I know you used to love to swim."

"No duh. I still love to swim," she admitted with a warm chuckle, enjoying his reminiscing. "And I totally like to camp. My dad used to bring my mom and me up here a lot when I was younger. I've never been on a horse though."

"One of my uncles in Lexington owns a horse farm, so I grew up riding horses," Alan explained, adding with a twinkle in his eyes, "If you'd like to learn to ride, I'm sure I could teach you."

Elizabeth permitted her own eyes to linger a moment longer with Alan's. She vividly imagined her and Alan riding together on a horse though the surrounding woods. As she pictured his big, strong arms wrapped around her, as they galloped along, something stirred deep within her. "That'd be gnarly," she replied, suddenly breathless. She broke all eye contact and began trying to dispel the picturesque image floating in her mind.

As Alan steered the car over the hill, the lake came into view. With the sun setting, it looked beautiful even to Elizabeth, who had seen it many times. The greenish-blue water sparkled, as if it contained millions of tiny diamonds, and the rose and orange sky fell to perfectly intermingle with it. The new, spring leaves on the trees glowed a brilliant green.

"There are some picnic tables down by the water if you would like to get out of the car," she informed Alan, pointing in their general direction.

"Getting out of this car for awhile sounds good to me." She was grateful to hear Alan say. "Maybe we could go for a walk down by the water."

Elizabeth realized, within the next fifteen minutes, the sun would be hidden by the trees. Then it would get fairly dark down by the lake. Regardless, she felt she could trust Alan to take care of them both. "A walk sounds like the ticket," she agreed.

Alan had already pulled his Monte Carlo into a parking space by the picnic area. He got out of the car and walked around to Elizabeth's door. He opened her door, and she scrambled from the car.

Alan pulled her hand into his, leading her closer to the lake. At that particular moment, it felt so utterly fitting Elizabeth would have allowed Alan Michaels to lead her anywhere. She wished the night would never end, and it had only begun.

Minutes later, as they strolled along the bank in silence, Elizabeth settled in close to Alan's side. As he stared out into the water, Elizabeth studied his handsome, intent profile. Watching strands of his shiny, blond hair rise with the gentle breeze, Elizabeth could not help but envision running her fingers through it. She forced herself to look away, embarrassed by the wild thoughts flowing freely through her mind.

They had only been walking a short time before the sun disappeared behind the tress, bringing dark shadows to everything. Alan came to a stop, turning to focus his full attention on Elizabeth. "Well, unfortunately, it's getting dark. We better start back. The last thing I want is for you to stumble over something and hurt yourself," he said. Placing a supporting arm behind her lower back, he turned them both.

"We'll have to come back again when we have more time," he suggested as he led them back toward the car. "I'm glad you chose this spot to show me first. If you don't make it as an actress, an excellent second career for you would be a tour guide."

Elizabeth's heart skipped a beat. As if the touch of Alan's brawny arm along her tingling back were not enough to speed her heart, hearing yet another invitation from him to spend more time together sent it racing off the scale. She yearned to know if Alan really wished to spend more time with her or if he just made idle conversation.

They strolled back toward the car, each intently studying the ground in front of them for hidden obstacles. When they reached the car, Alan walked Elizabeth to her door. He unlocked her car door and pulled it open. Elizabeth reluctantly climbed inside the car. She did not want to leave yet. She enjoyed her time alone with Alan.

Alan shut Elizabeth's door and made his way back to the driver's side of the car. He promptly joined her inside. "Are you ready to go?" he asked, settling behind the steering wheel and sticking the key in the ignition.

"Could we, like, sit here and talk some more?" Elizabeth proposed.

A strange silence reigned in the car for a moment, with only the clinking of keys as Alan toyed with his keychain. Alan finally spoke, saying, "I want to be truthful with you, Elizabeth. I've really enjoyed being with you tonight. And, I think, if all you truly want to do right now is talk, maybe we better go someplace like *Antonio's*, where it's light and we would have other people around us. Because if we sit here in the dark, with the way I'm feeling right now, I will have a hard time keeping my hands off of you."

Touched by Alan's honest profession, Elizabeth found it new and refreshing. Usually, guys would bring her to the lake and just start pawing her. Then they would get angry when she asked them to stop. Since she had run into this problem time and time again, she did not have a steady boyfriend.

"I'm sorry, Elizabeth," Alan apologized, removing his hands from his jangling keys. He mistook her prolonged silence for anger. "I guess you think I'm a creep now. I didn't mean to come across that way. It's just that I'm attracted to you...and you smell great...and sitting in this secluded, dark spot tempts me to do more than just talk."

"I don't think you are a creep at all, Alan!" Elizabeth refuted, pulling her seatbelt around her. It clicked as it latched. "Quite the opposite. You can't imagine how much I appreciate your straightforwardness. It for sure attracts me to you that much more."

"I'm glad to hear that. So what do you say we head out?" Alan proposed.

"Yeah. I think we should," Elizabeth admitted with disappointment. Part of her wanted to stay in this private spot with Alan and steal a kiss – or two.

Starting the car engine, and turning on the radio, Alan asked, "How about we get some dinner? *Antonio's* again maybe?"

"Sounds like a rad idea to me," Elizabeth agreed, happily settling back against her leather seat and enjoying the song which was playing – Human's League's *Don't You Want Me Baby*. At least her evening with Alan was not going to end, even if she would not have him all to herself. He seemed like such a great guy, and Elizabeth did not want to do anything to blow things with him. *So off to Antonio's we go!* she accepted.

Chapter 3
First Kiss

Nothing is ever as important, or as nerve-wracking for that matter, than a first kiss from that all special guy.

~ Sissy Marlyn ~

They spent the rest of their first date in engrossing conversation at *Antonio's*, sharing pizza and facts about one another's lives. Elizabeth's heart ached when Alan revealed his mother had been killed in a car accident, by a drunk driver, when he was thirteen. She reached across the table and squeezed his hand in sympathy, and Alan seemed touched by her caring nature.

Noticing the time, 10:30, he asked, "Do you think we could do something again tomorrow night? Or have you got plans already?"

"No, I don't," Elizabeth admitted, without hesitation. Thrilled by the prospect of spending another evening with Alan, she rattled, "Do you like to dance? There's a gnarly under-21 dance club in the heart of town. Or we could for sure do something else, if you don't like to dance, or don't want to be around a bunch of teenagers."

"Dancing sounds great to me. As far as it being an under-21 club, it will be kind of nice to go dancing without alcohol all around. I'm not much of a drinker," he revealed. "What time does the dance club open?"

"At eight. And it closes at eleven," she informed him.

"Then how about I pick you up at seven and we get a bite to eat first?" Alan suggested with a friendly smile.

"That sounds awesome!" Elizabeth chirped, her eyes twinkling.

"Okay. That's all settled then. I better get you home. I don't want to upset your folks…"

"Yeah. I know they are a little overbearing. I'm sorry about that."

"They just care about you, that's all," Alan responded, as they scooted out of their booth and stood. "You are young, and there are a lot of jerks out there."

"For sure. I'm not all that young. I'll be eighteen in a month. I've met a lot of those jerks you just mentioned," Elizabeth volunteered, as she walked by Alan's side toward for the door .

"Oh, is that so?" Alan chuckled, opening the door for her.

"Yes," she confirmed, stepping outside. She waited on the walkway as Alan continued to hold the door for some people entering the restaurant. When he walked out, joining her again, Elizabeth smiled and said, "I like you, Alan. You seem different."

"I'm not all that different," he admitted as they walked across the parking lot to his car.

"Why do you say that?" Elizabeth questioned, stopping by the passenger door.

Alan unlocked her door and pulled it open. "Hold that thought," he said as he watched her slide inside the car. He shut her door and went around to his side of the car and climbed inside with her. After he started the engine, he picked their conversation back up. "I was seventeen once. And I behaved the exact same way as these 'jerks' you are talking about. They have only one thing on their minds, right?"

"Yeah. For sure," she confirmed. "So are you saying you *don't*?"

He had backed the car out and headed across the parking lot. He stopped to wait for cars to clear so he could pull out onto the street. He looked over at Elizabeth and said, "I'm not going to lie to you, Elizabeth. It's still pretty high on my list. But…" He looked out the windshield as he pulled out onto the street and headed toward her house. "I'm not looking for that with you."

"Why not me?" Elizabeth surprised herself by asking. *What is wrong with me? I sound like I'm saying I want him to be.*

Alan laughed then. "I didn't mean that the way it came out. I just meant I'm not in any hurry with you. I don't intend to force myself on you, like some of those 'jerks' you mentioned. I just want to hang out and get to know one another. How's that sound?"

"Awesome!" she cooed.

"Good," Alan said.

When they got to her house, Alan got out of the car and came around to open her door. Very pleased and impressed with his manners, so far, Elizabeth liked everything about Alan Michaels. She hated for their night to end.

Alan walked Elizabeth up the sidewalk to the door, past the picture window. Moonlight, a porch lamp, and the flash of a television screen from inside, lit their path. As he took both her hands into his, Elizabeth insides quivered. *Is he going to kiss me?* she wondered. *I hope so*, she wished.

"I really enjoyed tonight, Elizabeth, and look forward to seeing you again tomorrow. Thanks for being my tour guide, and for being such a sweet girl. You've really grown into quite a fine lady."

"Thanks," she said with a slight giggle, embarrassed by his compliments, even though they made her day.

Alan began to draw near. Elizabeth's heart hammered in her chest. She was nervous and expectant all at the same time. *Kiss me!* her mind pleaded.

Alan did kiss her, but only on the cheek. However, he held her in a long embrace, caressing her back. He could feel Elizabeth's heart pounding. It made him want to kiss her like a woman should be kissed, on the lips, but he would not allow himself. *Slow! She's young. Take it slow*, he cautioned himself. "You have a great night. I'll see you tomorrow," Alan said, slowly releasing her from his embrace.

"Y…you too, Alan," Elizabeth replied in an unsteady voice. She could still feel his arms around her, and she wanted to be held by him again. Shaken by her overpowering attraction to this man, she uttered, "See ya."

Alan merely smiled and waved, as he started down the sidewalk to his car. Elizabeth did not open the door and go inside until she watched Alan climb into his car and back out of the driveway. She waved one last time, and he blinked his headlights at her. She felt all warm and toasty inside as she entered the house and ended her first date with the most incredible guy she had ever met.

* * * *

Elizabeth's bliss abruptly ceased. She skidded to a halt as she almost ran directly into her mother on the other side of the door. "Mom," she gasped. "What were you doing by the door?"

"What do you think I might have been doing? I was watching you and your new boyfriend," she confessed without disgrace.

"No duh. Why would you do that?" Elizabeth questioned in disbelief, pushing the door shut.

"Because I wanted to make sure your college graduate kept his hands to himself," her mother also revealed with frankness.

"Alan was...like...a perfect gentleman, mother. A lot more than I can say for the majority of high school dweebs I've gone out with. He asked me out again tomorrow night. He wants to take me to the under-21 club in town."

"Why would a young man of drinking age want to go to an underage club?" her mother grilled, skepticism written all over her face.

"Because he isn't into drinking. Alan is totally awesome, mom. You should give him a chance before you condemn him."

I bet he would like for me to give him a chance. Something is fishy about an older man wanting to date a high school girl. This Alan is up to something, her mother suspected. She intended to keep a close eye on him. She had been deadly serious when she had told him she would not allow him to take advantage of her daughter. She had been young once. She knew how impressionable young girls could be.

"Is daddy still up?" Elizabeth asked.

"Of course. You know we both always wait up to see that you get in alright."

Elizabeth knew her mother always kept a close eye out. Although this date comprised the first time her mom had ever watched her out the front door. This behavior made Elizabeth very ill at ease.

What would she have done if Alan had given me a passionate kiss? Would she have charged out the door and told him to leave? Suddenly extremely worried about her *next* date, Elizabeth hoped and prayed there would be one. She realized she needed to get her father's acquiescence. He was usually on her side, and she believed he would be this time as well.

She went into the living room. Her mother followed closely behind. "Well, how was your first date, sweetheart?" her dad asked with a smile. He had been watching the beginning of the eleven o'clock news. A twenty-five inch RCA television, in a cherry cabinet, sat against the wall directly across the room from his and her mom's recliners. *She's home right on time*, her father noted, glancing at the pendulum clock on the wall over the fireplace on the other side of the room.

"My first date with Alan was awesome, daddy," she purred. She took a bouncing seat on the couch. "Alan was a perfect gentleman. He opened my car door every time, and he only kissed me on the cheek. He asked me to go out again tomorrow. He wants to take me to the under-21 club. Is it okay?" she wasted no time asking.

Elizabeth saw her father look to her mother for her advice. Her mother still stood in the entranceway to the living room. Her arms were crossed and her face locked in a hard scowl.

"What do you think, Gladys?" Elizabeth cringed as she heard her father ask. She hated that he never made a decision on his own.

"I think Mr. Michaels seems much too good to be true," she commented. "I don't like the age difference either, as you are well aware."

Did they talk about Alan while I was out with him? Elizabeth could not help but wonder.

"Don't have a cow, mom. If I find out he is putting on an act, I'll stop dating him," Elizabeth chimed in. "He was better to me than any of the high school boys I've dated. They are the ones who were all hands. That's why I haven't kept dating them. You guys can trust me," Elizabeth promised.

Her dad had a very hard time saying no to Elizabeth when she genuinely wanted something. Going out with Alan again seemed essential to his daughter, so he could not squelch her dream. A good girl, Elizabeth had given them absolutely no reason not to trust her. "Okay. You can go out with Alan again tomorrow," he told her.

Elizabeth sprang off the couch, dashed over to him, and threw her arms around his neck. "Thank you, daddy!" she exclaimed, also giving him a kiss on the cheek.

"Why'd you even ask my opinion?" Elizabeth's mother grumbled as she finally entered the room. She took a seat in the recliner beside Elizabeth's father. She stared at the television as if suddenly caught up in the news stories being broadcast. She dismissed them both.

"Chill, mom. It will be alright," Elizabeth assured her as she passed in front of her, heading out of the room.

"If it's not, it isn't on my head," she mumbled, not even looking at Elizabeth.

Elizabeth continued out of the room. When certain she was out of sight of both her mom and dad, a smile spread across her face. She shook both her clenched hands in front of her, and declared under her breath, "Yes!" She had never been so excited about a second date. She wondered if she would get any sleep at all that night. She attempted to decide what she would wear and how she would style her hair tomorrow.

Chapter 4
Getting to Know You

No one ever forgets their first love.
That person will always hold a very special place in the heart.

~ Sissy Marlyn ~

*P*ervasive thoughts of Alan encompassed Elizabeth's mind all day Saturday. It seemed the longest day of her life as she waited for the magical hour of his arrival. True to his word, Alan showed up at 7:00 p.m.

At Elizabeth's suggestion, they went to *Mariah's 1818*. "It's in the Mariah Moore House," she told him. "The House was originally built in 1818 by Elizabeth and George Moore at an astronomical cost, for that time, of almost $4,000. After the house was built, George and Elizabeth had five children, including Mariah, who never married and occupied the house until her death in 1888. Thus it became know as the Mariah Moore House. The house is listed on the National Register of Historic Places. It is one of the oldest standing brick structures in Bowling Green. The restaurant opened in 1979, so it's been around for three years now. I think you'll like both the atmosphere and the food."

"I'm sure I will. And I appreciate you sharing some more of the history of Bowling Green with me as well," Alan said with an admiring smile.

When they got to the restaurant, Alan took a second to appraise his surroundings. The wood floors had been stripped to their original look; the fireplaces and mantles had been refurbished; several walls had been stripped back to their original brick. There were also many antiques and additional woodworking all around. "Are all the antiques and woodworking original stuff?" he asked.

"A lot of the stuff here is original, for sure. But most of the antiques and some of the other woodworking were, like, purchased from other historic buildings," Elizabeth replied. She was proud to know the history of this house and restaurant.

"This is a great place," he told Elizabeth with an enormous grin, as they settled in at the table they had been led to by one of the restaurant's hostesses.

"I'm glad you like it. Wait until you taste the food."

"I can hardly wait," he said with an approving smile.

* * * *

They left the restaurant around 8:30, after both had a meal consisting of a burger and fries and comfortably relished being together again. Elizabeth immensely hated to leave. She thoroughly enjoyed being alone with Alan, and she decided to tell him so. "I for sure love to dance, but I like having you all to myself," she admitted with a satisfied smile as they slowly strolled hand-in-hand toward his car.

"I like being alone with you too." Elizabeth thrilled at hearing him respond.

They got in Alan's car and headed to the club. It was not far from the restaurant.

* * * *

At the club, she and Alan ran into Kathy and her date almost immediately. Dressed in a short, plaid kilt, white lacy leggings, and a white cotton shirt with red ribbons around her neck with yellow alligators on them, Kathy screamed 'in style'. To complete the look, she had her teased hair pulled up in a banana clip, so her long, dangly earrings showed, and she wore high-heel, red, pixie, ankle shoes on her feet.

Elizabeth, in contrast, had on layered T-shirts, Capri jeans, ruffled socks and jelly shoes. The only thing the two girls had in common were their teased, curled bangs. Alan had on cotton Bugle Boy pants, an unbuttoned, long-sleeved shirt with a T-shirt underneath, and Bass shoes.

Popular music – *Come on Eileen*, *Beat It* and *Hungry Like the Wolf* – blasted from several, gigantic speakers. Elizabeth and Alan shouted to try and talk above the music, as did everyone else there. A strobe light flashed across the painted, concrete block walls and upon the shiny, wooden, dance floor.

The dance floor overflowed with teens. When a slow song – *One On One*, by Hall & Oates – finally played, Alan asked Elizabeth to dance. When the song ended, they went into the dimly lit concession area, off to the side. They bought some soft drinks, sat at a small table for two, held hands, and talked and laughed. They waited out some more fast songs. Then when another slow song played, Alan stood, offered Elizabeth his hand and asked her to dance again. They danced nearly every slow song thereafter.

Each time Elizabeth and Alan slowly swayed to the music, everyone else at the club ceased to exist. Amazed by how comfortable and fitting Alan's strong arms felt around her, Elizabeth wished she could remain in them forever. Unfortunately, all too shortly, the time came for Alan to be taking her home.

Walking her up her front steps, Elizabeth breathed a sigh of relief that the porch light was not on. *Hopefully mom isn't watching out the front door tonight*, she wished.

Alan warmly took both of Elizabeth's hands in his own and told her, "I really enjoyed being with you again tonight."

"Me too," she hummed, returning his gaze.

"I'll call you," he promised, giving her hands a reassuring squeeze.

As he closed the distance between them, Elizabeth's insides quivered with expectation, excitement and nervousness. She found the smell of his cologne mouthwatering. As Alan's face drew near to hers, Elizabeth closed her eyes and waited. The gentle touch of his lips felt like heaven. She almost could not breathe for a second. The kiss was not long, but she was shaken when it ended.

As she watched Alan pull back, disappointment swept over Elizabeth. She wanted him to kiss her more. But instead, he stepped down one step and said, "I really hate to say this. But I better be going."

"I know," she agreed, feeling melancholy.

"Well, goodnight for real then," he uttered. He gave her hands one last, tender squeeze before releasing them. "I'll talk to you tomorrow."

"Bye," Elizabeth muttered in a regretful whisper. As with the night before, she remained standing on the porch. She watched longingly as Alan got in his car and drove away, amazed to discover she missed him almost instantly.

Thankfully, when she entered the house, her mother was *not* standing right inside the door. As Elizabeth passed by the entrance to the living room, she looked in and saw her mother and father sitting in their recliners, watching television.

Her mother had an unhappy expression on her face and did not acknowledge Elizabeth's presence. Her father, on the other hand, looked over and asked with a relaxed chuckle, "So how was your date, sweetheart?"

"It was awesome, daddy!" she declared. Her whole face lit up.

"Good. I'm glad you had a good time," he said. He looked back at the television. "Night, daddy. Night, mom," Elizabeth said, before she headed off toward her bedroom.

"Sweet dreams, sweetie," her dad said. Her mom merely nodded. She was obviously angry about something.

Wonder if dad banished her from standing by the door and spying on me, and this is what's set her off. Used to her mother's moodiness, Elizabeth did not care why her mom was upset. She merely wanted to go to her bedroom, lie in bed, go to sleep, and dream about Alan.

* * * *

Alan called Elizabeth Sunday evening. He also called her every other day during the week. Elizabeth was overjoyed. Alan seemed very interested in her.

Thursday, before they hung up from a rather lengthy conversation, he asked Elizabeth if she would like to go out with him again Friday. She delightedly told him "Yes!" She could not wait to see him again.

When he suggested they go to his apartment, order a pizza, and watch a movie on one of the cable movie channels, Elizabeth enthusiastically replied, "Sounds great!" She did not give this decision a second thought. She only wanted to be with Alan again, and she genuinely believed she could trust him no matter where they went.

* * * *

When they arrived at Alan's apartment Friday evening, Elizabeth began to feel a little uneasy. She had never been to a man's apartment before. She had gone to guys' houses before, but their parents had always been home. She would be all alone with Alan.

"Have a seat. What would you like to drink? I have Pepsi, milk or water."

"Pepsi sounds good," Elizabeth answered. She walked over and sat down on the sofa.

She watched Alan go into his tiny kitchen. The refrigerator squeaked as he opened it. Light from inside lit his profile for a moment. He pulled forth two cans of Pepsi, sat them on the counter with a clunk, and shut the refrigerator. He opened an overhead cabinet. The hinges on the cabinet also screeched. Alan pulled forth two glasses and sat these on the counter. He opened the freezer to retrieve a few hands full of ice. The glasses rattled as he filled them both about three-fourths full. Lastly, Elizabeth heard him snap open the two cans of Pepsi and the fizz and ice settling as he begin pouring them into the glasses.

She glanced around at the rest of the apartment. A nineteen-inch television and a VCR sat in a wood cabinet across from her. A stereo stood by the wall across the room with record albums and cassettes stacked on each side. A small table and chairs off to the side of the kitchen made up the dining area. All the walls, painted a bright white, were bare, and boxes still sat around here and there, waiting to be unpacked.

As Alan brought Elizabeth her soft drink, he noticed her looking about. "I'm still unpacking," he excused all of the boxes. "I haven't gotten around to decorating yet either. And I don't have much furniture. I do have cable hooked up, so I can watch movies. It's nice to have my own place, but it doesn't feel like home yet. Maybe when I get all unpacked, get a little more furniture and hang some stuff on the walls."

"For sure. It's still nice though," Elizabeth commented.

Alan sat his soft drink on the floor to the side of the sofa. Then he walked over to the television and turned it on. He handed Elizabeth the cable movie guide. "I have HBO and The Movie Channel. Look through the movies and pick out one you would like to watch. I'll go and order us some pizza. Is pepperoni and sausage alright?"

"Cool beans," Elizabeth replied, taking the small movie guide from his outstretched hand and starting to thumb through it.

A phone sat on the kitchen counter. Alan took a magnet off his refrigerator. It had the number for Pizza Hut on it. He called them and placed their order.

"It should be here within a half hour. Did you pick a movie yet?" he asked. He took a seat beside her on the couch.

Elizabeth picked out the movie *Tootsie*. She had heard it was funny, but she had not seen it yet. Alan had seen it, but he said he did not mind watching it again with her.

"Are you sure?" she asked. "I could pick out something different. *ET* is on HBO. We could watch it instead."

"No. I've seen *ET* too. I'd rather see *Tootsie*," Alan proclaimed. "I think you will really like it. It's hilarious."

He set the cable box to The Movie Channel. The movie came on at eight. It was quarter till, so they did not have long to wait. "So I guess you're glad to be graduating next week?" Alan commented, making conversation.

"For sure," Elizabeth answered. "I'm happy, but a little sad because it will all be over. Then we'll all go our separate ways."

"Yes, you will. But graduating is fun. I enjoyed it," Alan commented. "Both times."

His last statement made Elizabeth feel a little awkward, because it seemed to point out the age difference between them. "Well, you haven't been out of college that long," she quickly pointed out. "Do you like being through with school? Or do you miss it?"

"I like it, but I miss it too. It's fun putting to use what I learned, but it's a little scary from day to day too. So far I haven't screwed up anything though," he said with relief.

"That's always a good thing," Elizabeth agreed, with a small chuckle.

"That's a *very* good thing," Alan agreed. "So what are your plans for the summer?"

"I don't know. I'd like to get a job, but my mom isn't too stoked about that idea. I guess she wants to try and keep me under foot all summer. Who knows."

"Yeah. Your mom is a little intense," Alan confessed.

"For sure. A lot," she agreed.

She started to comment more on her mother, but Alan announced, "Oh…the movie is about to start." He turned up the sound on the television. Then he dropped his arm around her shoulder. Elizabeth totally relaxed and basked in the feel of his warm, strong arm. She felt like the luckiest girl alive.

* * * *

Their pizza arrived about fifteen minutes later. Alan paid the delivery boy, went to the kitchen and got some plates. He handed one of the plates to Elizabeth and sat back down on the couch. Elizabeth hated when he sat the pizza box on the sofa between them. She missed the pleasurable touch of Alan's arm.

She soon laughed at *Tootsie*, which she found very funny. Elizabeth also laughed at Alan. He persistently teased her. He would pretend to steal some pizza from her plate. She reciprocated by snatching some off his.

"Here, let me help you out," he finally offered. He held a piece of pizza in front of her face, by her mouth.

Elizabeth allowed herself a moment to gaze into his warm eyes. Then she snickered, opened her mouth, and took a large bite off the end of his gracious offering. She quickly reciprocated Alan's hospitality by holding up a slice for him to share.

Following Elizabeth's example, he also readily took a bite. They chuckled in unison, as they settled into comfortable play, taking turns feeding one another. When they finished their last bite of pizza, Alan pleasantly surprised Elizabeth by substituting his lips, for a lingering kiss.

When the kiss ended, Elizabeth found herself dazed and wanting more. Also shaken by the intensity of the kiss, Alan told her, "I believe you may be more delicious than the pizza." Desire shone in his eyes.

"Alan," she gasped. "I know this is going to sound lame. I realize we barely know one another, but I've never felt as close to a guy as I do you." *I feel like I'm falling in love with this guy.* Her thoughts scared her, but also pleased her.

Elizabeth's heart raced with elation as she heard him reply, "I feel really close to you too, Elizabeth."

"You know…I want you to kiss me some more…but I'm scared…"

"What are you scared of?" Alan asked, looking a little confused.

"I…I don't want to lead you on. We're all alone here, and if we start kissing, aren't you going to want to take things further?" she dared to ask. Her heart was beating in her throat now. "I'm not like most girls, Alan. I know a lot of girls do the nasty without even thinking about it. But I want my first time to be special…I want to…like…wait for my husband…for my wedding night."

Her eyes locked with his, pleading for understanding. Alan reached, took both her hands in his, and told her, "It's okay, Elizabeth. I meant what I said at the lake. I don't intend to try and take advantage of you. That hasn't changed just because I have you all alone in my apartment. I respect that you want to wait…"

"You do?" Elizabeth interrupted with wide-eyed amazement.

"Yes. But, I'll be honest with you; this isn't going to be easy!" Alan confessed. "You're pretty darn irresistible," he proclaimed with an admiring chuckle.

"Sorry," she responded, wanting to kiss him all the more. "You're no skank yourself."

"Thanks…I think," he laughed, rising to his feet. "I think I'll get us some more, *cold*, Pepsi to drink. You watch the movie. I'll be right back."

As he left Elizabeth's side for a few minutes to get their drinks, she appreciatively absorbed what Alan was trying to do for her. He proved he really intended to respect her wishes and try to keep his hands to himself. It was exceptionally hard for her to believe.

Could Alan possibly be the man of my dreams?, Elizabeth ecstatically wondered.

Chapter 5
Graduation

When God closes one door, he opens another.
A door always closes when one graduates from high school.
Life quickly changes: Some go on to jobs; some go to college;
some marry; some are footloose and fancy free.
Many paths are chosen as the quest to grow continues.

~ Sissy Marlyn ~

Elizabeth graduated from high school on May twentieth. Her emotions mixed on this day – happiness, sadness, excitement and nervousness – seeing Alan there seemed to make it all better. As she walked out the front doors of Western Kentucky University's Diddle Arena, into the parking lot, after her graduation ceremony, she was waylaid by Kathy and many other classmates. They all hugged and laughed, thrilled to be high school graduates.

"See ya at my house in a little bit," Kathy said, releasing her friend and rushing toward her mom.

When Elizabeth turned, Alan stood there. His warm embrace and admiring smile caused her heart to leap with joy. She could not wait for the summer to begin. She envisioned a lot of her time this summer would be spent with Alan, and this reflection brought her much delight.

"So how does it feel to be a high school graduate?" he asked her, reaching to toy with her tassel. Elizabeth wore a maroon cap and gown with a grey stole.

"It feels awesome!" Elizabeth announced, giving him a gleeful kiss and a wide grin.

Alan wore a striped Duck Head T-shirt, Levi button fly jeans, and Bass shoes without socks. "I can't wait to celebrate with you," he told Elizabeth.

"Well…don't plan too much of a celebration," Elizabeth heard her mother say. She reluctantly pushed out of Alan's arms and turned to find her mother and father standing behind her.

"Congratulations, sweetie," her dad said, folding her into a hug. "We're very proud of you."

"Thanks, daddy," she replied, giving him a smile as well.

"So where are you and Alan planning to celebrate?" her mother asked, as Elizabeth pulled back from her father.

"Kathy's mom is having a graduation party at her house," Elizabeth told her.

"This is the first I've heard of it," Elizabeth mother stated with a frown. She had made no attempt to embrace or congratulate her daughter.

"Don't have a cow, mom. Kathy just told me before the graduation ceremony. It's okay if I go, isn't it?" she asked, looking at her father for approval.

"I would think so," he answered, looking at Elizabeth's mom for her agreement.

Even though Kathy and Elizabeth had been friends forever, Elizabeth's mom had never liked Kathy's mom. Kathy's parents were divorced, and even though Kathy's mom had never remarried, she was seen about town with different men from time to time. Elizabeth's mother did not approve of this type of behavior, and she did not find Kathy's mother a very good role model for Kathy.

"I suppose it's okay if you go," Elizabeth's mother agreed with noted hesitation.

"Thanks, mom," Elizabeth gushed, giving her a hug even though she had not initiated it.

Elizabeth's mom gave her daughter a slight squeeze, and then she released her.

"Let's get one thing straight though," she stated, fixating on Alan with a mean glare. "Just because Elizabeth's graduated, doesn't mean she is ripe for the picking."

"Oh, my God, mom!" Elizabeth sputtered in horror, her mouth dropping open as she glanced all about. There were people all around them – other members of her class, their parents, and friends. Fortunately, they all seemed to be absorbed with visiting with one another, talking loud and animatedly, and bestowing and receiving warm congratulations. They did not appear to be paying any mind to Elizabeth and her family.

"Don't say God's name in vain, Elizabeth! You stood here kissing Alan in a public place, and I saw the look he gave you, like he'd like to have you for dinner…"

"Mrs. Warren," Alan addressed her. "Elizabeth's graduation has not changed anything. I like spending time with her and she likes spending time with me. I still don't intend to take advantage of her in any way," he tried to assure her, embarrassed for Elizabeth. *This day should be nothing but special for Elizabeth, but yet her mother stands here embarrassing her*, Alan thought with annoyance. It also irritated him that Elizabeth's father allowed his wife to act in such a manner. *Why doesn't he say something?*

As if he had heard Alan's thoughts, Elizabeth's father said, "Gladys, I think Elizabeth will be fine. This is her special day. Let's not ruin it."

"Fine!" she snapped. "Let her go off and do whatever she wants, and let the cards fall where they may. At least she has one parent that cares about her future and isn't scared to speak up." She turned and stormed off then, almost colliding with several people as she weaved her way through the crowd heading to the parking lot.

"You kids have fun," Elizabeth's father said. He gave Elizabeth another brief hug. "Home by eleven, okay?"

"For sure," Elizabeth agreed. "Thanks, daddy," she said again. She greatly appreciated him stepping in. It was not often that he stood up to her mother. As he headed away, Elizabeth made her way back over to Alan. "Barf me out. Sorry about that," she apologized.

"Don't worry about it," Alan dismissed. "Let's get out of here and head to Kathy's. The party should be a lot of fun. You deserve to celebrate."

"For sure. I do," Elizabeth agreed with him, half teasing. She wanted to put aside the humiliating encounter with her mother. She never ceased to be amazed at how unruffled Alan was by her mother. It made her love him all the more. She had not said these words to him, but Elizabeth was certain she loved Alan Michaels, and the more time she spent with him the more convinced she became of this fact. Happy to have graduated, she could not wait to get on with her life – a life that included this very special man. Elizabeth allowed Alan to sweep her away through the crowd, toward the parking lot, eager to get on with the afternoon and evening at hand.

Chapter 6
Summer of Love

What does it mean to be willing to share one's soul with another? Some believe we each have a soul mate out in the world somewhere, and all we must do to find that person is search. You will know when the search has concluded. It is when you find the person who makes your life whole.

~ Sissy Marlyn ~

On a perfect Saturday in June – cloudless, vibrantly sunny, temperature in the low eighties – Alan picked Elizabeth up around noon and took her to Barren River Lake. As he had mentioned on their first date, he wanted the pleasure of being able to teach Elizabeth how to ride a horse. She was both nervous and excited.

Alan had suggested it to her a couple of times, and Elizabeth declined his invitations, because she was a little scared. Alan had raised the issue again last night. And as Elizabeth snuggled securely in his strong, able arms, her fear suddenly seemed silly. Elizabeth found herself agreeing to try. The beautiful weather, showcasing a dazzling blue sky and a warm, gentle breeze, seemed to be the perfect sign she was making the right decision.

As soon as they got out of the car, Alan rushed to Elizabeth's side, taking her hand securely in his. He attempted to alleviate the uneasiness written all over her face. "Don't worry, Elizabeth," he soothed, slowly leading her in the direction of the stables. "I came out here last weekend and talked to the guy who runs things here. He helped me pick the perfect horse for you. I called him this morning, and he's holding that horse just for you. He's really tame and well-behaved, so you have absolutely nothing to worry about."

"The guy who runs things is really tame and well-behaved, or the horse?" she teased with nervousness.

"Ha. Ha. You are so funny. You know what I meant," Alan mocked. He gave her hand a gentle, reassuring squeeze. "Both the horse and the guy who owns him better be well-behaved, or I'll shoot them both."

Elizabeth stared at the foreboding horse stalls – a series of wood enclosures with openings at the top, in a redwood barn building. As they drew nearer, she could smell the hay and a slight manure stench. She could also see some horse heads looking out at her. "Just making sure that I don't…like…break my neck will suffice," she told Alan with a slight smile, studying his face.

"That I will promise you. I have no plans on getting rid of you," he asserted. "Besides, I have a special fondness for this beautiful neck in particular," he flirted. Elizabeth had her hair pulled back in an attractive French braid today, so he had a great view of her lovely neck.

Alan's warm affirmations made Elizabeth's insides shudder. Determined to trust him, she attempted to put all her silly fears aside. *He won't let me get hurt*, she convinced herself. "You definitely know how to schmooze me," Elizabeth declared with a contented giggle. She stopped and wrapped her arms around Alan, giving him a rewarding kiss on his lips.

They walked the last few yards in a cozy embrace. Their eyes carried on a silent, caring conversation. As usual, Alan calmed all of Elizabeth's reservations and made her feel secure.

They were met by Robert, the stable owner. Robert, a tall wiry man in a black cowboy hat, worn blue jeans and a denim shirt, had sunken cheeks and dark circles under his eyes.

Can I trust this man? Elizabeth wondered, as she and Alan dropped into pace with him.

Robert led them to a specific horse's stall. This stall held the horse he and Alan had previously selected for Elizabeth. "This is Dudley," Robert told Elizabeth. "Dudley likes everyone, so you need have no fear. He just likes to get out and be ridden. Come here, and let me introduce you to him."

Elizabeth hesitantly walked over to Dudley's stall. She directed her attention away from Robert and instead focused on the horse beside her. She stared into this animal's big, tame, brown eyes. Robert unexpectedly took Elizabeth's hand, turned it palm up, and put some little carrot pieces in it. "Just hold your hand up to him, straight out like you've got it," he instructed, demonstrating with his own hand.

Elizabeth watched the horse eat the carrot pieces out of Robert's hand. She listened to him chewing – chomp, chomp, chomp. She very slowly raised her own hand. It shook a little as she got it closer to Dudley's head – and the teeth she was certain would be very sharp. She closed her eyes and silently prayed the horse did not bite her. A second later, Dudley's tongue began to tickle her hand, as he gladly accepted her offer. When he had consumed all the carrots – chomp, chomp, chomp – Dudley appropriately thanked Elizabeth with an appreciative whinny.

"Now reach up and pat his neck. He loves that," Robert further explained.

Elizabeth once again obeyed. At the touch of her hand, Dudley lowered his head closer to her, and once again whinnied gratefully. Elizabeth could not help but smile. She patted the horse's neck again, and he happily whinnied a third time.

Robert swiftly proceeded to open the stall door and lead Dudley from this area. He was dark brown, with perfect long legs and a golden mane and tail. Elizabeth found him pretty. He looked like a Kentucky Derby horse. Completely won over by Dudley, Elizabeth, for the first time, looked forward to riding a horse – *this horse anyway.*

Robert fitted Dudley with a bridle and some reins and then he said, "Let's get ya up on his back."

Elizabeth glanced anxiously at Alan and saw him nod. Elizabeth watched as Robert interlaced his hands and directed, "Put yer foot in my hand and I'll hoist ya up. Yer boyfriend will be on the other side to help stabilize ya. We won't let ya fall."

Elizabeth felt her heart beating in her mouth as she lifted her leg and placed her foot in Robert's hand. As promised, he lifted her off the ground. "Pitch yer leg over the horse's body," he directed.

Elizabeth did as directed. As she slid onto the horse's back and took a firm grip on the reins to stabilize herself, she looked down to see Alan looking up at her on the other side. He stood ready to catch her should she slip. She smiled at him. As Alan adeptly climbed on behind her, Dudley continued to stand perfectly still and wait.

"Thanks, Robert," Alan said, enveloping Elizabeth securely in his arms. His arms and his sturdy chest felt delightful to Elizabeth. Alan reached to place his hands responsibly on top of Elizabeth's on the reins.

"You kids have fun," Robert called after them, as Alan taught Elizabeth how to make Dudley start to move.

* * * *

They rode for two hours, listening to Dudley's hoofs rhythmically clomping along the trail, enjoying the trees, the balmy gentle breeze, the sunshine, the magnificent views of the lake, the smells of spring, and one another's company. At first, Alan merely had Dudley walk along the path. After a while, when Alan was certain Elizabeth was comfortable on the horse's back, he made him trot. He even eventually allowed Dudley to take them for a short gallop.

Elizabeth had the time of her life. She hated it when she had to finally climb down off the horse's back. She also terribly missed having Alan's supportive arms wrapped around her body and his great smelling, warm body resting against her back.

"So how was it, kids?" Robert asked, coming over to tend to Dudley. He needed to remove his bridle, hose him down, and get him back in the stable.

"It was awesome!" Elizabeth shrieked in delight.

"That says it all," Alan commented with a happy grin. He squeezed Robert's shoulder and said, "Thanks for all your help, man!"

"It was my pleasure," Robert said, taking Dudley's rein to lead him away. "Hope you come back soon."

"We will," Alan said.

"For sure!" Elizabeth agreed, reaching to stroke the side of Dudley's face one last time before Robert took him away.

Alan put his arm around Elizabeth's shoulder and began leading her in the opposite direction. "Next time, you get to ride Dudley alone," he told her, as they strolled leisurely toward the car.

He warmly rubbed the back of her neck. He also missed their bodily contact. He tried not to think about it, because the movement of the horse, the occasional whisper of her perfume, and their bodies moving together in perfect harmony had aroused him.

"You didn't enjoy having me in your arms?" Elizabeth pretended to pout, popping her bottom lip out and looking pitifully into his eyes.

"Well, when you put it that way, maybe we *will* ride together again next time," he agreed, eagerly sliding his arms around her shoulders and drawing her in for a long, passionate kiss.

When he finally pulled back, the awed expression on Elizabeth's face turned Alan on all the more. "Um…we should be going," he wisely suggested, tucking his fingers through the front belt loops of his jeans and rocking back on his heel a bit.

Elizabeth did not want to leave, but she realized it was the smart thing to do. She wanted to wrap her arms around Alan and allow him to kiss her over and over. But she knew behaving in such a manner would only tease him. Suddenly exceedingly confused, she wondered, *How can I possibly wait for years to be intimate with this guy?* The thought floated through her mind, and it scared her, but Elizabeth had to concede these were her feelings.

"Let's go get a bite to eat," Alan said, interrupting her thoughts.

"O…okay," Elizabeth replied a little shakily. She allowed herself to be led away to his car, hoping to escape her wayward stirrings.

* * * *

The next weekend, they went riding again, and Elizabeth did indeed ride Dudley alone. She and Alan rode side by side on the trail, their horses' hoofs clomping in unison. However, they occasionally held hands. "Do you feel comfortable over there riding alone?" he inquired, after they had been riding for a short while.

"For sure, but not as much as when you were behind me," she mischievously admitted with a wicked smile and wild, dancing eyes. "It's not nearly as warm."

"Well, I'll just have to do something about that," Alan eagerly replied, staring happily into her eyes. He carefully pulled his horse over to Dudley until their sides softly touched. Dudley lowered his head and whinnied, and Alan's horse swished its tail. "Make Dudley stop."

Elizabeth commanded "Whoa!", and Dudley promptly obeyed, with just a gentle tug of his reins. Alan stopped his horse completely even with Dudley. He reached out and secured one arm behind Elizabeth's back, and then he brought his face and hers together for a tender kiss. "Is that better?" he asked with a lighthearted grin, a warm breeze raising strands of his hair.

"I don't know. Could you do that again? Then I'll let you know my decision," she continued to playfully tease, a frisky smile plastered all across her face.

Alan promptly bent his face to hers again. However, this time, he kissed first Elizabeth's forehead, then her nose, and finally settled greedily upon her lips, fierily probing the inside of her mouth with his eager tongue.

When Alan finally pulled back, Elizabeth swayed slightly on Dudley's back. Alan tightened his grip on her waist. "Are you okay?" he asked.

Elizabeth was not sure. Alan had made her dizzy with desire. She swiftly decided not to share these thoughts with him. Instead she played it off in a teasing manner.

She feigned a bad English accent, grabbed Alan's hand and held it tightly to her side, and uttered, "Don't release me yet, sir. I fear I may swoon." It was not far from the truth.

"You don't have to ask me twice," he replied in a decisive, husky voice, gazing at her with yearning. He then, quite unexpected, added, "How about if I hold you for the rest of your life?"

As if the intense tingling from Alan's kiss were not enough, his words and the lingering, attentive gaze of his eyes made Elizabeth's body flutter even more. *I wouldn't mind if he held me for the rest of our lives*, she honestly accepted. Her heart overflowed with emotion.

Still feeling she should keep the mood light, Elizabeth responded, "I for sure wouldn't mind it if we stayed like this forever, but poor Dudley and your horse would get awfully tired. Don't you think?" As if

Dudley knew he was being talked about, he whinnied again, and both horses shuffled.

Alan chuckled. "I suppose you definitely have a valid point there," he agreed. "I guess we should probably ride on then. That is, if you are warm enough over there now."

"For sure. You accomplished raising my body temperature very well," Elizabeth chuckled, returning his contented smile. She released his hand, and Alan slowly removed his arm from behind her back. However, he reached out and took her hand again as they started moving their horses together farther along the trail. As Elizabeth scrutinized Alan's warm, lingering eyes, she felt he was telling her, without words, that he cared as deeply for her as she believed she did for him.

* * * *

After Elizabeth and Alan had been dating about a month, just after her eighteenth birthday, she was summoned into the living room for a meeting with her parents. As usual, they both sat in their recliners. But the television was turned off.

"What's up?" Elizabeth asked, as she took a seat on the couch. She took note of her mother's rigid face.

"I guess that is what we would like to know," her mother stated, giving her a hard stare.

"Would you like…be more specific?" Elizabeth questioned in confusion. Her mother was always deliberately evasive, which made having a mature conversation with her virtually impossible.

"Well…you've been going out with Alan Michaels quite a bit lately. We'd like to know where you see this thing heading," her mother narrowed down.

"This *thing* as you put it is called going together," Elizabeth stated, sounding cross.

"Don't get smart with me, young lady," her mother called her down.

"I'm not getting smart. I wish you'd take a chill pill. Alan and I are dating. What's the big deal?"

"The big deal is he is several years older than you. Has he pressured you to have sex with him yet?" her mother finally got to the point.

"Oh my God…"

"How many times do I have to tell you not to say God's name in vain, Elizabeth!" her mother chastised.

"It's just an expression, mother," she started to argue. Seeing the disapproving frown on her mom's face, she added, rolling her eyes, "Sorry, but you are the limit…"

"What's that supposed to mean?"

"It means you never cease to barf me out. You always think the worst of everyone."

"That isn't necessarily what is happening here, honey," her dad finally spoke up. "It's just that your mother and I can't help but be a bit concerned about the age difference. You seem to like Alan a lot, and we don't want you to get hurt."

"And what else could a boy his age want from a younger girl than sex?" her mother brashly chipped in.

"Maybe he actually likes who I am and likes spending time with me," Elizabeth disputed, angered by her mother's continued insinuations.

"I'm sure that is true," her father agreed. "But with him being older, he may have experienced a few more things than you. We just don't want to see you pushed into something you aren't ready for," her father tried to pacify again.

"Neither of you need to worry," Elizabeth assured them. "Alan is *not* trying to push me into anything. We've talked about my beliefs about sex, and how it should be within marriage, and he totally respects my feelings."

"He told you this?" her father clarified.

"Yes. And he's proven it. If things…" she hesitated because she feared she might be straying into forbidden territory. But she felt she needed to expound on this topic, at least to her dad. "He's only kissed me. If things seem to be heating up any more than that, then Alan does something to distract us both. He's totally the most decent guy I ever been out with."

"And this could all only be an act to get you comfortable, and then he'll take advantage of you," her mother falsely accused.

"Or he could genuinely care about Elizabeth's feelings," her dad countered.

45

"You always think the best about everyone," her mother pointed out with repugnance.

"And you always think the worst," her dad murmured, almost under his breath.

Elizabeth heard it and smiled. Her mother also heard it. Her face had an ugly contortion to it now. "Fine. If she winds up pregnant don't blame me!" she snapped. She hopped to her feet and scurried out of the room.

"Gladys," Elizabeth's dad called after her, but she did not stop. He looked up toward the ceiling, shook his head and exhaled.

"Are we...like...through?" Elizabeth asked.

"We are for now," her dad agreed. "But, Elizabeth, just know your mother and I love you, and we don't want you to get hurt. If it gets confusing with Alan, I want you to know you can come talk to me. Men and women a lot of times want different things. You are spending a lot of time with Alan, and you seem to like him a great deal. We just want you to stay true to yourself. Don't compromise who you are or what you want for any man."

"No duh, daddy. I won't," Elizabeth assured him. She stood and went over and gave him a hug. "I love you too. Alan is an awesome guy though. You guys don't need to worry."

"Okay, sweetie," he said and gave her a kiss on the cheek.

He hoped Elizabeth was right. The age difference between her and Alan bothered him too. He knew Alan was likely to want sex from Elizabeth in a nearer future than four years – her years of college.

He did not know how it was all going to work out. He only hoped Elizabeth would not get into a sexual relationship with Alan too soon or rush into marriage and end up not following her dreams and going to college. These were his gravest concerns. But for now, he decided to trust Elizabeth's intuition and give their relationship a chance. They would take it little by little and see how it went.

* * * *

The Fourth of July fell on a Monday that year, so Elizabeth and Alan spent a long weekend together. Barren River Lake had a fireworks show, so she and Alan packed up hamburgers and hotdogs for grilling, chips, and plenty of soft drinks. They staked their claim in the picnic area about two o'clock that day. They were far from alone.

Barren River Lake was known for its beautiful fireworks display. The show would start about 9:45, and it would be over in forty-five minutes. As usual, for a Fourth of July in Kentucky, the weather was hot and muggy.

Alan finished setting their picnic spot up. He covered their grill with aluminum, put a plastic tablecloth on their picnic table, and sat a cooler at both ends to keep it from blowing off. Then he easily persuaded Elizabeth to take a swim in the lake with him.

Even though the lake was crowded with bodies, men, women and children, Elizabeth and Alan soon settled into easy play. Alan even picked Elizabeth up and sent her plunging into the water, as he had when they were kids. When they finished their fun frolic in the water, like many others, Alan spread a blanket out on the grass, so they could let the sun dry them.

"Would you like me to put some suntan lotion on you?" he offered with a wicked grin, as they settled themselves on the ground.

"For sure, but only if you let me do you too," Elizabeth proposed, indecently thinking about the feel of his bare chest and back under her hands.

"You got yourself a deal!" Alan eagerly exclaimed. He leapt up and went to retrieve a bottle of suntan lotion from the bag they had brought. When he returned, he knelt down behind her, gently flipped her hair over one shoulder, and slowly began massaging her shoulders, arms, and the rest of her back with warm, open palms. The touch of his gentle hands on her bare back caused excited ripples along Elizabeth's spine and all throughout her body. She hated it when he eventually removed his wondrous hands.

When he had finished, Alan crawled around and sat in front of her, handing her the bottle of lotion. "I've done all I can," he announced and added both playfully and with obvious desire, "I would love to do this side, but there are children present." He allowed his eyes to swiftly scan her scantily-clad, water-pearled body. She looked magnificent in a bikini. Elizabeth had a truly lovely body.

"Grody. How about I do your chest and back instead?" Elizabeth asked a little breathlessly.

"Sounds like a plan," he agreed with haste. A large smile came to his handsome face, and his eyes lit up with amorous anticipation.

"Turn around. I better do your back first," she directed, anxious to place her hands on his skin.

"Aye, Aye, captain," he agreed with a slightly nervous chuckle, quickly turning his back to her.

Elizabeth took her time spreading the lotion along Alan's back, wanting him to enjoy the touch of her hands as much as she had his. She also greatly enjoyed touching his bare skin and feeling his ample muscles. She began at the very bottom of his back by his trunks and slowly made her way up to his neck.

Then, vigorously working her thumbs back and forth in a hearty massage, Elizabeth seductively worked down his neck, across his shoulders, and along his arms toward his hands. When she proceeded back up his arms, slid her hands around to the front of his neck, and started descending his chest, Alan reached up and intercepted his hands, solicitously encircling both her wrists.

"I have to stop you before you give me a heat stroke," he panted. "Another excellent career choice for you would be a masseuse."

"Grody," she fussed again. "I was only trying to make you feel good," she argued, reluctantly removing her arms. She took a shaky seat beside him. She had not wanted to stop touching him. Her whole body tingled and stirred deep within.

"You definitely succeeded in making me feel good," Alan assured her in a rather hoarse voice. Turning to face her, he whispered, "If I had let you make me feel much better, things might have gotten out of hand. I would have hated for us to have gotten arrested."

Elizabeth knew he was teasing, but in his eyes, she could also see the obvious, strong desires she had haphazardly aroused in him.

"Maybe I better get us both something very cold to drink," Alan wisely suggested. He gradually rose to his feet, without waiting for Elizabeth's response.

Alan returned a second later with an icy can of soda for both of them. They sat side by side, slowing drinking the cold liquids and silently looking out at the lake. Each attempted to calm the furious passion they had accidentally kindled in one another.

* * * *

Later, they went for another long, refreshing swim. When they had finished, they went up to the campground restrooms and changed into some dry clothes. Afterwards, Alan promptly fixed up the grill and set to the task of preparing their hamburgers and hot dogs.

After they had eaten, they toyed with sparklers, firecrackers and bottle rockets for awhile, like many all around them. When they had extinguished their supply of miniature fireworks, they settled on the blanket to await the aerials.

As the first rocket burst into the air, a brilliant red, which vibrantly reflected in the water, Alan put his arm around Elizabeth and pulled her tight.

"Awesome!" Elizabeth exclaimed.

"Just like you," Alan complimented, kissing her temple.

They stared wondrously into the sky, watching more exquisite fireworks – brilliant blues, sizzling reds, loud whites. They listened to others 'Ow' and 'Ah' all around them.

"You know…I'm really glad I decided to move to Bowling Green," Alan said.

"Any reason in particular?" Elizabeth dared to ask.

"Why do you think?" he replied with another question. He also drew her to him for a lengthy, very expressive kiss.

"I'm really glad you moved to Bowling Green too," Elizabeth said with a giggle when the kiss ended.

"I don't think I can ever remember enjoying a fireworks show as much as I am this one. Do you know why?" Alan questioned, giving her another squeeze.

"It's beautiful?!" Elizabeth both stated and asked, watching several more, spectacular shells explode, lighting up the water, their faces, and the faces all around them.

"*You're* beautiful – inside and out," he professed, warming Elizabeth's heart. "You've made me really happy since I've come to Bowling Green, Elizabeth."

"Me? Make you happy?" Elizabeth asked. "I think that's totally the other way around. I'm stoked to the max every time I'm with you. You make everything ten times better."

"Only ten times?" he teased, kissing her nose.

"Okay…a hundred times. Or maybe a thousand times. Or maybe even a million times," she declared, laughing and drawing him in for a kiss again. *God, I love you*, she thought. She had to fight to keep from saying it. She had to fight to stop kissing him as well.

The loud boom, boom, boom and the bright flashes of some explosive shells drew their attention back to the sky again. "We've got a great thing going here, Elizabeth," Alan murmured.

"For sure," Elizabeth readily agreed, almost purring like a cat she was so happy and her heart was so full.

Alan squeezed her to his side, and they continued to watch the show, occasionally sneaking kisses here and there.

They relished the grand finale – shell upon shell, upon shell. It lit up everything in its path. The sky, the water, the landscape and their faces all radiantly glistened. As the show ended, they would have liked to snuggle and kiss a while longer, but they would have been trampled by the anxiously exiting crowd of hundreds.

So Alan protectively pulled Elizabeth to her feet. They gathered the blanket and the rest of their belongings and fell into pace with the rest of the excited crowd. They all headed for cars in the parking lot.

Elizabeth knew she would never forget this Fourth of July. Like so many things she experienced with Alan, it would become one of her happiest memories. She looked forward to making many more with this very special, unique man.

Chapter 7
Advice

When others give us advice, it is shaded by their own past experiences and perceptions. Therefore, personal advice should always be taken with extreme caution.

~ Sissy Marlyn ~

August first rolled around fairly quickly – time for Elizabeth to go through orientation and final registration for her fall classes at Western Kentucky University. Classes began the last week of August. She and Kathy rode to the university together. Happy to be spending time again with her friend, Kathy wanted the scoop on Elizabeth's relationship with her cousin. They had talked very little that summer, because Elizabeth had always been out with Alan when Kathy called.

Kathy wasted no time bringing up the subject. "So what's the story with my totally rad cousin and you?" she curiously asked.

Elizabeth glanced away from the road, smiling at her friend and replied in a half-teasing manner, "Eat my shorts, Kathy. You know a lady doesn't kiss and tell." She reached to turn up the car stereo. Olivia Newton-John's *Physical* bellowed out of the speakers.

"I'm so sure. Does that mean it's serious?" Kathy further questioned. Reaching to turn the radio back down a bit, she specified,

"What I'm getting at is…are you still a good Catholic girl or are you and Alan boinking?"

If Elizabeth had not been so well acquainted with Kathy, she would have been shocked by her brazen question. However, she knew Kathy had lost her virginity their freshman year and had slept with a few other boys since. Unfortunately, Kathy never stayed with a boy long after she began sleeping with him. Kathy always labeled the guy boring, or she said she did not want to get tied down. Despite their friendship, Kathy and Elizabeth had totally different views of relationships and sex, and Kathy was well aware of this schism.

"Chill, Kathy. You know me too well not to know the answer to that question," Elizabeth replied with a smirk, looking disapprovingly at Kathy as she squeezed the steering wheel a bit.

"For sure. I know you alright," Kathy confirmed, a disparaging tone to her voice. "But, from what I hear from my dad, he says he has never seen Alan so stuck on someone before. So I would say it's true love. So how about it, Elizabeth? Are you just playing with my poor cousin's heart, or am I right?"

"I know that what I feel for Alan is something I have never felt for anyone else," she answered cautiously, knowing whatever she said to Kathy could easily get back to Alan. Honestly, she believed she loved Alan, and she would have liked to openly declare this to her friend. But, Elizabeth wanted to wait until Alan told her he loved her first.

"In other words, you're head over heels," Kathy hastily interpreted. "As you say, I know you well enough to see that. And from what my dad says, it sounds as if Alan feels the same way. So what in the world is keeping you from doing the nasty with this guy?"

"Kathy!" Elizabeth distastefully exclaimed. "Gag me with a spoon!"

"I'm not asking you to give a play-by-play description, Elizabeth," Kathy argued with determination. "It just doesn't make sense to me, that's all! I could see you playing hard to get with other guys you dated. You didn't give a hoot for them, and they only wanted one thing from you. But Alan totally seems to be the one you've been searching for, so why are you keeping him waiting? Don't tell me you are going to make this guy marry you first. No way!"

"Way!" Elizabeth challenged, a touch of anger in her eyes now.

"Totally grody! You might as well eat shit and die," Kathy professed. "You don't want to put Alan in a position where he will marry you to get a little, and then turn around and divorce your ass," she angrily stated. "Guys don't think like we do, Elizabeth. They totally think from between their legs. So why don't you boink Alan a little and see what you get in return. If it's not what you expect of him, then you can move on. Alan seems to actually be interested in falling in love. So why make the poor guy suffer? Doing the nasty with him could only work to your advantage."

"Barf me out, Kathy. For your information, Alan respects how I feel about sex," Elizabeth truthfully explained, finally getting a word in edgewise. "He for sure cares about me enough that he will wait until I say I am ready. That may be when we are married, if he decides he wants to marry me. But, if he asks me to marry him, it won't be just because of that. We already have a lot more than just *doing the nasty* going on between us."

"No shit, Sherlock. That still doesn't answer my question as to why you won't let him boink you. In fact, if he's that considerate of your feelings and you love him, then how can you not satisfy his needs? Not to mention the fact that you totally must want to do it with him too. I think you've had too much Catholic bullshit pounded into your head by your mother, airhead. I got news for you, Elizabeth, your mother and father would like you to totally practice abstinence for the rest of your life. Parents have a hard time imagining their kid ever doing anything like that, and they use the Catholic Church to try and keep us pure and virginal. I'll for sure bet your parents even did it before they were married. Marriage is just a piece of paper, especially to a guy. If the sex isn't good, they will walk."

Elizabeth knew Kathy's parents had divorced because her dad left her mom for another woman. So she sadly understood Kathy's bitterness about men and sex. But, Elizabeth's parents, still wed, proved that not all men left their wives. However, Kathy's referral to Elizabeth's abstinence as being cruel to Alan and not considering his feelings did disturb her.

Elizabeth loved Alan, and she certainly wanted him to be happy. Now, Kathy's hurtful comments made Elizabeth worry about her fairness to Alan. *After all, wasn't it more difficult for a guy to abstain than a girl?*

"Look, don't get pissed at me," Kathy said, interpreting Elizabeth's silence for anger. "I'm just trying to tell you how to keep Alan as your steady boyfriend, that's all," she justified. "You know I'm your friend, Elizabeth, and I've never seen you care about anyone like you do Alan. I'm only trying to save you from being hurt. You don't want him to find relief with someone else, do you?"

"I'm so sure," Elizabeth commented, starring intensely into her friend's determined eyes. "I appreciate you caring, Kathy. But what happens or doesn't happen between Alan and me is just between the two of us, okay? You and I have totally different views about sex, and I would appreciate it if you would respect my decisions. I've never come down on you about anybody you have slept with."

"Okay. Fine," Kathy begrudgingly agreed. "I just hope you know what you're doing."

"I for sure do," Elizabeth earnestly declared. However, for the first time, Kathy's words implanted doubt in Elizabeth mind.

* * * *

As diligently as Elizabeth tried to forget Kathy's tormenting words, they still managed to haunt her each night as she talked to Alan on the phone. *He sounds happy,* she decided. *But what if Alan isn't telling me how he truly feels? Won't he eventually get tired of waiting on me?*

Elizabeth also had to admit Kathy's statement, about her wanting Alan too, definitely applied. Some nights, after they had been together, when Elizabeth lay down in bed, she fought from vividly picturing what it would be like for her and Alan to make love. After clutching her pillow inseparably to her, she would finally fall into a fitful sleep. *It has to be worse for Alan. Maybe I am being insensitively cruel,* she mulled over with anxiety.

* * * *

Friday night, Elizabeth suggested they go to Alan's apartment and watch a movie. She had no idea how, but somehow, she intended to find out exactly where Alan stood on the two of them having sex.

54

Alan, always integrally attuned to Elizabeth's feelings, noticed almost immediately that something seemed to be weighing heavily on her mind. "You're awfully quiet tonight, Elizabeth. Is something wrong?" he asked with obvious concern. He slid closer to her on the couch.

As if Alan's intent expression would give her answers to all her troubling questions, Elizabeth extensively examined his eyes for a few, silent moments. Then she replied, "I've just really missed you this week. I totally couldn't get you off my mind."

"Well, you've definitely been on my mind all week too. But, then again, you always are," he warmly assured her, reflexively reaching out and placing one of his hands of top of hers. He noted her joined hands, held uncharacteristically against the waist of her Chic jeans. "Did everything go okay with registration? Did you get all the classes you wanted?"

"It...college is fine," she replied. Then she requested, "Alan...will...will you just hold me?"

Without answering, he instantly gathered her into his soothing arms. Elizabeth wrapped her arms around Alan's neck and relaxed her weary head on his shoulder. Resting securely in Alan's strong, reassuring arms, Elizabeth's heart filled with love for him. *But if I truly love Alan, then why shouldn't I allow him to make love to me,* she wondered in silent agony.

Raising her chin off his shoulder, Elizabeth began to kiss the side of Alan's neck. Then she greedily sampled his lips. His urgent, invigorated response told Elizabeth all she needed to know. *Kathy is right. I should have considered how much of a sacrifice Alan has been making for me.*

They had spent all summer together, and he had not even tried to touch her in a compromising way. Alan had certainly proved he was not just out to lay her. *So why have I been so cruelly holding back?*

"Alan," she gasped and then kissed him temptingly once again. "Do you...like...want to touch me?"

Without waiting for a response, Elizabeth swiftly took his right hand and placed it deliberately on top of her left breast. She instantly became conscious of Alan's eager fingers delightfully massaging her nipple through her T-shirt and bra, gently pinching the end.

Elizabeth ecstatically rocked her head backward and exhaled a sweltering breath toward the ceiling. Alan easily lit an unquenchable torch within her. When she lowered her head, he locked his lips hungrily upon hers with such unexpected, unbridled force Elizabeth effortlessly propelled backwards on the couch.

"Alan, I love you so much!" Elizabeth adamantly proclaimed.

Abruptly, without warning, Alan pulled away, awkwardly coming to a seated position again. "E...Elizabeth," he exclaimed hoarsely, his face showing a mixture of passion and surprise. "What's going on here?! Why'd you just do that?!"

Elizabeth also slowly slid herself back into a sitting position. She promptly reached out, took his right hand, turned it palm up, and demonstratively kissed it with steamy lips. "Alan," she addressed in a husky voice full of yearning. "I...I'm in love with you. I just needed to tell you how I felt. And...that I...I'll do *anything* for you."

"Including sleeping with me?" he asked incredulously, eyeballing her strangely.

"Yes," she eagerly agreed, gripping his hand more firmly. "I so totally want you to be happy."

"What makes you think I haven't been happy? Have I done or said something to make you think you have to do this for me?" Alan inquired with confusion and concern.

"No," she assured him, affectionately kissing his thumb, before seductively placing his hand between her breasts, securely on top of her excited, racing heart. "You've been absolutely awesome! That's one of the reasons I fell in love with you. I just want to make sure I'm being fair to you."

"Being fair to me? First you said you would sleep with me to be sure I'm happy, and now it's so you're fair to me. Where is all of this coming from all of the sudden?" Alan inquired with obvious frustration.

"Well...Kathy...she...well...she just sort of said some things to me that made me think," Elizabeth grudgingly admitted.

Alan gazed into Elizabeth's troubled eyes, shaded by her full, curled, stiff bangs. He reluctantly removed his hand from her chest. Instead, he took one of her hands and kissed the palm, as she had his earlier. "Look, I don't know what Kathy said to you, but I think I've gotten a pretty good idea. But basically, it's none of Kathy's business what does…or doesn't…go on between the two of us. As far as you making me happy or being fair to me goes, you shared with me that you wanted your first time to be something very special. I care about you enough that I want it to be just that," Alan professed, squeezing her hand in assurance. "In fact…I…I love you too."

His confession of love profoundly touched the deepest part of Elizabeth's heart. "Oh, Alan!" she exclaimed, excitedly kissing his lips. "I have wanted so badly to hear you say you love me and to be able to tell you I loved you. Right now, hearing you say how you feel, I don't see how making love with you could be anything but special. I know you're the person I've been waiting for."

"Okay," he said a little doubtfully. "But tell me this. How have you always envisioned your very first time? Something tells me it wasn't on a couch in your boyfriend's apartment, and then being taken home to your parent's right after."

Elizabeth realized Alan had a very valid point. She had always imagined her first time being with her husband on their honeymoon. It did indeed take all the romance out of it when she thought about the two of them on this couch and then him taking her home afterwards.

"Why don't you let me tell you what I have imagined for you, and you see if you don't think it might be worth the wait?" Alan lovingly proposed, sliding right beside Elizabeth again and dropping a secure arm around her shoulders. "Lay your head on my shoulder, close your eyes, and try to picture in your mind what I'm about to say."

Elizabeth willingly did as Alan requested. When she comfortably settled against his body, he began in a soft voice, "I picture just the two of us away somewhere. I'd say we need at least a week. I picture it being a warm place with a beach or a cold place with a fireplace and Jacuzzi. I can see us spending the whole day laughing and having a good time together. Then, as it starts to get dark, we go back to our room together. We spend the whole night making love, and in the morning, when you wake up, you find yourself still in my arms. We spend the rest of the week together doing the same thing. Just the two of us, with all the time in the world, finding out everything we need to know about how to make each other happy in a whole new way. Isn't that more the way you've always imagined it?"

Elizabeth terribly hated to open her eyes and respond, because she vividly pictured all that Alan had just so wonderfully described to her. He did know her, oh so well, because this was definitely the way she imagined her first time with him. "That's exactly what I've dreamed about," she admitted, staring wondrously into his eyes once more. "The only thing different is you would be my husband."

"So you actually want to wait until you are married?" Alan inquired, sounding a bit surprised.

"I guess...when you make me envision what I've always dreamed about," she admitted with obvious confusion, breaking eye contact for a second to pensively study her lap. "But, I love you so much, and I honestly don't know if I want to wait that long. I plan on going to college, so that means it could be another four years before I get married."

"Four years...huh?" Alan shakily repeated, with a mocking grin. "Well, I tell you what we'll do. We will plan to have our wedding ceremony right after your college graduation. Then we'll skip the reception and go straight to the honeymoon."

"Alan! Eat my shorts!" Elizabeth declared with a snicker and playfully swatted the top part of his closest arm.

"Not for another four years," he continued to tease, kissing her lightly on the tip of her nose. He grew gravely serious again and admitted, "I can't decide for you whether you should wait or not, Elizabeth. But I can promise I won't pressure you into having sex with me. If it ends up being four years and we've gotten married first, before it feels right to you, then we'll wait four years. The important thing to me is that you are absolutely sure when it happens. I don't want you having any regrets."

Upon hearing his caring profession, Elizabeth's heart overflowed with love for Alan. She could not help but seriously wonder how she could possibly ever regret anything that might happen with him. "Do you have any idea how happy you make me?"

"Happy enough that I'm the one you will want to marry in a few years, I hope," he confessed with a nervous chuckle.

"For sure. I can't imagine ever wanting to marry anyone but you. I can't imagine ever loving anyone but you," she uttered, gazing deeply into his eyes.

Alan bent forward and the two shared another, rather lengthy kiss. "I plan on seeing to it that you always feel that way," he promised.

The young lovers sat warmly cuddling for a lengthy time, content with their newfound understandings and honest professions of love for one another.

Chapter 8
Truth

Truth can be a hard pill to swallow sometimes. But then again, sometimes it answers questions we've had in our minds for a very long time.

~ Sissy Marlyn ~

Only a week later, Elizabeth started her college classes. The enormous overload of reading and homework kept her much busier than she had ever envisioned. Terribly dismayed, Elizabeth discovered keeping up with her courses not only did not allow her time to see Alan much during the week, but it even forced her to spend some crucial time away from him on the weekends.

One bright spot in her new, hectic schedule, Elizabeth had been accepted as a freshman apprentice actress at the university's Drama School. They only accepted a few freshmen to their team, so Elizabeth felt extremely grateful, and lucky, to have been chosen. Likely she would not star in any of the plays this year, yet she could still audition and learn from working behind the scenes.

Even though Elizabeth could not spend as much time with Alan as she certainly would have liked, Alan supported Elizabeth's new routine one hundred percent. So, regardless of things being extremely different than Elizabeth originally thought, she still remained very happy.

Elizabeth proudly finished her fall semester with a 4.0 grade point average, which enabled her to make the Dean's List. Needless to say, Alan and her parents beamed with delight over her success. Her mom wanted to see Elizabeth's college successes continue. She maintained a close eye on her daughter's relationship with Alan Michaels from behind the scenes.

* * * *

Spring semester, Elizabeth had another delightful thing happen. Auditioning for an important, lead role in *The Graduate*, the university's most current theatre production, she had been selected as an understudy for the role of Mrs. Robinson. Chances were slim she would see any real stage action, but Elizabeth still relished having been selected to be a part of the show.

Her mother detested this turn of events. She still wanted Elizabeth to put acting aside. She believed Elizabeth could better do without acting and having Alan Michaels in her life. She quietly kept both these observations to herself.

Fate fortunately seemed to be on Elizabeth's side, and not her mother's. After the first performance of *The Graduate*, Sheila Greene, the girl whom Elizabeth was an understudy for, could not fulfill her obligation. She regretfully had to leave town for a family emergency. Sheila had no idea when she might return.

While Elizabeth truly felt terrible for Sheila, she could not help but feel grateful for her own good fortune. These circumstances meant Elizabeth would be starring in her first college play. Ecstatic, Alan was equally thrilled for her. Her dad was as well. Her mother's words fully expressed how she felt about this turn of events, "Well…it seems your time could better be spent on your studies, but I guess we all need some downtime and diversions."

* * * *

"This is just one step closer to you becoming that famous actress you want to be," Alan told Elizabeth with an adoring smile, locking eyes with her. Saturday evening, they sat on the couch in his apartment. He held her securely around her slim waist as she sat sideways on his lap like a little girl. Sunlight streaming through the front windows provided the only light in the room. Bread's *Lost Without Your Love* cassette played in the stereo. This album had been popular when Alan was in high school, and he still loved the songs. Elizabeth enjoyed Bread's music as well. "We should celebrate your success!" he suggested.

"Hold up on any celebration until the play finishes and we know if I was a success or not," she wisely instructed, sounding extremely nervous. "I'm used to grade school and high school plays where you only had to be great for one night. This runs for three nights. Sheila, the girl I'm replacing, was there for the first night. But, I'm on tonight, and then tomorrow as well. My stomach is knotting up just thinking about it"

"I'm sure you'll be great!" Alan assured her, strategically placing both his hands across her flat stomach and gently massaging her nervous tummy. "Since we saw the play last night, I'll be able to compare Sheila's performance to yours. I have a feeling yours is going to be much better."

"I'm so sure. I think you are a little biased," Elizabeth pointed out with a touched smile, craning her neck so she could meet his warm lips in gratitude.

"Can't argue with you there," he agreed with a satisfied laugh, affectionately kissing the side of her neck. He also massaged her stiff shoulders. "I can hardly wait to see you on that stage tonight. And I bet everyone else in the audience is going to love you too."

"Oh well! Whatever happens, I know at least one person will love me, because I'll know you are in the audience. So how can I possibly go wrong?" she declared, gazing into his handsome, bright blue, believing eyes once more.

"I'm telling you, you'll be terrific," Alan attempted to persuade her, squeezing her against his robust body.

He allowed Elizabeth to remain in his comforting arms for over half an hour, alternately rubbing her back and softly kissing her neck and lips. Shortly after, he drove her to the Ivan Wilson Fine Arts Center, which housed the theatre where she would be performing *The Graduate*. Nervous, Elizabeth's hand trembled as Alan led her into the darkened theatre.

Elizabeth glanced around her as if she had never been inside this building before. She looked at the rows and rows of empty chairs and envisioned them full of people – folks who would be clandestinely critiquing her performance. Her eyes scrutinized the students on the lighted stage, making final, last minute preparations of the set. *That's where I should be. Helping to get things ready. I'm only a freshman. Sheila is a senior. Can I possibly hope to be even half as good?*

"It will all be okay," Alan reassured her once again as they reached their point of separation. Elizabeth needed to go backstage to get ready. Alan bent to give her one last, supportive kiss. Then he released her hand. "Break a leg," he said, wishing her luck in theatre talk.

Elizabeth inhaled a deep breath, trying to muster her courage and settle her upset stomach. Then she parted from Alan and went backstage, while Alan took a seat in the front row to anxiously await her performance.

* * * *

The audience gave *The Graduate* two standing ovations, and when Elizabeth made her final appearance and bowed for them, they cheered and clapped even louder. The director came onstage and presented Elizabeth with a bouquet of congratulatory flowers. The crowd of still very attentive onlookers whistled and applauded once more. Proud to be amongst them, Alan glowed with happiness for Elizabeth.

When the big, black, satin curtain swooped closed the final time, Alan leapt to his feet and eagerly pushed through the large crowd, trying to make his way backstage to congratulate Elizabeth. He found her animatedly talking to the director. As Alan managed to draw closer, he could hear what the man said, "You truly have an enormous talent, Elizabeth. The audience lost themselves in your portrayal of Mrs. Robinson, and that's a rare gift. You can go far in theatre if that's what you desire, and I'll be ever so happy to be the director of any of the other plays you star in."

"Oh, thank you so much, Stuart!" Elizabeth gushed, displaying an ear-to-ear smile and giving him an appreciative hug.

"No. Thank you, my dear!" Stuart countered, taking her hand and brusquely kissing the top. Then he swiftly left her to go and congratulate the rest of his cast. "I'll see you at the celebration party at my place," he invited over his fleeting shoulder.

Only then did Elizabeth notice Alan standing there. She dashed toward him, throwing her arms around him in elation and planting rough, welcoming kisses on his lips. She also bounced against him with such force she almost knocked him down.

"Um…unlike the college graduate in the play, I feel a little funny kissing mom," he teased in a loud voice, trying to be overheard above the loud commotion of excited talking and greeting going on all around them. He also toyed with the gray wig she still donned.

"I'm so sure!" Elizabeth laughed, kissing him again.

"Congratulations!" he shouted. "Didn't I tell you that you would be wonderful?!"

"Stuart thought I was wonderful too!" she exclaimed, literally jumping up and down. "He says I have a gift!"

"Is Stuart the guy I saw kissing one of your hands? Should I be jealous?" Alan asked, only half teasing. Stuart looked to be in his mid-thirties, but he was not a bad looking man – tall, full head of gleaming black hair, and dark brown eyes. Alan's eyes studied Elizabeth's facial expression a little too sternly.

Elizabeth drew in close to Alan's ear, so as not to be overheard, and clarified with a knowing giggle, "There'd be more chance of me being jealous of him chasing you. Stuart is a proclaimed homosexual."

"Oh…okay," Alan replied with a chuckle of his own.

Elizabeth pulled back and gave Alan another reassuring brush of her lips. "He's also the director for all the campus plays. That means if he thinks I'm good, I'm almost sure to get a starring role in more plays. I'm stoked!" she declared, looking like the cat that had just swallowed the canary.

"Well, that's great!" Alan agreed. "You certainly deserve it. I heard what Stuart said about the audience losing themselves in your character, and I'm here to tell you it's absolutely true. I didn't even feel like I knew you. It was like you had the same face and body, but you were a totally different person. You're so good, you actually scare me."

"That's the ticket, but I can assure you I'm still the same person you love," Elizabeth promised. Her eyes met his with warmth, and she reached to trace his lips with her finger. "I love you even more for being here and sharing this with me."

"I wouldn't want to be anywhere else," he proclaimed with a wide, toothy smile. He gently removed her hand from his face and warmly kissed the palm.

"Neither would I," Elizabeth's dad said. He had walked up behind Alan.

Elizabeth released Alan and sprang into her father's arms instead.

"Great job, sweetie!" he said and squeezed her to him, kissing her on the cheek.

Alan wondered where Elizabeth's mother was. Elizabeth wondered the same, asking, "Where's mom?"

"Um…she wasn't feeling well tonight," he explained, seeming a little ill at ease.

I'll bet, Alan thought with a bit of malice. *Seeing her daughter live her dream is probably sickening to Elizabeth's mom.* Angry she was not there, Alan quickly concluded she would not have shown Elizabeth her support anyway, so perhaps it was best she was not there.

"Oh," Elizabeth muttered. *I wonder if she really is sick, or just didn't want to come,* she could not help but ponder. Surprised to discover her mom's absence hurt a little, Elizabeth's smile became more of a frown. Her mom never overly supported her acting, but at least she usually made an appearance at her plays.

"So are you and Alan going someplace to celebrate?" her dad asked, swiftly changing the subject. He had seen a trace of pain in Elizabeth's eyes, and he did not like his daughter to be hurt.

"I believe we are going to a celebration party at the director's house," Alan answered for Elizabeth.

"You don't mind going?" she asked, stepping back from her dad and studying Alan's face.

"He invited you, didn't he? I guess it would be alright if I escorted you, right?"

"For sure!" Elizabeth assured him.

"Well, before the play, I told you we needed to celebrate. This is the perfect opportunity. You can introduce me to the other cast members, and I can see what they are really like," he enthusiastically suggested.

"They're really nice people. You'll like them," Elizabeth shared.

"Sounds like you kids have it all figured out," her dad stated. "What time will you be home?" he surprised Elizabeth by asking.

"What time?" she repeated. "Eleven?" she answered and asked all at the same time. This had been her curfew forever.

"It's already after 9:00. You're in college now. If you want to stay out a little later at this party, then I don't see a problem with it. I think I can trust Alan to look out for you."

"Thank you, sir," he replied. "I definitely will. How about I have her home at midnight?"

"Midnight it is," Elizabeth was surprised to hear her dad easily agree. But then again, her mother was not there to argue the point. Elizabeth was suddenly glad her mother had not showed up.

"Thanks, daddy," Elizabeth said and gave him another grateful hug.

"You've earned it. I've very proud of you!" he bragged, tightening his embrace. "Now go and have a good time."

"We will," Elizabeth agreed with a glowing smile. She reached to take Alan's hand and began pulling him with excitement toward the exit door. Very happy, all seemed right with Elizabeth's world.

* * * *

Stuart had an apartment about a mile from campus. Another man answered the door. His hair was a wavy platinum blond, and he had on a flowery, pink shirt and formfitting slacks. His high-pitched voice and exaggerated wrist movements led Elizabeth and Alan to assume this man was Stuart's boyfriend. Alan felt a little strange about this situation, but he secretly breathed a sigh of relief that Stuart was gay. He knew, as Elizabeth got more roles, she might be spending a lot more time with Stuart, and it was good to know Elizabeth definitely was *not* his type.

* * * *

Monday, the campus newspaper printed a very positive review of the play. It said that freshman actress, Elizabeth Warren, overshadowed Sheila Greene's opening night performance. The article went on to say that it was almost certain that not only Western Kentucky University, but the theatre world as a whole, could count on seeing a lot more of Elizabeth Warren. Needless to say, Elizabeth was thrilled to death by the news.

Stuart called to congratulate her again and said he wanted to talk to her. She agreed to meet him later that evening, at his apartment. When Alan heard news of the meeting, he was again immensely glad Stuart was gay.

* * * *

Alan met Elizabeth at *Antonio's* after her meeting with Stuart. As soon as he walked through the door, he was greeted by Elizabeth's enormous smile. As usual, Elizabeth's smile always seemed to brighten the room a bit more. Leaping from the booth, filled with uttermost excitement, she nearly pulled Alan's arm out of socket, as she drew him into an embrace.

"Well, I take it Stuart had something good to tell you," he concluded with an amused grin, when their extensive kiss had ended.

"He sure did!" she enthusiastically declared. "Stuart told me he used to work for MGM out on the West Coast. He said he still keeps in touch with them, and if he knows of a part they have available, he occasionally sends them someone for a screen test, if he thinks that person is really gifted. He said he thinks I'm gifted enough! Me, Alan! Can you believe it?!"

"I have no problem believing he thinks you are gifted, because you most definitely are. But what does he mean about sending you for a screen test? Is he planning on floating you the money to fly to California?" he skeptically questioned with concerned eyes, as he released her from his embrace and had a seat in the booth. Elizabeth sat down across from him.

"No, you dweeb!" Elizabeth giggled, lightly swatting one of his arms. "I guess I did make it sound that way. I'm just so excited, I'm rambling to the max! MGM is coming to the Galt House Hotel in Louisville. They are supposed to be producing a new movie called *Bardstown*. It'll be a romance drama, centering on a wealthy, bourbon industry family in Bardstown and a farm girl who gets involved with one of the sons. Stuart said they are looking for Kentucky ladies around my age for one of the main acting parts. He says MGM plans on filming the show on location in Bardstown. Doesn't that sound perfect?! I wouldn't even have to leave the state!" She stopped for only a second to catch her breath and then zealously proclaimed, "It all sounds so gnarly to me! I know it's a long-shot that I would actually be chosen for anything. But just the thought of actually taking a real, live, screen test for a movie role makes me so excited I can hardly stand it!"

"It does sound like your dream's coming true," Alan agreed, sharing a grin and taking one of her hands supportively into his.

A waitress approached the table. "What can I get you to drink?" she asked. Elizabeth already had a plastic Coke glass sitting in front of her.

"Coke," Alan answered, giving the server only the slightest attention. He was much more interested in Elizabeth and her exciting news. "So when are you supposed to go to Louisville to have this screen test done?"

"This Saturday," Elizabeth enthusiastically chirped.

"So is Stuart planning on going with you?" Alan curiously inquired.

"No. But I was hoping you would," Elizabeth readily invited.

"I'd love to!" Alan eagerly agreed. "It'll be fun to be out of town together, even though Louisville is only an hour and a half away."

"Oh, Alan! This opportunity just keeps getting better and better!" she declared, throwing her arms securely around his neck and smothering his face with excited kisses once more.

* * * *

The next day, when Elizabeth shared the news about the movie audition with her mother and father, true to form, her dad was tickled and her mom was perturbed. "Well, I hope you don't think you are driving to Louisville by yourself," she said in a stern voice.

"No. Alan is going to take me," Elizabeth informed them.

"You are going out of town with Alan?" Elizabeth's mom verified. Her icy blue eyes looked even more pronounced, because of her paleness. She had not just bugged out of Elizabeth's play; she really was ill.

"Veg, mom. We're just going to Louisville. It's only an hour and a half away," Elizabeth replied. "The screen test is at noon at the Galt House Hotel. We'll drive back afterwards."

"I think it'll be okay," her dad said, glancing at her mom.

"You think it's okay for your daughter to go out of town with an older man to a hotel?" she questioned. "Sounds like a plan to me. Alan will have her right where he wants her. So much for her finishing college and making a life for herself."

"Mom...I wish you would take a chill pill!" Elizabeth exclaimed. "If Alan wanted to take advantage of me, he's had plenty of opportunity. He has his own apartment. We don't have to go out of town to some hotel. He's taking me for an audition; that's it! He's very excited for me. Why do you always have to think the worst?"

"I don't feel like arguing about this," her mom stated, getting up from her chair and heading out of the room. "I won't always be around to keep an eye out on you anyway."

"Gladys!" Elizabeth's dad bellowed. "Please don't talk like that." She shook her head and continued to meander out of the room.

"What's going on, dad?" Elizabeth asked, noting the worried expression on her father's face.

"Your mom's sick, Elizabeth," he answered, looking down at his feet.

"I know..."

"No. You really *don't*," he contradicted. "She...your mom has cancer, sweetie. She...she didn't want you to know. She's been fighting it for some time now, and she thought she had it beat. But..."

"Dad, what are you saying?" Elizabeth questioned in shock. She took a seat in her mom's recliner beside him.

"I'm...I'm saying...your mother is dying, Elizabeth," he replied, couching back a sob.

Stunned, Elizabeth's eyes bulged and her mouth gaped open. *How could this be?*

"She wants to see you have a happy life. It's why she is so hard on you. I have something to tell you, Elizabeth. I think you are old enough to hear it."

Something else? She was still reeling from the last pronouncement. "Wh...what?" she asked even though she really did not want to hear anything else.

"Your mom has reason to be so worried about Alan. The reason she reacts the way she does is because I got her pregnant when she was eighteen. She never got to go to college and follow her dreams. She wants different for you. She loves you a lot, Elizabeth. Even if she doesn't always know how to show it."

Struck dumb, Elizabeth could not respond.

"I'm sorry to dump all this on you. But it's well past time that you knew."

"So...you're saying there is no hope for mom?" Elizabeth asked, disregarding her dad's last disclosure. She needed to deal with one shocking revelation at a time.

"They've begun giving her radiation. But it's for the pain...not as a cure. That's all the doctors can do for her now – control her pain. It will only be a matter of time now," he sadly relayed, looking down at his feet.

Elizabeth could still not believe her ears. She did not know what to say. "Should I go talk to her?" Elizabeth questioned, looking toward the archway leading out of the living room. "Should I tell her I know?"

"Ah...I'll tell her that I've told you," her dad replied, giving her a sheepish glance. He knew Gladys was going to be very upset that Elizabeth knew about her illness. But Elizabeth needed to know the truth – all of it, including Gladys' out-of-wedlock pregnancy. It was important that Elizabeth understand why her mom overreacted so much to her relationship with Alan.

"Okay..." Elizabeth replied, sounding very unsure. "So what should I do?"

"Just go about your normal routine," her father answered. "It's all we *can* do. Your mother doesn't want our pity. She's a strong woman. We need to stay strong too."

"Okay," Elizabeth numbly responded once more. But she felt anything but strong. She felt as if the world had just come to a screeching halt. Physically, she felt ill all at once. She was cold; she was sick to her stomach; her head throbbed.

She jumped when the television erupted in sound all at once. Looking back at her father, she saw he had gotten up and turned the television on. He escaped through watching TV, and that was what he was doing right now. Their conversation was over. Elizabeth stood and quietly crept out of the room – confused and dazed.

* * * *

Elizabeth went to her room. She sat on the side of her bed, picked up the phone from the bedside table, and called Alan.

"Hey, what's up?" he said in a chipper voice recognizing her voice.

"Alan…could you come and pick me up?"

"On a Tuesday night? After seeing you last night at *Antonio's* for a little bit? This is a rare treat. Since when do I get to see you so much during the week? Don't you have homework, or some quiz or test to study for?" he lightheartedly inquired.

"I have both," she answered rather matter-of-factly. "But I can't concentrate on either right now. I…I need you."

Alan picked up on the turmoil in her voice then. Instantly concerned, he said, "I'll be right over."

"Okay. I'll see you in a few," Elizabeth replied, feeling a bit of relief. Everything always seemed better when she was with Alan. She counted on this comfort now. She hung up the phone and waited anxiously for his arrival.

* * * *

At her house within fifteen minutes, Alan found it even more unsettling when Elizabeth did not even invite him in. She walked out the door as soon as he rang the bell. Without even saying hello, she waltzed past him and headed for his car, trancelike.

Alan turned and followed at her heel. He unlocked her car door, opened it, allowed her to settle herself inside, and then closed it. He hurried around to the driver's side and clambered inside himself.

As he started the car and put it in reverse, he noticed Elizabeth stared straight ahead out the windshield. Very concerned about her, he asked in a soft voice, "Where do you want to go?" He had pulled the Monte Carlo out onto the street.

"Your apartment," she answered in a near monotone.

"Okay," he replied, putting the car in drive and heading in that direction. The car radio played *Come on Eileen*. A very upbeat song, both he and Elizabeth liked it. But Elizabeth did not move to the beat this evening. She still looked straight ahead, expressionless.

Alan stepped down on the gas a bit more. In a hurry to get to his apartment, he hoped to get to the bottom of what troubled Elizabeth when they got there. For now, he remained silent, giving her space. He figured if she wanted to talk then she would. He did not want her to feel forced to do so. But it drove him nuts not knowing what had her so upset. He drove on, anxious to arrive home. He would get to the bottom of things once they got to the apartment. Of this, he was determined.

* * * *

Elizabeth walked directly over to the couch and sat down as soon as they walked into Alan's apartment. Normally, Alan would have turned on the stereo. Their favorite station, WBGS, played a good mix of Top 40 songs. He also might have turned on the television; they watched a lot of MTV. They particularly liked Michael Jackson's *Thriller* video. But this evening, Alan turned on neither the stereo nor the TV. This evening, he merely took a seat beside Elizabeth on the couch.

"What's wrong, Elizabeth?" he asked.

Elizabeth turned toward him, slid herself into his arms, laid her head on his shoulder, and began to softly cry. Alan wrapped his arms around her and held her tight, stroking her back to comfort her. He patiently waited.

Several minutes later, Elizabeth pulled back from him. "Thank you for being here with me, Alan," she said, wiping away a few remaining tears.

"I'm glad to be here for you. But can you tell me what's wrong?" he asked again.

"I…I found out tonight that…my mom…my mom is dying," she managed to utter. The words still felt strange to her. She still had a hard time believing them.

Alan dropped his head a little; his eyes darkened and his lips parted a bit. "Did…did you say…she's dying?" he repeated.

"Yeah," she answered. "I know…I'm still in shock too. She's evidently had cancer for some time and has been keeping it from me. My dad says there is no hope…"

"Jimenez, Elizabeth…I'm so sorry," Alan said, pulling her back into an embrace. He felt awful for her. He wanted to fix things, but he knew he could not.

"And you want to hear something else?" she asked, pulling back from him. Her eyes looked a little cold now. "My dad also told me mom got pregnant with me before they were married. So now you know why she is such a nutcase toward you. She doesn't want me to make the same mistake. I guess I ruined her life," she stated, sounding bitter.

"You changed her life," Alan stated, squeezing her shoulders and locking eyes with her. "But you certainly didn't ruin it. And I don't think your mom thinks that way either. If she didn't love you, she wouldn't be so concerned about you. She wants you to have things she couldn't..."

"Yeah...things she couldn't have because of *me*," Elizabeth pointed out, choking up again. She hurt. She hurt that her mother was dying, and she hurt because she felt betrayed. She knew her mother had married her father when she was eighteen, but she had always believed they married because they loved one another – not because they had to. Now, she viewed their whole relationship in a far different light.

"Look...I can't speak for your mother," Alan said. "But I know she loves you. And I know you love her. You need to talk to her about all this." *Before it's too late*, he thought, but did not add.

"I've never been able to talk to my mom like I can my dad," Elizabeth admitted. *Now I understand why. Alan thinks my mom loves me...but she probably hates me, or at the very least, resents me. And what a hypocrite she has been about Alan and me.* "Alan, I think we should spend the night in Louisville," she strangely blurted out.

"Why would we need to spend the night? Your interview is at noon, and Louisville is only an hour and a half away..."

"We don't *need* to spend the night there. I *want* to spend the night. I want to stay in a hotel room there with you. I want for the two of us to make love."

"Whoa!" Alan exclaimed. "I know you are hurt by what you just learned, Elizabeth. But...you can't throw your values out the window because of this."

"What values? The values I've believed in...have been taught...have all been a sham. So why am I holding back? I know you want to be with me, and I want to be with you," she proclaimed, framing his face with her hands.

"I do want to be with you," he professed, drawing in to give her a brief kiss. "But not like this. Not to avenge your mother. When the two of us make love, I want it to be for the right reasons."

"And what are the right reasons?" Elizabeth questioned, her eyes very serious.

"Because you love me. Because I love you. Because it's the right time."

"We have all that," Elizabeth argued, drawing in for another kiss – this one packing heat.

When Alan finally pulled back, a little dazed, and unceasingly searched Elizabeth's eyes, she could almost hear the gears in his mind churning. "Elizabeth," he finally spoke, after several minutes of meditative silence. "I know, these last few months, I've gone a little bit farther with you, but I didn't do that to frustrate you. I just love you so much I'm having a hard time not touching you. You opened Pandora's box that night you placed my hands on you. But, I promised I would never push you to do anything you didn't want to do, and I intend to keep that promise. In Louisville, at the Galt House, is not the right time…"

"So when is the right time?" she challenged.

"According to your words…when we get married. Which will be when you get out of college."

"But what if I've changed my mind, and I don't want to wait until after we are married?"

"That would be fine, if you had given this a lot of thought. But you haven't. You are just reacting to a bad turn of events. Are you trying to follow in your mother's footsteps? Do you want to get pregnant?"

"No!" Elizabeth exclaimed, looking shocked by Alan's question.

"Well, you know the facts of life as well as I do, and if we sleep together this weekend, then there is a possibility of that happening. You didn't think about that, did you?"

"No," she had to admit, looking down at the couch cushion.

Alan reached to gently raise her chin. "I love you so much it hurts sometimes, Elizabeth," he uttered. "I wish I could take away the pain you are feeling, but I can't. All I can do is be here for you. And not let you do something you might regret. The last thing I want to happen is for you to regret our making love. I'd rather wait four years. Wouldn't you, when you get right down to it?"

Elizabeth looked him directly in the eyes. His eyes shone with love for her. Her heart swelled with love for him. *He's right*, she could not help but acknowledge. "Just hold me, Alan," she said and slid back into his arms.

He wrapped his arms around her and stroked her back again. "I'm here, Elizabeth. I always will be," he promised. And Elizabeth could not help but believe him.

Chapter 9
The Audition

What happens when presented with a special dream? Does it overshadow everything, and everyone else, in our lives? Or does having someone special in our lives, make the dream that much sweeter?

~ Sissy Marlyn ~

T hey arrived at the Galt House at 11:00 a.m., even though testing was not supposed to begin until noon. Alan walked his highly nervous girlfriend through the spacious, wood-grained lined lobby, up a wide, carpeted staircase, and to a large conference room where the screening was to take place. Elizabeth was surprised to find several other, young women already waiting to test as well.

A man with a clipboard quickly took her name, home address, and telephone number. He then brusquely told Elizabeth to have a seat and wait for her name to be called, motioning to some nearby, vacant chairs.

Alan tried unsuccessfully to convince Elizabeth to sit with him. But, high strung, she mostly paced back and forth in front of him, practically wearing a hole in the carpet. They started calling names around 11:30. However, Elizabeth, still agonizing, waited for a little over an hour before she fearfully heard her name. Alan gave her a fleeting kiss for luck, and she swiftly disappeared behind a curtained-off area, consciously fighting to keep her knees from embarrassingly knocking.

"Elizabeth Warren?" asked a rather tall, slim, white-haired man, in a grey, tailored suit. He sat in a chair behind a shiny wooden table.

"Yes. That's me," Elizabeth answered a little shakily.

"I'm Arthur Goldbloom. I'll be producing *Bardstown* for MGM. I take it, by the way you are dressed, you have been briefed a little about the character you will be testing for?"

Elizabeth donned coveralls. She had borrowed these from WKU's costume department. She wanted to look like a farm girl. She also had on very little makeup and had her hair haphazardly pulled back into a ponytail.

"Yes, sir," she answered in a quiet voice, looking him directly in the eye and trying to give the illusion of confidence. "I go to Western Kentucky University in Bowling Green. Stuart Lyons, who used to work for MGM before coming to the university to direct and teach, sent me for this screen test. He keeps in touch with certain individuals at MGM, and he sometimes sends prospective actors and actresses to try out for certain parts. He told me I would be testing for the part of a farm girl."

"Stuart Lyons, huh?" Mr. Goldbloom repeated, folding his hands and leaning back in his seat a bit. He added with a bittersweet smile, "I remember Stuart well. How's he doing? He decided Hollywood was a little too unreal for his likening, so now it appears you young people are able to benefit from his expertise. He's a fine man."

"He's doing great!" Elizabeth enthusiastically told Mr. Goldbloom, delighted to hear he had actually known Stuart. "We're proud to have him as our director."

"As well you should be," he genuinely stressed his high opinion of Stuart. "Well, Elizabeth, I'm very anxious to see your test now. Because Stuart wouldn't have sent you to us if he didn't truly believe you had talent." Arthur Goldbloom honestly explained, and then swiftly proceeded to hold out a script to her.

Elizabeth stepped forward and carefully took it from his outstretched hand. Another man came over and directed her where to stand. Then Arthur instructed, "Take a few minutes to study this scene and prepare yourself to be filmed. You just tell us when you think you are ready. Then I want you to look directly at the man standing beside that camera over there. He will give you a countdown from ten. On the word, 'action', I want you to look directly into the camera lens, and give this scene your best shot. Good luck!"

"Thank you," Elizabeth said with a meager smile as she quickly and thoroughly began to scan the few pages Mr. Goldbloom had given her.

When she finally, nervously announced her readiness, Elizabeth concentrated so hard on portraying her character and truthfully eliciting the emotions the scene called for, she barely heard the director's important countdown. On the word, 'action', however, she triumphantly propelled herself right into the scene, successfully blocking out everything else around her.

Moments later, as she convincingly delivered her very last line, Elizabeth had engrossed herself so deeply in her intense presentation, it took her a few seconds to snap back to reality. Since the scene called for her to get emotional, she mustered her feelings about her mom's illness. Her mom and her still had not talked. In fact, they seemed to be avoiding one another. Elizabeth got so caught up in the passionate speech, actual tears stood in her eyes when Arthur Goldbloom joined her again.

"Very Nice!" he freely complimented, flashing her a pleased smile. "Have you ever done any other acting, Elizabeth?"

"Not professionally," she honestly admitted, eagerly returning his smile. Delighted by his praise, Elizabeth added, "I just completed my first college play a little over a week ago."

"I'm quite certain you probably did a very fine job with that play as well," Mr. Goldbloom continued to candidly commend, much to Elizabeth's delight. "Thank you for coming in to audition today, Elizabeth. We'll be screening all week, so we probably won't make our decision on who to cast until at least next Saturday. If you don't get this part though, I would still suggest you keep on trying. Because Stuart was right to send you. You have an enormous acting talent. I haven't seen the film of you we just shot, but I have a strong feeling the camera probably loves you as well."

"Oh, thank you again!" Elizabeth gushed, springing forward to firmly grasp Arthur Goldbloom's hand. She gave it a hearty shake, and then she excitedly rushed from the room to share the exhilarating news with Alan.

* * * *

When Elizabeth got home from her audition, she found her mother sitting alone in the living room. A cloudy day outside, the room was dark, since her mother did not have any lamps turned on. Elizabeth started to walk on past and go to her room, but her mother called to her. Uncomfortable, Elizabeth made her way into the darkened living room.

"Can we talk for a moment?" her mother asked. Her eyes looked tired and sad.

"Where's daddy?" Elizabeth asked. Surprised not to see him there, she was looking for a way out of this confrontation with her mother. She wanted to run and hide. Basically, other than the audition today, she had been putting her mother's illness and her betrayal out of her mind.

"Your dad went to the store for me. I think the two of us need to have a chat," her mother said, getting them back on subject. She stared at her hands. She looked as ill at ease as Elizabeth.

Elizabeth took a seat on the couch. She joined her hands and fidgeted with her high school ring. Several moments of awkward silence passed.

"So, what's on your mind?" her mother asked, breaking the silence at last.

"The audition I just finished," Elizabeth answered, giving her mom a glance. She knew this was not the answer her mother sought.

"Oh..." her mom replied. She looked a little hurt. "Anything else," she fished.

Suddenly finding it hard to breathe, the air in the room felt thin to Elizabeth. She squirmed a little in her seat. "Dad told me about you having cancer," she answered, forcing herself to look at her mom again. She saw her flinch, so Elizabeth averted her eyes again.

"And he also told you about him getting me pregnant before we were married," her mom added, changing the subject a bit. This topic concerned her more than talking about her illness.

"Yes," Elizabeth confirmed, looking her in the eye again.

"And how do you feel about that?" her mom dared to ask, gnawing at her bottom lip a bit. She championed the art of asking pointed questioned.

"Like it explains a lot," Elizabeth honestly answered.

"Like what?" her mother further questioned.

"Like why you and I have never been close. I…I ruined your life, right?" Elizabeth asked, breaking eye contact again. She suddenly felt like crying, and she fought her emotions.

"Elizabeth, look at me," her mother commanded.

Elizabeth slowly raised her head. Her mother's eyes bore holes into her. She wanted to look away again, but she forced herself to maintain eye contact. "What?" she asked. She wanted more than ever to bolt from the room.

"I need for you to understand something. You did *not* ruin my life. *I* messed up my life…"

"Yeah, by getting pregnant with me," Elizabeth stated. Her emotions got the best of her then, and she began to cry.

Her mom slowly arose from her chair and came over to the couch, sitting down hip to hip with her daughter. When she put her arm around Elizabeth and pulled her close, Elizabeth lost all control. As if a dam burst, tears splashed down her cheeks, and her body shook with sobs. Her mother's unusual affection caused this emotional meltdown.

Elizabeth cried more when she heard her mother's voice soften and say, "Shh…it's okay. I love you, Elizabeth. You didn't mess up my life. My choices did. That's why I want so much more for you."

Elizabeth slowly reigned in her emotions. "Wh…why didn't you just tell me the truth, mom? I feel like everything I've always been taught was such a lie now. Like how I should wait until I get married."

"I know it seems like I've been a hypocrite. But…I do want you to wait. I want you to finish college and do whatever makes you happy before you have to settle down with a baby…"

"Like you did."

"Yeah, like I did. But don't think that I don't love you, because I do."

"And daddy. Do you love him too?" Elizabeth dared to ask, intensely scrutinizing her mother's weary eyes.

"Of course."

"Even though you had to marry him?"

"We both still had a choice, Elizabeth. Your father could have shirked his responsibility, but he loved me, and I loved him. And we both love you."

Elizabeth looked away again. Still not accustomed to her mother sharing her emotions, she could not look her in the eye and not want to cry again. "So what do you want from me?" Elizabeth asked.

"I want for you to be happy. I want for you to have whatever future you want."

"And what if that future is with Alan?" she challenged.

"Are the two of you sleeping together?" her mother dared to inquire.

"No. And do you know why? Alan wants our first time together to be special. He doesn't want me to have any regrets. He's a great guy, mom."

"Sounds like he is," Elizabeth was surprised to hear her admit. She looked over at her mom as if she did not know her. "Take it slow, honey. That's all I ask. I have to start trusting you to make your own decisions and your dad to look out for you..."

"I wish you wouldn't say that, mom," Elizabeth said, tears standing in her eyes again.

"I know, but it's true," she said, reaching to pat Elizabeth's hand. "I know I haven't told you...but...I'm very proud of you, Elizabeth. You can make big things with your life if you want to. It's all about making the right decisions. Don't think that I'm saying I regret having you, because that's *so* not true. I only regret having you too soon. I think I could have been a better mother to you if I had been a little older. Can you forgive me for that?"

"Mom, I love you," Elizabeth said, choking up again. She threw her arms around her mother and folded into her. She heard her mom start crying. The two embraced and cried for awhile, but they realized a wall had come down between them. Elizabeth had never felt so close to her mom, and her mom had never felt so close to Elizabeth. Their relationship had taken a hard turn, and both of them were happy about this change. The only thing both of them wished for now was more time. Something they sadly could not have.

* * * *

Disappointed when she heard nothing from MGM the following Saturday, Elizabeth still relished having had the chance to audition. She had never really believed she would actually get the part. She would not soon forget Arthur Goldbloom's kind encouragement, however. Elizabeth was more determined than ever now that acting was what she wanted to do with her life. Her mom even seemed to be supporting this dream more now, and she was also being much nicer to Alan.

Sunday afternoon, attentively engrossed in reading a chapter in her Sociology book, for an early, Monday morning class, Elizabeth was startled when the phone rang. Figuring it was probably Alan, she was surprised when she was met by a stranger's voice on the other end of the line.

"Hello. Is Elizabeth Warren there?" the man's voice asked.

"This is she," Elizabeth politely answered.

"Elizabeth, this is Arthur Goldbloom," the man's voice informed her.

Elizabeth was so shocked by the sound of his name she nearly dropped the phone.

"Hello," he repeated, obviously puzzled by her strange silence. "Are you still there?"

"Ah...yeah. Yes, I'm still here. Hello, Mr. Goldbloom. It's really nice to talk to you again," she finally managed to ramble, when she could find her voice.

"Please call me Arthur," he kindly directed. "After all, we will be working together. Congratulations, Elizabeth! The director and the rest of my crew agree that you fit the part we are looking for to a tee."

"I...I...I'm sorry," Elizabeth stuttered, not believing her ears. "But did you just say I got the part? Please tell me this isn't some sort of joke."

"I can assure you this is most certainly not a joke,' he said with a slightly amused chuckle. "We will begin filming the middle of next month in Bardstown. So that will give you a few weeks to have a lawyer look over the contracts I'll be sending you and to return them to us."

"Cool beans! I can't believe this is actually happening to me!" Elizabeth excitedly shared in an uncontrollable, animated voice. "I think I may need to pinch myself to make sure I'm not dreaming this."

"You're not dreaming," Arthur attested with a hearty laugh. "But I'm truly delighted to hear you are so excited about joining us, and I look forward to the pleasure of working with you."

"Oh, the pleasure will most definitely be mine!" Elizabeth exclaimed. "I can't thank you enough, Mr. Goldbloom!"

"I told you, it's Arthur, to those I work with," he corrected in a light voice. "Anyway, after we get your signed contracts back, my secretary will be in touch with you. She will provide you with the time and date we'll need to see you in Bardstown, and she can give you directions to the set. So, as I already said, I look forward to working with you in a few weeks."

"I look forward to working with you too!" she zealously agreed in a happy, excited voice.

"Great. See you soon. Goodbye," Arthur concluded their conversation.

"Goodbye," Elizabeth reluctantly replied, slowly lowering the receiver. However, as she let her revealing talk with Arthur sink in, she snatched it from its cradle and called Alan to share her splendid news.

Chapter 10
Initiation

If at first you don't succeed, try, try again.
Easier said than done! But if you want something
bad enough, you'll find a way to make it happen.

~ Sissy Marlyn ~

lizabeth received the contract the following day via express mail. She promptly telephoned Stuart, and he gave her the name of an attorney friend. Elizabeth passed on this attorney's name to her father, and he called the man and set up an appointment for all three of them to sit down and look over the contract.

The attorney's office was in Louisville, so Elizabeth got to make another trip there, albeit with her father this time. The attorney sported an office on the twenty-fifth floor in the Citizen's Plaza building. Stepping into the building, Elizabeth and her father stopped in the lobby, looking around. Considering the Citizen's Plaza was a large building, they did not know which direction to go in.

A woman who had come in behind them stopped and asked, "Excuse me, but did I hear you say you are looking for the twenty-fifth floor?"

"Yes," Elizabeth's dad answered. He had just been discussing this fact with Elizabeth as they walked through the doors to the building. "We have a meeting with an attorney named Aric Peterson."

"With Grayson & Associates?" the woman clarified.

"Yes," Elizabeth's dad agreed again.

"That's where I am heading. I'm Jackie Lynn Greathouse. I'm also an attorney with this firm. I'd be glad to show you where to go."

"Thanks. We'd appreciate that," Elizabeth's dad said with a smile.

They quickly fell into pace behind this woman. She led them to a set of elevators on the far side of the building. The elevators were marked 12-29. Jackie Lynn pushed the *25* button when they got on the elevator.

The shiny brass posts, wall-sconce lighting, and dark walnut walls which greeted Elizabeth and her father when they stepped off the elevator gave reference to this law firm's elite status. Known to deal exclusively with high wealth clients, Aric was only meeting with Elizabeth and her father as a favor to Stuart.

Jackie Lynn led them up to the receptionist. "Amy will show you to Aric's office," she told them with a smile.

"Thanks for helping us find the elevators," Elizabeth's father said.

"No problem," Jackie Lynn replied with another smile. She headed off down the hallway, headed for her own office.

Elizabeth and her father were then greeted by the receptionist, a young woman dressed impeccably in a wrinkle-free, black skirt and cream, silk blouse. "May I help you?" she asked, giving them her undivided attention.

"We have an appointment with Aric Peterson," Elizabeth's father said.

"And your name?" the woman asked.

"Bill Warren and his daughter Elizabeth," he replied.

"Thank you," the woman responded, picking up her phone. She called into Aric Peterson's office and relayed, "Mr. Warren and his daughter Elizabeth are here to see you." He must have okayed their visit, because the next thing the woman uttered was, "I'll bring them right back."

She stood then. "Mr. Peterson is expecting you," she told them. "If you will follow me, I will take you to his office."

Elizabeth's father nodded, and they began following this woman down a carpeted, wood paneled hallway and into Aric Peterson's office. Aric sat behind a large, imposing, walnut desk in a big, black leather chair. A window with a spectacular view of the Ohio River was situated right behind his desk, providing natural light to the room.

When Aric stood, Elizabeth noted he was a tall man. He had on a navy pinstriped suit, which complimented his shiny, silver hairline. The pale blue dress shirt and navy tie he wore showcased his dark blue eyes. He reached to give a firm handshake to both of them. Then he motioned to two chairs in front of his desk.

Elizabeth's father handed him the contract for his perusal before he sat. Elizabeth dropped to a seated position beside her father. Aric was the last to be seated. They were all silent as Aric read through the pages.

When he finished, he looked up at Elizabeth's father and explained, "Mr. Warren, the contract states that your daughter, Elizabeth…" He glanced at Elizabeth then, before continuing, "agrees to six months of filming for the movie *Bardstown*. The majority of the filming will take place on location in Bardstown, Kentucky. Some of the filming, at the director's discretion, will be filmed at MGM studios in Florida. MGM agrees to pay all of your daughter's expenses relating to filming, lodging, and travel expenses. In addition, Elizabeth's salary will be $25,000, paid in weekly installments of $4,166.66. If filming continues for more than six months, then Elizabeth will still continue to be paid $4,166.66 a week until filming is complete."

Elizabeth's mouth dropped open in shock when she heard the sum of money. She could not imagine being paid so much for doing what she loved.

"There is only one other thing I would suggest," Aric said. "It's called a gross participation clause. This would entitle Elizabeth to a percentage of every dollar the film grosses over and above whatever amount she has already been paid. So in other words, if the film makes a million dollars, and MGM agrees to pay her a gross participation of…say one percent, Elizabeth would make another $9,750. She deserves to make a percentage of profits, especially should the film be a big hit," the attorney advised.

Elizabeth glanced at her dad. He appeared to be awestruck by the numbers as well. "O…kay…how do we go about getting this gross participation clause added?" he asked.

"I'll draw up an addendum to the contract. Then we'll forward everything back to MGM. If they agree to the terms, they will sign off on it and send it back. Then all Elizabeth has to do is sign, and she's on her way."

"And if they don't agree?" Elizabeth's dad questioned. He did not want to do something to anger MGM and mess up his daughter's big chance. Extraordinary that she had been offered this opportunity, he understood the same offer would not likely come about again.

"If they don't agree, they will let me know, and Elizabeth can sign the contract as is."

"They won't back out of the deal if we ask them for something more?" he clarified.

"No. They are used to negotiating. The worst that will happen is they will turn down our counter."

"Alright, then," Elizabeth's dad agreed. "How much to do an addendum?"

"$500," Aric answered. This was a lowball figure for him, but then again, he was doing this service as a favor to a friend.

"Okay," Elizabeth heard her father agree.

"Are you sure, daddy," she questioned, looking him in the eye. "Five hundred dollars sounds like a lot of money."

"You can always pay me back," he said with a lopsided grin, patting his daughter on her shoulder. He would have paid even more to see his daughter get this opportunity. He was very happy for Elizabeth.

"I *will* pay you back," she agreed.

"Draw up the papers," Elizabeth's dad instructed, focusing his attention on Aric again.

"I'll have them out to MGM tomorrow. I'll be in touch," he said. He stood and offered his hand again. Both Elizabeth and her father also stood and shook Aric's hand once more.

"Thank you," Elizabeth's father said.

"Thank you. Good luck, Elizabeth. I look forward to seeing you in *Bardstown*," Aric said, giving her a smile for the first time.

"Thanks," she said, giving him a giggle in embarrassment. She still could not believe she would be acting in a movie.

As they left the office to drive back home, Elizabeth could hardly wait to call Alan and share the latest news with him. She knew he would be happy for her. She was so excited she could hardly stand it. Things were coming together wonderfully.

* * * *

MGM agreed to the new terms of the contract without complaint. So the second week of April, on a Sunday afternoon, Alan drove Elizabeth to Bardstown. Expected to report to Lincoln Plantation – the set for Bardstown – at 5:00 a.m. the next morning, Elizabeth needed to be nearby. That being the case, MGM reserved a nearby cottage for her stay.

Since Elizabeth would primarily be in Bardstown during the week, her college course load had to be temporarily put on hold. It was not feasible for her to attend college courses at WKU and be in Bardstown every day. She promised her mom she would return to college once filming for *Bardstown* completed, but her mother doubted this turn of events. She also hated the fact that Elizabeth would practically be living out of the house. Even though Elizabeth was eighteen, her mother did not feel she was old enough to be in a strange town on her own.

"It will be okay, Gladys. Elizabeth has a good head on her shoulder," Elizabeth's dad tried to persuade her. In the end, Elizabeth's mom had no option but to let her daughter go. She worried in silence and vowed to keep an eye out on her daughter whenever she could – for as long as her health allowed her to do so.

When Alan pulled up in front of the small cottage, Elizabeth smiled. A pink weatherboard house with a white picket fence around it, the cottage looked like something out of a fairytale. "Well, I guess this is home-sweet-home for about six months," Elizabeth commented.

"Kind of seems that way," Alan said with a bittersweet smile. He also had a problem accepting that Elizabeth would be living an hour away from him most of the time.

He vacated the car, went around to Elizabeth's side, and took her hand in his when she had climbed out of his Monte Carlo and he had shut her door. He walked her up the brick walk and the three brick steps. Reaching in his pocket, he extracted a key. They had picked this key up at a rental office in downtown Bardstown before coming to the cottage.

Alan unlocked the door for Elizabeth and pushed it open. Elizabeth walked inside. Sunlight streamed across the shiny wooden floor and reflected off of the glass on an old antique clock which sat atop a fireplace mantel. A massive stone fireplace resided underneath. Ancient black-and-white photographs decorated the walls. An oriental rug adorned the hardwood floor in front of a cloth, blue-and-white-striped sofa. There were also two black leather recliners in the room, a coffee table, two side tables, and a television. Elizabeth noted that the house had a pleasant, homey smell to it – almost as if someone had recently baked cookies.

"It's nice," she said.

"Yeah," Alan agreed. "I'll go get your suitcases. You find the bedroom, and I'll put them in there for you before I go."

"Okay. Thanks," Elizabeth said. "Alan…" she said, clutching his hand before he separated from her.

"Huh?"

"Thanks," she said again, and drew in to give him a kiss. "I appreciate you driving me here."

"I didn't want you to come here alone," he said, sounding dejected. "I don't even like the idea of leaving you. But I guess I have to do what I have to do," he stated. Lowering his eyes, he toed the floor with his shoe. He reluctantly released her hand and turned to go back out the door.

Elizabeth walked through the living room and down a hallway. She came to a bedroom with a full-size bed in it first. Then she came to a bathroom. At the end of the hall, on the other side, resided the master bedroom. A four-poster, king-sized bed, adorned with a maroon and blue, Wedding Ring, handmade quilt, took up most of the room. An oak cabinet with a television inside sat against the wall across from the foot of the bed. There was also an oak chest of drawers and nightstand in the room.

Alan came up behind Elizabeth a few moments later with her two bags. He held one in his hand and had the other slung over his shoulder. "Where do you want me to put these?" he asked.

"Just sit them both at the foot of the bed," she told him.

He walked forward into the room and discarded the bags. Turning, he noted the odd expression on Elizabeth's face. "What?" he asked.

"There are two bedrooms," she answered.

"Yeah...and?" he questioned, not sure why this configuration would bother her. "Did you want to sleep in the other room instead? It's a smaller bed. Is the king too big?"

"No," Elizabeth replied. "I was just thinking...maybe...well... would you like to stay here tonight, since there are two rooms? Or would that be too awkward? You seemed kind of bummed about me being on my own," she pointed out.

"I am," he admitted.

"I know you have to be at work tomorrow, but I'll be up at 4:00 a.m. We could have breakfast together, and then you would be back in Bowling Green in plenty of time. What do you think?"

"I think..." he repeated, closing the distance between her and folding her into an embrace. "that I like the way you think."

"So would you like to stay?" she asked with a smile.

"Of course, I would," he agreed, returned her smile and playfully kissing the end of her nose.

Elizabeth was happy to hear that Alan would be staying with her. Truth be known, she had been a little ambivalent about being alone in Bardstown herself. Plus, he would help to calm her nerves. She drew in and gave him another appreciative kiss.

* * * *

As arranged, MGM sent a car to pick Elizabeth up the next morning. They picked her up at 4:45 a.m. Alan walked her out to the car. He had given Elizabeth a farewell-and-good-luck kiss in the cozy kitchen. They had drunk coffee and eaten Danishes, provided compliments of the cottage owner. Both of them were quiet, because neither were used to being up this early.

"Drive safe," Elizabeth told him, as she settled herself into the comfortable, leather backseat of the black Cadillac MGM had sent for her.

"Have a great first day," Alan wished, giving her one final peck.

He stepped back then, and let the driver – a tall man in a dark suit and chauffeur's cap – close Elizabeth's door.

A few minutes later, the Cadillac comfortably floated down the highway. The easy ride almost lulled Elizabeth back to sleep. It was much too early to be up, but she knew she needed to get used to rising at this deplorable hour.

Ten minutes later, the chauffeur pulled the Cadillac to a black, iron-barred gate. A gold plate hanging on the gate read: *Lincoln Plantation*. Elizabeth heard the power window buzz. A security guard greeted the driver. "I'm bringing Elizabeth Warren to the soundstage," he told the guard.

"Wow, security and all. I'm impressed already," Elizabeth told the driver.

"Yes. It's pretty impressive," the man agreed, glancing at her in the rearview mirror, as the security guard checked his clipboard, found Elizabeth's name, and opened the gate to allow him to drive through.

"If you think that is impressive, wait until you have to hire your first bodyguard," the driver made further conversation.

"I'm so sure. That's a little hard for me to imagine," she admitted with an excited giggle.

"Well, if this movie is a hit, it won't be hard for you to imagine for long," the chauffer informed her.

Elizabeth really could not imagine having to have a bodyguard. She was just happy to be where she was at, doing what she was doing. It was still very unreal to her at this point.

"Thanks for your vote of confidence. I hope this movie is that successful," Elizabeth admitted.

She noted the shadows on the car and on the pavement. They were driving past several tall trees. It almost seemed they were going into a forest. Elizabeth was relieved when, at last, a large house came into view. It looked like a mansion.

Seconds later, the Cadillac pulled to a stop in front of this building. The driver vacated the car and came around to open Elizabeth's door. "Have a good day, Ms. Warren," he said, as she stepped from the car.

"You too. Thanks for the lift," she said. She felt a bit awkward. She was not sure if she was supposed to offer a tip to this man or not. When she took her purse off her shoulder, the driver said, "No need for that, ma'am. MGM takes care of all gratuities too."

"Oh…okay," she chuckled, throwing her purse back over her shoulder. "Well, thanks again. I guess you'll be picking me up when filming is through for the day?"

"Our company will be. I'm not sure whether it will be me or not," he answered. "You take care."

"You too," she wished again.

She watched as he walked back around the car and climbed back inside. As he slowly pulled the Cadillac away, Elizabeth stood and watched it disappear into the dark horizon. Only then did she hesitantly turn and begin to make her way into the unfamiliar house. She suddenly felt terribly alone and very frightened.

As Elizabeth opened the large wood door, the light from inside almost blinded her. A large, sparkling chandelier hung from crystal ropes overhead, brilliantly illuminating the white granite floor in the foyer. She also noticed the smell of the house – a bit musty.

Arthur Goldbloom's instant, cheerful greeting helped to settle Elizabeth's nerves a bit. "Hello again, Elizabeth. Welcome to the set of *Bardstown*," he cordially received her. He stood by a winding, marble staircase a few feet in front of her. As he advanced a few paces in her direction, Elizabeth noted the clip-clop of his shoes on the hard floor.

A short man – five-foot-five at the most – with shoulder-length, copper-blond hair, dark brown eyes, and dark-framed glasses also approached.

"I don't know if you remember my director from your audition, but it's time you two meet. This is Ryan Axman. Ryan, this is Elizabeth Warren. She will be portraying Julia Parks."

"Nice to officially meet you, Elizabeth," the director said with a smile and offered his hand in welcome.

Elizabeth nervously shook his hand. "Nice to meet you, Mr. Axman," she greeted in a quivering, unsure voice.

"We'll all be on a first name basis around here, Elizabeth," Arthur quickly corrected her. "So you can just call him Ryan. You'll meet the rest of the cast and crew all throughout the day. Right now, you just need to go down that hall and into the third door on your left. They are waiting for you in *Makeup and Wardrobe*."

"Okay. Thanks," she mumbled and swiftly started in the direction he pointed.

The third door on the left had a shiny brass sign posted which plainly stated *Makeup and Wardrobe*. Opening the door, Elizabeth beheld what looked rather like a very fancy beauty salon – rows of chairs, each with a mirror surrounded by bright lights directly in front of it. Two of the chairs already occupied – one with another young woman and the other with a young man – a team of individuals scurried around the actors. One person applied makeup and the other styled their hair.

"Well, what are you waiting for?" A woman said to her, tapping her on the shoulder from behind. "If you are part of my crew being filmed today, then have a seat, so we can start getting your hair fixed and your makeup done. Otherwise, you are in the wrong place. What's your name, honey?"

"I'm Elizabeth Warren," she stated. Turning to face this strange woman, Elizabeth discovered a robust, older woman with gray bouffant hair. "I'm supposed to be portraying Julia Parks," Elizabeth further clarified

"Aw…congratulations," the woman stated with sarcasm. "If that's the case, then will you please choose a makeup station, so we can get started? We don't have all day, you know."

Elizabeth promptly walked to the vacant chair beside the other young woman and had a seat.

"What size are you, sweetheart?" the woman with the bouffant hair asked. "I would guess about a seven or an eight."

"Eight is right," she agreed with a slight smile.

"George," the woman called. A man hurried over. "Would you bring in the rack of size eight dresses for Miss Warren?" The man nodded and immediately disappeared from the room.

"My name is Tammy," the woman finally introduced herself. "I'm going to help you pick out the clothes you will need for filming today. Then, after you've changed for the first scene, my friend Michelle, working on your co-star beside you here, will do your makeup and hair for you," she explained pointing to the other woman standing right beside her, busily working on Elizabeth's co-star's face. Michelle looked to be an older lady as well. She appeared to have lived a hard life. Her cheeks were sunken, and her long, light brown hair hung in dry, damaged strands.

Elizabeth merely nodded. A few moments later, Tammy sent her across the room to one of the dressing booths, where she put on a beautiful, shimmering, ankle-length, red, formal dress. As she proudly emerged from the changing place, gracefully sauntered across the room, and contentedly studied herself in the mirrors, Elizabeth truly believed she looked like a queen. All of her earlier fears instantly vanished. *Acting in Bardstown is going to be more fun than I ever imagined*, she decided.

"Oh, this one is going to be a sheer joy to prepare, Michelle," Tammy declared with satisfaction, directing Elizabeth to have a seat once more. "She looks lovely. And you haven't even started your magic yet."

"I'll second that!" Elizabeth heard her male co-star say, as he abandoned his makeup spot. Strutting to stand directly in front of her, he leered from head to toe with a careful eye. "Allow me to introduce myself. I'm Bradley Reed. Did I hear you say your name was Elizabeth?"

"Yeah," she replied, noticing for the first time that he was dressed in a tux. She glanced back over at her female co-star and saw she was also costumed in a formal dress. "I'm Elizabeth Warren. Nice to meet you, Bradley. Which role are you undertaking?"

"I'll be playing Jake Tully. I believe we get to share a kiss on film today," he confessed with a wicked smile. "I can honestly say I'm looking quite forward to that."

Bradley, a dark-haired, well-built, young man, normally would have been someone Elizabeth would have found attractive. But something about him made the hair on the back of her neck stand up. Elizabeth was not quite certain why she instantly disliked Bradley. She supposed it centered around the fact he was so openly coming on to her. Elizabeth had never liked brash guys.

"Okay, studly," Tammy mockingly addressed him. "You can worry about your love scenes with this young lady later. Right now, she is Michelle's. I think we have done all the damage we need to do to you, so you can go on out."

"See you on the soundstage, Elizabeth," Bradley said with an eager smirk, proceeding to leave the room as requested.

"Don't pay any attention to him," her female co-star finally spoke. "He's one of those men who think he's God gift to women. He may be looking forward to his love scenes with us, but I, for one, am not overly anxious. I would say, judging by the look on your face, you aren't dying for them either."

"For sure. Is it that obvious?" Elizabeth asked with a nervous giggle.

"Yeah. But not to that stud," she pointed out and rolled her eyes in distaste. "Oh well! What else can you say? Anyway...to coin Bradley's phrase, allow me to introduce myself. I'm Patricia Meyers. But please call me Pat."

"Nice to meet you, Pat," Elizabeth said, offering her hand and a friendly smile. Pat reminded Elizabeth a little of her friend Kathy. She had long, glistening blond hair and twinkling blue eyes. However, Pat was much slimmer than Kathy; yet she had a bigger bust line.

Pat eagerly shook Elizabeth's hand, but before they had a chance to converse more, Michelle promptly interrupted saying, "I'm sorry to interrupt, ladies. But I really need to get started on Elizabeth's makeup and hair...even though you haven't left me much magic to work. Pat wasn't much of a challenge either. I believe I have you finished," she addressed Pat, glancing from her to the door.

"Thanks, Michelle," Pat responded with an attractive smile, rising to her feet.

"See you on the set, Elizabeth," Pat cordially said before she strolled out of the room.

Pat seems nice, Elizabeth thought. She hoped they became friends. She knew she could certainly use a friend here. Bradley had made her even more uneasy about being away from Alan.

As Michelle started to prepare her makeup and hair, Elizabeth tried to relax once again and put all of her insecurities aside. *I'm here to act, which is something I love*, she reminded herself. She was not going to let someone like Bradley spoil that for her.

Michelle pulled Elizabeth's hair into a stylish roll on top of her head, expertly applied her makeup, and sent her to join the others. However, when Elizabeth opened the door and hastily stepped into the hallway, she narrowly escaped colliding with a man who walked past. When she got a good look at him, her breath caught in her throat.

The man was Jameson Thornton. Elizabeth had idolized Jameson Thornton when she had been a little younger. She had been twelve years old when Jameson had been in a very popular, television series – *West Coast*. She and many other girls her age, and a little older, had watched this show religiously.

A huge poster of Jameson had hung on Elizabeth's bedroom door. She had only taken it down a few years ago, when she began to think she had grown a little old to be fantasizing about someone she did not even know. Yet, here Jameson Thornton stood right in front of her. Elizabeth could hardly believe her eyes.

"Are you okay?" she heard Jameson ask. "I didn't mean to scare you. They should have windows in these doors, before someone gets hurt."

Dumbstruck, Elizabeth just stared at him in silence for several more moments. Part of her felt she should be asking Jameson for an autograph. She finally managed to stutter, "I...I'm fine." She could not make her mouth function to say anything more. She just kept staring at Jameson's adorable, real face. She also caught a whiff of his cologne. He smelled as good as he looked – *scrumptious!*

"Well, I take it by the way you are dressed and the fact you just came from makeup, we are about to be working together," he correctly assumed. "You might know who I am. But I haven't had the pleasure of meeting you."

Instead of telling him her name, Elizabeth idiotically declared, "You're Jameson Thornton!"

"By golly, I think you are right," he joked with an amused smile.

His smile melted Elizabeth's insides. *He's even better looking in person than in his pictures.* His wavy, jet black hair formed a stunning contrast to his dark navy eyes. The only thing that surprised Elizabeth was Jameson's height. He was shorter then she had always envisioned, standing only as tall as her.

"I would rather you call me James," he further expounded. "And you are?" he tried again.

"I'm sorry," she apologized, feeling foolish. "I'm Elizabeth...Elizabeth Warren. I'm supposed to play Julia Parks. I didn't know there was going to be anyone famous in this movie."

"Thanks for the compliment," Jameson said with a flattered chuckle. "I don't know that I would classify myself as famous. Though, I did have one pretty decent television series and had a little luck with one movie. I'm just hoping this movie will be a smash. I think you are slated to be my Juliet. I have the role of Jason Tully. From what I can tell from the first script, I believe we are supposed to be in love, but can't be together. Sounds rather interesting, don't you think?"

Upon hearing she would be working directly with Jameson, Elizabeth suddenly felt very inadequate. Never had she anticipated in her wildest dreams that she would be working with someone like him. She figured all the actors and actresses chosen for *Bardstown* would be inexperienced and unknown like herself. She suddenly was scared to death about this whole undertaking.

"Well, I was headed to the soundstage for the filming of the first scene. I'd be more than happy to escort you there," Jameson graciously offered, holding out his arm to her.

"O...okay," Elizabeth agreed, tensely hooking arms with him and allowing herself to be led further down the hall.

Elizabeth's heart beat so loudly she hoped Jameson could not hear it. Her legs suddenly felt like jelly, and her stomach churned. She apprehensively thought, *What am I doing here? I'm not good enough to be acting in anything Jameson Thornton is in.*

"So where have you been hiding yourself, Elizabeth?" Jameson asked, interrupting her erratic thoughts. "I don't recall seeing you in anything before. Is this your first role?"

"Y...yeah. I've never done anything professionally before," she admitted, purposely avoiding eye contact with him. "I've only done grade school, high school and college plays. Never film."

"Well...you know...everyone who ever wanted to be an actor got their start in some school play," Jameson pointed out. "Don't be nervous,

Elizabeth. I bet, after this first week, you'll feel like you've been doing film forever."

"I sure hope you're right," she mumbled, as they reached their destination, a large room within the house, which had been transformed into a rather elaborate ballroom.

Crystal chandeliers hung overhead. Swooping, red velvet drapes dressed up the windows. The wood floor shined so elaborately that the light reflecting off of in it, from the chandeliers, almost hurt Elizabeth's eyes. In addition to the chandeliers, as if these did not provide light enough, ample stage lights were positioned all about. Elizabeth had never seen such a beautiful set in her life. She stood looking around her, awestruck.

Ryan, the director, broke the spell when he promptly came over to her and Jameson and began explaining in detail what he expected from them for the first scene. He walked them step by step through all of their expected movements. When he finished talking and asked, "Have you got all that?", Elizabeth nodded, even though she was not at all sure she did 'get all that'. Her stomach knotted even tighter.

"Great!" Ryan praised with a slight smile. "Elizabeth, if you will just go stand in the doorway, I will give you a countdown from ten. When you hear the word 'action', begin walking slowly toward the sofa, looking directly into the camera."

Elizabeth timidly walked away and positioned herself in the open doorway under a mobile hanging microphone. Her mind rushed a million miles a minute. She suddenly could not remember a single line from the script she had so tirelessly memorized for today's scenes. Her stomach lurched, and she truly feared she might be sick.

As she heard the director's countdown begin, she fought vigorously to regain control of her senses and her body. At the word, "action", instead of gracefully making her entrance, she stumbled forward, almost falling flat on her face.

"Cut!" She heard Ryan shout.

"I'm sorry," she instantly apologized, feeling stupid and inadequate.

"It's okay, Elizabeth," Ryan said with mild understanding. "These things happen. Just get back in place, and we'll start again."

Elizabeth swiftly took her place by the door again. She realized she needed to pull herself back together, and quickly. *For whatever reason, these people saw something in me that was special enough that they hired me for this role. I need to be an actress now and stop being a scared, insecure, nitwit.*

Elizabeth took several, deep breaths and told Ryan, "I'm ready now." *I'm no longer Elizabeth Warren,* she determinedly told herself. *I'm Julia Parks, and I'm about to walk across the room to meet the man I love. I have nothing to be nervous about.*

This time, when Elizabeth heard the word, "action", she gracefully waltzed across the room, holding her head high with confidence, and looking directly into the camera lens with a slight, satisfied smile. She successfully stopped where Ryan had instructed her to and looked longingly across the room at Jameson.

Despite the fact she had managed to triumphantly throw herself into her part, when Jameson came seductively toward her, it promptly broke Elizabeth's illusive spell. As he came to stand directly in front of her, reaching out to take her hands in his, Elizabeth totally tensed up again. When she opened her mouth to say her first lines, her mind went completely blank again. Even though there was a TelePrompTer to help with her lines, Elizabeth still said, "Hello, James", instead of his character name, Jason.

"Cut!" Ryan screamed again, sounding totally exasperated. "His name is *Ja...son*, Elizabeth. We are acting here; remember?!" he snapped, sharing his frustration at her errors.

"Sorry," she meekly uttered, wanting to crawl in a hole somewhere and not come back out.

"So am I," he replied. Then mumbled under his breath, "Sorry we hired an amateur."

"Hey, Ryan," Jameson called, walking over to him and placing his arm on his shoulder. "Can we give Elizabeth a little bit of a break?" Jameson questioned. He had overheard Ryan's last snide remark. "This is the first time she's done film, and to make matters worse, I think she may be a bit intimidated by having to work with me. Am I right?" he asked Elizabeth, studying her face with sympathetic eyes.

"Yeah," she honestly admitted, and added, talking exclusively to Jameson, "You're just so unreal to me. I idolized you when I was younger. I used to have a poster of you hanging on my bedroom door. But I certainly never expected to actually meet you, much less be working with you."

"I'm real," he assured her with a dazzling smile. He walked back over to her and took her hands in his once more, squeezing them reassuringly. "I'm just a man. You're looking at me like I'm some sort of god. You're a beautiful woman, and they wouldn't have hired you if they didn't think you had talent."

"I know," Elizabeth agreed, but did not sound convinced.

An inspired thought came to Jameson all at once. "A pretty girl like you must have someone special in her life. Right?" he asked.

"For sure," Elizabeth answered in a quiet voice. Her mind instantly registered a pang of guilt. She had not thought of Alan since she had laid eyes on Jameson.

"Well, that's great!" Jameson unexpectedly declared. His straight, white teeth glistened. "Do you love this special guy?"

"Yes, I do," she answered. Her eyes relayed her confusion at this line of questioning.

"Good. Because your character, Julia, is supposed to be in love with Jason, which is who I happen to be portraying," he said, placing his hand on his chest. "So…all you have to do is fixate your mind on the guy you are in love with, and transform your real feelings of love into your scenes with me." He tapped his chest again. "This guy you are in love with should be the most important man in your life, so I won't look so almighty to you anymore. And the love scenes should be great!" he explained with a devilish glint to his eyes.

Elizabeth knew what Jameson said was true. She was already prevalently thinking of Alan now. In her college play, which had led to this role, she had been so successful with the love scenes, Alan had been jealous. As Elizabeth had told Alan, her acting had been so authentic, because she had pretended her lover in the play had been him.

Elizabeth looked at Jameson and realized he was just a fellow actor. Granted, he was a very good actor. But, perhaps she could be as well, if she really gave it her all. Jameson's rejuvenating confidence in her gave Elizabeth the small boost she sorely needed. She could concentrate again now, and she was all at once determined to give this opportunity her very best shot.

"Do you think you are ready to try again?" Jameson asked her after a few moments of silence, staring discerningly into her eyes.

"Yeah," she agreed with renewed assurance, returning his warm smile for the first time. "Thanks, Jameson."

"You're more than welcome, Liz. Do you mind if I call you that? I think you may very well be the next Elizabeth Taylor," he playfully complimented with a satisfied grin. "And please, call me James. Jameson is just for the public."

"Okay...*James*," she quickly corrected, feeling much more comfortable with him now.

"We're ready now, Ryan," Jameson informed the director, wearing a very smug expression.

Ryan had been patiently waiting and attentively watching them. He had not said another word. Elizabeth was expendable, but Ryan certainly did not want to do anything to make Jameson unhappy. His presence in the movie was sure to draw ticket buyers, and if they could create an instant following, *Bardstown* was sure to become a blockbuster movie.

When they started the scene over, this time, thanks almost entirely to Jameson's professional coaching, Elizabeth carried through beautifully. The only other strife she experienced that day was filming her kissing scene with Bradley. This turmoil worked to Elizabeth's advantage, however, since Bradley was supposed to be forcing himself on her in the scene.

He smelled like he had bathed in Brute cologne, and Elizabeth found she disliked him even more when he deliberately stuck his tongue into her mouth. It took every ounce of her restraint not to chomp down hard on his uninvited tongue. Instead, Elizabeth forced herself to endure his rash intrusion and finish the scene. At the word, "cut", Bradley actually had the nerve to say, "Thank you, Elizabeth."

Then Bradley happily strutted away with an arrogant smile. Thankfully, right after that difficult moment, Ryan wrapped up filming for that day, telling them all to have a great night, and he would see them bright and early the next morning.

Chapter 11
The Dream

A dream come true is being able to do
something you have wanted to do your entire life.
But dreams aren't always everything we imagined them to be.
However, the only way to discover this is through experience –
accepting the bad with the good.

~ Sissy Marlyn ~

W hen Alan called that night, Elizabeth lay on her stomach across her king-sized bed religiously studying her lines and visualizing scenes for the next day.

"So how did it go today?" he asked, sounding truly interested. "I couldn't wait any longer for your call. So I decided to call you."

"I'm sorry," she quickly apologized. "I was just working on learning my lines for tomorrow, and I guess I lost track of the time."

"That's okay," he said in an understanding voice. "But you still haven't answered my question. How was your first big day as a professional actress?"

"Grody," Elizabeth honestly admitted. "Right after the chauffeur dropped me off, I had a near panic attack. And I came really close to totally blowing it during the filming of my first scene. If it hadn't been for one of my co-star's help, I think I might have broken down into tears and run off the set."

"Jeez! That sounds terrible," Alan commented. "Who was the co-star who helped you? I should thank this person for taking such good care of you for me."

"For sure. Do you remember the guy who used to star in *West Coast* several years ago?" she inquired a little evasively.

"Do you mean, Jameson Thornton? The guy you practically slobbered over in that movie, *The Fraternity*, we watched on cable? Didn't you refer to him as your first love? Please tell me this isn't the guy you are now working with," Alan interrogated, a tinge of worry now evident in his voice.

"Chill, Alan! You know I was just teasing you about him. I idolized him when I was younger. But it turns out he's really a very nice guy and a terrific actor," she praised.

"So what you are telling me is he's not only a hunk, but a nice guy too. You aren't purposely trying to make me jealous, are you?" Alan asked very insecurely.

"I am so sure! I barely know James. Yes, he's good-looking and nice, but so are you! And you already have sole possession of my heart," she fervently professed.

"Did you just call him James?" Alan questioned.

"Ye...ah, because that's what he told me to call him. He said Jameson is just his public name," Elizabeth explained. She also did not volunteer that Jameson had given her the nickname of Liz, which she honestly kind of liked. "We just work together. There's totally nothing for you to worry about. No more so than the female co-star I made friends with today named Pat."

"So who does James play? Do you have to do love scenes with him?" Alan further grilled.

"James has the part of Jason Tully. And even though we didn't have any love scenes today, I'm sure we eventually will, since he's supposed to be playing the man I love," she truthfully confessed. "But it's just acting. I don't want you to worry about this. Now, can you just veg?! I told you I had a rough day, and you aren't making it any easier by being so ridiculously jealous!"

A few moments of strained silent passed before Alan finally uttered, "I'm sorry. I know I'm acting like a goof, but give me a break here. The thought of you in some other guy's arms, with his lips touching yours is really going to be a hard thing for me to get used to. Especially knowing it will be with someone you already told me you were attracted to."

"You are just going to have to focus on the fact that I love you with all my heart. And remember…only what's between you and me is real. Acting is all illusion," she tried to assure him.

"I know you're right," Alan grudgingly agreed, after a few more minutes of illusive silence. "I love you with all my heart. And I really am happy for you and glad you are getting to do what you have always wanted to. I guess I've just got some things I need to work through."

Before Elizabeth could respond, he intentionally changed the subject and lightened the mood. He relayed something funny that had happened to him earlier that day. Since he was calling long distance, Alan did not talk to her much longer.

Elizabeth promised she would not forget to call him tomorrow evening. She did not like the fact that Alan had gotten upset about her working with Jameson. She was determined to do everything in her power to try and alleviate his jealousy pangs.

* * * *

Elizabeth made it through the next two days without many problems, other than Bradley's overwhelming cologne and his continued, unsubtle advances each time they filmed a scene together. Thursday, however, she was faced with a new dilemma, her first bed scene with Jameson. More upsetting than filming a bed scene was their choice of wardrobe for her – nothing but her underwear.

"You're kidding, right, Tammy?" Elizabeth asked the wardrobe lady, in shocking disbelief. Tammy held up a slim, strapless bra and very skimpy underwear. "Gag me with a spoon. They don't actually expect me to strip down to just this, do they? If it's a bed scene, then why can't we just pull the covers over us? Then filming won't show that I have on clothes under the covers."

"Look, doll, I just pull the clothes they tell me to," Tammy explained, looking a tad aggravated. "If it helps any, you get to wear a robe over your underclothes for the beginning of the scene," Tammy tried unsuccessfully to settle her. "You have a beautiful body, so you actually have absolutely nothing to worry about."

"For sure. I'm not ashamed of my body, but I don't want it on display for all of America to see either," Elizabeth argued, getting even more upset. "This is bogus! I can't go on the set like this, and that's all there is to it! Who do I need to talk to? Ryan?"

"Wow! This is refreshing!" Michelle noted, butting into his friend's conversation and placing a supportive hand on one of Elizabeth's rigid shoulders. "You're an actress who actually has a conscience. Most of the gals in here nowadays would bear their entire body if it meant they might get ahead. Tammy, you need to go talk to Ryan for her."

"I'll be back," Tammy told them, throwing her hands in the air in defeat. "I can't fight the both of you. But I can tell you that Ryan isn't going to like this. And, unfortunately, what he says goes."

"Just give it your best shot. You can be very convincing when you want to," Michelle further urged. When Tammy had left the room, Michelle said to Elizabeth, "I really do admire you for standing up for your beliefs. Nudity is highly overrated anyway. Not every movie needs to show a woman's tits to be a hit. If the movie is really good, people will go to see it without naked bodies everywhere."

"Can they fire me if I refuse to do the scene this way?" Elizabeth worriedly inquired.

"Well…it depends on what they want *Bardstown* to be rated. Love scenes will be expected, and you have to do them. But, hopefully, the amount of clothes you are wearing will be debatable. Fortunately, Arthur Goldbloom is a decent guy, so I think he will give you a little leeway. Some producers are terrible. If you don't do exactly what they ask, they will not only fire you, but your name will be mud for any other professional acting jobs."

Before Elizabeth had a chance to reply, the door opened, and Tammy returned, followed closely by Jameson.

"Michelle, you want to go get some coffee with me?" Tammy asked. "Jameson wants a moment alone with Elizabeth."

"Sure," Michelle agreed. The two swiftly left the room.

Elizabeth could not help but stare at Jameson's body. He did not have a shirt on, and he wore only boxer shorts. The bulky muscles in his broad chest, stomach and legs proudly introduced themselves to her. It was almost as if they had a voice that was screaming, 'Touch Me!' Elizabeth had to force herself to look away.

"I guess you are already dressed for the bedroom scene," she theorized, evasively studying her shoes. "Do you get to keep on those shorts, or do you have to lose those too?"

"Honestly, I would say they will most likely film them falling to the floor," he confessed, sitting down in one of the makeup chairs and swirling to face her. When he noticed Elizabeth's shocked, worried expression, he quickly added, "Don't worry, I have on other underwear underneath these shorts. We're not allowed to actually be nude. We are just supposed to appear that way for the audience's pleasure. I learned a long time ago that they are not only making money off of my extraordinary acting talents, but also off of my biceps and other assorted muscles on my well-seasoned body."

"And you're okay with them exploiting you like this?" Elizabeth questioned, locking eyes with him and trying to force her mind to forget he was practically naked. *I'll focus entirely on his caring eyes*, she persistently told herself.

However, Jameson unknowingly drew her attention back to his body with his honest reply, "I'm proud of who I am. I work hard to keep my body in shape, so if ladies like to see it all across America, I have no problem with that. It isn't as if I'm doing porno. I'm not showing off anything more than your average, decent looking guy does on the beach."

Elizabeth stared at his muscles again for a few seconds. Then she said, "Well, I guess it's probably different for a guy. To me, the thought of being filmed in nothing but my underwear is downright embarrassing. And I can't help but feel like I'm doing something a little bit dirty, almost like porno."

"Well, being embarrassed about your first bed scene is the most natural thing in the world. I was a total wreck the first one I ever filmed, but it gets easier. After a while, it's second nature. No different than filming any other scene," Jameson alleged, with a slight grin, obviously reminiscing. "Do you feel dirty wearing a bikini? You do wear bikinis, don't you?"

"For sure. But there is a big difference between them and underwear, even if they cover you about the same," she argued, meeting his eyes again in exasperation. "If I went strolling on the beach in my underwear, people would definitely stare."

"I would imagine most men would be staring regardless," James remarked, making a quick, approving analysis of her with his roving eyes.

Noticing both his verbal compliment and his uninvited, visual examination, Elizabeth became even more uncomfortable. They were supposed to be just two actors working together. They were not supposed to be attracted to one another. She had Alan. She did not want to be attracted to anyone else.

But yet, she found herself admiringly studying his stocky, upper body yet again, and suddenly, Jameson seemed to be sitting much too close to her. Elizabeth crossed her arms protectively across her chest and began to anxiously pace the room, focusing her eyes once more on the floor.

"Look, Liz, I like working with you, and I think you are enormously talented," she heard Jameson say. She still did not stop pacing or make eye contact with him. "Would you be terribly uncomfortable being filmed in a tube halter top and short shorts?" he asked.

"No duh. That's clothes, not underwear," Elizabeth proclaimed, mocking.

"Okay. I'll go talk to Ryan. There is no reason they can't make it appear you are nude by just filming your bare shoulders and legs. Your first bed scene is going to be hard enough without you being concerned about what they are making you wear."

"You'd do that for me? Talk to Ryan?" Elizabeth asked, looking attentively into his face again and finally halting her anxious marching. "You must think I'm a real dweeb."

"No, I don't," he truthfully protested, his eyes showing only warmth and no sign of aggravation. "And neither will Ryan. I have some leeway with both him and Arthur, so don't worry. You trust me, right?"

"For sure. How could I not? This will be the second time you have gone to bat for me in a week. I owe you big time," she pointed out, displaying a grateful smile and relaxing her crossed arms. She allowed them to drop comfortably to her sides once more.

"I'm just glad to see you smile again. Acting is supposed to be fun, remember?" he pointed out, standing and promptly heading toward the door. "I'll send Tammy and Michelle back in. Tell Tammy to look for a tube top and some very short shorts. I'll see you on the soundstage."

Elizabeth watched Jameson leave the room, feeling very grateful to him. He was so totally sure of himself, but he certainly had a right to be. Jameson had already proven he was a star. What amazed Elizabeth, though, was the fact that he unselfishly seemed to want to help her become one also.

* * * *

The bedroom scene was indeed one of the hardest things Elizabeth had ever attempted to film. While trying to pretend to passionately kiss Jameson and make love to him, Elizabeth still had to be vitally aware of how to stand and lay so that the lighting was perfect and the camera could accurately capture the correct angles.

Ryan had to stop them at least ten times to reposition them. When Elizabeth heard the magical words, "That's a wrap!", she was very relieved. However, Ryan warned them, "I'll have to preview the film to see if things looked absolutely right. So just be prepared to possibly redo some, or all, of this scene tomorrow."

Thankfully, this scene was the last one of the day for both Elizabeth and Jameson. Elizabeth was extremely glad. She was exceedingly tired, after working so hard on her bedroom charade.

"Can I give you a lift back to where you are staying?" Jameson asked, falling comfortably into stride beside Elizabeth. They both headed back to their dressing rooms to change into their clothes. "Seems everyone else has abandoned you. Pat went with Bradley to get some dinner. She has been giving you a ride, hasn't she?"

"Yeah," Elizabeth admitted, surprised Jameson had noticed. She and Pat had even gone to dinner together the last few evenings. It had been good to have the company, and Elizabeth felt she was making a new friend in Pat. "Arthur told me there's always a car available anytime I need transportation while I'm working," she informed Jameson.

"Yes, I know. The car I'm driving is compliments of MGM. I would be more than happy to be your chauffeur for the evening. I'll even treat you to dinner," he graciously offered, displaying a playful smile.

Since she had been aware Pat had left the set after filming of her scenes, Elizabeth had decided, for dinner, she would just have the chauffeur go through the drive-through at one of the fast food restaurants in town. She had intended to eat alone in the cottage. She had been more than a little surprised to hear that Pat was having dinner with Bradley. She did not think she even liked him.

"Well, what do you say, Liz? Will you keep a lonely, out-of-town actor company for a short while this evening? You said you owed me one. This would be a good way of paying me back," he pointed out, as they both stopped in front of Elizabeth's dressing room.

Elizabeth was very hesitant about leaving the set with Jameson, and most especially about allowing him to buy her dinner. This would seem like a date, instead of just a simple meal between two co-stars and friends.

Strangely, she realized, for the first time, she really was beginning to view Jameson in this manner, as a friend. *How could I not? After all he's done for me.* Elizabeth really did not want to let him down. *What could having dinner with him hurt? We could discuss tomorrow's script,* she reasoned. "Okay, James. I'll agree to let you be my driver, and I would enjoy joining you for dinner. But, I'll pay for my own meal. *Friends* don't generally let other *friends* buy their food, unless one is totally broke. And I'm totally making the big bucks now," she pointed out with a chuckle, studying his face.

"Sounds good by me," he agreed with a happy smile, seeming totally at ease with her terms. "I'm going to run down the hall to my dressing room to find my clothes and shoes. I'll just meet you out front whenever you are ready."

"That's the ticket," Elizabeth readily agreed with an amused chuckle, looking down and noticing Jameson was barefoot. He was also still dressed in only boxer shorts, but after filming the love scene with him, Elizabeth did not find his essential nakedness nearly as discomforting as before.

As he hurried away to make himself presentable, she opened the door in front of her and went inside her room to do the same.

* * * *

When she met Jameson outside in front of the house, he was dressed in layered, alligator polo shirts, with both collars folded upwards around his neck. A kelly-green polo shirt was on the outside, and a pink polo was underneath. He had on Bugle Boy shorts, a baseball cap, and Birkenstock sandals. He also wore Ray Bans, even though it was an overcast day.

"Like my disguise?" he asked, noticing Elizabeth's odd scrutiny. "It's the only way I can go out in public. Otherwise, we would be hoarded by people everywhere we went. Don't get me wrong. I love my fans, but I still need my privacy some of the time. You'll understand after *Bardstown* becomes a hit. Then everyone who sees you will be asking *you* for your autograph or wanting to touch you like you are some god."

"I'm so sure. I can't imagine that for myself. But I do understand it where you are concerned. When I was younger, I used to…like…stare at your posters hanging on my walls and dream about what I would say if I ever got the chance to meet you. I totally spazzed on you," she confessed with a shy grin.

"Well, did I fulfill your fantasies when you finally did meet me? What exactly did you dream about?" Jameson questioned, returning her smile, his eyes dancing mischievously.

Suddenly embarrassed by her past thoughts and confessing her fantasies to Jameson, Elizabeth coyly lowered her eyes from his playful gaze. She not only used to fantasize about meeting Jameson, but she used to dream they instantly hit it off, and he naturally fell in love with her. "I was just a kid," she answered. "I was only twelve and you were twenty. I read all of the teen magazine articles about you and believed every word…like every other girl my age." *You were my first love, as least in my vivid imagination*, she thought but did not share.

The word *love* instantly made her think of Alan. He was the one who had taught her what true love was. Alan was the real man who had fulfilled all of her fantasies. "It still seems a little unreal to me sometimes that I'm actually working with you," she truthfully confessed, making eye contact again, and adding with a relaxed smile, "But I really am happy to have met you. You really are a nice guy."

"Awww... how sweet,' Jameson poked fun at. "I'm a nice guy! You just made my day."

They reached the car then, a black Trans Am. Jameson opened Elizabeth's door for her and ushered her inside. When he had joined her inside, he asked, "So do you like chicken, Liz?"

"For sure. I love chicken," she truthfully replied. "Do you have a specific place in mind?"

"Uh-huh." he responded, eagerly nodding his head. "I think so anyway. Are you game?"

"You're the driver. I'm willing to go anywhere you choose to take me," Elizabeth agreed with a trusting smile.

* * * *

About ten minutes later, Jameson whizzed off the roadway, wound around a few blocks, and then abruptly turned into a gravel driveway which led back to an old, large brick house. The name on a sign in the yard said *Rosewood Bed & Breakfast.* Jameson pulled up beside the side door to the house.

An older gentleman, who had been pruning some roses, instantly greeted them, saying, "Good evening, Mister Thornton." The man also tipped his John Deere hat in an obvious gesture of respect. Then he went right back to tending his flowers.

"Um...James, where are we? I thought you were taking me to dinner someplace," Elizabeth commented in confusion.

"Relax, Liz," Jameson said, reaching over to lightly tap the top of one of her hands in reassurance. "I'm not some high school boy who is trying to pull a fast one. I'm a twenty-six-year-old man that is trying to take a young woman, who I happen to respect, to my home-away-from-home to treat her to one of the best chicken dinners she may have ever had in her entire life. Nothing more; I promise. You can trust me. Remember, you said I was a nice guy."

"I just thought we were going out to a restaurant. You never said anything about going to a...bed...and breakfast," Elizabeth pointed out, still feeling very uncomfortable.

Jameson swiveled his body to face Elizabeth. Intensely studying her face, he grilled, "Do you trust me or not?"

"For sure. It's not a matter of whether I trust you or not," she argued, staring downward at her lap. She paused for a second, taking time to decide how best to phrase her next statement. "It's just...there's a very big difference between being in a busy restaurant with lots of other people and being at a bed and breakfast."

"So? Don't you trust yourself?" he further interrogated, and then rather playfully added, "What's wrong? Are you afraid you will try and make your childhood fantasies about me come true? What about your boyfriend?"

"My boyfriend wouldn't like me being alone with you here either. That's another part of what's making me uncomfortable about being here," she truthfully acknowledged, locking eyes with him again.

"Does he mind you going to dinner with Pat?" Jameson rapidly fired another question. "Because we are just friends too. I know you already have a man in your life, and I respect that. I'm telling you I'm just offering dinner, nothing more. So you still make me wonder if you are afraid of yourself."

"I'm so sure!" she defiantly exclaimed, her face set in a determined scowl. "I love my boyfriend, Alan, very much. So much so, in fact, that I don't even think of anything ever happening with another man. I can assure you that I just look at you as a friend and work partner!"

"Then what exactly is the problem here? Can't two friends and work partners have an innocent dinner together at a bed and breakfast?" Jameson persuasively argued. The smile had disappeared from his face.

Elizabeth had to concede that Jameson had a valid point. *If we are just friends, then why can't we be alone together and enjoy a meal? Am I just worried about how Alan will react?* He already seemed a little jealous of Jameson, and Elizabeth certainly did not want to give him any reason to worry. *But do I really have to tell him that James and I had dinner at his bed and breakfast? Couldn't I just say we had dinner together and leave it at that?*

"Look, Liz, if you are really that uncomfortable being here, then maybe I should just take you home. Maybe it's not a good idea for us to have dinner together at all. I don't want to cause problems between you and your boyfriend. I've obviously given you the wrong impression of myself at some point," he stated with just a hint of aggravation. He rotated his body to face the wheel again and reached to turn the key.

"No, James," Elizabeth quickly protested, gently grasping his hand to stop him from starting the car. The last thing in the world she wanted to do was hurt his feelings. Jameson had been nothing but kind to her. "I'm sorry. You haven't given me a bad impression of yourself at all. All you have ever done is be good to me. I would love to join you for dinner. I can't wait to see if this chicken is as good as you claim it is."

"Are you sure?" he skeptically questioned, fixating on her eyes.

"Yeah," she tried to assure him, lightly squeezing the arm she still held. "I was just acting lame. Like you said, there is certainly nothing wrong with two friends having dinner alone together. And you've certainly proved yourself to be my friend."

"Well, I hope you'll like the chicken then. I'm a little biased, because it reminds me of my mother's," he told her with a satisfied grin. He opened his door and hopped out of the car.

Elizabeth promptly followed suit and walked with Jameson to the side door. When they stepped inside the house, they were warmly greeted by a woman in an apron. Like the man in the yard, she was an older lady. She had gray hair, pulled back into a neat bun on the back of her head. "Good evening, Mr. Thornton. Good evening, ma'am," she said and stepped back to let them pass.

Elizabeth could not help but favorably notice the respect which people automatically gave Jameson and also at how well she was treated just because she was with him.

"Martha, I hope you don't mind that I brought a guest for dinner," Jameson addressed the woman.

"Of course not, Mr. Thornton," she told him with a warm smile. "The more the merrier. We always fix plenty of food around here."

"Elizabeth, this is Martha Rosewood. That was her husband Elmer who greeted us outside. This is their home."

"Nice to meet you," Elizabeth said and offered her hand.

"Nice to meet you, Elizabeth," the woman replied, picking up on her name from Jameson. "Welcome to our home. I hope you enjoy your meal tonight. Do you like fried chicken?"

"Yes, ma'am, I do," Elizabeth told her. "James has ranted about how delicious your chicken is, so I can't wait to try it."

"Good. Dinner will be ready in about a half hour."

"Sounds great!" Jameson said. "I'll just show Elizabeth around the place a bit."

"We'd love it if you did?" Martha offered with a smile.

She seemed like everyone's grandmother – warm and loving. Elizabeth suddenly felt very comfortable here. She was glad she had let James talk her into staying. She was looking forward to sampling this woman's cooking as well.

Jameson led Elizabeth out of the kitchen area then and into the rest of the house. She stood gawking in the entranceway to the parlor, trying to take it all in. The old was preserved along with the new. There was a sofa, a recliner, and a large television. But the wood floor, cultured stone fireplace, antique, glass-panel lamps, and oil paintings of My Old Kentucky Home and Old Talbot Tavern added a historic charm to the room.

"This place has a homey feel to it," Elizabeth commented.

"Yeah. It's like being in grandma's house," Jameson added with a reminiscent smile. "Do you want to sit down? We can turn on the television. Or there's a stereo in the bookcase over there," he pointed.

"Sure," she agreed.

"Do you want anything to drink? They always have iced tea or soft drinks in the fridge."

Elizabeth had to smile. It almost sounded as if she *were* at Jameson's grandparents' house with him. "Ice tea would be nice," she answered.

"Okay. You have a seat. I'll be right back," he said.

Elizabeth made her way over to the sofa and Jameson turned and headed back to the kitchen. Elizabeth's eyes caught sight of a cable movie guide on the side table. She smiled again at the many contrasts of the house – all the modern conveniences with old-time charm.

Jameson came back a second later with two glasses in his hands. He handed one to Elizabeth. "So what's your pleasure? Do you want to watch television or listen to the stereo?"

"It doesn't matter to me," Elizabeth replied, taking a sip of her tea. It tasted good – not too sweet; just right.

"Okay," Jameson said, switching on the television. *Wheel of Fortune* was on. He left it on that station.

Both decompressing from their day, they silently and mindlessly watched the game show. It had just ended when Martha appeared in the entranceway to the parlor to call them both to dinner. Elizabeth was glad; she was hungry, and she could smell the fried chicken emanating from the kitchen.

They followed Martha into a large dining room. The cream alabaster and brass ceiling lamp provided brilliant shine to the walnut table underneath it. Elizabeth and Jameson seated themselves. A stoneware plate, polished silver knife, fork and spoon, and a crystal goblet sat on a lace placemat in front of them. Elizabeth sat her half-empty glass of tea beside her crystal goblet.

Elmer came from the kitchen, holding a platter full of the tasty-smelling, fried chicken. Elizabeth's mouth automatically began to salivate.

"Madam, which piece would you like? Breast, thigh, or wing?" Elmer asked her, obviously playing the role of waiter.

"Breast please," she answered with an appreciative smile.

Elmer carefully lifted a chicken breast from the platter, with his silver meat thongs. He placed it on Elizabeth's plate. Then he waited upon Jameson as well. Jameson also requested a breast.

Elmer sat the rest of the platter in the middle of the table. Then he vacated the room to help his wife carry in the sides and a bottle of wine. They sat bowls of corn, mash potatoes and slaw upon the table.

"Help yourselves to the sides and some wine," Martha said, as she and Elmer also took a seat at the table.

Jameson picked up the bottle of white wine and opened it. He poured some in his crystal goblet and also some in Elizabeth's. "There is nothing better than White Chablis to compliment chicken," Jameson explained. "Try it. I think you will like it."

Elizabeth picked up her glass, wondering if her facial expression displayed her indecision. She tried to decipher whether she should tell Jameson that she did not drink, or if she should just try a little wine with the chicken as he suggested. She realized the reason she did not drink was because neither her parents nor Alan drank. She really had no idea whether she liked wine or not. *What could drinking one glass hurt? At least I'll find out whether I even like it or not*, she reasoned.

"Is everything okay?" Jameson questioned with a hint of concern, instantly noticing her sudden pensiveness. "You haven't tried the chicken yet."

Elizabeth promptly picked up her knife and fork and carved a slice off the side of her breast. Placing the meat in her mouth, she instantly tasted the delightful seasonings, savoring it for a moment before she swallowed. "Yum! This is really is good!" she announced with a grateful smile.

"Thank you," Martha replied with a pleased grin.

"Top it off with a sip of your wine, and it will taste even better," Jameson advised.

Elizabeth did as he directed. The wine tasted sweeter than she had imagined. It did seem to compliment the chicken. She took another sip before returning her glass to the table.

Enjoying her meal and the wine, Elizabeth managed to drink two glasses in no time. As she finished her meal and consumed a third glass, she began to suffer the alcohol's effects. Everything Jameson had to say was suddenly very funny, and when she stood to leave the table, she immediately discovered her legs had a very strange, rubbery feel to them.

As she unexpectedly staggered sideways, Jameson leapt from his chair and joined her side, taking one of her arms in his. He led her back to the living room parlor and over to the couch.

"Wow! I think I maybe shouldn't have drank that last glass of wine," Elizabeth confessed with an exaggerated giggle. "I'm not really used to drinking. I feel all warm and fuzzy."

"You'll be fine." Jameson assured her with a slightly mischievous smile. "You just have a little buzz, that's all. You just relax here on the couch for a little bit. In fact...while you're so relaxed...why don't we practice a scene for tomorrow."

"I guess that's okay, but I think I better not do any dancing scenes. I'd certainly trip us both," she told him, laughing hysterically.

"No dancing scenes. I promise," he said with an amused chuckle. "Actually what I had in mind was a love scene."

"Do we have another one of those again tomorrow?" Elizabeth asked, her speech a bit slurred.

"I think we will," Jameson shared. "I have a strong feeling that Ryan is going to make us redo our bed scene tomorrow," he confided.

"Why? He said he was going to look at the film first, didn't he?" Elizabeth asked, trying unsuccessfully to clear the fog from her brain.

"Yeah. And that's exactly what makes me think he wasn't happy with it. How many other scenes has he said he needed to look at the film of to make sure it was okay? Something about the scene must not have looked right, or real, to him," Jameson knowingly pointed out. Then he quickly added, "So...what I was thinking is...why don't we just run through that scene again tonight? While you're feeling no pain. That way, even if we don't have to redo it tomorrow, we'll be ready for the next love scene. Because I'm sure there will be many more. If we can get it right without the cameras and the pressure from Ryan, then you'll have something positive to draw from the next time a love scene rolls around."

"Practice here? What if one of the Rosewoods walk in? What would they think?" Elizabeth questioned. Her head still swimming; she was having trouble reasoning things out. She knew she felt more relaxed right now than she should.

"Don't worry about the Rosewoods. They stay to themselves in the cottage out back and give me my privacy. MGM has rented this whole bed and breakfast for me. The Rosewoods are just the cooks and groundskeepers, even though this is really their home," Jameson assured her. Then he asked, "You and Pat have helped one another rehearse, haven't you? That's all I'm proposing. You have an enormous, acting talent, and there is no reason you should have to struggle so hard to get through a scene. I think I can help. But if you are uncomfortable, then maybe I should take you back to your place, and you can try and work it out by yourself."

117

"No, James," she quickly retorted without giving it a lot of thought. "I really appreciate all you have done for me, and if you think we should practice our love scenes to make them more realistic, then I trust your judgment. And it would definitely be easier without Ryan barking orders at us constantly. He's such a nerd!" Elizabeth honestly exclaimed, bursting into laughter once more and playfully swatting one of Jameson's legs.

"Okay then," Jameson agreed, drawing in very close to Elizabeth. "Put your arms around my neck. Now when I draw in to kiss you, I'll always lean my head right and you always lean your head left. Ready?"

"As I'll ever be," Elizabeth stated hesitantly, placing her arms around Jameson's neck as requested.

Jameson slowly drew Elizabeth into a tight embrace and the two locked lips for a long, lip-entwining kiss. When the kiss ended, Jameson very slowly began easing Elizabeth backwards on the lengthy couch. When her back touched the couch, he brought his lips into contact with hers again, kissing her lips a little more roughly this time, trying to show desire and passion.

Elizabeth could feel the tip of Jameson's tongue against her lips, so they parted almost automatically in a warm, natural response. Furthermore, she allowed her tongue to also touch not just his lips but the inside of his mouth as well. Jameson seemed to savor her lips a few moments more before moving his mouth to attentively kiss the side of her neck.

Elizabeth felt a pleasant, familiar tingle within her body. She loved having her neck kissed. She responsively dropped her head backwards a little and smiled contently in response. So relaxed and uninhibited from the alcohol, it took Elizabeth several more minutes to finally realize she responded much too authentically to Jameson's pretend lovemaking.

"James!" she suddenly shrieked, coming to her senses and pushing him away rather forcefully.

"Wh...what?! What's wrong, Liz?" he asked, his perplexed eyes levelly meeting her shocked ones.

Intently analyzing his concerned face, it suddenly dawned on Elizabeth that maybe only *she* felt that what had transpired had been too real. Jameson may have totally still been in character and thought she was acting as well. She did not want to sound as if she was accusing him of doing anything improper. After all, it was not his fault she had allowed alcohol to impair her judgment.

I shouldn't have drank that wine, she chastised herself.

"Liz, is everything alright?" Jameson inquired, seeming to be unnerved by her prolonged silence. "Did I do something wrong? You look upset."

"No," she declared, frustrated with herself for having been so stupid and irresponsible. "I...I just think that might be enough for tonight. I think I've got an idea what Ryan might like to see now. And I still need to study my lines for tomorrow," she tried to diplomatically explain.

"Okay," he promptly agreed without argument, sitting back up on the couch and offering her a hand to pull her to a sitting position as well. "I think you were doing great though. You just need to learn to relax and do this in front of the camera and you'll have it made."

"Yeah. For sure," Elizabeth concurred, trying to sound enthusiastic. However, she was very concerned by her thoughts. She realized now she had really been kissing Jameson and allowing him to touch her because she wanted to. She suddenly felt overwhelming guilt and just wanted to be alone. "Well, I guess you really should be taking me home," she prodded again, trying to remove the urgency from her voice.

"Well...since I've been drinking too, I'm going to call for a car. But I'll ride along with you and escort you back home," he offered with a warm smile,

"No," she protested a little too strongly. Then she added in a surprisingly level voice, "I just mean...there is really no reason for you to come along. After all, you need to study your lines for tomorrow too, and I've taken up enough of your time for tonight."

"Okay," he reluctantly agreed again. He was still on good terms with Elizabeth, and he wanted to stay that way. He got up off the couch and walked across the room to the phone. He picked it up and called the chauffeur service for Elizabeth.

"Thanks," Elizabeth said when he had hung up the phone. She rose to her feet, gathered her purse, and started hurrying toward the door as fast as her unsteady legs would allow. Her head still felt a little hazy, but her scene with Jameson had helped to sober her up considerably.

She felt really ashamed and guilty about both her actions and ensuing thoughts. She had wanted to find out whether she liked to drink or not, and she had graphically gotten her answer. Elizabeth had always heard that people made colossal fools of themselves when they drank. Now, she knew the accuracy of these reports firsthand. *At least I'll know better in the future*, she wisely concluded. "Bye, James. Thanks for dinner," Elizabeth said.

"Where are you going?" he asked with a confused expression on his face. "The car won't be here for a few minutes," he reminded her.

"I'm going to wait outside," she explained.

"By yourself? I'll go with you," he offered.

"No," she protested a little too strongly. "It's nice outside. I need the air to clear my head. The wine still has me a bit disoriented. I'll be fine waiting for the car by myself. Why don't you go and start studying your lines for tomorrow."

Jameson could tell that Elizabeth wanted to be parted from him. Once again, he wisely decided not to push the issue. He had enjoyed his night with her, and he hoped for many more. But he knew if he came on too strong right now, he would push Elizabeth completely away.

"Okay," he agreed one last time. "I'll see you tomorrow on the set. Have a good night."

"You too," she said. She turned and hurried away as fast as her unsteady legs would carry her. She was relieved when she escaped through the side door and stood outside by herself. The cool spring breeze felt nice. It helped to sober her up even more. She waited impatiently for the car to arrive. She could not wait to get away from this place and hide in her cottage for the night.

Chapter 12
Jealousy

Nothing is worse than when the ugly head of jealousy
rears itself. Jealousy can wreak havoc
on even the strongest of relationships.
Real or imagined, jealousy is a force to be reckoned with.

~ Sissy Marlyn ~

*S*afely in her cottage, studying her script for the next day, Elizabeth could not stop thinking about what had occurred with James. She felt ashamed of her actions.

The next day, when Elizabeth reported to the appropriate soundstage to film her first scene of the day, she found Jameson and Ryan involved in a lengthy discussion. When they parted, Ryan motioned for her to come to him. "Elizabeth, I viewed yesterday's taping, and I'm sorry to say that I still have a few problems with your and Jameson's love scene. I've already told Jameson that I've decided we have no option but to re-tape it at the end of the day today. He told me he helped you practice last night, and he thinks you both could definitely do it better."

Elizabeth glanced nervously at Jameson over Ryan's shoulder. He gave her a knowing smile and a thumbs-up. "Well, if you think we need to do it again, then I guess we will have to," Elizabeth grudgingly told Ryan. "I'll try to give you what you want next time."

"I'm sure you will do just fine," Ryan reassured her with a friendly grin and a slight pat on the shoulder. "Jameson has utmost confidence in you, so I have to also," he told her. "Now let's get on with the filming for today," he ordered, promptly proceeding to point them to their appropriate spots.

An impending dread remained in the back of Elizabeth's mind. She hated that, when today's scenes concluded, she would have to do her bed scene with Jameson again. *It certainty won't be as good as last night's performance, because I have no intention of letting things get so out of hand between us again*, Elizabeth decided. She walked over to where Ryan asked her to go and prepared to begin filming for that day.

* * * *

Time passed swiftly, and before Elizabeth could hardly grasp it, she had successfully completed her last new scene of the day. Time to re-tape her bed scene with Jameson, Elizabeth reluctantly headed off to wardrobe.

When she came back from wardrobe in her halter and short shorts, Jameson came over and comfortably dropped an arm around her shoulder, whispering, "Just relax, Liz. Pretend we are alone like last night, and you'll do great."

"I hope so," Elizabeth said, allowing Jameson to lead her over to the bed.

They sat down on the side together. She purposely tried not to think about the night before.

As Jameson began to kiss and caress her, Elizabeth tried to totally focus her mind on the fact that she was *only* acting. However, when Jameson kissed her neck and shoulder and pushed her softly back onto the bed, memories of last night's genuine passion vividly flooded back to her.

Elizabeth wanted to push Jameson away once more, but she knew she could not. *This isn't James!*, she concentrated. *This is Jason Tully and you are Julia Parks, his lover. You're just getting caught up in this scene!*, she frantically tried to convince herself.

"That's a wrap!" she finally was overly relieved to hear Ryan call. "Perfect! Beautiful! If I didn't know any better, I would think you two really were lovers," Ryan raved, clapping his hands enthusiastically.

Jameson gave Elizabeth one last hug and an appreciative kiss on the cheek. "I knew you could do it, Liz!" he gushed. "You'll be fine from now on. I'm glad we practiced together alone last night. It made all the difference in the world."

To Elizabeth, Jameson's dancing eyes seemed to linger a little bit too long. She quickly averted her head. Still feeling stunned and overcome by the emotion the scene had easily arose in her, Elizabeth remained strangely silent. She wanted to tell Jameson she wished last night had never happened, but of course, she did not.

Jameson released her from his arms and stood to leave the soundstage. He graciously offered her an assisting hand, which she hesitantly took and stood up beside him. It was only as she started to make her way away from the bed that she noticed Alan stood only a short distance away. Off to the side, he intently watched them.

Casually dressed in shorts, a red and white baseball jersey, and black, high-top tennis shoes, he had come to pick her up. She had left his name at the guard station so he could come onto the property. But Elizabeth had not expected to see him watching her film scenes.

Especially this particular scene. Why does he have that strange expression on his face?, she nervously wondered. *Or is it just my guilty conscience making me think he is looking at me oddly?* She found herself wondering exactly how long Alan had been standing there. *Did he watch my love scene, and hear what Ryan and Jameson said to me?*

Elizabeth managed to muster a deceiving smile and eagerly rushed over to where Alan stood. "Alan!" she shrieked, throwing her welcoming arms securely around him. "I'm so happy to see you!"

"Are you?" he asked, sounded very doubtful. As Elizabeth pulled back a little and closely studied his face, she could tell he definitely was angry with her.

"This must be the *boyfriend,*" Elizabeth heard Jameson say. She looked up to see him approaching. He pulled a T-shirt over his head as he closed the gap between them. He still remained un-shoed.

"For sure. James, this Alan. Alan, I believe you know who Jameson Thornton is." Elizabeth made introductions between the two men.

"Nice to meet you, Alan," Jameson greeted with an enormous smile, offering his hand in a friendly gesture. "I've heard so much about you from Elizabeth that I feel like I already know you."

"I guess I could say the same about you," Alan brusquely commented, giving his hand a halfhearted shake. Elizabeth noticed Alan's voice had a stern edge to it. She also noted that Alan did not return Jameson's smile.

"Well…I'll leave you guys alone. I know you must be anxious to spend some time together after being separated all week," Jameson commented. "Enjoy your weekend, Liz, and I'll see you Monday. Again, nice meeting you, Alan."

"Yeah," Alan acknowledged almost under his breath. As Jameson started away, Alan turned his attention solely to Elizabeth. "I guess you are going to change before we leave, aren't you?" he asked in a matter-of-fact voice, scrutinizing her skimpy clothing.

Suddenly very self conscious, Elizabeth was glad she had not allowed MGM to film the scene in just her underwear, as they had wanted to at first. "Yeah," she replied, anxiously studying Alan's taunt face again. He would not make eye contact. *He must have viewed the love scene and heard what Ryan and Jameson said to me*, she concluded with a sick feeling in the pit of her stomach. "My dressing room is just down the hall. Do you want to see it?"

"No. I think I need some fresh air," he admitted.

Only glancing at her face, it was long enough for Elizabeth to see a mixture of anger and hurt in his eyes. Her heart wrenched, and her conscience gave her a vicious attack of renewed guilt. The very last thing she wanted to do was hurt Alan.

"Just meet me outside when you are ready to go," Alan requested.

"Okay," she agreed and turned to hurry away. She wanted to get changed and join Alan as quickly as possible. She owed him an explanation for what he might have overheard and what he might be thinking he had viewed.

* * * *

When Elizabeth emerged from the house a few minutes later, she found Alan already sitting in his car. Instead of watching for her, he stared pensively out the windshield and tightly gripped the top of the steering wheel. Elizabeth had no doubt that he was extremely upset with her. She gingerly climbed into the car beside him. She badly wanted to put her arms around him and reassure him that everything was okay, but she sensed he did not want to be touched by her. Without saying another word, as soon as Elizabeth shut her door, Alan started the car and pulled away.

"Alan, are you okay?" Elizabeth mustered the courage to ask after another few minutes of tense silence between them.

"Am I okay?" he repeated in a gravelly voice, allowing his eyes only a very rapid glimpse of her and then staring straight ahead again. He drove along the tree-lined private roadway, heading for the highway. "Why would you think I wouldn't be okay? I mean there is nothing like missing somebody so badly it hurts for a week, and then when you finally see that person again they are in bed with another man. Real refreshing!"

"Don't have a cow, Alan!" Elizabeth exclaimed. "I know how my love scenes upset you, and I'm sorry you had to watch me filming one. But you have to remember that you were on the soundstage for a movie. It's not like you walked in on me with another man in my cottage. It wasn't real," she tried to assure him, feeling terrible for his pain, especially since she honestly knew she had put too much into the scene he had viewed.

"But it even looked real to the director who, I quote, said 'If I didn't know better I would think you two really were lovers'. And what is this crap about you and lover boy practicing love scenes alone together?! That seems pretty damn real to me! And then the jerk has the nerve to come over to me and shake my hand. I wanted to break his face!" Alan angrily exclaimed in a raised voice, pounding the steering wheel twice with the palm of one of his hands to release the steam that had been building since he had watched Elizabeth and Jameson together.

"Alan, you know I love you, don't you?" Elizabeth questioned in a shaky voice, reaching to lightly touch his upper arm, in hopes that he might remove his hand from the steering wheel and take hers.

Alan remained rigid, but he did allow his eyes to make brief contact with hers before he focused on the roadway again, as he pulled out onto the state highway.

"I've missed you too," she declared, massaging his stiff bicep. "The scene you viewed we filmed yesterday, but I couldn't get it right. For one thing, they wanted me to go before the camera in nothing but a bra and some very skimpy underwear. James went to bat for me, just like he did my first day when I kept messing up. Anyway, I've never done a bed scene before, so I just couldn't get it right. It just didn't look real to Ryan. That's why I was practicing alone with James, away from the cameras and Ryan's pressure. And that's why Ryan went on so about it looking so real this time. But, as I told you before, you are the only person I'm interested in doing any real love scenes with. I'm sorry I'm such a good actress, but nothing you saw was real. I love you! And when I make love I want it to be with you...and only you...for the rest of my life."

"So you are telling me that you honestly have no attraction to Jameson Thornton at all?" Alan grilled, sounding only the slightest bit calmer. While they were stopped at a red light, he turned his head to intensely study Elizabeth's eyes, anxiously awaiting her important answer.

"Alan, I'm not going to lie to you. Of course, I think James is handsome," Elizabeth reluctantly admitted, returning his intensive gaze. "He's a sex symbol. Most women would say they find him attractive. But, regardless of his looks, he's a friend and nothing more. I'm so totally in love with you, there could never be anything more with James," she tried to assure him. She quickly added, "James understands this. He respects the fact that I've got a boyfriend. He's happy for us."

"What do you mean by him respecting the fact that you have a boyfriend and that there won't be anything more than friendship with him? Has he come on to you?" Alan asked with obvious concern.

"No," Elizabeth firmly professed. "The only thing James has done for me is to help me become a better actress."

"So if he's only interested in friendship with you, what's the story with him? Is he involved with another woman?" Alan further interrogated, looking very doubtful.

"I don't know," Elizabeth truthfully replied, realizing for the first time that she had never really asked Jameson much about his personal life. "He's never mentioned anyone. But we don't talk much about our personal lives. We just basically have our job in common."

"Then how's he know so much about me?" Alan suspiciously asked.

"Everyone knows about you. Because you were on my mind constantly, I talked about you every chance I got," she confessed with an honest smile.

Alan gazed deeply into Elizabeth's eyes a few seconds more, as if trying to determine the sincerity of her responses to his heated questions. A car honked in back of him, and he realized the traffic light was green. He turned his head to stare absently out the windshield again. He did, however, remove his right hand from the steering wheel and take Elizabeth's hand, giving it a gentle squeeze. Elizabeth took this as a hopeful sign that his anger was finally subsiding, even though he remained silent for the rest of the journey back to her cottage.

Alan finally spoke to her again when he had parked the car in the driveway to her cottage. "Elizabeth, I don't know how I'm ever going to get used to seeing other men kiss you and you kissing them," he confessed, refraining from making eye contact and still grasping the steering wheel with one hand.

Elizabeth quickly slid across the seat so she could be as close to Alan as possible. She reached up and carefully placed the palm of her hand on Alan's opposite cheek, gently turning his head to face her. When she saw that he was not going to resist her, and that his eyes no longer held anger, she locked her hands behind his neck and drew him into a tight, reassuring embrace, warmly kissing the side of his mouth. Alan instantly responded, finally removing his other hand from the wheel and affectionately running his fingers through the back of Elizabeth's hair.

They shared an extended, pursuing, heat-filled kiss, before Elizabeth pulled away a little. Massaging the sides of Alan's head, she convincingly commented, "You have to remember that only what I give you is real. Now why don't we concentrate on showing each other how much we missed one another? Only this is real!" she heartily proclaimed and swiftly locked her lips hungrily upon his again.

"Man, have I missed holding you and kissing you!" Alan earnestly professed when they separated again several minutes later.

"Maybe that's what made me even more nuts when I saw you kissing and touching Jameson."

"Shhh!" Elizabeth commanded, placing a finger over his lips. "James is part of work for me. I don't want to think about him anymore until I have to on Monday. I want to concentrate only on you. Why don't we go inside, and I'll teach you what a genuine love scene looks like. Hopefully, when I'm through, you will never confuse the two again."

"One can certainly hope," Alan eagerly responded, displaying a slight smile for the first time and speedily following Elizabeth out of the car.

Chapter 13
Secrets

Are secrets lies? Ever hear of the lie of omission?
Yet, what harm can a little secret do? Only time will tell.

~ Sissy Marlyn ~

Alan spent the night with Elizabeth at the cottage Friday night. It was difficult for the two to part and go to separate bedrooms, but they did. Alan was still determined to respect Elizabeth's virginity.

Saturday morning, Alan drove Elizabeth back to Bowling Green and took her to her house. Elizabeth was shocked by her mother's appearance. Her hair had thinned a great deal, as well as her body. Dark circles stood under her eyes. Elizabeth enveloped her in a hug, and her mother hugged her back. It felt good to finally have this affection between them, but it hurt Elizabeth a bit to know it would be short lived.

"So how was your first week at professional acting?" her mother asked, seeming genuinely interested.

"It was...o...kay," Elizabeth honestly replied.

"Just okay?" her mother questioned. She looked over Elizabeth's shoulder at Alan, as if he could provide some explanation. He sat on the couch. Elizabeth's mother sat in her recliner. Her dad was beside her in his chair.

"She had kind of a rough week," Alan explained. Then he added with a smile. "But working with her all-time idol helped to smooth out the edges. Why don't you tell your mom and dad who your co-star is?"

Elizabeth turned and looked at Alan. Mindful of his jealousy toward Jameson, she downplayed a bit, "It's Jameson Thornton."

"The young man you had posters of on your wall?" her dad questioned, looking both surprised and impressed.

"That's the one," Elizabeth replied. She walked over and sat down hip to hip with Alan. She wanted to be close to him to ease any insecurity he might feel about them talking about Jameson. Alan seemed to be fine right now, and Elizabeth wanted to keep it that way. She wanted their weekend together to be a good one.

"Wow! Both the television show and the movie that young man was in were quite a hit!" her mother pointed out. She was impressed that Elizabeth was working with a star.

"Yeah," Elizabeth answered, still not reacting with an overwhelming amount of excitement. "He's a really nice guy. He helped me learn the ropes this week. And I had a lot to learn. Doing film is a lot different than acting on stage," Elizabeth explained.

"Well…we missed you," Elizabeth was surprised to hear her mother say. "It's good having you home. Even if it is only for one night. I worry about you being out on your own."

"I'm fine, mom," Elizabeth assured her.

"Just be careful, and remember all you've been taught," her mother warned.

"I am doing both," Elizabeth maintained.

"Good," her mother replied.

Elizabeth was still unsettled by the change in her mother's behavior. She had been all prepared for her mother to start interrogating Alan about whether he had been staying in Bowling Green with her or not. Her mother's silence was almost harder to take than her pointed questions. Alan must have sensed Elizabeth's uneasiness, because he reached to take her hand. She gave him a slight smile. It was actually good to be home, even if it was only for one night.

* * * *

Elizabeth's weekend passed swiftly. Sunday afternoon rolled around too soon, and Alan drove Elizabeth back to Bardstown. She once again invited him to spend the night at her cottage.

"I'm not sure that would be such a good idea," she was surprised to hear Alan say.

"Why?" she asked, sounding more than a little disappointed.

"Because..." he replied, drawing in close and giving her an impassioned kiss. "You make me crazy. That's why. We got pretty carried away Friday night. It was *really* hard to separate from you," he confessed, his eyes full of desire.

"Maybe we were wrong to separate," he was surprised to hear Elizabeth say. Her eyes held a mirror of his desire.

"What are you saying?" Alan asked.

"I'm saying...I'll be living in this house for six months. You could stay here with me. It would almost be like we were married."

"Almost...but not quite," Alan argued, even though he did not want to. "We would only be playing house. Is that what you want?"

"I don't know," Elizabeth said with frustration. "I believe sex without love is morally wrong. But I love you from the bottom of my heart. How could the two of us making love be wrong?"

"Ah...I don't think anything that happens between the two of us could ever be wrong..." Alan said, seeming to agree with Elizabeth.

"For sure. So are you saying...you are going to stay?" Elizabeth questioned.

"No...," Alan begrudgingly disagreed. "Because deep down, I know you still want your first time to be with your husband. And I'm not your husband...yet! I want your first time to be all you've ever dreamed about."

"But all I dream about now...is you," Elizabeth honestly uttered. She drew in for another persuasive kiss.

"Elizabeth...you really are rattling me!" Alan confessed, sounding winded. "I should go." *Before I change my mind*, he thought. He pushed himself out of Elizabeth's arms.

"Okay," she agreed with reluctance. She knew she was being a terrible temptress, but her desire to be with Alan grew more and more each day. She did not see how they could put off being together much longer.

"Look…you have a great week," Alan said, his voice still husky. He stepped down one step to put a little more distance between them. His body was screaming for him to change his mind and take Elizabeth up on her offer. But his love and respect for her was too great to be overcome. "I'll call you every night, and I'll see you on Friday. I'll miss you like crazy."

"I'll miss you too," she uttered. *Don't go!* her mind screamed.

"See ya soon," Alan said, and began making his way down the sidewalk toward the car. He turned and waved before he climbed inside. "I love you!" he called.

"I love you too!" she declared. "You drive safe. Call me when you get home."

"I will," he agreed.

Alan climbed into the car and started it then. Still early spring, the temperature outside was not hot, but Alan turned on the air conditioner in the car regardless. He needed to cool himself off and clear his mind. He put the car in reverse and headed out before he changed his mind. He even turned on the radio to further distract himself as he sped off down the road.

* * * *

The next morning, when the driver dropped her off at work, Elizabeth eagerly entered the house and walked assuredly toward *Makeup and Wardrobe*.

What a change over the Monday before, she realized, thinking about how scared and unsure she had been then. This week, she was merely excited to see what lay ahead. Elizabeth had a great deal more confidence in herself than she had the week before. She knew she owed most of the credit for this newfound self-worth to Jameson and his constant, unwavering support and belief in her.

Very relieved to have put Alan's jealous fears to rest this weekend, Elizabeth also believed she had come to terms with her feelings toward Jameson as well. She might be attracted to him, as any young woman would be, but all she and Jameson would ever be was friends.

She loved Alan much too deeply for there to ever be any other relationship with Jameson.

Elizabeth did not have a scene to film with Jameson until a little later in the day, so she did not see him until then. They were dressed formally again, because the scene called for them to be at a fancy dinner party. Jameson looked very handsome in a jet black tuxedo, which matched the color of his wavy hair to a tee. All of the dark coloring seemed to make his navy eyes glow brilliantly in stunning contrast. Elizabeth could not help but stare.

"You look very lovely," Jameson told her with a slight, appreciative smile, approaching her before the filming began. It was quite obvious he was thoroughly checking her out as well. Elizabeth wore an ankle-length, royal-blue, formal gown. The only thing she did not like about the dress was the very low-cut, cleavage-bearing, V neckline. "Blue certainly must be one of your colors, Liz."

"And black yours, you handsome devil," she teased. Determined to stay relaxed around him, she comfortably returned his smile. *We are going to have a great work relationship and a wonderful friendship*, she determinedly convinced herself.

* * * *

Wednesday, Elizabeth was asked to film her first bathing suit scene. Of course, the bathing suit had to be a very skimpy bikini. Elizabeth was uncomfortable, but since they had allowed her to film love scenes in more clothes then they had originally planned, she readily accepted their choice of bathing suit.

However, to her surprise, after they had finished filming the scene, Ryan pulled her aside.

"What's wrong? Did I look as uncomfortable as I felt being filmed in this string you guys gave me to wear?" she questioned.

"No. Your acting was fine," Ryan told her. "But one of the cameramen said you look a little heavier on the film. Have you put on a little weight?"

"Maybe. I don't really know. Not that I've really noticed. But if I had, it would totally show in this thing. It's probably just that the cameraman has...like...never filmed me in so little clothing," Elizabeth argued, crossing her arms defiantly across her chest.

"That's true," Ryan agreed. "But I bet you don't realize that the camera adds ten pounds, do you? I'm not saying you look fat. Just that every extra pound will show. You might want to watch what you eat and exercise a little more. You're a beautiful young lady, and we just want to be sure you film that way no matter what you are wearing. You might want to consider losing say…five or ten pounds."

"Okay. If you think so," Elizabeth agreed, sounding very skeptical. This was the first time in her life anyone had ever said she needed to lose weight. In high school, her friends had always seemed envious of her figure, always commenting on how she could eat whatever she wanted and never seem to gain a pound.

"Don't let my comments upset you, Elizabeth," Ryan instructed, noticing her pensiveness. "Like I said, you still look great. We just want you to look your absolute best," he said, pushing his glasses all the way up on his nose, as if he was taking a closer look.

"Alright," she conceded again. Elizabeth left Ryan's side, making her way back to the *Makeup and Wardrobe* room to change from the much too revealing bikini to her outfit for her next scene. She found Pat in the room also making a change.

"So how'd your first bathing suit scene go?" Pat asked, seeming genuinely interested.

"Okay, I guess," Elizabeth replied, sounding a little unsure. "Actually, I'm a little bugged."

"How come?" Pat inquired, buttoning up her blouse and tucking it into her jeans.

"Well, Ryan said he thinks I need to lose about five or ten pounds. I've never had to diet in my life. But he said the camera adds weight. The problem is I don't know if I can go without eating the way you do," Elizabeth confessed. "I guess I'll just have to exercise myself to death when I can find the time."

"You just need to reign in your appetite, that's all," Pat helpfully shared, threading a belt through her belt loops. "I have some great diet pills that help me stay on track. I can give you a few to try if you want. They not only help you eat less, but they will give you more energy to get that extra exercise."

"Pills? I'm so sure. I'm not much on taking pills for stuff," Elizabeth honestly admitted with obvious hesitation.

"Well, if you change your mind, let me know," Pat said with a smile, zipping her jeans and starting out of the room. "They've made a world of difference for me. Do I ever look like I'm dragging to you because I haven't eaten a lot?"

"No," Elizabeth had to admit. As she set to the task of changing her own clothes, she wondered if it would hurt to take a few pills from Pat. *If I don't like them, I could always stop taking them*, she reasoned.

At the end of the day, Pat joined Elizabeth for dinner. As Elizabeth watched her friend eat her usual, tiny meal, comprised of salad and fruit, she told Pat she thought she would like to try a few of her miraculous diet pills. Pat eagerly removed a container of pills from her purse and emptied a few out for Elizabeth.

"It'll make a new woman out of you," Pat promised with a knowing grin, as Elizabeth stored the pills safely in her purse.

* * * *

Taking Pat's advice, Elizabeth waited until the next morning to take her first pill. Pat had explained that taking them in the evening could make it hard to sleep, because they gave you extra energy. Elizabeth noticed an enormous difference almost immediately.

Usually, it took her a while after getting to work to feel fully awake. However, today, she not only felt totally awakened but could not wait to get started. She took another pill before lunch, because she was beginning to feel tired, and almost instantly, her momentum picked right up again.

By the next day, she found she could indeed make it through the day even though she was eating only a bare minimum of food. Elizabeth could not believe the energy she had and that she did not even feel hungry when she ate. She thanked Pat profusely for sharing her wonderful secret with her.

* * * *

Friday, after Elizabeth had taped her final scene for that week, she found Alan patiently waiting near the soundstage to whisk her away for their stolen weekend. She happily showered him with welcoming kisses.

This time, Alan allowed Elizabeth to show him around a bit. She took him to the small room that served as her dressing room.

The room was not much bigger than a large walk-in closet. It had a rack for Elizabeth to hang some clothes, and there was a chair, a vanity and a mirror. Regardless of its small size, Elizabeth was proud to have a room with her name on the door, and Alan, as usual, was happy for her.

He waited outside this room, in the hall, as Elizabeth changed clothes, eager for the weekend to begin. During their car ride to the Old Talbott Tavern – a nearby restaurant – Elizabeth continuously chattered with excitement about the week's events. Alan could barely get a word in edgeways.

When they got out of the car, Elizabeth snatched Alan's hand, surging forward in an excited jog toward the entrance door of the historic stone building which housed the restaurant and several guest rooms. Alan knew Elizabeth liked visiting historic places, and the Old Talbott Tavern had been around since the 1700s. He guessed that her excitement had something to do with visiting this place.

"Elizabeth, you don't have ants in your pants tonight, do you?" Alan inquired with an amused smile. They had been seated by a hostess in period costume, and Elizabeth still fidgeted in her seat.

"I just feel like I'm totally on top of the world! Do you know what I mean? Of course, you don't! I mean I just feel soooo good! My dreams are all coming true! It's awesome!" Elizabeth spurred forth another analog of nonstop words.

Alan chucked and commented, "I swear, if I didn't know you as well as I do, I would think you were high on something."

"For sure! I am! I'm high on life! And *most especially*, I'm high on you!" Elizabeth deliriously shrieked. She reached across the table to interlace her fingers through one of Alan's hands.

"Well, the feeling is very mutual," he professed with a warm smile, as their waitress reappeared, sitting a glass of iced tea in front of both of them.

"I'll give you a few minutes to look over the menu, and then I'll come back for your order," she told them with a welcoming smile.

"Okay. Works for me," Elizabeth replied with a giggle, snatching up her menu. Elizabeth studied it for only a moment. Then she bounced it back and forth in her hands as she impatiently waited for the waitress to come back.

"I guess I'm just tired from working all day and the drive here. Sorry I'm not as bouncy as you," Alan said, as he laid his menu down on the table.

"You're fine!" Elizabeth assured him. She dropped her menu, grabbed Alan's hand and brought it up to her mouth, kissing it. "I'll be settling down in awhile. I'm still just keyed up from a good week on the set."

"Well, I'm certainly glad to hear it's all going so great for you," Alan said with sincerity, flashing her a warm, toothy grin.

The waitress came back to their table to take their order. Alan ordered the fried chicken, which their hostess said was a specialty. Not hungry, Elizabeth knew she needed to eat something, so she merely ordered a house salad.

"That's all you are going to eat is a house salad?" Alan asked after the waitress had left with their order. His serious eyes scrutinized her face, conveying his concern. "Are you feeling alright?"

"For sure! I don't just feel alright. I feel great!" Elizabeth proclaimed with exhilaration. She displayed another wide smile and pumped Alan's hand enthusiastically. "I just need to watch what I eat a little better. Ryan said I could stand to lose a few pounds."

"Ryan actually told you to lost weight? Is he crazy?! You look wonderful!" Alan argued, his irritation toward Elizabeth's director plainly obvious. Alan's handsome grin promptly turned into a tight, disapproving frown.

"Thank you, sweetheart. I think you look pretty rad too. Although I think you would look even better with a smile on that handsome face," Elizabeth coaxed, trying to persuade Alan to be a little less serious. She quickly tried to explain, "The reason Ryan said I need to lose a little weight is the camera makes me look ten pounds heavier. So I need to be a little underweight."

"That's ridiculous!" Alan further protested, ignoring Elizabeth's playful suggestion to loosen up. "Even if you put on another ten pounds, you would still be beautiful. If that clod can't see that, then he must be blind."

"Do you suppose you might be just a little prejudiced?" Elizabeth pointed out with an astute grin. She affectionately gave his hand yet another squeeze, and she swung his whole arm playfully back and forth, still determinedly trying to lighten his mood again. "Anyway, you don't have to worry about me. It's just a few pounds. Neither of us will miss them."

"I will. I like you just the way you are. In fact, I love every pound of you," he assured her.

Elizabeth was touched by his words and the adoring look in his eye. She sprang up from her chair, which resided across the table from Alan, and bounced into the chair beside him. She threw her arms around his neck, and she drew him in for a kiss. "I love every pound of you too," she professed when the kiss had ended. "Thanks for worrying about me. But you don't need to. Losing a little weight isn't going to hurt me. I promise."

Alan still was not happy about Elizabeth having to diet, but he let the subject drop. She was very giddy this evening, and he did not want to spoil her happy mood. He looked forward to their weekend together. He gave her another kiss and then dropped an arm around her shoulder. Elizabeth's body quivered. He was glad to see her so excited and happy. He loved her so much that her happiness brought him joy as well.

* * * *

Once again, the weekend passed quickly, and on Monday, Elizabeth started her third week of filming. After work Monday, Pat told Elizabeth she was going to join Bradley for dinner again. Elizabeth was once again surprised. Pat and Bradley never seemed to have much to do with one another during the day, but yet, Pat occasionally seemed to want his company in the evenings.

Elizabeth had a hard time understanding this strange behavior, but she tried not to judge Pat too harshly. The one good thing that had come out of Pat dating Bradley was he had finally stopped trying to proposition Elizabeth. This change made working with him far less of a chore.

As Elizabeth left her dressing room that day, she found Jameson waiting for her in hallway. "So are we both all alone again tonight?" he asked with a crooked smile. "Bradley told me he thought he had convinced Pat to go out with him again. So, I was wondering if you might like to join me. I heard through the grapevine that you are trying to shed a few pounds. Believe it or not, there is a great workout room in the basement of my B&B. I'm going to spend an hour there before I go grab a bite to eat. You certainly aren't overweight, so it sounds like you just need to tone up a little."

"Who'd you hear that from?" Elizabeth asked, sounding guarded.

"Actually I saw Ryan pull you aside last week after the bathing suit scene. I thought maybe he was giving you a hard way to go, so I asked him what was up. He told me what he had said to you. I just want to help. I don't want you to start starving yourself like Pat," Jameson told her.

"Now you sound like Alan," Elizabeth observed with a slight smile. "He got really upset this weekend because I didn't want to eat much. He thinks it's ridiculous for me to lose any weight. I was afraid he would come in and tell Ryan off."

"Alan's kind of hot-headed, isn't he?" Jameson unexpectedly questioned, a very somber expression on his face.

"No," Elizabeth quickly protested, her face also becoming very serious. "He's just very protective of me."

"Protective…or controlling?" Jameson dared to inquire, his eyes piercing hers.

"Most definitely protective!" she firmly asserted, coming to Alan's defense. "I may make him sound controlling, but he's not! He's been very supportive of my acting, even though we are spending a lot of time apart. I just don't like to do things that upset him. I guess that's because I love him so much."

"I'm sorry. I don't mean to be attacking the guy," Jameson clarified, seeing he was upsetting Elizabeth. "It's just that every week he seems to get upset about something that has happened here. First, it was your love scenes, and now, it's because they asked you to shed a few pounds. He's going to have to get used to the fact that you may be doing some things he doesn't like."

"No shit, Sherlock. He knows that," Elizabeth confirmed. "He's working on being less jealous, and he said if I felt I needed to lose a few pounds, he would support me in doing that also. What more can I ask?"

"Well...I'm glad to hear Alan is willing to change for you. It's hard on relationships when one person isn't in the business," Jameson commented, giving her a slight grin once again as he quickly changed the subject. "So how about it, Liz? Are you going to make it easier on Alan and go work out with me? That way I guarantee you won't have to starve yourself."

Silent for a few moments, Elizabeth mulled over Jameson's suggestion. Any diet she had ever seen called for exercise in addition to watching what you ate. Going with Jameson could help her reach her goal weight even quicker. Then, she could stop taking the diet pills, at least so often. *Besides,* she reasoned, *I'm still very keyed up from the last pill I took a few hours ago, and working out would help use up that excess energy.*

"Okay. Let's go," she agreed.

"Great!" Jameson chirped, leading the way down the hall toward the door. He was glad to have Elizabeth's company for the evening again.

* * * *

Elizabeth worked out with Jameson's two more times that week. She had to admit that she enjoyed working out with him, riding stationary bikes, doing sit-ups, leg and arm workouts, and even lifting a few weights. Not once did he seem forward in any way. He was just a friend to her.

As the week came to an end, Elizabeth felt great. Due to her eating much less and exercising, she had already lost over five pounds. She decided she would not need to take any more diet pills. Even if she gained a pound or two, she could lose the weight again while exercising with Jameson during the week.

Saturday afternoon, however, Elizabeth found herself to be very lethargic. She also had a severe headache and felt very uptight. She was at Alan's apartment with him. Alan, always exceptionally attuned to her, asked if she felt okay. "You look tired," he told her with obvious concern.

"I have a bad headache," she explained, holding her throbbing forehead. She also felt a slight bit nauseated. She wondered if she was coming down with something.

"Do you want me to call your parents and tell them we won't be at Mass? Maybe you should take an aspirin and lay down for awhile," Alan tried to helpfully suggest.

They were supposed to join her parents in a couple of hours for Saturday evening Mass. Alan had just begun to go to church again, and Elizabeth was very happy about this fact. He told her he figured if they had kids, he would want to raise them Catholic, so he thought he should start practicing the faith again. He also didn't want to spend even one hour apart from her, and Elizabeth always went to church with her parents, so going to Mass had become yet another activity for them to share on their stolen weekends. Elizabeth's mother was happy to have Alan going to church with them as well. She was growing to like this young man more and more, and she was relieved to accept this fact.

Even though Elizabeth realized Alan was trying to be helpful and kind by offering to call her parents and change their routine, she was so irritable that he also seemed somewhat patronizing. "I already took an aspirin," she snapped without meaning to. "And a headache and being tired wouldn't be reason enough for my dear mother to accept me missing Mass."

"Okay," Alan agreed in a sympathetic voice, patting her arm. He sat down beside her on the sofa. He got the impression that she did not want him around, but he wanted to be there for her anyway. "Is there anything I can do?"

Elizabeth bit her tongue to keep from meanly telling him to stop hovering over her and leave her alone. She felt guilty for her nasty thoughts. She could not understand what was wrong with her. She had been fine yesterday.

Elizabeth wanted what little time she had with Alan to be good. She suddenly wondered if taking one of her diet pills would help her to feel better. They usually gave her a burst of energy. "Thanks for offering," she finally said, trying to make her voice sound far less harsh. "I think I'll take another aspirin."

"I'll get you one," Alan offered, instantly rising to his feet again.

Just like a trained dog, Elizabeth viciously thought. "No," she retorted. She slowly arose to stand beside him. "They're in my purse. I don't want you rummaging through everything trying to find one. You just stay put. I'll be right back."

Elizabeth went and got her purse, located her diet pills, went into Alan's small kitchen, took a Pepsi out of the refrigerator, and rapidly washed the pill down. She thought maybe the caffeine in the soft drink might wake her up a little also. At least she hoped so. She did not like the way she was feeling right now or her subsequent behavior.

By the time she and Alan left for Mass a few hours later, Elizabeth felt and was acting like a totally different person. Not only had her headache totally subsided, but she had plenty of energy now. Alan was more than a little surprised by the radical change in her so quickly.

"Maybe I just needed a little caffeine," she tried to explain and added with a giggle, "You know I don't get much sleep at night when I'm with you. Not that I'm complaining." They stayed up past midnight each night, trying to squeeze in as much time together as possible.

Elizabeth made a secret mental note to ask Pat exactly what was in the diet pills. *They must be loaded to the hilt with caffeine.* Right now, Elizabeth was just glad to be feeling like herself again and able to spend some more quality time with the man she loved.

* * * *

The following week, after spending many, long hours perfecting scenes for *Bardstown*, Elizabeth also spent each evening with Jameson vigorously working out. By Thursday, when Elizabeth weighed in, she victoriously found she had reached her goal weight.

"We should celebrate," Jameson enthusiastically declared with a proud smile. He handed her a towel to wipe the sweat away with. "There's some champagne in the refrigerator."

"I'm so sure," Elizabeth said, returning his smile. "I really am not much of a drinker. Thanks for the offer, but I'd just as soon drink some iced tea."

"Celebrate with iced tea? That's a new one! So is that how you celebrate things with Alan too? You are going to have a very strange wedding night if that is the case. You do realize that sharing champagne with your husband on your wedding night is supposed to be a tradition, don't you?" Jameson pointed out in a teasing manner.

"We will probably share sparkling apple cider instead, and start our own tradition. Alan's mom was killed by a drunk driver and his dad partakes a little too much, so Alan doesn't drink at all," Elizabeth freely shared.

Since she started exercising with Jameson, Elizabeth felt even more comfortable with him. She really did consider him a very good friend now. However, she still had not told Alan she was spending so much time with Jameson away from the set. *I will eventually*, she kept telling herself. *I just don't want to take the chance of making Alan jealous over nothing.*

"So do you not drink because of Alan? Or is it something you don't agree with either?" Jameson interrupted her thoughts asking, intently studying her eyes. "You seemed to enjoy wine that one night."

"For sure, but I have a confession to make. The wine I shared with you was the first alcohol I've ever drank," Elizabeth shared. She shyly averted her eyes from his serious scrutiny. "My parents have never drank. Neither do my friends yet or Alan. So it's not really that I'm against it or don't drink because of Alan. I just haven't really been exposed to it before you."

"Well...I'm glad I introduced you to something new which you were able to enjoy. But since you did seem to enjoy the wine, why not share a glass of champagne with me now? I'm not talking about us going on a drunken binge here. Just one glass apiece. What's the big deal? Are you afraid Alan wouldn't approve?" Jameson questioned, puzzled.

Jameson had a definite talent for being able to make Elizabeth think about things in a completely different light. Actually, she did not think a glass or two of champagne would hurt her at all. However, she had learned her lesson well about being alone and drinking with Jameson.

She now knew how quickly she could allow things to get out of control. They were forming a very nice friendship, and Elizabeth certainly did not want to chance doing anything that could harm their relationship.

Alan also was part of the reason Elizabeth did not feel right sharing a glass of champagne with Jameson at his B&B. She knew without a doubt that Alan would not like her drinking, especially with Jameson. Elizabeth quickly made a silent promise to herself, *I will tell*

Alan this weekend about exercising each night with James. That way there would be no secrets between the two of them.

However, at this present moment, Elizabeth felt it was Jameson she needed to be honest with. "I don't feel right drinking with you," she cautiously admitted.

"Why?" Jameson asked with a very concerned expression, gripping both ends of the towel which rested around his neck. "Did I do something last time to make you uncomfortable?"

"No. It wasn't you," Elizabeth explained, trying to assure him by maintaining direct eye contact. "I relaxed a little too much because of the wine, and I may have gotten into our love scene a little too much. I realize you stayed in character, but the lines blurred a little for me. Anyway, I know that Alan just totally wouldn't understand me drinking with you. He's having a hard enough time accepting us doing love scenes. I sure don't want to do anything else that might make him even more jealous."

"And I guess you feel you need to tell him everything you do?" he questioned with a slight, disagreeable grimace on his face. "Seems to me, some things would better not be said. But... regardless of what I might think, I don't want you to do anything that is going to make you uncomfortable around me. I really value the friendship we've formed."

"For sure. Me too," Elizabeth agreed with a warm, satisfied smile, reaching out to reassuringly pat one of his hands. "So how about it? Do you want to get yourself a glass of champagne and me a glass of ice tea and we'll toast my reaching goal weight?"

"If that's what the lady wants, then sure," Jameson agreed with a smile.

They headed for the stairs then to go up into the kitchen and get their drinks. Elizabeth felt very satisfied and content. She was happy with the friendship that she and Jameson shared and glad he was part of her life.

* * * *

Elizabeth's last scene Friday included Pat, so Elizabeth was finally able to introduce her to Alan. "Hi, Alan. I'm so glad to finally meet you," she greeted with a friendly smile, and warmly patted his arm.

"I've heard so much about you from Elizabeth that I feel like I already know you."

"Likewise," he admitted, returning her smile. He immediately placed his arm around Elizabeth and pulled her to his side. "I understand you keep Elizabeth's evenings pretty busy. You're her dinner partner, and the two of you help memorize lines together. That used to be my role before we were separated all week. I'm glad she has somebody to keep her company though."

"Yeah, me and Jameson," Pat enthusiastically and quite innocently spurted out. "Don't you think Elizabeth looks great though? She really took the weight off fast after spending three or four nights a week working out with Jameson."

There was a brief, strained pause as Elizabeth noticed Alan glancing from Pat to her. His eyes darted much too fast for her to decipher if what Pat had just revealed upset him in any way. She just wished she had already told him about going with Jameson to work out occasionally.

Now, since he had not known about it, it almost made it seem as if she was purposely trying to hide it from him. Which, in a way, was true. Elizabeth had not told Alan because she feared he would be upset about her spending so much time alone with Jameson, even though it was all very innocent.

"Well, now, maybe Elizabeth can go back to eating normal again," she finally heard Alan reply. She could not hear any anger in his voice, so she hoped this was a good sign.

"Don't count on it," Pat contradicted. "In this business, eating normal and being a normal weight is frowned upon. But you'll get used to the new and better Elizabeth. Basically, you don't have a choice. MGM runs her life now."

Alan did not respond. He only nodded his head, as if in agreement, and glanced quickly at Elizabeth's face again. "Well, it was nice meeting you, Pat," he finally said, obviously ready to leave.

"Nice meeting you too. You two have a wonderful weekend. I'll see you Monday, Elizabeth."

Elizabeth waved goodbye to Pat, and she walked with Alan toward the door. He left his arm around her, but he was suddenly, strangely quiet. Elizabeth knew he had to be wondering why she had not said anything about exercising with Jameson. However, right now, at least he did not seem angry about her omission.

When they were settled in the car, Alan finally broached the subject. "So you've been working out with Jameson, huh?" he asked rather matter-of-factly. His eyes studied her, but still did not display any anger or hurt. "When did this start?"

"He asked me for the first time last Monday. Pat has been seeing Bradley, the other young actor who works with us. So I was free that night. I rode one of those stationary bikes, did sit ups, and even lifted some weights. James agreed with you that I'm not overweight. He said I probably just needed to tone up a little. I enjoyed the first night so much that when he asked again Wednesday and Thursday, I went then too," she explained.

"So this is actually the second week you've been going?" he further clarified, briefly glancing away and then carefully analyzing her eyes again. He seemed to be anxiously awaiting her answer.

"Yeah. I was surprised, but I did enjoy working out. James wouldn't let me overdo anything. He said he didn't want me to get hurt. When I told him you were upset about me dieting, he convinced me, if I just started exercising, I wouldn't have to starve myself, like Pat. Then you wouldn't have anything to be upset about," Elizabeth further explained.

"Gosh! How thoughtful of him," Alan uttered in a voice laced with sarcasm. He also looked away from Elizabeth.

"Alan, please chill," Elizabeth pleaded, placing her hand on his arm. "You have absolutely no reason to be jealous of James. He's just a good friend, and he helps me every chance he gets."

Uncomfortable silence reigned for several moments. Elizabeth could tell Alan was thinking intently about what he wanted to say next. She braced herself for the worst. "So, do you consider Pat a friend?" he finally asked in a very level voice, scrutinizing her face once again.

"Yes," she truthfully answered. Her eyes immediately displayed puzzlement. She wondered what Alan might be getting at.

"And I pretty much hear about all of the things you do with her, right?" he questioned, adding, "I bet you would have told me if Pat and you started exercising together."

His eyes were so ardent they seemed to be piercing Elizabeth's. She glanced down at her lap as she replied, "Yeah, probably, but..."

"But what?" Alan abruptly interrupted, sounding a tinge angry for the first time. "Why didn't you tell me you were spending so much time with Jameson? After all, he's just a friend just like Pat, right?"

"I was planning on telling you tonight," Elizabeth informed him. She really had been. Once again, she wished she had not waited so long and given someone else the chance to tell him. "Look, I understand why you might be angry with me right now. But I only hesitated in telling you because I know how jealous you have been of Jameson. I really wanted to keep from getting you upset again."

"Well, that's just great!" he snapped. "So that means if you think you might be doing something that might upset me, mum is the word. I guess as long as I don't know anything about it, everything will be just hunky dory! Ignorance is bliss, right?!"

"Oh, Alan!" Elizabeth wailed, placing both of her hands over her face in frustration for a few, brief moments. "If you just wouldn't let your jealousy get the best of you every time I do anything with Jameson, then I wouldn't have to worry about telling you everything we do together."

"So you're justifying lying to me?!" he fired back, his face clenched in absolute fury now. He seemed to want to fight.

"I didn't lie to you about anything!" Elizabeth quickly contradicted. "I just didn't tell you right away what I was doing, but I really want to be able to freely share everything with you as it is happening. These hellacious outbursts of yours really upset me. It's like you don't trust me at all. Do you?!"

"I used to. But, I feel like if you are going to start hiding things from me, then I'm not sure whether I can trust you or not! Just how would you feel if you found out I had been hanging out with another woman in Bowling Green every evening?!" he growled in an animated voice, his face turning red.

"If it was someone who I knew, and you told me she was just a friend, then I would have to trust you. I might not like it, but I would hope I wouldn't rant and rave about it like you do!" she snarled, wanting to make her point as badly as him.

"Well, I guess I just need to find me a lady friend to keep me company while you are gone. You don't mind if I don't discuss what we might do together, I suppose?" he meanly proposed, trying to further drive his original point home.

His thoughtless barb managed to do much more than merely make a point. Alan's words managed to wound. Elizabeth's face turned a bright shade of red, and she quickly turned her face from his view, staring aimlessly out the side window. "Okay, Alan. You win," she conceded in a very feeble, defeated voice. "If you don't trust me, and you want to see someone other than me, then maybe you aren't even sure you love me anymore. Is that what this argument is all about?"

"Don't you try to turn this around on me!" he ordered, still fiercely propelled by anger. "I haven't done anything to make you doubt my love for you!"

"Neither have I!" she vehemently argued, turning to face Alan again. It was only then that he saw the tears that streamed down her cheeks. "You're making it...it sound like James and I are...are having an affair and...and you'd like to ch...cheat on me to get even! Why don't you just tear my heart out?! That would be a lot kinder! How many times do I have to tell you that you...you are the only man I love, and the only man I ever want to...to love! I don't guess it really matters though if...if you really don't...um...don't trust me anymore."

Elizabeth's tears quickly dissipated Alan's anger. He suddenly felt very guilty for having hurt her so badly. It certainly had not been his intent. He quickly slid across the seat and pulled her tightly against his chest. Elizabeth laid her head on his shoulder and sobbed.

"I'm sorry, Elizabeth," he apologized, rubbing the back of her head to try and soothe her. "I don't really mean that I don't trust you, and I certainly don't want to see anyone else. It's just that...well...you and I could always talk about everything. When I feel like you are hiding things from me, it makes my crazy. I want you to share everything with me. Can you understand that?"

"For sure. But James is really just a friend, Alan. You are the only man in my life," she affirmed again. "I'm sorry I was so stupid. The last thing I ever want to do is make you doubt your trust in me. I just want all of our time together to be good, because we have so little time together since I started filming *Bardstown*. And it seems like we are taking up more and more of that time arguing. That's why I wasn't overly anxious to tell you I was spending time with James away from the set. But, I swear, I really was planning on telling you tonight. And I wish to God I had told you last week. I've learned my lesson. Please don't be angry with me anymore."

"I think it's impossible for me to stay mad at you about anything," Alan professed in a quiet, comforting voice, gently brushing Elizabeth's tears from her cheeks. "You forgive me for hurting you, and I'll forgive you for keeping things from me. Have we got a deal?"

"For sure," she quickly agreed, kissing the hand which had seconds before been lovingly stroking her wet cheeks. "I promise, from now on, I'll tell you everything that happens between James and me, just as soon as it happens."

"And I promise to try and not behave like such a jealous jackass all the time," Alan professed, giving her a tight, reassuring squeeze.

After holding her and continually caressing her head and back for several more moments, he finally released Elizabeth to slide back over behind the wheel and start the car. Elizabeth swiftly slid over beside him and placed her head on his shoulder.

"I love you, Elizabeth," Alan said, gazing into her bloodshot eyes.

"I love you too, Alan. From the bottom of my heart," she pledged, drawing in to give him a demonstrative kiss.

"Let's go enjoy our weekend," Alan suggested, placing the car in drive to finally head out. He hated that he had hurt Elizabeth, but he hoped that from now on, she would be completely honest with him about everything. Trust was essential for their relationship.

As Elizabeth slid back over to her side of the car and buckled her seatbelt around her, Alan switched on the radio. *Come on Eileen* was playing. Alan smiled at Elizabeth, as he turned the radio up a few more notches. He knew she loved this song.

As Elizabeth began to move to the music and sing a bit, Alan decided, *It'll be a good weekend after all. It's our time now. No more arguing. Only happy times.* He chimed in on the song, and sped on down the highway, headed to Bowling Green, leaving Bardstown far behind again for a while.

Chapter 14
Changes

Sometimes change is good.
Some change, however, is neither welcomed by the person who
the change is happening to or by those closest to them, and
sometimes, neither are fully aware of the change until
it's too late to prevent the damage that may occur.

~ Sissy Marlyn ~

*M*onday, Elizabeth decided to start weaning herself off of the diet pills. She had not tried on the weekend, because she knew it would make her crabby and tired, and she wanted the rest of her time with Alan to be nothing but enjoyable. She figured she would not miss them as much anyway if she was busy filming scenes at the set. She was wrong, and it did not take her long to discover this fact.

By Wednesday, Elizabeth not only moved as if she was sleepwalking, but her facial features showed the strain as well. Michelle had to put extra makeup on her, but even that did not totally disguise her awful fatigue.

Elizabeth's mind focused on when she would be able to take her next pill. She only allowed herself one in the middle of each day. Therefore, the mornings seemed to drag by and so did the evenings. She also had a great deal of difficulty sleeping and had very severe headaches.

Thursday, when Elizabeth missed her mark five times in a row during the filming of one particular scene, Ryan had finally had more than enough. Elizabeth was moving way too slowly, and she did not seem to be able to pay attention.

"Elizabeth," Ryan called, motioning for her to join him away from the set.

She crept off the soundstage and over to his side. "I'm so sorry, Ryan," she apologized. "I've had the most awful headache this week. I'm really having trouble concentrating."

"And what do you think is causing this headache?" he interrogated, shoving his glasses up against the bridge of his nose. Elizabeth noted the angry glint in his eyes.

"I don't know," she lied.

She wished she had never started taking diet pills. When she had questioned Pat about what they had in them, Pat had been strangely evasive. Now, convinced she had become addicted to these pills, Elizabeth resolved to kick the habit as soon as possible.

"Look, Elizabeth, not only is your acting suffering, but you don't look so hot either. So whatever you are up to, I want you to knock it off. I know I asked you to drop a few pounds, but enough is enough. If you are starving yourself, then you have no energy for the brain, and this will cause bad headaches. Do you understand?" Ryan explained in detail. His irate eyes seemed to burn a hold in Elizabeth's weary, drawn face.

"Yes," Elizabeth listlessly agreed.

With some measure of relief, she realized it was almost lunchtime – the time she would allow herself another pill. She knew she would soon feel much better. At least she would feel better for a little while, before the pill's effects wore off. "I'll try to eat more sensibly," she mumbled with downcast eyes as she started to slowly edge away from Ryan.

"See that you do," Ryan sternly ordered in dismissal. The two officially separated with Ryan turning his back on Elizabeth to say a few quick words to one of the cameramen.

Elizabeth lumbered away, heading to *Makeup and Wardrobe* to get ready for her last scene before lunch. She mustered extra energy from the happy realization that she only had one last scene to film before she would break for lunch and finally get to ingest the drug her body so urgently craved.

* * * *

That weekend, Elizabeth went back to taking three diet pills a day. She did not want to be distracted, tired or sick feeling while she was spending time with Alan. It never seemed they had enough hours together on the weekend, and she knew if she only took one pill per day, her main focus would not be on Alan. Her entire focus would be on taking another pill.

Elizabeth desperately hoped, by the end of the next week, she would have the strength to take only one pill on the weekends as well, without missing them so greatly. However, so far, her craving for them did not seem to be lessening any.

She barely slept a wink Friday night. Yet, on the ride back to Bowling Green Saturday morning, she was so agitated she squirmed in her seat.

"My, we've really got ants in our pants this morning, don't we?" Alan finally asked. He studied her with perplexed eyes. He had watched her change radio stations several times, and she still seemed oddly dissatisfied. "Is everything alright?"

"I just get so excited when I'm with you that I can hardly wait for what's going to happen next. I just don't want to waste a moment of our time together," Elizabeth rattled, trying to cloak her strange behavior.

She released her seatbelt and bounced across the seat, giving him several, reassuring pecks on his cheek and the side of his mouth. Her whole insides seemed to be fast-dancing, so it was literally impossible for her to sit still. She turned the radio louder and pretended to be singing along with Michael Jackson's *Beat It*, actively moving her body to its rhythm.

When they finally got home – a trip that seemed unmercifully long to Elizabeth – she immediately suggested they go horseback riding. She thought maybe the constant motion would be good for what ailed her. Alan eagerly agreed. Not only was it a beautiful, sunny, and warm day, but he never tired of horseback riding. Being on a horse was second nature to him, and he loved the fact that Elizabeth enjoyed it as well now.

They had not been riding long, however, when Elizabeth unexpectedly challenged Alan to a race. Without waiting for his response, she kicked Dudley's sides and took off in a wild gallop. Dust flew up from the trail; they whipped past trees and brushed against low hanging tree branches.

When Elizabeth saw Alan quickly gaining on her, without thought, she kicked Dudley much more savagely, thoughtlessly pushing him to go even faster. Dudley was not used to such vigorous running, and he certainly was not used to the rough treatment. All at once, quite uncharacteristically, he bucked, trying to expel Elizabeth from his back in rebellion. Fortunately, Elizabeth had a tight hold on his reins. Miraculously, she managed to stay on Dudley's back. She pulled back hard on the reins to bring him to a halt.

Alan galloped up beside the bucking, angry horse. Expertly pulling his horse to a skidding, prompt stop, he immediately jumped to the ground, tightly grabbed the side of Dudley's bridle, and forcefully pulled downward. In a serious, authoritative voice, he talked to the horse, "Whoa, boy! Calm down! It's okay!"

"Blublublu," the horse fussed, his nostrils flaring, as he raised and lowered his head a few times and scratched his front hoof in the dirt.

Alan continued to talk to him in a soothing voice and stroke the side of his face, calming him. Dudley, tame by nature, whinnied loudly in protest one last time. Then he stood perfectly still, staring at Alan with docile, kind eyes, as if to say, "Thanks".

"It's okay, boy," Alan further reassured. He gently rubbed Dudley's neck, making certain he was completely calmed.

When Alan was absolutely sure that Dudley's nerves had settled, he carefully led not only Elizabeth's horse, but his own, to a nearby tree and securely tied them both to it. Then he cautiously helped Elizabeth down off her horse. No sooner had Elizabeth's feet happily found the safety of ground than Alan took a viselike grip on her arm and swiftly pulled her a short distance from the horses.

With obvious anger, he barked, "What in God's name were you thinking of?! Do you realize you could have been killed?! At the very least, you could have hurt poor Dudley. This is real life, Elizabeth. You're not on some film set here!"

"I'm sorry," she swiftly apologized, feeling very foolish. "I just wanted to have a little fun. And show you how well you've taught me to ride."

"I never taught you to ride stupid," he argued. "If that horse had caught his hoof in a hole or decided to leave the path and run you into a tree...phew..." he exhaled. "I don't even want to think about what might have happened. As it was, you're just lucky he didn't throw you off his back and break your neck. Thank God, you managed to hang on!"

Finishing his concerned narrative, Alan leaned his tense back against a nearby tree and impulsively pulled Elizabeth into his arms to securely hug her with obvious relief. "What possessed you to kick that horse like you did?" he further interrogated, clutching both of her shoulders and pushing her slightly away so he could study her eyes. His eyes displayed disapproval and some remaining fear.

"I just wasn't thinking," Elizabeth replied, not elaborating on what really might have caused this lack of judgment. "I treated Dudley like we were running the Kentucky Derby. Poor horse! You don't think I hurt him, do you?"

"No. You made him mad is all," Alan knowledgeably explained. "Him and me. I'm telling you right now, if you ever pull anything like that again, you won't have to worry about the horse killing you, because I'll break your pretty neck," Alan threatened, his remaining anger dissipating as he released his grasp on her shoulders. Instead, he wrapped his arms around her, giving her a relieved squeeze.

Quite plain she had genuinely scared Alan, Elizabeth felt bad. "I'm really sorry, Alan. I promise it won't happen again," she swore and added, "Thank you for being my hero, though."

She pulled her head off his shoulder and allowed her lips to find his for a lingering, thankful kiss.

"I'm just so glad you are okay," he admitted, giving her one final, long hug before allowing Elizabeth to pull back where she could study his facial expression once more. "I honestly don't know what I would do if anything ever happened to you."

"The feeling is mutual," she agreed. She locked eyes with him. Elizabeth was warmed by the gleam of love which shown from Alan's handsome blue eyes.

He held her, affectionately running his fingers through the back of her long hair for several more, gratifying seconds. Then, glancing momentarily at his watch, he announced, "It's getting late. We better finish our ride and get these horses back to the stable. I need to get you home. I know your mom and dad want to spend some time with you today too. You're in real demand."

"Yeah, so it seems," Elizabeth giggled. "Do you think Dudley has forgiven me? Will he let me ride him again?"

"Dudley is pretty tame...and probably has forgiven you. But I want to trade horses...just in case. That way if Dudley is still a little skittish, I'll be able to calm him. I don't want to take any more chances with you today. I want a nice, quiet ride back. Understood?"

"For sure," she agreed without hesitation.

Alan carefully untied the horses, helped Elizabeth atop of his, and expertly straddled Dudley. They slowly made their way back to the stables. Alan held Elizabeth's hand the whole way.

Elizabeth vowed even more firmly to stop taking the pills. *I wouldn't have behaved so irrationally today if I hadn't felt so restless,* she honestly accepted. She silently pledged, *Next weekend, I won't be taking any more pills.*

* * * *

During the week to follow, Elizabeth went back to taking only one pill a day. By Wednesday, however, she was feeling the full effects of withdrawal again. Her head absolutely throbbed, and she felt as if she had to push herself to do even the simplest of tasks. When Jameson picked her up at her cottage that evening to go exercise with him, she was in dire hopes that working out would miraculously help her to get some energy back.

However, halfway through her vigorous workout, all at once, the room began to spin and everything simultaneously turned black. When her eyes could focus again, Elizabeth found herself looking up into Jameson's slightly blurry face. As she slowly became aware that she was lying on the floor and he was kneeling beside her, she foolishly tried to sit up, but Jameson instantly protested with a loud, "No!"

He gently pushed her back down, placing a cold rag on her forehead, and checked her pulse at one of her wrists. "Wh...what happened?" Elizabeth sluggishly inquired, bewilderingly studying Jameson's serious eyes. She thought she beheld a hint of anger in them.

"You tell me," Jameson grumbled in aggravation. "Did you eat lunch today?"

"Yeah," Elizabeth verified.

"And just what exactly did you have?" he further interrogated.

"I don't know. What does it matter? I wasn't very hungry, so I just ate an apple and a granola bar," she admitted, irritated by his questions.

"That's exactly what I figured," Jameson concluded with a grimace. "And I bet you didn't have dinner either. Do you think you can sit up?"

"Yeah," she said, starting to rise again.

"Slowly," he ordered, placing a restraining hand on one of her shoulders. He allowed her to sit up at a snail's pace.

When she had been sitting for a few minutes and he was relatively certain she was not going to pass out again, Jameson rose to his feet. "Stay right there," he directed, pointing his finger at her. He walked over to the steps, poured some Gatorade into a plastic cup, walked back over to Elizabeth, and handed her the glass. "Drink it slowly," he further instructed.

Elizabeth did as asked. When she finished the drink, she held the glass back up to him. "I'm through with my Gatorade. Can I get up now?" she asked.

"Sure," he agreed, offering her his hand. Elizabeth grabbed hold of Jameson's hand and allowed him to help pull her to her feet. She noted she still felt a little dizzy, so she stood in place for a few more seconds. "You're probably right. I probably do need a good meal," she agreed.

"Well…you know you can get that here," he reminded her. "I'm sure there are some leftovers from dinner in the refrigerator upstairs. Let me help you up the steps, and I'll warm you something up."

"Okay," Elizabeth agreed.

Jameson took hold of her arm and the two began making their way across the room and up the stairs. In desperation, Elizabeth wondered if she should take another pill. Doing so would undoubtedly give her back the energy she sorely lacked.

However, she knew the only way she was going to be able to stop taking them permanently was to totally avoid them. *Surely, I'll feel a little better once I've eaten,* she tried to rationalize.

In the kitchen upstairs, Jameson pulled out a chair for Elizabeth, and she quickly took a seat. He went over to the refrigerator and started pulling out plastic bowls with leftovers in them. "I'll have you something whipped up in a few minutes," Jameson told her. "I'll also get you some more Gatorade."

"I think I'd rather have a soft drink. I could use the caffeine," Elizabeth told him.

"Caffeine, huh?" Jameson strangely questioned.

Elizabeth watched him remove two glasses from the kitchen cabinets and fill them with ice and soft drink. He walked over to the table, handing one of the glasses to her. "Do you really think caffeine will be a strong enough stimulant?"

Elizabeth studied Jameson's eyes, which she found to be oddly scrutinizing her. "What do you mean by that?" she replied a little defensively. Jameson was not smiling, and his eyes seemed to be piercing right through her.

"I think you know what I mean." he answered, walking back across the room. He put some food on a plate and placed it in the microwave. Then he walked over to the counter, snatched up Elizabeth's purse from its resting place, and brought it back across the room with him. Thrusting it in her face, he questioned, "Do you have any of your wonder pills with you tonight?!"

"W…wonder pills?" she stuttered in alarm, wondering how he could possibly know.

"Look, Liz, you don't have to worry about telling me about them. I've been around for awhile. I made a television series and a movie in Hollywood. So…I've seen people high as kites. I know what it looks like. And I know what withdrawal looks like," he explained, his eyes showing sympathetic knowledge. "You're doing speed, aren't you? Who gave it to you? Pat?"

"Speed?! Of course not!" she instantly protested, feeling offended. "Pat did give me some pretty powerful diet pills, so I could lose weight really quickly. They are loaded to the max with caffeine, and

I have to admit that I seem to be hooked on the extra energy bursts they give me. I'm slowly weaning myself off of them though. I've only been taking one at lunch each day, but they kill my appetite. That's why I didn't eat much today, and I guess that's why I fainted tonight. I'll really be glad when I get them out of my system."

"Do you perchance have any of these *diet* pills with you?" Jameson asked, sounding suspicious. He began to intrusively unzip her purse to conduct a search without her permission.

"Yeah. As a matter of fact, I do," Elizabeth replied with aggravation.

She reached to jerk her purse from Jameson's unwelcome hands. She promptly reached inside, located her container of pills, and thrust it out, waving it innocently in Jameson's face.

"Mind if I take a look at them?" Jameson questioned, confiscating the container.

"Suit yourself," Elizabeth told him, sounding exasperated now and giving him a disgruntled look.

She watched Jameson open the container and dump a few of the pills into his hand. Glancing from the pills to Elizabeth's unknowing face, he slowly sat back down beside her. "You really believe these are just diet pills, don't you?" he asked incredulously.

"For sure," Elizabeth earnestly declared. "I asked Pat about them after I had taken a few and noticed how hyper they made me. She said they are an appetite suppressor loaded to the hilt with caffeine. She said they put so much extra caffeine in them so that you'll feel great even though you are eating a lot less. I think I'm addicted to the caffeine now though."

"I can't honestly believe Pat has done this to you!" Jameson angrily declared, dropping the pills back into the container and sitting them on the table. "Where does Pat buy these? Have you been to the store to get them with her?"

"She has them sent from a friend in Chicago. She said we could get them cheaper that way," Elizabeth explained, suddenly beginning to doubt Pat for the first time. "Do you know what speed looks like?"

"You just saw it," he resolutely proclaimed, pointing to the bottle of pills prominently sitting on the table. "And I'll bet you Pat knows damn good and well what they are too. Real appetite suppressors are sold in boxes in drug stores, not in pill containers like those. Those are speed. I'm positive of that."

Elizabeth stared with alarm at the container on the table in front of her. "But why would Pat have lied to me like that? What would she have to gain by giving my speed? How do you know what speed looks like?" she fearfully rambled, unable to pull her eyes away from the offensive pills.

Elizabeth had never taken illegal drugs. She had seen some of the kids in high school smoke pot, but she had never even tried it. She had not even been thrilled with the idea of taking diet pills, and now Jameson was telling her she had actually been taking speed the whole time. She simply could not believe it was true.

"I know what speed looks like because I've taken some before," Jameson honestly confessed, without remorse. "I told you I've been around the block. You can get just about any drug you want in Hollywood, and I've tried quite a few."

Profoundly shocked, suddenly, Elizabeth realized she did not really know much about him or Pat. She had thought Pat was her friend and that she could trust her, and now, Jameson had severely shaken her confidence in him as well.

Elizabeth suddenly wanted to leave. In fact, she wanted to bolt from the room. Before she had a chance to get to her feet, the microwave beeped, and Jameson arose to retrieve her dinner. *I really do need to eat something*, she reasoned. *Then I'll leave.*

Her feelings were so ill at the moment that she surprisingly wanted to leave not only Jameson's B&B, but also Bardstown. She wanted to rush home to Alan and have him hold her in his big, strong arms and tell her everything was going to be okay. She had always dreamt about being an actress, and she loved to act, but if it meant she could not trust any of the people around her, Elizabeth truly was not sure she wanted this dream after all.

"Liz, are you okay?" Jameson asked, as he sat a plate full of food in front of her – ham, green beans and mashed potatoes. Her face had turned completely white. Jameson feared she might faint again.

"I...I'm a little rattled, that's all," Elizabeth confessed, picking up a knife and cutting up her ham. She put a bite into her mouth. She really had no appetite for any food, but she began to eat it anyway. *The sooner I eat, the sooner I can leave*, she decided, chewing much faster. The ham actually did taste very good. Martha was an excellent cook.

"I'm sorry I had to shock you like that. I didn't think you were the type to abuse drugs," Jameson commented, sitting down again.

"I never would have thought you were either," Elizabeth freely admitted, swallowing her food and taking a drink of her Pepsi. "I guess I really don't know you either."

"Okay...I can tell you are upset by the fact that I've done drugs," Jameson said, looking her straight in the eye. "You don't feel like you know me now. But I'm telling you that I am who you think I am. You just don't know much about my past. I'm not hiding anything though. I'll tell you anything about myself, and I won't lie. I'm really sorry Pat has betrayed you. I know you considered her a friend too."

Elizabeth went on eating in silence for a few moments, only glancing briefly at Jameson. Then she finally admitted in a quiet voice, "I just don't know what to think anymore. Or who to trust."

"Liz, I promise you can trust me," Jameson heartily professed, reaching across the table to briefly give her hand a reassuring squeeze. "I was a kid when I was in that television series. Drugs were all around me, so I got involved to go along with the crowd. I was lucky though. I never got hooked on anything. I think speed may have a little hold over you though. I want you to know that I'm here to help."

"You don't do drugs anymore?" Elizabeth questioned suspiciously, scrutinizing his eyes.

"Not very often," he truthfully confessed.

"N...not very often?!" Elizabeth echoed incredulously, looking down at her plate once more. "You still take speed?"

"No. I have been known to smoke a little pot sometimes, and occasionally, I toy with some coke," he replied, being brutally honest once more.

"C...coke? Do you mean cocaine?!" Elizabeth nervously questioned.

"Yeah," he confessed.

Elizabeth flashed him a shocked glance once again, and then seemed to be eating much faster. She just wanted to get her food down and get out of Jameson's B&B. She felt as if her skin was crawling, or she was in over her head and drowning.

"Liz, I'm being honest with you because I want you to know you can totally trust me. I would never trick you into taking drugs like Pat did. If you're not into them at all, that's okay," he thoughtfully assured her.

"Cocaine is a big deal to me," Elizabeth promptly admitted, sadly looking into his eyes once again. "People die from drugs like that."

"Yeah," Jameson surprisingly agreed. "And I've seen people who are addicted to it, and that's scary. But I don't use it that often, and I can take it or leave it. It's similar to speed in that it's a stimulant, but I don't think it makes you near as fidgety."

"I'm so sure. If you can take it or leave it, then why do you still do it?" Elizabeth bravely inquired.

"I've always been a thrill seeker," he confessed with a slight smile, adding, "I scare you when I drive, because I enjoy racing. I've parachuted from a plane, and I like to scuba dive. Coke gives me that high instantaneously. It taps into the pleasure area of your brain. Sometimes, in Hollywood, I would get really lonely, and coke was the friend I knew would never let me down. I understand how you are feeling right now about how Pat has done you. I've had many people betray me. When you become a star, it will be even harder to know who to trust."

"Then I'm not sure I want to be a star," she earnestly admitted, down casting her eyes again.

"That's understandable," he agreed. "But, if you are talented, it just happens. And I can tell acting is in your blood. You just need to hang on to the people in your life that keep you grounded, and you'll be fine."

"Who keeps you grounded?" Elizabeth curiously interrogated, staring at his face again.

"People like you who I know are my true friends. When I find someone I feel good about trusting, like you, I really value that. That's why I've tried so hard not to do anything that would jeopardize our friendship," he professed, reaching out to lightly squeeze her hand again and maintaining direct eye contact to reinforce his honesty.

Elizabeth lowered her eyes again in confusion and studied her plate. She took a moment to try and allow Jameson's heavy revelations to totally sink in. She honestly did not know what to believe anymore. *Can I really trust Jameson? He has admitted he is a drug user, and he obviously still enjoys it. It isn't merely something that was part of his troubled past.*

She began to shovel what was left of her food into her mouth. Her basic human instinct to fight or flee was in full gear. She wanted to flee. She could feel Jameson's eyes boring holes through her, and this just served to make her even more nervous.

Thankfully, Jameson remained silent. Elizabeth did not want to hear anymore. She just wanted to finish her food, go back to her cottage, and be alone. She felt dangerously close to tears.

As she washed down the last of her food with her soft drink, she forced herself to look at Jameson again. "I feel much better now," she lied. "You must have been right about me needing to eat a decent meal. Can you take me home now? I feel like I need to be alone to rest and let everything that I've learned today completely sink in."

"Sure," he agreed, to Elizabeth's immense relief. He picked up his glass and finished off the rest of his soft drink. Then he rose to his feet, offered her a hand, and said, "I'm ready any time you are."

Elizabeth took his hand and slowly stood. She still felt very weak, and since she had eaten, she now felt a bit nauseated. It made her even angrier to realize that her prevalent weakness and nausea was due to her body wanting another fix of speed. *I simply won't have it*, Elizabeth silently resolved. *The pill I look at lunch will be my last, if it kills me.*

The ride back to her cottage was very quiet. When Jameson pulled up in the driveway, Elizabeth thanked him for watching out for her, and then she swiftly vacated the Trans Am.

Jameson got out of the car as well and walked her up to her door. "I know you have a lot on your mind, Liz," he said. "I really do consider you a good friend, and I hope you still feel the same about me. I'll do whatever I can to help you."

"I appreciate all you have done," she told him sincerely, pitying the lifestyle he had chosen. She unlocked the door to her cottage then. "Goodbye, James," she said as she walked through the door.

"Bye, Liz. I'll see you on the soundstage. Call me if you need anything."

She nodded, but deep down, Elizabeth knew Jameson would be one of the last people she would call. She shut the door, practically in his face, and locked it. Sad, she made her way over to the couch in the cottage's living room. Dejected, she took a seat on the sofa, dropped her head in her hands, and tried to sort through all she had learned. Being an actress suddenly seemed a very lonely, destructive world to be in. A world she honestly, really was not sure she wanted a part of anymore.

Elizabeth laid her head back on the sofa, closed her eyes, and attempted to block out the rest of the world. She decided to try and let her exhaustion lead her into sleep. She just wanted to sleep and escape from all the cruel realities of the world she had entered.

Chapter 15
Confrontation

What do you say to someone you considered to be a friend, who betrays you? Confronting betrayal is a very difficult thing. Only the true strong-at-heart will do it. The others will run and hide.

~ Sissy Marlyn ~

The next day, Elizabeth waited right inside the front door and immediately caught Pat as she walked into the house.

"Good morning!" Pat greeted in a chipper voice and flashed her friend a warm smile. Pat had her hair pulled up with a banana clip and she was wearing a baggy, cropped top T-shirt, calf-length pants and clogs.

"Is it a good morning?" Elizabeth instantly countered with aggravation.

"Oh my! Sounds like someone sure got up on the wrong side of the bed this morning. You don't look so hot either," Pat commented, the smile quickly disappearing as she intently studied Elizabeth's haggard face. She looked pale and she had circles under her eyes.

"Maybe I just need another diet pill. That should *speed* me right up! Wouldn't you say?!" Elizabeth barked, carefully scrutinizing Pat's face for some sign of guilt.

Pat's eyes betrayed nothing, however, and her mouth was now set in a tight, dismayed grimace. "Whatever works," she flippantly replied, starting to walk away and leave Elizabeth standing there.

Before Pat could get away, Elizabeth's arm flung out and she gained a tight clutch on Pat's arm. With determination, she forced Pat to turn back around to face her, viciously sinking her nails into her arm. "What in the hell is wrong with you?!" Pat screamed in protest, hastily wrestling her arm free and protectively covering Elizabeth's attack marks with one of her hands.

She glanced from the painful, red streaks to her friend's face in obvious confusion and anger.

"Oh, I think you know only too well exactly what is wrong with me!" Elizabeth growled. She also thrust the container of speed from her purse and flagrantly waved it in front of Pat's eyes, within an inch of her face. "Maybe I'm suffering from withdrawal from these non-addictive diet pills. What do you think?"

Elizabeth immediately noticed Pat glancing nervously around to see who might be within ear range. Fortunately, the hallway was empty. But Ryan's voice could be heard in the great room, instructing the cameramen for the filming of the first scene of the day.

Observing Pat's paranoid behavior, Elizabeth was convinced Pat had indeed known all along that she was giving her speed. "What I want...no...what I *need* to know...is...why? Why didn't you tell me these weren't just harmless, diet pills?" Elizabeth questioned in a voice which, all at once, sounded very weary.

"Look, Elizabeth, can we get out of this doorway, and go someplace more private to talk?" Pat asked in nearly a whisper, lightly placing one of her hands on top of one of Elizabeth's wrists to guide her away.

"That's fine by me," Elizabeth agreed. "As long as you're willing to talk. To tell me everything I need to know."

Pat nodded and started sprinting away from the doorway, because there they could easily be observed and heard by many. Elizabeth allowed herself to be led along. Pat headed up the hall, past *Makeup and Wardrobe*, to one of the vacant rooms that they filmed bedroom scenes in.

When Elizabeth entered the room, she turned on the overhead light and carefully closed the door. Walking past floor lighting that was not turned on, and dodging hanging microphones, Elizabeth strolled over to the bed, resting her back against one of the high bedposts, craving its support.

"Now, do you want to tell me what your little outburst is all about?" Pat questioned with irritation, defiantly crossing her arms across her chest, facing off with Elizabeth.

"Don't start playing stupid with me!" Elizabeth warned, irate again. She took a few, threatening steps closer to Pat. "I want to talk about why you passed off speed as a simple diet pill. How could you lie to me like that?! You know I wasn't even happy about taking diet pills. So you are bound to have figured that I never would have taken speed. What was your motive?"

"How'd you find out it was speed?" Kate asked, dodging Elizabeth's question once more and looking uneasy.

"What does that matter?" Elizabeth replied with annoyance. "The point is, I know. And I demand to know why you did this to me! What did I ever do to you?"

"Why are you making it sound so tragic? You needed a little help losing some weight, and I tried to help. If you don't like taking the pills, then give them back to me," Pat suggested with obvious indifference.

"So you see absolutely nothing wrong with giving someone illegal drugs without telling them?" Elizabeth interrogated, incredulous.

"I think you are being way too overdramatic. I could tell you were one of these people who would be scared to try the pills, but you needed the help. You should be thanking me instead of attacking me. You accomplished what you needed without drawbacks. Where's the harm?" Pat argued.

"The harm is...you tricked me. The harm is...you lied to me," Elizabeth told her, counting off her sins on her fingers. "And the biggest harm is...I'm having a hell of a time trying to stop taking the pills. Speed is addictive, but I'm sure you knew that. You're right when you say I wouldn't have tried the pills if you had told me upfront what they were. But I wasn't given a chance to make that choice. You had absolutely no right to force speed on me by presenting it as something it wasn't. I considered you my friend. I trusted you. But you stomped all over my trust. And if I can't trust you, then I guess I don't count you as a friend after all," Elizabeth informed her.

She tossed the vial of pills at Pat in exasperation. Pat reflexes good, she caught the container. She swiftly concealed it in her purse. "So you think you are addicted to speed now?" Pat asked, showing the first trace of concern. "How many are you taking each day? I told you they were powerful stuff, even if I didn't tell you they were speed. I've been taking speed on and off for years and haven't gotten addicted. I swear if I had any idea you might get hooked, I would have told you upfront what the pills were."

"If you've been taking speed for years, then it sounds like you definitely have a problem too," Elizabeth pointed out. She suddenly felt sorry for Pat. *At least I accept that I'm having a problem with the pills.* Pat did not seem to have the slightest concern about herself.

"I said *on and off*," she argued. "I only take the pills when I need a little help to stay ultra- slim like they expect you to be in this business."

"Well, I'm through with them. I took the last one I ever intend to yesterday at lunch. Please don't try to offer me any more of your unsolicited help. I'll know better next time," Elizabeth warned with disgust.

"That's just fine," Pat agreed, sounding surly. She showed not the slightest trace of remorse for what she had done. "I'm sorry you feel I took advantage of you. Like I said, I was only trying to help. Are you sure you don't want a few of these in case the headaches and shakes get too bad?"

"I'll manage to make it through without anymore speed," Elizabeth vowed. Another wave of pity for Pat washed over Elizabeth. *She wouldn't know about headaches and shakes unless she's already gone through withdrawal too*, she sadly concluded.

"Suit yourself," Pat said. She turned and promptly left the room without another word.

Elizabeth remained in the room alone for a few moments after Pat had departed. She could not believe Pat had not even seemed upset. Pat had no qualms whatsoever about her deceitfulness. Elizabeth felt very bad for Pat.

Even though Elizabeth had not known Pat long, she still felt regretful sorrow over having lost a friend. She only hoped her trust in Jameson was not a farce also. Since he had confessed to using drugs too, Elizabeth certainly had reason to feel very unsure about him as well. All at once, she felt incredibly lonely.

The only light at the end of the tunnel was that it was Friday, and she would be seeing Alan again that evening. She missed him desperately. Like the day she found out her mom was dying, she yearned to feel his strong, reassuring arms around her. Snuggling in those arms, Elizabeth could convince herself that everything would somehow be okay. Thinking of Alan, Elizabeth mustered the newfound strength to leave the bedroom set and head for *Makeup and Wardrobe* to begin her day.

Chapter 16
The Mistake

Compounding mistakes never makes things better. But the only way to discover this fact is to do this very thing.

~ Sissy Marlyn ~

By that afternoon, Elizabeth began to feel extremely awful. Her head throbbed without mercy, and her legs trembled. As if that was not bad enough, her hands began to quiver, and she feared it would soon be noticed.

Regardless of her physical impairments, she fiercely struggled to film her scenes. However, entirely impossible for her to concentrate, even with the TelePrompTer, she kept messing up her lines. Ryan finally, roughly pulled her aside.

With clear displeasure, he barked, "Elizabeth, it's bad enough you look like crap, and no amount of makeup can fully cover for you. But, now it's clear that your mind is screwed up too. I don't know what drug or drugs you are messing with, but you better clean up your act fast! Or this will be the last warning you'll ever hear from me! You'll be packing and heading back to Bowling Green for good."

"Maybe that's exactly what I should be doing," Elizabeth mumbled in weary despair. She rubbed her aching forehead with the side of her hand. "I'm not really sure I'm cut out for this world."

Before Ryan had a chance to reply, Jameson deftly joined Elizabeth's side, interrupting her frustrated tirade. "Can I talk to Liz for a moment, Ryan? I think I might be able to help her out," he offered.

"Be my guest, Jameson," Ryan conceded. Walking away, he flailed both his arms in the air. "I sure hope you can get through to her. Because, I'm telling you, she is coming very close to throwing her acting career away."

"Trust me. Everything will be fine," Jameson assured him, taking a firm grip on Elizabeth's upper arm.

He led her away from the soundstage. He walked her down the hallway to his private dressing room. As soon as they were both in the room, Jameson shut the door and locked it.

His dressing room was much larger than Elizabeth's. It had a large leather sofa against one wall with a coffee table in front of it. He also had a desk, a closet, and a window looking out on the grounds. The sunlight it allowed in hurt Elizabeth's head, so she averted her eyes from looking in this direction. She quickly headed to the couch and plopped down, putting her head in her hands.

"You're feeling terrible right now, aren't you?" Jameson questioned, staring at Elizabeth with concerned eyes.

"No shit, Sherlock," Elizabeth sassed, looking up at him and rubbing her temples. "I need some more speed. But you know that, right?"

"Yes, I do," Jameson admitted.

"God," Elizabeth swore, dropping her head in her hands again. In a muffled voice she said, "I've, like, loved acting all my life and dreamed of filming a movie. But I totally never anticipated this."

"I know," Jameson agreed, walking over and taking a seat on the couch beside her. "Do you have any more pills?"

"No, I don't!" she snapped, running her hands down her face as she slowly exhaled. She opened her eyes and looked at Jameson again. "I gave the pills back to Pat. Now, I just need to find a bed somewhere, curl up in a ball, and ride this out, or die, whichever comes first."

"Liz, please let me help you," Jameson pleaded, taking one of her trembling hands into his. "Ryan is no fool. He knows what's going on with you. And if he talks to Arthur about it, Arthur could fire you. Don't throw away everything you've dreamed about because Pat did something stupid to you. You're too good of an actress. I know you don't think you know me that well, or I you. But I think I know you well enough to tell that you will regret giving this part up for the rest of your life."

"What other choice have I got?" she asked in a small, defeated voice. "My body is fighting me, James. It wants more speed, but I'm not going to take any more. So unless I can take time off...however long it takes for this hellacious drug to work its way out of my system...then maybe I should just quit."

"It'll probably take a few days, and filming is on a tight schedule..."

"Then I guess it's over," Elizabeth concluded, looking very sad. "I can't concentrate, so I can't act."

"It doesn't have to be that way," Jameson told her. "I can give you something that will make you feel better almost instantly. You won't need the speed anymore, and no over will ever know you had a problem."

"I'm so sure. What are you talking about?" Elizabeth asked with puzzled eyes.

"I'm talking about helping you save your career and possibly even your relationship with Alan. He doesn't know you are addicted to speed, does he?" Jameson asked. He rose from his seat, swiftly walked across the room, and retrieved something from a desk drawer. "If you quit now and go home, Alan will weather the worse of the withdrawal with you. Are you actually willing to put him through that?" Jameson questioned, studying her intently with very determined eyes.

"I need Alan by my side to be able to make it through all this. But I don't want him to see me like this. His father drinks a lot, and I've seen how upset he gets when he calls him drunk. God, James! What am I going to do?! I can't believe I'm in such a mess!" Elizabeth wailed, dropping her head down into her open palms again and succumbing to frustrated, exhausted tears.

"Alan doesn't have to see you like this, nor do you have to take any more speed," Jameson told her in a reassuring voice.

Coming back over and sitting back down beside her, he rubbed her back for a few moments until she could contain her emotions. When

Bardstown

Elizabeth looked back up at him, he opened the palm of his hand to reveal a small packet of white powder.

"Please tell me that's not what I think it is," Elizabeth said, glancing from his hand to his face with noted disgust.

"I'm not like Pat, Elizabeth. I'm not going to lie to you, and I would never give you coke if I thought it might hurt you. I swear one hit will not make an addict of you. Please, Liz! You need something to help you through this. You can trust me. Have I ever done anything to make you think otherwise?"

"No. But neither had Pat," she pointed out, staring fixedly at the tiny package. She really felt terrible, and Jameson was telling her it could get worse. She suddenly was very afraid. *But, how can he guarantee I won't get hooked on cocaine as well?*

"Liz, please trust me," he begged. As she curiously looked on, he picked up a handheld mirror from the table beside them. He carefully poured the drug out on top of the glass, and with a straight edge, arranged the white powder into two, fairly perfect lines. "I care about you. I really do. And I like working with you. I'm not going to let you mess up your life with *any* drug. This will just help you through right now. Just try it. How could things get any worse?"

He handed her a tiny straw, and she hesitantly took it from him. Her hand shook, partly from withdrawal and partly from the fear of what she was overwhelmingly tempted to do.

"It will be okay," Jameson continued to persuasively console, holding the mirror steady under her chin. "Just bend your head down and try it. You won't believe the difference. You'll not only be able to concentrate, but you'll never have to worry about speed having a hold over you again."

Elizabeth was thoroughly disgusted by the hold that speed had over her, but she was painfully exhausted from her body betraying her so wretchedly. She took a hard look down at the white powder spread out so neatly and invitingly in front of her. It looked so harmless. Yet, she was wise enough to know it was not.

Elizabeth's mind raced wildly. Part of her intellect urgently warned her to push the mirror far away, quit her job, run home to

Bowling Green, and hide in the safety of Alan's strong arms. *He surely will understand when I explain how Pat tricked me.*

The other half of Elizabeth's torn mind frantically wanted all of the intense pain to instantly vanish. This part of her did not want Alan to ever find out what she had so foolishly allowed to happen. This part of her absolutely loved being an actress in *Bardstown*. This part of her wisely perceived she would indeed regret it if she threw this role away over something so stupid. This part of her wanted to have it all.

"Trust me," Jameson said again, watching her struggle with herself.

Elizabeth gave him a hard stare. Then she lifted the straw to her nose. "Don't you let me get hooked on this," she half demanded.

"I won't," he pledged.

Before she could change her mind, Elizabeth hastily lowered her pain-filled head over the mirror, and inhaled the lines of coke up her nostrils. The inside of her nose burned for a few seconds. However, within moments, she began to feel the astonishing effects of the drug.

As if someone had raised the pillow which had been smothering her, she magically felt better. In fact, she suddenly felt as if she could conquer the world. She shut her eyes, laid her head back against the sofa, and allowed the drug to take full control of her. The high she felt was truly incredible.

"That's a girl!" She heard Jameson cheering. She opened her eyes to see his gleaming, white teeth. "Now you are feeling much better! Aren't you?!"

Better was not the word Elizabeth would use to describe what she currently experienced. Absolutely euphoric, she was once again filled to the brim with energy and almost overwhelming utmost happiness. A little scared to be able to change moods so quickly, her drug-induced bliss easily overshadowed her fear.

"Why don't we go tell Ryan you are feeling much better and are ready to continue?" Jameson instructed, sounding very chipper himself.

He eagerly stood and offered his hand to pull her to her feet beside him. Elizabeth left the room with a smile on her face. All fine with her world again, she was thrilled.

Chapter 17
That's a Wrap!

The dream is brought to fruition...
or is a nightmare just beginning?

~ Sissy Marlyn ~

Elizabeth used cocaine to completely overcome her speed addiction. Jameson gave her only one packet to take with her for her weekend with Alan. She did one line Saturday and another Sunday, and this usage warded off almost all of the horrible withdrawal she would have otherwise experienced.

Thereafter, she fell into a deceptive, standard routine with the drug. Three times a week, on Monday, Wednesday, and Friday, both she and Jameson got high together in his dressing room. Then they happily and energetically went about filming their respective scenes.

Since Elizabeth did the drug only a few times a week, and not several times a day like she had speed, she decided to cease worrying about its use. *When I stop filming, I'll totally stop using the drug*, she told herself. For now, she felt as if cocaine had truly been a lifesaver for her.

* * * *

Elizabeth's last, several weeks of filming needed to be completed in Lake Buena Vista, Florida, at an MGM soundstage within Disney World. Alan hated to be separated from her for over a month, but he consoled himself with the fact that Elizabeth would be through filming after this time period. *Then she'll be all mine again. No more splitting our time with MGM and Jameson.*

Alan drove her to Standiford Field Airport in Louisville. This airport seemed enormous to Elizabeth, since the airport in Bowling Green was so small – mostly servicing small planes and not jets. Elizabeth was glad she did not have to navigate the Louisville airport alone.

Alan checked her bags at the curb and handed her the baggage claim ticket. He explained, "You'll need this when you claim your suitcase in Lake Buena Vista, Florida. The number on the claim ticket will correspond to the tag on your suitcase. A lot of suitcases look alike, so be sure and check the number."

Elizabeth was both amused and pleased by Alan's protective explanations. They went inside then, and Elizabeth stood in front of the glass doors looking all about for a few moments. Counters and counters and counters, with people standing in line in front of most all of them met her eyes. She bet the whole airport in Bowling Green, including a runway, could fit into this gigantic place.

"We need to head to the Delta counter," Alan told her, pointing down the way a bit.

He took her hand and began leading her there, as if she were a little girl. They stood in their own short line in front of the Delta Airlines counter for a few moments. Then a woman in a Delta Airlines uniform checked Elizabeth in for her flight.

Alan walked her as far as he could. Before they separated – Elizabeth going to a specific gate for her flight and Alan back to his car – Alan pulled Elizabeth in a tight embrace and told her, "I'm going to miss you."

"I'll miss you too. Like crazy," she assured him, gazing longingly into his eyes. "It'll totally go fast though."

"Not fast enough for me," Alan honestly professed. "You be sure and call me every evening."

"I will," she promised, giving him another kiss. "I love you, Alan."

"I love you too. I'll see you soon."

They shared one final kiss, and then Elizabeth turned and sadly separated from Alan. Her heart ached at the thought of their separation, but another part of her thrilled at the prospect of going to Florida to film her final scenes for the movie. She turned and waved a final goodbye to Alan, and then she rushed forward toward her gate and new adventure.

* * * *

Elizabeth's last weeks of filming some of her happiest, she felt more confident as an actress. This newfound confidence easily showed in her work. Ryan praised her at least once a day.

Elizabeth believed she had Jameson to thank for her happiness. He had always been there to completely support her, and that had helped carry her through all of her rough times. She truly surmised she would have been fired long ago if it had not been for his constant, unwavering help. She would miss Jameson's friendly companionship.

As October came to a close, Elizabeth and Jameson comically filmed the last scene for *Bardstown* on Halloween. Ryan rushed to Elizabeth's side, gave her a grateful hug, and praised, "Great Job!"

Then Jameson grabbed her and pulled her into another, tight embrace, giving her a brief, friendly kiss on her lips before releasing her. "I'll be seeing you in a few months for the Hollywood premiere of *Bardstown* at Mann's Chinese Theatre," he told her, displaying a broad smile.

"I can't wait," Elizabeth chirped excitedly. Her eyes danced and she gave Jameson a wide, toothy grin, declaring, "I want to thank you once more for all you did for me. As I told you, I couldn't have made it without you."

"As I said, it was certainly my pleasure," Jameson replied, giving her another, brief hug which he ended with an affectionate peck on her forehead. "I look very forward to working with you in the future, my friend."

Elizabeth stared warmly into his eyes and clutched his hands for a few more, grateful moments. "I totally look forward to working with you again too," she confessed. Then she slowly released his hands.

She felt a peck on the shoulder, and she turned to find Bradley standing behind her. "Do I get a farewell hug too?" he asked with an impish grin.

"Sure," Elizabeth replied. Despite her initial dislike of Bradley, the two had been able to forge a decent work relationship. She opened her arms, and Bradley pulled her to him for a tight hug.

"I hope we get to work together again too," he told her. However, when he reached to softly pinch her butt, Elizabeth pushed out of his arms. "Just a little pinch for good luck," he said with a chuckle.

"Yeah. I'm so sure," Elizabeth replied, rolling her eyes and shaking her head. Bradley would never change. "See ya around," Elizabeth said, turning to say her goodbyes and congratulations to others in the cast.

She spied Pat approaching her. "It's been a good run," Pat said.

"Yes, it has," Elizabeth agreed. She offered no smile or no hug. She and Pat had been on a work-only basis since Elizabeth's confrontation with her about the speed she deceptively gave her.

"I'm sorry I wrecked our friendship," Pat admitted. Her eyes looked remorseful. "I wish you all the best with all your other endeavors."

"I wish you the same," Elizabeth said. She could tell Pat seemed to want a farewell hug from her, but Elizabeth could not make herself acquiesce. Pat had broken her trust and hurt her. Elizabeth felt no warmth toward her at all anymore, and she saw no reason to illicit affection. "See ya around," she muttered, as she had with Bradley.

"See you," Pat said with a bittersweet smirk. She turned and continued on her way to talk to some other cast members. Elizabeth did the same. It was a thrilling and depressing day all rolled into one.

* * * *

As Elizabeth entered Standiford Field Airport, she searched for Alan in the crowd. She quickly found him. He looked so handsome and relaxed in his faded Levi jeans, tennis shoes and hooded sweatshirt.

She sprinted across the hallway, weaving through other travelers, and warmly wrapped her arms around his neck. Eagerly showering him with excited kisses, she exuberantly proclaimed, "It's over, Alan! I did it! I made a movie! Now we have the rest of our lives to spend together!"

"Amen!" he hastily agreed. His face all smiles, he gleefully pulled Elizabeth to his chest. Bringing his lips to hers, he gave her a warm, lingering, congratulatory kiss.

"If that's your way of saying congratulations, I totally like it!" Elizabeth enthusiastically commented, her voice sounding a little husky when the very lengthy, probing kiss finally concluded. "Take me home, Alan! Drive me back to Bowling Green," she said with longing, eagerly tugging at one of his arms.

They rushed off through the airport, each eager to get on with their future together.

* * * *

Elizabeth's mom and dad were glad to have her home for good as well. Elizabeth's mom appeared to be doing better, even though her prognosis was still terminal. Some of the hair she had lost had grown back, and she had even put on a little weight. Elizabeth was happy to see these changes.

"You look awesome, mom!" she told her with a smile.

"So do you, sweetheart!" her mom replied, giving her an affectionate hug. "We're glad you're home."

"Me too," she admitted. She would miss the privacy of the cottage in Bardstown, but oftentimes, it was lonely being there. Bowling Green would always be her home, no matter what.

"Well, sit down and tell us all about your last few weeks," her dad invited.

"For sure!" Elizabeth agreed. She followed her parents into the living room, eager to share details about her time away.

* * * *

Elizabeth found herself awakening at 3:30 a.m. Monday. It felt strange not to have to get up at this hour now. She tried to go back to sleep but found she could not.

She finally got up about 6:00 a.m., after tossing and turning in frustration. Not wanting to disturb her parents – retired, neither of them would get up until about nine or so – she turned on her desk light and sat at her desk. She found herself thinking of Jameson.

She could not help but wonder if he would get high today on coke, even though she was not there to share the extreme bliss with him. Elizabeth found herself going to her closet. Opening a shoe box, she lifted out some concealing shoes and extracted a cosmetic pouch.

Her last day on the soundstage at MGM, Jameson had led her to his dressing room and given her a small stash of cocaine. Even though Elizabeth had tried to resist taking the coke from him, it had not taken much persuasion on Jameson's part for her to change her mind.

Now, as Elizabeth sat down on the side of her bed, she slowly unzipped the bag and stared temptingly at the pleasure packets before her eyes. *I should zip the pouch back up and put it safely back in its hiding place. I don't need to get high*, she told herself.

However, she just could not make herself fasten the zipper and put the bag away. Instead, she reached inside and retrieved a package of coke. Alluringly holding it up in front of her nose and sniffing the outside of the package with yearning, an expectant shiver ran menacingly through her.

Even Alan can't provide me with as much pleasure as this one, little package, a wicked, little voice in her head told her. *What could it hurt to use it one more time? No one will ever know.*

She rose from the bed and went over to her vanity table. She spread the miraculous powder on the face of a handheld mirror, and quickly sat down in front of it. Before she consumed the drug, she promised herself, *This will be it. I'll give the rest of the packets back to Jameson when I see him again, or I'll throw them out.*

However, she could not stand the temptation for just one more time.

* * * *

Alan was supremely happy to have Elizabeth home again. His life had seemed to be missing some vital element while she was away. He planned to propose to her soon, even if they still would not be getting married for several more years. He did not care if they had a long engagement, but he longed to claim Elizabeth as his fiancé.

Elizabeth registered for the winter semester at WKU. She had to plan her life as if her filming was over for good. If *Bardstown* became a hit, and she was asked to star in more movies, then she could always drop the college courses she had enrolled in. However, right now, she sought to settle back into her old life before *Bardstown*.

But 'settling back in' was not as easy as Elizabeth had imagined. She gravely missed being in front of the cameras and being able to act each day. Her life suddenly seemed to be missing fundamental excitement.

Unfortunately, Elizabeth compensated for this new, strange boredom and unrest in her life by forsaking her promise not to use cocaine anymore. Since she only used the wonder drug occasionally, she decided not to worry that she had broken her promise to herself. Cocaine was not interfering with her life or her relationship with Alan, so Elizabeth could truly see no harm whatsoever in using the drug every so often.

* * * *

Promotional previews for *Bardstown* began to run on television late January 1984. Together the first time they saw one of these commercials, Elizabeth and Alan had just finished watching a movie on cable in his apartment. Alan happened to switch back to a local channel, and their attention instantly riveted to a glimpse of Elizabeth's and Jameson's faces on the screen.

The ad ended with a steamy, love scene between Jameson and Elizabeth. Locked in a passionate embrace, they kissed one another. Several other snippets of love scenes had been shown as well.

Held spellbound by the preview, it felt really strange to Elizabeth to watch herself on television. It finally made all of her hard work authentic. Proud of how real it all looked, she glanced at Alan expectantly with a proud smile. She was met by a rather somber, shocked expression.

"Well, what do you think? Does it look like it will be a hit movie?" Elizabeth asked rather cautiously, studying his serious eyes.

"I don't know," he answered without thinking, his mind still preoccupied with the love scenes he had just watched. "I really don't like the ad's description of *Bardstown* as one of the hottest, new movies of the year or the scenes of Jameson and you that they picked for that matter. Makes it look like soft porno. I know sex sells, but that bothers me when my future wife's involved."

The satisfied smile vanished from Elizabeth's face as quickly as it had appeared. Alan's harsh, thoughtless words instantly diminished her momentary joy. She wanted him to share her happiness.

Even though Elizabeth realized Alan hated the fact that she had to do love scenes, it still hurt her feelings that he had nothing good to say about seeing her on television. It had been very exciting to her. Now, she felt very alone and slightly betrayed.

Alan noticed the change in her demeanor, and he knew, without Elizabeth saying a word, that he had said the wrong thing. He realized how much she loved acting and how hard she had worked on *Bardstown*. He also was certain Elizabeth expected him to show his pride in her and not his petty insecurities.

Alan desperately wished he could take back his thoughtless words. *I just need to say something to show that I* do *support her*, Alan decided. "Hey, where'd that smile go?" he asked in a much lighter voice, gently caressing one of her cheeks.

Alan turned her head to face him. Elizabeth's eyes looked sad and hurt, and her disharmony tore at his heart. "Hey…I didn't mean to say that I thought *Bardstown* wasn't going to be a hit or that you weren't great, even in those few clips they showed. I was picking on the guys who put that commercial together. But, I should have told you how great you looked. You know I've always thought you were a wonderful actress. Come on; let me see that beautiful smile again?"

Despite the fact that Alan's first words had drastically diminished Elizabeth's exuberance, the love she saw in his adoring eyes brought a smile to her face again. *At least he's trying to overcome his jealousy.* She hoped, in time, after watching her love scenes many times, Alan would come to accept them as nothing more than acting. He still let them bother him way too much.

"That's much more like it, my little star to be." he commented, lightly tracing her smiling lips with one of his thumbs before he drew her to him and sealed his mouth to hers for several, heated moments.

Even as he kissed her, however, Alan could still distastefully envision Jameson kissing and touching her. As much as he wanted Elizabeth to be happy and be able to act some more, part of him still hoped, in betrayal, that *Bardstown* did not become a hit movie. Selfish, he liked having Elizabeth all to himself too much.

Elizabeth, however, was thinking the exact opposite. After seeing the preview, it made her long to film more. Part of her also missed

Jameson. He would have been ecstatic for her. He understood how much acting meant to her, because it was in his blood as well.

Elizabeth loved Alan and liked having more time with him again. However, she wanted her other life as an actress as well. She vehemently hoped she could have both. Only time would tell.

* * * *

The following week, Alan and Elizabeth were at a local restaurant having dinner together when a heavyset woman, who neither of them knew, hesitantly approached their table. "Excuse me," she said, sounding a bit bashful and nervously wringing her hands in front of her. "I don't mean to interrupt your meal. But aren't you the girl I've been seeing in previews for a new movie called *Bardstown*? If you aren't, you certainly could be her twin."

"Yeah, that's me," Elizabeth proudly answered, a gigantic, pleased smile instantly materializing on her face. "Hi. I'm Elizabeth Warren," she promptly introduced, offering her hand in friendly greeting.

The woman firmly clasped Elizabeth's hand in between both of hers and excitedly shook it. "Wow!" she gasped with a giddy chuckle. "Are you from Bowling Green? If not, what's a movie star like you doing in Kentucky?"

"I was born and raised here in Bowling Green and still live here," Elizabeth replied. Extremely tickled that someone actually seemed to be awestruck by seeing her on television, Elizabeth also liked the woman's reference to her as a movie star.

"Well, could I trouble you for your autograph?" the woman excitedly requested, releasing Elizabeth's hand with hesitance.

She pulled her purse from her side, sat it on the side of their table, unzipped it, and began to frantically look for something Elizabeth could write on. She looked as if she was afraid Elizabeth might change her mind and go skirting away.

Elizabeth smiled in amusement at Alan. He also watched the woman with a grin. She quickly located an address book and a pen and eagerly thrust them toward Elizabeth.

"Who should I make the autograph out to?" Elizabeth questioned, comfortably playing the role of movie star. However, she chuckled a little when she glanced at Alan again.

"Please make it out to Joan," the woman swiftly answered with a wide, happy smile, obviously excited. "And could you date it please? I may be one of the first persons to have gotten your autograph before you become a big star."

"Thanks for the compliment and your confidence in me," Elizabeth declared, as she wrote a small message in the woman's book and signed her name, putting the date below it."

"Oh, thank you so much. Miss Warren!" Joan chirped, clutching her address book possessively to her chest, as if it were now extremely valuable. She backed slowly away, staring transfixed at Elizabeth and grinning broadly.

When she was finally out of sight, Alan and Elizabeth looked at one another and shared a hearty laugh. He admitted, "I didn't have the heart to tell good ol' Joan that I was actually the first person to officially get your autograph before you became a star. Maybe I should frame it now. What do you think?"

"Oh, for sure!" Elizabeth agreed with a hearty laugh, warmly thinking about the first night she and Alan had met, when he had *indeed* asked for her autograph. "I can't believe a stranger just, like, asked for my autograph. Now I know, if *Bardstown* doesn't make it, I can always totally become a star just doing commercials."

"Do you have your sunglasses with you? I think maybe you should disguise yourself before we get mobbed," Alan playfully teased, choking back giggles.

Elizabeth pulled her sunglasses out of her purse and quickly slipped them on. "Will you be my bodyguard, sir?" she played, standing from the table to indicate she was ready to leave the restaurant. "I'll need someone to keep a close eye on me."

"I'll do you one better than that," Alan professed, as he also promptly vacated his chair and draped an arm securely around her middle. "I'll literally cover your body as much as possible."

"Hmm...I think I'm going to like having your services, sir," Elizabeth replied with a very mischievous grin. "Maybe we should go somewhere where you can show me your exact techniques."

"I like the way you think, Miss Warren," he pestered with a toothy, playful smile. The two impatiently made their way up to the front to pay, so they could go somewhere and be alone.

Chapter 18
The Premiere

Let the Good Times Roll! But watch out for the downside.
There always is one.

~ Sissy Marlyn ~

The first week of June 1984, on a Thursday night, at 8:00 p.m. Pacific Standard Time, the premiere showing of *Bardstown* aired at Mann's Chinese Theatre in Hollywood. Flown to California by MGM, Elizabeth and Alan arrived in Beverly Hills early Wednesday. A limo awaited them, also compliments of MGM. Fitted for a formal gown and shoes at exclusive shops on Rodeo Drive, and loaned a breathtaking, diamond necklace and bracelet from Tiffany's, Elizabeth felt like royalty. Brought to Hollywood by MGM to be Elizabeth's companion, Alan's tuxedo was also paid for and provided by them.

The same limousine took them to the theatre that evening for the premiere. When they pulled up out front, as soon as the chauffer opened the door, Elizabeth gazed out at bright lights, roped off red carpet, and a large group of people. As they stepped from the limo, photographers and reporters closed in, microphones thrust at them, and cameras flashed in all directions.

The reporters began to shout at Elizabeth. "Miss Warren, how does it feel to be on the throes of becoming one of America's newest movie stars?", "Miss Warren, how was it working with heartthrob

Jameson Thornton?", "Miss Warren…" Their voices all blended together.

"Awesome!" she replied to all of them with a radiant smile, spinning her head from side to side. Dizzy and a bit overwhelmed, she continued her forward saunter toward the doors to the lobby, glad to have Alan's reassuring arm around her to help calm her nerves.

Photographers captured beautiful images of her and Alan for their television shows, magazines and newspapers. Elizabeth looked like Cinderella going to the Ball. Her hair, makeup, and nails had been professionally done at a beauty salon on Rodeo Drive. She wore a shimmering, ankle-length, emerald gown and black, satin, high-heeled pumps. Alan donned a black tuxedo, emerald bow tie and cummerbund, shiny black dress shoes, and a ruffled, white shirt. MGM had spared no expense.

Several other reporters shouted questions at Elizabeth, but she and Alan were moved swiftly forward by a bodyguard. Jameson's limo had just pulled to the curb, so the reporters' and photographers' emphasis was about to change.

Elizabeth and Alan made their way inside the lobby. The quiet inside a huge contrast to the noise and unrest outside, they stood glancing all about. Tall, wide, orange, marble columns met their eyes, as well as gigantic, black, iron-rimmed, hanging lights; sculptured, stone, temple dogs; and orange carpeting with a bright yellow dragon in the middle.

Only allowed a few seconds to take in their surrounding, they were whisked into the dimmed theatre. They soon climbed stairs to their seats in the balcony. Red, plush, comfortable chairs awaited them.

They were not seated for long when Jameson Thornton and his female companion made their appearance in the balcony. Alan was glad to see Jameson had a date with him. "Hello, Liz. Hello again, Alan," Jameson spoke, as he and his date had a seat in the row behind them.

"Hi, James," Elizabeth replied. They made no further conversation.

Bradley and his date – a voluptuous blond, with more hanging out of her gown than covered – sat beside Jameson and his lady friend. Pat and a tall, Hispanic man were the last of the main cast to arrive. They sat beside Elizabeth and Alan.

"Hi. How have you guys been?" Pat asked Elizabeth, making friendly conversation.

Alan was surprised when Elizabeth only made brief eye contact with Pat and curtly replied, "Fine." He had always sensed Elizabeth and Pat had had a falling out, but Elizabeth had never elaborated on what might have happened to bring about this disruption in their friendship.

The theatre below soon filled with many others, among them esteemed movie critics and stars. "Oh my God, Alan! John Travolta is here for the premiere!" Elizabeth whispered, pointing. "And over on the other side is Madonna! Cool beans!"

Jameson leaned forward, tapped her shoulder, and commented with amusement, "Better get used to seeing these celebrities, Liz. You might soon be working with one of them."

Elizabeth did not reply to his banter. She merely gave him a glorious smile. Alan placed his arm around her shoulder and gave her a possessive squeeze. Jameson settled back into his seat. He still had a grin on his face.

As Arthur Goldbloom and Ryan took their places in front of the movie screen, Arthur announced, "Ladies and gentlemen, MGM welcomes you for the premiere of *Bardstown*. Enjoy!"

With that, the lights dimmed to dark; the enormous, orange curtain slid open; and the familiar MGM lion appeared. His loud, authoritative roars, splitting the silence, caused Elizabeth to shudder in her seat. Alan gave her another squeeze, as the opening scores began to play and scenes from the movie flashed upon the screen.

Most everyone in the theatre was fairly quiet the whole run of the movie – right at two hours. The many steamy love scenes with Jameson made Elizabeth uneasy. She made a special point to give Alan's hand a reassuring squeeze each time something came on she thought might upset him.

Elizabeth, of course, critically analyzed how she could have done things better. Alan, on the other hand, was amazed at how realistic it all looked. *Bardstown*, an attention grabber, with an interesting story line, was not just a chick flick, although it had a lot of romance in it. It also delved into the liquor industry in Bardstown, and Alan found this facet of the movie captivating.

Believing *Bardstown* to have been well done, Alan thought it could very well go over big with the general public. For the first time, he feared what *Bardstown* could do to his relationship with Elizabeth if it did become a hit show. *Will she still have room for me in her life if she becomes a famous movie star?*

When the movie finally ended and the lights in the theatre came up, a flurry of talking and activity erupted. Most everyone leapt from their seats, excited about what they had just seen. They shared their comments and congratulations with those around them. Reporters sought out Ryan and Arthur to get their comments on the premiere.

Even though Pat, Bradley, Jameson, and their dates all seemed to be on the move, Elizabeth and Alan remained seated. Anxious to know what Alan thought of the movie, Elizabeth studied his serious eyes, questioning, "Well? Tell me honestly, what did you think?" Alan's opinion always meant a great deal to her.

Alan truthfully was stunned. He stared oddly at Elizabeth's lovely face, and he found he had to touch her to make sure she really sat there beside him. He slowly rubbed the palm of his hand along one of her soft checks. "I think you just confirmed what I've always told you," he answered with a proud smile, continuing to affectionately caress her face. "You're a wonderful actress!"

"Thanks for the compliment," she replied, mirroring his smile with a happy one of her own. "But I actually meant what did you think of the movie? Did it seem good enough to be a hit?"

"It was very good!" Alan declared honestly. "And I'm not just saying that because I happen to love one of the main characters. Even if you weren't in it, I would want to watch it again. If a bunch more people feel the same way, then I wouldn't doubt if it became a big hit."

"Oh, Alan!" Elizabeth exclaimed, and threw her arms around his neck, showering him with kisses. "I was hoping you would say you liked it and that the love scenes wouldn't upset you too much. I love you so much! Thanks for sharing this with me!"

"It's always a pleasure to share anything with you," he proclaimed, feeling truly happy for her. "I love you too, my little movie star!" he told her before drawing her to him, lengthening their kisses.

"Hey...hey, you two," a voice interrupted their private interlude. "You better save that for later."

Elizabeth pulled back from Alan to see Jameson smiling down at them.

"How'd you guys like the premiere?" he asked, taking the liberty to squeeze Alan's shoulder.

"It was awesome! Truly awesome!" Elizabeth declared. Her face was all smiles.

"You guys did a great job," Alan praised, looking over his shoulder at Jameson.

"So are you guys ready to celebrate now?" he asked.

"For sure!" Elizabeth replied.

"The party will be in Beverly Hills at Arthur Goldbloom's house," Jameson informed them.

"For real?" Elizabeth questioned.

"Oh, yeah!" Jameson said with an enormous grin of his own. "The limo will take you there, but first we have to brave the crowd of reporters and paparazzi outside. So prepare yourself," he warned.

"Right now, I think it's totally gnarly," Elizabeth said with a giggle.

"Well...that will all soon change," Jameson knowingly told her.

Alan and Elizabeth vacated their seats then, headed for the stairs and for the mayhem outside the theatre walls. Stopped several times, just walking through the lobby, by reporters and photographers, a shot of her and Jameson together was requested. She reluctantly left Alan's side and joined James' instead.

Alan's insecurities began to raise their ugly head again. A fish out of water, he did not look forward to the rest of the evening. Quite the opposite, Jameson seemed to thrive in this environment.

Alan tried to put his uneasiness aside. Happier when Elizabeth and he were safely alone inside the limo, driving away, he realized he still had to face a Hollywood party in Beverly Hills. *For Elizabeth I'll grin and bear it*, he told himself. He feared this party would be only the first of many more to come. *I might as well get used to it*, he reluctantly decided.

* * * *

The limousine climbed the peaks into Beverly Hills, taking them to Arthur Goldbloom's dwelling. Elizabeth requested that the driver leave the divider between and her and Alan open. She wanted to be able to see out the front glass.

She watched with interest and excitement as they pulled to a large, wrought-iron gate with a lion's head in the middle. A gold plate just above the lion's head read: ***Goldbloom Estate.*** As the driver rolled down the window, inserted a card in a card reader, and the gate slowly swung open, Elizabeth's insides tingled, and she wiggled a bit in her seat.

"Excited?" Alan asked.

"I'm stoked to the max!" she said with a gleeful smile, only giving him a glance.

Her attention still riveted out the front glass, she watched as they drove along Arthur's private driveway for several moments. A large, lighted fountain, decorated with cherubs, met her eyes first. His massive house stood overlooking this fountain.

The limo circled the fountain and pulled up in front of the mansion. As Elizabeth stepped from the car and stared up at the grand estate, she shielded her eyes. Ground floodlights brilliantly illuminated the ivory estate, sparkling in the wall of arched windows, and giving the red tile roof a gleam. It blinded like sunshine on new fallen snow.

"Ready to go inside?" Alan asked, taking her hand.

"No duh. For sure!" she chirped, scurrying forward along the pathway leading to the door.

A man, in a black tuxedo with tails, opened the large, wooden, front door for her and Alan. Stepping into the foyer, Elizabeth almost gasped out loud at the beauty that greeted her – a shiny, black-specked, marble floor; enormous, white, Ionic columns; a double marble staircase; and a stained-glass skylight with a gigantic, sparkling, Waterford chandelier hanging in the center high above.

Another gentleman, also in a black tux with tails, quickly approached them. "Who may I say is calling?" he asked, sounding very stately.

"I'm Elizabeth Warren, and this is my boyfriend, Alan Michaels," she replied.

"Very well," the man responded. "Please follow me."

190

He turned and walked forward. Elizabeth and Alan fell into pace behind him. The click of all of their shoes could be heard on the marble flooring as they made their way down a quiet hallway, lined with collector oil paintings.

As they approached the entranceway to another room, the melodic sound of a grand piano could be heard as well as voices raised in conversation. In the archway to this new, vast room, Elizabeth once again took a moment to savor her surroundings.

She glimpsed a carved marble fireplace across the room from her, with a huge, Picasso painting above it. Off to the side, in an alcove sat a man in a light blue tuxedo playing the piano. Triple gold-gilt moldings lined the vaulted ceiling. Antique Parquet flooring graced the floor.

"Miss," the gentleman in the tux called to her.

"Sorry. I was just, like, admiring…ah…everything," she told him.

She stepped forward into the room.

"Miss Elizabeth Warren and her escort Alan Michaels," the man proclaimed in a loud baritone voice.

Those standing about the room took a second to glance over at them. Some nodded. Then they went right back to drinking from their crystal goblets, sampling Hor'duerves, and carrying on conversations. Elizabeth saw Arthur Goldbloom approaching.

"Elizabeth," he said, reaching for her hand. As she raised her arm, he ensconced her hand between both of his. "Welcome to my home. And, Mr. Michaels, you also are very welcome."

"Thanks," Alan replied, reaching to shake Arthur's hand. "You've got quite a place here. I think Elizabeth is speechless."

"For sure," she admitted with a giggle.

"Well, I'm glad you like it. Please make your way out onto the Grand Terrace. It's through those double, French doors over there," he pointed. "Servers will be coming around with drinks and Hor'duerves. Help yourself to all you would like."

"Thank you so much, Arthur. For inviting us here…and…for everything!" Elizabeth uttered.

"It was my pleasure. I hope to be privileged to work with you again, Elizabeth. Although I'm sure you will be deluged with offers once

Bardstown becomes a hit. Oh…that reminds me." He reached into a pocket and pulled forth a card. "This is the name of an agent friend of mine. I'd advise you to give him a call. You'll need a good agent to field through the offers and get you the best deals."

"Thanks again, Arthur," Elizabeth replied. She placed the card in her clutch purse. Then she spontaneously put her arms around Arthur's neck and embraced him.

"Once again…my pleasure," he bantered as he released Elizabeth. "Take good care of her, Mr. Michaels," he said to Alan, giving his upper arm a light pat as he started away.

"I intend to," Alan said with more confidence than he felt at the moment. Arthur's mention of a deluge of offers and Elizabeth getting an agent had him more than a little flustered.

"You want to go outside?" Elizabeth asked him, interrupting his disturbed thoughts.

"Sure," he agreed. It suddenly felt stuffy in here to him.

Elizabeth grabbed his hand and began leading him across the large room toward the double French doors Arthur had pointed out. Out on the Grand Terrace, they came face-to-face with a garden paradise. Manicured hedges, weeping willows, palm trees, ferns, flowers and tropical plants embellished by brightly, lit, winding brick pathways. Greek statues ornately interspersed with the greenery. The piano music from inside drifted in the air through well-positioned speakers.

"This place is *so* beautiful!" Elizabeth exclaimed, still trying to take it all in. She could not imagine living here.

"Yeah. It sure is something," Alan agreed. He took her hand and led her over to a vacant stone bench under one of the willow trees.

They had no more than sat down than two waiters approached them – one with a tray of drinks and another with a tray of Hor'duerves. Alan waved off the goblets of wine. "I'd rather have water if I could," he told the gentlemen.

"Of course, sir," he agreed. He reached to the side of the tray and handed Alan a goblet with ice water in it.

Elizabeth wanted to take a glass of wine, but she also asked for water. They both took a snack off of the Hor'duerves tray. "Yum…this is good," Elizabeth commented, chewing hers up.

"Yeah. It is," Alan agreed, having no idea what he might be eating. He was sure Elizabeth did not either. He just hoped it was not snails. He had heard of these being served at elite parties.

Alan had just begun to relax when Jameson Thornton and his girlfriend made their way onto the Grand Terrace. "Liz," Jameson called when he spied her. He came toward them with his girlfriend in tow. "How do you like being at your first party in Beverly Hills?"

"It's totally rad!" she purred, a smile spanning her face.

The waiter came over and Jameson and his girlfriend each took a glass of wine from his tray. "You need to mingle a bit, Liz. Alan, do you mind if I walk Elizabeth around and introduce her to some folks?"

He wanted to say, 'yes', but he did not want to spoil Elizabeth's evening. "No. I'll just wait here."

"I'm so sure. You can come along," Elizabeth said as she stood.

"No," he disagreed. "They don't care about meeting me. It's you they want to talk to. I'm fine here. It's a beautiful garden and the weather is great. I'll just sit here and enjoy the warm breeze and the view."

"That's a sport," Jameson commented with a grin. "Come on, Liz," he said, taking her hand. Beginning to lead her away, he promised, "I won't steal you away for long. Donna, do you want to wait here with Alan?" he asked, almost as an afterthought.

"Sure," his female companion spoke for the first time. She seemed as ill at ease as Alan. Alan could feel for her.

"We'll both be right here waiting," Alan said. "Donna, I'm Alan Michaels," he said introducing himself. He offered his hand.

She shook his hand and said, "I'm Donna Clark." She took a seat on the bench beside him.

Elizabeth looked back at them as Jameson led her farther away. She hated leaving Alan – *especially with another woman...an attractive one at that!* "It'll be okay, Liz," Jameson assured her, taking her hand and leading her back inside the house.

* * * *

Once inside, Jameson proceeded to introduce Elizabeth to many movers and shakers in the movie industry, television industry, and media. She smiled and made small talk with all of them, pretending to be fascinated by what they had to say, even though many times they talked about subjects over her head.

After about twenty minutes of meet-and-greet, Elizabeth reminded Jameson, "Alan and your girlfriend are, like, waiting for us outside. We should totally get back to them."

"I agree," Jameson said, but he had a mischievous smile on his face. "After you share one dance with me."

Without waiting for her reply, Jameson took Elizabeth's hand and led her to an area by the piano where couples slowly moved to the music. Taking Elizabeth in his arms, the two of them began to sway to the music as well. "So tell me, Liz, are you happy?" Jameson asked a second later, pulling back from her a bit, so he could see her face.

"To the max!" she confirmed, giving him another radiant smile. She had smiled so much this evening that her jaws hurt. But Elizabeth felt as if she was living her dream.

"Good! This is only the beginning," Jameson commented.

"I'm so sure!" Elizabeth exclaimed with a gleeful chuckle. "It's like, as soon as I think it can't get any better, something else totally rad happens. Does it ever end? Don't tell me yes, you dweeb. I'm enjoying this feeling way too much!"

Jameson pulled her close once more and whispered in her ear, "Well...if it does end, you know there are other ways to get the high you are feeling now," he reminded her.

Elizabeth instantly felt a strong, familiar, unwanted yearning. She had convinced herself she was through with coke for good. The highs incredible, Alan's love and trust were more important to her. She was not going to do anything else that she could not share with him.

"What's wrong, Liz?" Jameson asked, pushing her back again and looking into her taut face.

"Nothing," she replied. She pulled back in close and murmured, "It's just...I've, like, decided not to do coke anymore." Pulling back she further elaborated, "Alan and I got even closer since you and I filmed *Bardstown* together, and I totally don't want to do anything that could hurt that. Besides, everything is so awesome right now, I'm on a *natural*, constant high."

"It's great that you are so happy, Liz," Jameson proclaimed. Drawing his mouth to her ear again, he inquired, "So did you use any of the coke I gave you? Or did you just quit after you stopped being with me?"

"I...like...used what you gave me," Elizabeth admitted, ashamed she had even wanted more when that ran out. But she had slowly gotten over her craving...that was...until now. She wanted to stop talking about that part of her life. "But I'm totally done with that now," she declared with more conviction than she felt.

"Okay," Jameson agreed with an approving grin. He pulled her close one more time as the song, and the dance, came to an end. "We better get back to our dates," he said.

"That's the ticket," Elizabeth agreed. She allowed Jameson to lead her through the crowd toward the French doors leading to the Grand Terrace, anxious to get back to Alan and away from Jameson and his talk of cocaine. That vice had been put behind her, and that was where she intended for it to stay.

Chapter 19
The Interview

Can you really become a nervous wreck? No, but a bad case of nerves can lead us to do things we really wished we hadn't.

~ Sissy Marlyn ~

Life, as Elizabeth had known it, ended that night. *Bardstown* became a hit. Suddenly thrust into the limelight, Elizabeth could not go anywhere that she was not instantly surrounded by curious, fawning admirers, male and female alike. These people asked for her autograph and excitedly gazed at her as if she were some kind of god. While part of Elizabeth happily basked in her newfound notoriety, another part of her desperately missed having privacy.

Even Elizabeth parents were hassled. The local paper was full of headlines about **Bowling Green's Own Movie Star**, so it did not take strangers long to find out where she lived. Fans started appearing at her parents' house, knocking on the door and asking to see Elizabeth. Her parents even had to get an unlisted phone number because the phone rang almost nonstop.

When Elizabeth ventured out, she either tucked her hair under a baseball cap, which Alan had given her, or she donned a blond wig, she had purchased. Of course, she always disguised her face with dark sunglasses either way. Living life in disguise was not something Elizabeth enjoyed. She missed the freedom she had enjoyed before *Bardstown* hit the big screen.

Elizabeth called the agent Arthur Goldbloom suggested. His name was Christopher Nelson. He wasted no time getting in touch with her, eager to represent Elizabeth. Only a week later, he called Elizabeth's with her first opportunity, "Elizabeth, I have some good news for you," Christopher shared.

"And, like, what might that be?" she prodded, anxious to hear.

"Barbara Walters contacted me. She would like to interview you and Jameson together for an upcoming special of hers. Needless to say, being on her show will be good publicity both for *Bardstown* and also for your career."

"That sounds really awesome!" she purred. "When do I do this?"

"Next week," he revealed. "Since Barbara wants to take some shots of Jameson's house in West Palm Beach, she plans to do the interview there. I spoke with Mr. Thornton, and he says he has more than enough room at his house to put you up for a few days."

"You...like...want me to stay at James' house?" Elizabeth asked, sounding concerned.

"If you would be comfortable with it. Jameson has a small mansion – beachfront – so I think you would enjoy staying there. But if you prefer, MGM will put you up at a secure hotel nearby. It's certainly your call. It would just be easier on everyone, I think, if you stayed with Jameson," Christopher told her.

"I think I'd totally rather stay in a hotel," Elizabeth told him.

"Suit yourself," Christopher said, sounding a little disenchanted. "I'll work out the details and get back with you."

"Thanks," Elizabeth said.

About ten minutes later, the phone rang again. This time it was Jameson. "What's this about you staying at a hotel and not my place?" he asked. He sounded a little perturbed.

"I, like, don't want to put you out," Elizabeth stated.

"Put me out? Please! My house is big enough that you wouldn't even have to see me if you don't want to," Jameson revealed. "It would be my pleasure to have you as a guest for a day or so. I have a maid and a cook, so it would be just like being at a nice hotel, only much more personal. And it's completely secure, so you wouldn't have to have a bodyguard standing watch like you would at some hotel. Come on, Liz, say yes! You can enjoy the private beach in back while you're here. West Palm Beach is really beautiful, Liz. I know you would enjoy being here."

"You put forward a very excellent argument, Mr. Thornton," Elizabeth said with a chuckle. "Plus, I totally spaz on the beach and the ocean."

"Then what's holding you back?" Jameson prodded. "I promise I won't bother you, and you'll have your own space. You're going to hurt my feelings if you say no."

"I'm so sure. I certainly wouldn't want to do that to a dweeb like you," she teased, believing Jameson was being a little overdramatic. "Okay. I'll stay," she agreed. Elizabeth trusted Jameson and considered him a friend. *What could staying with a friend hurt?* she reasoned.

"Good," he said. "That's all settled then. I look forward to having you as my guest."

Elizabeth dreaded breaking this plan to Alan. She knew he did not trust Jameson and was jealous of him. *If he gets too upset, I can always change plans*, she decided. But for now, she planned to take Jameson up on his offer. The allure of a private beach and a chance to play in the ocean for a day was too much temptation for Elizabeth to resist.

* * * *

Jameson's beach house was indeed a mansion, at least to Elizabeth. He proudly showed her around. The house sported an enormous living room, dining room, office, kitchen, two-and-a-half bathrooms, and six bedrooms.

Elizabeth considered Jameson's bedroom a bit drab, because of the dark colors. It had brown carpet and tan walls, and his bedspread and the few pictures which adorned the walls had dark colors in them also. *But this does look like the bedroom of a bachelor*, she concluded a little sadly, wondering again why Jameson had no, one, special lady to share his life.

The rest of the bedrooms bright and airy, they pleased Elizabeth's eye more. They seemed to have an ocean theme to them, with white wicker tables, glass-based lamps with seashells, and bedspreads with dolphins or ocean items on them.

Jameson graciously told Elizabeth she could have her choice of bedroom. Five of the bedrooms were upstairs and only one was downstairs. Three of the upstairs' bedrooms faced the beach. Jameson's was the one in the middle of these. The sole bedroom downstairs also faced the beach.

Elizabeth chose the first floor bedroom, figuring this would give them both all the privacy they could possibly need. As Jameson had mentioned, it was almost like being in two separate houses. Elizabeth would stress this point when she talked to Alan, since he had not been happy with her staying at Jameson's house. Trying to overcome his jealous streak, Alan had not made a major issue of Elizabeth accommodations. But Elizabeth knew he was uneasy and displeased about her staying with Jameson.

Since it was late when Elizabeth arrived at Jameson's house and she was tired from her flight, she turned in for the night shortly after picking out her bedroom. Jameson courteously walked her to her room, wished her a good night's sleep, shut her bedroom door, and she never heard another peep from him.

Elizabeth felt completely safe and comfortable staying at his house. Elizabeth truly loved Florida and being near the ocean. She let the calming sound of the waves meeting the beach lull her into a peaceful sleep.

* * * *

At 7:30 the next morning, Elizabeth awakened to a knock on her bedroom door. "Hey, sleepyhead," Jameson called in a loud, cheery voice. "The sun is coming up and lighting up the ocean, and it's going to be a beautiful, warm day. I told the cook we would like breakfast served on the patio, so whenever you are dressed, come out back and join me. I'd like for you to take a stroll on the beach with me after we eat. Sound good?"

"For sure," Elizabeth agreed in a voice still groggy with sleep. With nervous excitement, she quickly remembered where she was and why she was there. She was going to be interviewed by Barbara Walters this evening in Jameson's living room. That still left a few hours this morning to enjoy Florida's sunny skies, ocean, and beach.

"I'll see you in a few minutes out back," Jameson concluded in a friendly voice. "Dress comfortable."

Elizabeth could hear him walking away down the hall. She sat up on the side of the bed, stretched and yawned, ridding herself of the last remnants of sleep. Rising, she happily padded over to the wide window and pulled back the drapes, so she could view the ocean. She found the view exquisite. The brilliant blue water glistened brightly, appearing to have millions of dancing diamonds in it.

It was going to feel strange taking a walk on the beach with Jameson, because Elizabeth felt it should be Alan beside her. However, she supposed she should be able to enjoy Florida with a friend as well, so she would take a stroll with Jameson after breakfast and enjoy watching the ocean roll in and all the other sights, sounds, and smells along the beach. Elizabeth pulled the drapes back shut and went in search of something light and comfortable to throw on to have breakfast in and a walk on the beach.

* * * *

After they had strolled comfortably on the beach for about an hour, Elizabeth joined Jameson by his roomy, S-shaped pool for some sunbathing. By noon, the temperature had risen to a pleasant eighty degrees.

The only time Elizabeth felt uncomfortable with Jameson was when he offered to put suntan lotion on her back. He did not linger over her or touch her in any inappropriate way. He merely spread the lotion completely across her entire, exposed back, and then handed the bottle back to her. But in Elizabeth's mind, putting suntan lotion on her body should be Alan's job. She found she missed him.

* * * *

At 1:00 p.m., Jameson and Elizabeth came in out of the sun to shower and begin to get ready for Barbara's arrival, even though the interview was not until 4:00 that evening. Elizabeth hoped she had picked up a little color from the sun. She usually tanned fairly easily.

Two hours later, Jameson knocked on her bedroom door for the second time that day. "Liz, the film crew is here," he announced in an eager voice. "Barbara's makeup people would like to see us. No shiny faces on Barbara's shows. And when they are done with us, which shouldn't take long, Barbara wants to meet with us to run through the questions she plans to ask."

Elizabeth stood from the side of the bed and reluctantly walked across the room toward the closed door. She had changed clothes at least three times, and she still was not certain she was happy with what she was wearing.

Jameson had told her to choose something neat, but casual, preferably shorts and a T-shirt or a short sleeve blouse. Elizabeth had gotten out every piece of clothing she had brought. *What if none of it is right?* she agonized. *I'm used to wardrobe people choosing the appropriate clothes for me.*

Elizabeth begrudgingly opened the door to face Jameson's smiling face. "James, I don't... like...think I can go through with this," she confided, trying to keep her voice low.

She looked from side to side as if she fully expected someone from Barbara's film crew to snatch her from the room. Her stomach felt like it contained tiny gymnasts who were doing cartwheels over and over. Elizabeth genuinely feared she would be ill.

"Liz, it's natural to be nervous before your first interview," he told her in a soothing voice, reaching to touch her arm. It was trembling. "I'll be right there beside you, and everything will be just fine."

"I'm so sure. How do you think me, like, totally throwing up in your lap with go over?" she asked, no trace of humor in her statement.

Elizabeth frantically clutched her betraying stomach, which had begun to churn even more. "I'm in deep shit, James. I'm going to be sick!" she wailed.

Elizabeth turned and raced across the bedroom to the connecting bathroom. There she dropped to her knees and bent urgently over the toilet bowl. When she emerged from the restroom a few seconds later, Jameson had just opened the door and was re-entering the room.

"Will you please go tell them I'm sick? Or is that, like, where you have been?" she asked him, dabbing at her clammy face with a cool washrag.

Jameson promptly made his way across the room to where Elizabeth weakly stood. "Sit down," he instructed, pointing to the side of the bed.

Elizabeth quickly did as he ordered, grateful to be getting off of her much-too-wobbly legs. Jameson proceeded to reach into one of his short's pockets and instantly retrieved a packet of coke. "You just need something to help settle your nerves," he told her.

He turned and walked over to the vanity table. Picking up a mirror, he hastily emptied the package on the glass, forming two, all too familiar, white lines. "This will make you forget you were ever nervous. Then we can go meet with Barbara's crew."

"James, I know you are totally trying to help, but I told you that I didn't plan on using coke anymore," Elizabeth staunchly declared, looking away from the drug and trying to concentrate solely on his serious face.

"This isn't play time, Liz," Jameson quickly protested, an angry edge to his voice. "If you never use coke again, I don't really care. But, right now, you need to get a grip. Barbara and her crew flew to Florida today to interview *both* of us, and it will make you look very bad if you stand them up. So just try the drug and see if you don't feel much better."

When Elizabeth still hesitated, Jameson forcefully thrust the mirror in her face. "Go on," he ordered in stubborn aggravation, pointing to the drug which her downcast eyes temptingly observed.

She really did not want to miss the interview with Barbara Walters, but Elizabeth did not see any way she could meet her in the condition she was in now. Just the thought of sitting in front of Barbara and answering her questions, without a script with the given answers, made Elizabeth's stomach start to erratically whirl all over again.

On the other hand, she knew coke would probably ease all of her exaggerated fears and give her the confidence she sorely needed. However, Elizabeth feared, if she used the drug again, she would definitely be tempted to use it again in the future. *And I made a promise to myself not to do drugs anymore or keep any other secrets from Alan,* she mused.

"Liz, they are waiting on us," Jameson reminded her with urgency. He took one of her hands and placed the tiny, drug receptacle in it. "I know deep down that you would hate yourself if you missed meeting Barbara today. Taking coke once more won't hurt anything. I promise. You've always trusted me before."

Elizabeth knew only too well that this was true, and she had to truthfully admit that trusting Jameson had always enabled her to come through all of her other, seemingly impossible situations with flying colors. She certainly did not want to let him down now, and she could see that this interview was very important to him. It was important to her as well.

Despite the logical objections still floating through her mind, Elizabeth slowly lowered her head over the mirror. Hesitating only a second more, she quickly sucked all the powder up her eager nostrils. She lie completely back on the bed and let the drug fully set in.

When she sat back up, she could not help but smile. She had vaguely forgotten how wonderful coke could make her feel. Jameson took the mirror and put it back in its place. Then he extended a helpful hand in her direction, hastily pulling Elizabeth to her feet. "Let's go see Barbara's folks," he coaxed, displaying a satisfied smile for the first time. "Once you meet Barbara, you'll wonder what you were ever so nervous about."

"Gnarly. I could, like, honestly care less right now," she truthfully admitted, showing a wide, drug induced grin and giggling wickedly. "Thank you so much, James!"

"I'll always be here to help you, Liz," he assured her, taking one her hands into his own and swiftly leading her from the room.

* * * *

A few days after she had returned home from her successful interview with Barbara Walters, Alan came over to visit her and handed Elizabeth an inflammatory copy of the National Enquirer. One of the mechanics at the dealership had thoughtlessly flaunted the paper in his face, asking Alan how it felt to be in a tug of war with Jameson Thornton for his girlfriend's heart.

Without permission, the scandal sheet had printed three, very insinuating photographs of Elizabeth and Jameson, as well as a photo of her by Alan's side. Across the top of the front page, in big bold letters, was a large caption which read: ***Bardstown Star, Elizabeth Warren, Embroiled in Heated Love Triangle Between Hunky Car Salesman in Kentucky and Sexy Co-star Jameson Thornton.***

Under the condemning print, two pictures of Elizabeth leapt off the page. One was an enlarged photo of her and Jameson walking on the beach. Jameson happened to have his arm draped chummily around Elizabeth's back. The other was a picture of her and Alan arm in arm, taken one night when she had been out with him before she had become wise enough to start wearing disguises.

As if this was not bad enough, inside, two more, quite cozy, pictures of her and Jameson appeared. The first was Jameson applying suntan lotion to her back at his house. The other was from the airport, displaying Jameson hugging her and planting a kiss on her cheek. He had merely been saying an innocent, friendly goodbye.

Totally unaccustomed to being attacked and having her privacy so thoughtlessly violated, Elizabeth was distraught. *For a photographer to have taken these pictures, I must have been secretly watched all the time for some time now*, she ascertained.

The whole episode was even more unsettling because Alan had been cruelly and unfairly taunted because of it. "Oh, Alan, I am so totally sorry!" Elizabeth quickly apologized, adding, "I wish these reporters would just eat shit and die. They took pictures of innocent events and totally blew everything out of proportion. How can these cheesy people get away with this?!"

"It really wouldn't surprise me if Jameson didn't plan this whole thing," Alan stated with a deep frown. "He probably paid the photographer to take these photos and turn them over to the National Enquirer."

"Oh…let's…like…not go there," Elizabeth pleaded, with a disapproving grimace on her face. "I totally don't want to argue about Jameson. I'm for sure he had nothing to do with this."

Alan sensibly realized that continuing to tongue-lash Jameson would get him nowhere. However, the pictures of Jameson's hands, arms, and even lips on Elizabeth's body had served to enrage him. He twisted the offensive paper in a frustrated knot with both hands and said, "Look, we both know this story isn't true. Unfortunately, because you are a famous star now, I think you are going to get used to being exploited by rag sheets like this one. So, with that in mind, we just need to learn to ignore crap like this. And, as a sign that we will at least try not to let stuff like this get to us, what do you say we symbolically burn this copy?"

"It totally won't be easy to ignore papers like this making up lies about me, but I for sure think burning this copy sounds like a winning plan," Elizabeth readily agreed.

Alan rose from the couch and helped Elizabeth to her feet beside him. Carrying the wadded paper, he led her into the kitchen. Her mother stood at the stove cooking dinner.

"Mrs. Warren, do you have an open burner," Alan asked her.

Looking a bit puzzled, she pointed to a burner in the back. "What did you need?" she asked.

"A big pan," he replied.

She slid out a tray under the oven and pulled forth a baking pan. She still eyeballed Alan with bewilderment as she handed him the pan.

"Could I have the use of your stove for a moment?" he asked. "I have some trash we need to burn."

"Trash? Burn?" Elizabeth's mother repeated, looking over at her daughter for an explanation.

"Some cheesy newspaper printed a butt-ugly story about me," Elizabeth explained.

"Oh," her mother replied, stepping back from the stove. She had some idea what newspaper and what article, because she had seen it at the grocery earlier when she stood in line to check out. She had tried to ignore it, but the content of the article had disturbed her. "Burn away," she said.

She pulled out a chair at the kitchen table and sat down. She watched as Alan placed the large cooking pan she had given him on the stove. He stuck the end of the paper against the hot burner and it caught fire. "Say goodbye to this piece of trash, and let's pretend we never saw it," Alan suggested, as he quickly dropped it in the pan.

They all triumphantly watched it burn together. Elizabeth's mom secretly worried, because she realized this story would probably be the first of many unsavory things that would be printed about her daughter. She was happy for the success Elizabeth had found, but worried about her at the same time. Unlike times in the past, she did not criticize

Elizabeth's choice of career. She and Elizabeth had finally formed a friendship, and she would do nothing to disrupt their new relationship.

* * * *

In the weeks that followed, it seemed Elizabeth was away from home more than she was there. She was flown to New York for magazine interviews: *People*, *Woman's Home Journal*, and *TV Guide*.

Then she was zipped off to Burbank for an appearance on *The Tonight Show*. Elizabeth was excited and thrilled to meet Johnny Carson. She also had the pleasure of meeting Cyndi Lauper, who was the musical guest for the night.

Elizabeth was not nearly as nervous about doing these interviews, and meeting these other celebrities, as she had been with Barbara Walters. She warded off her case of nerves each time by taking a hit of the coke Jameson had sent home with her. Jameson said he knew she would have other opportunities to be interviewed, and he did not want her to get another case of the uncontrollable jitters. Coke helped to squelch her anxieties, and thus gave her self-assurance in her answers.

Chapter 20
Proposals

The glorious high of a marriage proposal versus the glorious high from drug addiction – what's a young girl to choose?

~ Sissy Marlyn ~

*B*arbara Walter's special aired in mid-August on a Friday evening. Excited for Elizabeth, Alan invited her to his apartment to watch the show. They settled comfortably on his sofa, fully focusing on the television in front of them. He also had a tape in the VCR to tape the show. He had taped her appearance on *The Tonight Show* as well. He intended to capture and save as many of these first interviews as he could.

Out of three interview segments, naturally, Elizabeth and Jameson's was last. Barbara's first guest was Tom Cruise. They talked about his popular 1983 movie *Risky Business* and his upcoming 1985 movie *Legend*. Barbara also asked him some questions about his personal life. To the delight of his many female fans, Tom told Barbara there was no one special lady in his life.

Barbara's next interview was with Deborah Winger. Barbara raved about her movie successes: *Urban Cowboy, An Officer and a Gentleman, Terms of Endearment*, and her Oscar nominations. She asked what was next, and Deborah told her of some projects on the horizon. They also briefly discussed Deborah's relationship with Nebraska senator Robert Kerrey.

There was a commercial break, with what seemed like millions of commercials, and Elizabeth fidgeted in her seat. She could hardly wait to see her and Jameson's interview. Alan loved seeing her get excited. He looked forward to the interview as well.

Elizabeth and Jameson's interview finally came on. Barbara's director had seated them on Jameson's long, cushy couch, which faced the beach and ocean. Barbara sat in a chair across from them, which meant she had the bright, sun-sparkling ocean in her background when the camera focused on her. Naturally, this setup made Barbara look her very best.

Elizabeth and Jameson also looked relaxed and charming. Jameson had comfortably crossed his legs, placing a foot on top of the opposite knee. His arm rested across the back of the couch behind Elizabeth's head. His hand dangled a little too familiarly close to her opposing shoulder for Alan's likening.

Elizabeth also crossed her legs and laid her hands loosely, one on top of the other, in her lap. Both dressed appropriate for Florida; Jameson wore a bright, royal-blue, Izod, polo shirt, and tan shorts, and Elizabeth donned a pastel, lightweight, blue, cotton blouse and white shorts.

Elizabeth's dark hair shone, and her pretty, green eyes sparkled. Alan thought she looked beautiful. The only thing that spoiled the picture for him: the presence of Jameson Thornton.

Barbara began the interview with some general questions about *Bardstown* and its instant success. Then she asked Elizabeth if she could ask some questions about her personal life. Elizabeth, of course, said, with a dazzling smile, "That would be fine."

"So, Elizabeth, you're from Bowling Green, Kentucky, and you've only done college plays at Western Kentucky University before landing your role in *Bardstown*. What's it like to go from college plays to a successful big-screen movie?" Barbara began her inquisition with a friendly smile, both for the camera and for Elizabeth's benefit. "Weren't you absolutely awestruck when you first learned that you had landed the part, and you were going to be filming love scenes with Jameson Thornton?"

Elizabeth heard Jameson chuckle, and she had to turn her head and warmly return his reminiscent grin. She knew he contemplated her first day on the set when she had been so stunned to see him. That seemed so long ago now.

"Share what the conspiratorial giggle between the two of you is all about," Barbara swiftly coaxed, her gaze expertly sweeping from one to the other.

"I think James is thinking about when I first came face to face with him," Elizabeth freely shared, looking away from Jameson and focusing on Barbara and the camera again. "Awestruck is definitely a good word. I was so flustered that, not only did my tongue cease to function, my brain went dead. I couldn't remember a single line from the script I had memorized for that day. It was awful!"

"That certainly sounds like a harrowing experience," Barbara commented, "How were you able to overcome your fears?"

"I can honestly say I never would have made it through that first day if it hadn't been for James," Elizabeth earnestly proclaimed. "He helped me through every scene, and he made our director be patient. I needed a lot of patience, because I was not only a nervous wreck but so green. I think James and I became friends that very first day."

Elizabeth automatically turned her head in Jameson's direction again and flashed him a grateful smile. Jameson reacted by grinning back and reaching to gently squeeze one of her hands. "I think Liz gives me a bit too much credit," he told Barbara. "She is a very talented actress and that is why she was chosen for the role and why she would have made it through the day without my help. She was a pleasure to work with."

"Do you feel that you have chemistry between the two of you, and that's why the love scenes are so realistic in *Bardstown*?" Barbara expertly questioned, distinctly glancing at their joined hands with a presuming smile.

This question had made Elizabeth slightly uncomfortable during the interview, and its obvious implication made her even more unsettled now as she watched Barbara's show with Alan. She hoped this innuendo did not serve to arouse Alan's underlying jealousy again.

Glancing at him, Elizabeth was relieved to find Alan still appeared to be unruffled. He just intently watched the interview. Elizabeth continued to carefully scrutinize Alan as they listened to Jameson's response to Barbara's inquiry. "The answer to your question is a resounding, 'Yes!'. I think we definitely have chemistry, and I think that does show on the screen."

Thankfully, Alan still did not negatively react, but continued to watch the television.

"So did the two of you see each other away from the set?" Barbara pried, her voice obviously insinuating a romance or dating.

"Yeah, a couple nights a week," Jameson answered truthfully.

"We worked out together," Elizabeth quickly explained.

"Oh, I see," Barbara commented. Then she continued to instinctively probe, "So the two of you don't date?"

"I really don't think my boyfriend would like that much," Elizabeth swiftly shared, grateful to finally have a chance to mention Alan.

"Boyfriend? Do tell; who is this young man? What does he do for a living, and how does he deal with your 'hot' love scenes with Jameson?" Barbara continued to probe, appearing happy to have learned this new information about Elizabeth. She would be the first to report this fact to Elizabeth's new, adoring public.

"Oh...oh," Alan said, giving Elizabeth a glance. "I didn't know I was part of this interview."

"I told you I talk about you everywhere," Elizabeth replied with a smile, giving him a kiss on the cheek.

They listened as she responded to Barbara's questions about Alan. "His name is Alan Michaels, and he is an assistant manager at a local auto dealership in Bowling Green," Elizabeth freely shared with a proud, happy smile. "As far as my love scenes go, they do bother him, but he's getting more used to them. He's very proud of my success."

"So is it serious between you and this young man? Do you plan to marry? And will he give up his job to travel with you?" Barbara continued to fire questions.

"It *is* serious between us, and we do plan to marry," she replied with confidence. "Right now, we're working around my schedule to spend time together. Fortunately, he's very understanding and wants me to be happy."

"But there are bound to be other movies for you, and other interviews and the like. This will mean you may be on the road a lot.

How will the two of you handle the long separations that may ensue?" Barbara rapidly grilled.

"I guess we will cross those bridges when we come to them. Like I said, Alan is very supportive," Elizabeth candidly declared, hoping Barbara's questions about her personal life would end soon.

"Well, that's great," Barbara agreed. "I wish the two of you all the best and hope your relationship can weather the pressure that this business is bound to put it under."

"I always tell her the same thing," Jameson spontaneously added, giving her shoulder a squeeze.

"So how about you, Jameson? If you and Elizabeth are not an item, is there any other special lady you would like to tell us about? I know you've been linked to many in the past. But none of them seem to take a permanent hold. Are there any hopefuls on the horizon?"

Elizabeth had been anxious to hear the answer to this question as well, since she worried about Jameson being alone.

"I like keeping my options open," Jameson replied, displaying an immediate, mischievous, wide grin. "I'm in no real hurry to be tied down. It's much more fun playing the field."

"You're incorrigible," Barbara chastised him playfully. "But I'm sure a lot of young ladies out there are happy to hear that you are still available. Would you like to give out your address and phone number during this interview, so they can all visit you?"

"I would, Barbara, but Liz is my guest here. Since I liked having her as my co-star, and consider her a friend, I wouldn't want her to get trampled in the stampede which would undoubtedly instantly occur," Jameson boasted with a confident chuckle.

After sharing a laugh at Jameson's obvious conceit, Barbara decided to change the subject one last time before the interview concluded. She asked, "I couldn't help but notice that Elizabeth calls you James, and you call her Liz. Why the name shortening between the two of you?"

"Jameson is my theatrical name, but since I consider Liz a friend and wanted her to feel comfortable with me, I wanted her to feel free to call me by my real name, which is James. As far as me calling Elizabeth Liz, I couldn't help but give her that pet name, because I think she has talent enough to possibly become another Liz Taylor," Jameson explained.

"Elizabeth, how does your boyfriend feel about Jameson giving you a pet name? Does it bother him at all?"

Elizabeth hesitated briefly before replying. She did not want to admit that Alan, in fact, hated that James had given her the nickname Liz. Because of her prolonged pause, Jameson decided to answer for her, much to Elizabeth's further dismay.

"Alan isn't happy about the name at all," he candidly admitted.

"Alan prefers if James calls me Elizabeth," she defensively restated. "But it's really no big deal. He's slowly getting used to all the changes that my career has brought into our lives. I think me being called Liz by James is one of the least things that bothers him."

"Well, I think your nicknames for one another are cute," Barbara declared with a conspiratorial smile which made Elizabeth a little uncomfortable.

Barbara then concluded the interview saying, "I wish you both all of the best in your careers and hope you will both come back and talk with me about them in the future."

As Barbara's show went to another series of commercials, Alan turned toward Elizabeth and commented with a small grin, "Good interview."

"I'm sorry about the way some of Jameson comments, like, came across," Elizabeth said.

"I'm more concerned with your comments," Alan told her, his smile widening as he added, "You made me out to be a pretty supportive, understanding guy. I think I like that."

Elizabeth put her arms around his neck and gave him a grateful kiss. "I totally didn't say anything that wasn't true," she professed. "You are an awesome, supportive-to-the-max man!"

"I guess I just come by it naturally," Alan teased, as he kissed her again and held her warmly in his arms, glad to be able to share in Elizabeth's joy over being interviewed by Barbara Walters.

* * * *

The next big event for Elizabeth, the *People's Choice Awards*, was held at the Pasadena Civic Auditorium in Pasadena, California on

January 9, 1985.   As with the premiere for *Bardstown*, Alan was supposed to be escorting Elizabeth to this awards ceremony.

Elizabeth and Jameson had been asked to present one of the awards together.   They also both had been nominated for an award: Elizabeth for **Favorite Motion Picture Actress** and Jameson for **Favorite Motion Picture Actor**.   *Bardstown* had also been nominated for **Favorite Motion Picture**.   Elizabeth was excited and nervous about attending this ceremony, presenting, and possibly winning an award.

She and Alan flew to Pasadena early that day and checked into their hotel room.   They would be spending the night, since the award ceremony filmed live and would not be over until late.   Not the first time they had shared a bed without having sex, they had also spent the night in California after the *Bardstown* premiere in Hollywood.   It was getting more and more difficult for them to keep from making love.

Excited to be taking Elizabeth to the awards ceremony, Alan was even more excited about what he had planned to happen afterwards.   An added surprise for Elizabeth this evening, Alan intended to propose. Elizabeth's agent was looking over offers of more movies, and Alan did not want to keep being separated from Elizabeth.   He wanted for the two of them to marry, so he could travel with her all the time.   He also wanted to be able to freely make love to her.   He could not wait for the evening to progress.

However, when they got to their hotel room, at the Ritz Carlton, there was a message waiting on their phone.   Elizabeth retrieved the message and told Alan with concerned eyes.   "It was about your father. He's been taken to the hospital."

"What? Is it serious?" he asked in alarm.

"I don't know. You need to call and find out," she replied.

Alan called Kathy's house. She answered the phone. "What's up with my dad? Do you know?" Elizabeth heard him ask.

"Hemorrhaging!" she heard him exclaim next, his lips forming a circle as he loudly exhaled. "Crap!"

He said only a few more words before he concluded the call.

"It sounds really serious," Elizabeth commented with anxiety.

"It's his liver disease," Alan replied, a trace of anger in his voice. "He's abused his body with alcoholism for years. His body may just be giving out because of it."

"I hope not, Alan," Elizabeth said. "You totally need to fly home, don't you?"

"I guess so," Alan said, raking his nails through his hair.

"Do you…like…want me to leave with you?"

"What?…No," he answered. He stood, framed her face with his hands, and gave her a brief kiss. "But I love you for offering. You have an award show to present at, and hopefully receive an award…or two. I wish I could be there with you…"

"For sure. I know. I totally wish you could too. But your dad is more important," Elizabeth stated with empathy.

"That's why I love you. You have the biggest heart in the world," Alan stated, giving her another kiss, this one lingering a bit.

"I love you too," Elizabeth stated when the kiss concluded. "You, like, call and leave me a message as soon as you find something out about your dad."

"I will," Alan promised. He headed for the door. "Knock 'em dead tonight," he said with a smile, before he opened the door and left her for good.

When he had gone, Elizabeth sadly sat down on the comfortable, leather sofa. Her room a suite, it resembled a small apartment. There was a living room area, with plush carpet, couch, coffee table, side tables with crystal lamps, and a television. There was even a very small kitchen area, with a counter with stools and a microwave oven. The bedroom stood apart, in a separate room, with a bathroom off the side.

Elizabeth hated that Alan was not going to be there to escort her to the awards ceremony. It took a bit of the magic out of the night for her. She hoped his dad would be okay. She said a silent prayer for his recovery. Then Elizabeth picked up the remote control up off the coffee table and turned the television on to have some noise in the room, to occupy her mind with something other than worry, and to pass the time.

Chapter 21
Betrayal

What's it mean to betray someone?
In some cases, it means to break a heart in two.

~ Sissy Marlyn ~

*O*nly minutes before they were scheduled to be on stage and present the award they had been chosen to announce, Jameson and Elizabeth got high in his dressing room. Very anxious about doing live television, Elizabeth did not hesitate to partake.

When their names were announced, Elizabeth gracefully strolled to the podium on Jameson's arm, exuding confidence. The few lines of magic powder had made all right with the world again. Elizabeth felt she could do no wrong.

The camera absolutely loved both Jameson and Elizabeth. They made a very attractive couple. Elizabeth's hair had been pulled up and styled in a becoming, elegant, French roll. The low-cut neck in her sequined, royal-blue gown complimented her slim figure while also accentuating her bust line.

Jameson's black tuxedo, with light, baby-blue, ruffled shirt, made his dark blue eyes captivating. The lights of the studio rippled through the natural waves in his deep-black hair, embellishing its shininess.

Elizabeth stumbled over a few lines in her unrehearsed, cue card reading. But she merely laughed at herself, appearing totally unruffled.

She would have been mortified if it had not been for her use of coke to mollify her nerves.

An hour later, the award Elizabeth had been nominated for was preannounced before a commercial break. Realizing the effects of the coke she had consumed earlier had subsided, Elizabeth excused herself from her seat for a moment.

Fearful about possibly winning and having to take the stage again to thank everyone, Elizabeth desperately wished to alleviate her paralyzing fears once again. She escaped to the sanctuary of the ladies room. Hidden safely in a stall, without hesitation or remorse, she quickly snorted another few lines of coke. Moments after, she returned to her seat, feeling falsely indestructible once more.

Ten minutes later, Michael J. Fox and his co-star on *Family Ties*, Justine Bateman, took the stage to announce the nominees for **Favorite Motion Picture Actress**. "And the nominees are," Michael announced, handing the card to Justine.

Justine picked up with the names on the card. "Elizabeth Warren, *Bardstown*." She paused for a second to allow the cameraman to angle in on Elizabeth and for the applause. "Lori Singer, *Footloose*." The camera swung over to Lori, and she was clapped for. "And last, but certainly not least, Daryl Hannah, *Splash*. The camera captured Daryl's eager face and the audience erupted in hand-slapping praise once more.

Another few moments of tense silence passed as Justine handed the card back to Michael to unfold and announce the winner. "And the winner is...Elizabeth Warren, *Bardstown*!" He announced in a loud, excited voice.

Elizabeth swiftly rose from her chair. Applause, shouts and whistles flowed from the rest of the crowd. The camera followed her every movement, capturing her ear-to-ear smile. The camera also caught Jameson unabashedly hugging and kissing Elizabeth in congratulations.

When he released her, Elizabeth bounced up the few steps onto the stage, happily approaching the podium. Promptly handed her award trophy, the camera zoomed in on Elizabeth's happy face, making her white teeth sparkle all the more.

Elizabeth held the trophy triumphantly in the air in front of her and gaped at it for a few moments as if it would disappear. "Thank you!

Wow! This is so awesome!" she bellowed into the microphone, as the clapping finally died down. "I have so many wonderful people to thank for this. First off, thank you Arthur Goldbloom and Ryan Axman for giving me, an unknown, Kentucky actress, a chance. Next, I can't thank my co-star, Jameson Thornton, enough. Not only was he an awesome co-star, but his unwavering faith in me kept me going. And lastly, I want to thank all of you, my fans. It's because of you that I have this award. I love you all!" she proclaimed, as the music began to play, signifying her speech time had run out.

Led away by Michael J. Fox, Elizabeth sadly realized she had not gotten a chance to mention how grateful she was to Alan for his support. She knew he was taping the show for her. She hoped her thoughtless omission would not hurt his feelings.

Shortly after Elizabeth's win, Jameson won the award for his nomination: **Favorite Motion Picture Actor**. Equally thrilled for his success, Elizabeth offered him a hug and kiss as well. Jameson also sang her praises after he received his trophy.

Bardstown did not take home the award for **Favorite Motion Picture**. *Footloose* did. Regardless, elated at the success of his two stars, Arthur looked forward to celebrating their successes at his home in Beverly Hills.

* * * *

Elizabeth had smiled for so long, her jaws were sore. The effects from her last indulgence of coke had worn off, but she still remained high, because she so delighted in the evening's outcome.

In the limousine, on the way to Arthur Goldbloom's house, Elizabeth and Jameson shared a bottle of champagne to celebrate their successes. By the time they reached Arthur's house, Elizabeth had consumed at least four glasses and was feeling tipsy.

Jameson hooked an arm through hers and led her into the house. Elizabeth was truly grateful to have him to steady her. The marble floor seemed to be rising up to meet her as she walked.

"We'll get something to eat and you'll be just fine," Jameson assured her.

He escorted her directly to Arthur's elaborate dining room, where a large buffet of food invitingly awaited guests. The chandelier light looked much too bright to Elizabeth, and she giggled. "How about I fix you a plate and you have a seat?" Jameson wisely suggested.

Elizabeth quickly nodded her agreement. Her legs wobbly, she feared trying to support a plate and walk with it. Jameson swiftly led Elizabeth to a nearby chair and seated her. He returned to the buffet to attend to the task of preparing two plates.

Elizabeth did feel some better once she had consumed some food. She comfortably mingled with the crowd by Jameson's side, and he eagerly introduced her to many new people. She even finally got to meet her agent face to face. Up until now, they had transacted business over the phone and by mail carrier.

Christopher Nelson, a younger man than Elizabeth had envisioned, appeared to be only in his early thirties. He had red hair and golden brown eyes. Christopher enthusiastically congratulated both Elizabeth and Jameson on their awards.

After awhile, Elizabeth began to feel very sluggish and tired. Jameson noticed the change in her almost immediately. Wanting to help, he took her by the arm and led her quickly toward one of Arthur's bathrooms. "You're bottoming out," James told her.

"Well…it's, like, after midnight at home, even though it's only nine thirty here. Plus, I totally have jetlag from the flight in earlier today. I think I have a right to be getting tired, you airhead," Elizabeth justified. "I probably ought to be getting back to my hotel room anyway. Alan may have called with some news about his dad." Elizabeth had shared with Jameson about Alan's emergency and why he had to leave.

"Liz, you don't want to offend Arthur, do you?" Jameson asked in a rather stern voice.

He opened the door to the bathroom and pulled her inside, locking the door behind them. He reached inside his tuxedo jacket and pulled forth another packet on cocaine.

"James, I've had so much already. Plus, I've been drinking. I don't think I should use any more," she argued in a fatigued voice.

"So you just want to blow Arthur off? That's the thanks he gets for all he's done for you?" Jameson questioned.

"Well…of course not," Elizabeth begrudgingly agreed.

"Taking one more hit of coke isn't going to kill you, Liz. Or I wouldn't be offering it. You need to go out and enjoy the party Arthur is throwing for *us*," he persuasively argued.

Even though Elizabeth was very wary of taking more coke, the part of her that so liked cocaine and trusted Jameson won out. "Okay," she agreed. "But this is it. No more for the evening. Once I come down from this, I'm leaving."

"Okay," Jameson agreed with a smile.

He emptied the contents of the package on the marble vanity counter, arranged some lines, and they both took another hit. Moments later, euphoric again, Elizabeth's heart pounded wildly and her energy abounded.

She and Jameson joined the crowd again. Elizabeth talked animatedly with many people, including Arthur, who was proud to show off his award winning actors. When the live band began to play, Elizabeth happily danced with Jameson. She also irresponsibly drank more champagne.

* * * *

Groggily awakened by the sound of Alan's loud, shocked voice calling her name, Elizabeth forced her half-awake body to roll over on her back. She squinted when the offensive glow of a desk lamp across the way caught her eyes.

"Elizabeth, what in the hell is going on here?" Alan demanded to know.

She rubbed her hands over her eyes, trying to force them to focus and groaned, "Ow...mm." As she positioned her hands beside her body to push herself to more of a sitting position, she jumped as she noticed a form under the blanket in the bed beside her. Her eyes fully opened and focused. She gasped, as the last remnants of sleep quickly left her. Jameson Thornton lay in bed with her.

A sickening shudder ran through Elizabeth as she noticed his bare chest and then slowly realized she was naked beneath the covers. She looked back over at Alan. He stood less than a foot from the bed, his face a mixture of fury and confusion.

"A...Alan...this...this totally can't be what it looks like," Elizabeth unsurely commented, trying to convince herself as well.

She slowly slid herself to a sitting position, noting a slight soreness below her waist, a severe headache and some nausea. She tightly secured the sheet and blanket around her nude body. Jameson reacted to her movement. Stirring beside her, he opened his eyes to gaze longingly at her.

"Good morning, Liz," he greeted in a cheery voice, displaying a crooked smile.

He reached to affectionately touch her nearest arm. He obviously had no idea Alan resided in the room. Elizabeth was horrified.

"You son of a bitch!" Alan cursed in a guttural shout, causing Jameson's head to snap attentively in his direction. "What the hell are you trying to pull?!"

"Alan?!" Jameson exclaimed in honest surprise. "What are you doing here?! How did you get in this room?"

"Um...I have a key," Alan answered, holding it in the air and shaking it. "This is *our* room. The question is, what are *you* doing here?!"

Elizabeth wondered the same thing. She did not know why either man was in the room with her. Alan was supposed to be far away in Kentucky, and Jameson definitely was not supposed to be here, especially not naked in her bed.

Elizabeth's stomach knotted again. *Could I possibly have been so wasted last night that I did something unforgivable?* The last thing she remembered was drinking more champagne in the limo with Jameson on the way back to the hotel.

"You still haven't answered my question! What the hell are you doing in this room, you bastard?!" Alan demanded through clenched teeth, his hands balled into fists by his sides.

"Look, Alan, why don't you give Elizabeth and me a little privacy so we can get dressed. Then we'll meet you in the other room and talk about what's happened," Jameson calmly suggested, holding both of his hands up, palms out, to peacefully protest Alan's obvious, reasonable rage.

"I'm not about to leave you alone with Elizabeth for another second," Alan protested, stepping ominously closer to the bed. "You gather up your clothes and get the hell out of here! Or I'll gladly throw your ass out. I have no interest whatsoever in what you might have to say!"

"Liz, what do you prefer?" Jameson asked, courageously taking his eyes off of his furious nemesis and focusing his entire attention on Elizabeth's troubled face.

Even though Elizabeth wished she could have a second alone with Jameson to try and obtain a valid explanation of what had truly happened, she knew this would be viewed as another betrayal by Alan. Instinctively, without having it affirmed by Jameson, Elizabeth already feared the worst had happened anyway.

"James, I think it would be best if you left now. Alan and I totally need to be alone," Elizabeth replied, briefly glancing at Jameson and then quickly returning her gaze to Alan's angry form.

"Okay," Jameson begrudgingly agreed. He clutched the cover, yanked it loose from the bed and Elizabeth's grasp, pulled it around his lower half, and somewhat secured it as he stood. "I'll wait in the other room."

"Don't you even think about it! Unless you're looking to get the shit beat out of you!" Alan warned.

He charged at Jameson, giving him a challenging, forceful shove backwards. He wanted to provoke a fight. Pounding Jameson relentlessly with his fists would give Alan some pleasure amidst the turmoil that currently surrounded him.

"Alan! Let him go!" Elizabeth pleaded. "James, please leave. I'll talk to you later," she said, tensely watching the two men stare one another down.

"Alright, Liz. Whatever you want," Jameson agreed.

He intently watched Alan, ready should he attack. He hurriedly gathered his clothes and shoes from the floor. He headed into the bathroom to dress. Alan glared holes through the door until he saw it open and Jameson come back out.

"I'll talk to you later, Liz." He had the gall to say, as he headed for the door leading out of the suite.

Alan had to use every ounce of his restraint not to hurry after Jameson and try to kill him. Instead, he turned and focused all his attention on Elizabeth again. His only hope now was that she would tell him that nothing really happened, that it was all some sort of crazy misunderstanding, or that Jameson had somehow set the whole thing up to make it look as if something had happened between the two of them. However, Alan sadly braced to hear the worst.

"What went on here, Elizabeth?" he asked, his voice strained and nervous.

Elizabeth rubbed her throbbing forehead, hoping to miraculously stimulate her memory of the earlier morning's happenings. Suddenly aware of how fatigued she felt, Elizabeth figured this weariness was her body's way of getting even for the way she had so ruthlessly abused it yesterday.

Elizabeth felt she needed to do something to try and revitalize herself before she endeavored to explain things to Alan. *Maybe a shower will make me feel better*, she contemplated. She also hoped it might awaken her brain so she could recall what happened.

"Well. I'm waiting for an explanation," Alan demanded in a terse voice. Both his hands still clenched at his sides, he kept a safe distance from Elizabeth.

"Alan, I'm sorry. I totally want to try and explain things to you, but I'm…like…not feeling very well right this second," she honestly explained in a weak, half-pleading voice. "I think maybe a shower would for sure help. Can you please wait in the other room while I try that?"

"Do I have a choice?" he snapped. He crossed his arms across his chest and rocked back and forth on his feet.

"I promise I'll make it quick," Elizabeth vowed, climbing from the bed as quickly as her stiff, weary body would allow.

She pulled the concealing sheet along with her to the nearby bathroom. She locked the bathroom door. She needed this time alone and could not take the chance that Alan would barge in on her.

As she allowed the bed sheet to drop to the tile floor, and as she stumbled into the Jacuzzi shower, Elizabeth glimpsed traces of dried blood on her inner thighs. Even though the massager showerhead shot out a stream of hot water, she stood there shivering. Her stomach turned, and she gagged.

My God! It's true! She concluded in agony. Elizabeth stepped under the strong, steamy, coursing water and began to ferociously scrub her complete body, especially between her legs. With her eyes clenched shut, and tears running down her cheeks, she beat her hand against the stucco wall and stifled the loud sobs which threatened to escape. *How am I going to explain this to Alan?!*

Elizabeth scoured her offensive body and practically drowned herself as she upturned her face into the shower's continuous stream, washing away her anguished tears and stilling her sobs. When she finally forced herself to turn the shower off and step from the tub, she had scrubbed so hard, and for so long, her skin shown red and ached a bit.

The marks of my sin, she concluded, as she wiped steam from the mirror and studied herself with rightful disgust. Her heart breaking, Elizabeth's chest hurt. She loved Alan desperately, and she could not believe she could have so callously let another man take her virginity.

She realized drugs and alcohol were to blame for her acting so irresponsibly. Elizabeth softly banged her forehead against the framed mirror a few times. Then she let it rest forlornly against the steamed glass for a few moments more. She did not want to leave the sanctuary of the bathroom. She did not want to face Alan. She did not want to tell him the awful truth.

Even though she was repulsed by what drugs and alcohol had done to her life, Elizabeth was so weary and fearful that she longingly wished for a packet of coke. She needed something to give her the strength and courage she currently lacked. Elizabeth knew, without a doubt, that cocaine would help her get through the terrible confrontation that awaited her on the other side of the door. She was very ashamed of her weakness.

After a few more, nervous moments, Elizabeth pulled a long, white, terrycloth robe, crested with the Ritz Carlton logo, off a hanger and slid it over her naked body. She forced herself to unlock and open the bathroom door and slowly re-enter the bedroom. She turned the corner and went into the other room.

Alan sat on the couch, which directly faced the entrance to the room, so the first thing Elizabeth saw was his disappointed, somber face. She tightly clutched the robe around her body, relating to Eve in the bible. As Eve had covered her naked body from God's eyes because of her obvious sin, so Elizabeth felt she needed to do so from Alan. She could not bear for him to look at her deceitful figure now.

"Why are you being so bashful all of the sudden?" Alan observantly asked. "Are you trying to be loyal to Jameson now?"

"Wha..what?! No, of course not!" Elizabeth instantly denied. Guilty tears sprang to her eyes as she truthfully explained, "I can...like...hardly stand for you to look at me."

"Why?" Alan dared to inquire, his eyes hard. He already painfully knew the answer in his heart. He could tell by looking at Elizabeth's face. It was as if she had 'cheater' plainly written across her forehead.

"I think you already know the answer to that," Elizabeth replied honestly, with a sob. Weak, she leaned against the wall. Tears continued to stream down her face. "Please give me a chance to try and explain. I know you may hate me, but I have to tell you...to try and make you... understand why."

"Make me understand why you slept with another man?" Alan asked incredulously. "Why you lost your virginity...something you supposedly prized...and that I respected...to this man? You are going to make me understand this? That's rich!" he commented, shaking his head. Standing up, he declared. "Save your breath! It doesn't matter *why* you did what you did. It's just the fact that you allowed another man to touch you in...in that way. You've destroyed everything! Do you realize that?"

"No, Alan! Please don't say that!" Elizabeth zealously pleaded, folding her hands as if in prayer. "I...I love you! Last night never should have happened! It never *would* have happened if I hadn't been so strung out on drugs and alcohol. I can't believe I let another man touch me like that either. I'm disgusted by my behavior. I never would have done anything so horrible to you in a million years. I wasn't in my right mind!"

"My God!" Alan declared in horror, his face registering shock once more. "What are you saying? Did Jameson drug you? Were you raped?" he grasped at straws.

"I…like…so wish I could say this was true," Elizabeth replied in a quiet, ashamed voice, looking down at her bare feet. "Jameson did *not* drug me. I took the drugs freely, and I drank freely…"

"Jesus Christ, Elizabeth! Do I know you at all?!" Alan gasped. "First, I find you in bed with another man, and now…now, you tell me you were doing drugs and drinking. What the hell gives?!"

Before Elizabeth could utter a single word in reply, Alan threw up his hands in protest and started for the door, adding, "Don't bother to answer! I think I've already heard more than enough!"

"No, Alan!" Elizabeth screamed, charging forward after him. "Please don't go! I didn't mean for any of this to happen. Let me tell you the whole story!"

"We have nothing else to talk about!" Alan angrily declared, sending the door flying open. As he stepped out into the hall, he declared, "I hope you and your new lover are very happy." He brought the door closed with a loud slam.

Elizabeth crumpled to her knees in the middle of the floor. "No! No! No!" she exclaimed, beating the carpet with her fists. Her plentiful tears wet the plush fibers. She gagged and choked back bile. She sobbed so hard she could hardly breathe. Her world crashing at her feet, Elizabeth wished she could just roll up in a ball and die. She had never felt so wretched in her entire life.

Chapter 22
Sometimes Love Isn't Enough

Heartbreak is ending a relationship with someone we still truly love.

~ Sissy Marlyn ~

When Elizabeth finally pulled herself together, she packed her stuff, called her driver, and left the hotel at once. She hoped to catch Alan at the airport and possibly talk some more. But at the airport, she found no sign of Alan.

The airport very large, she had no idea what alternate flight plan Alan might have arranged. Her driver secured changes in her itinerary. Originally not supposed to fly out for several more hours, she wanted to leave as soon as possible.

When her flight touched down in Louisville at 1:00 p.m., Elizabeth was glad to have a limo available to drive her home to Bowling Green. Not only did she suffer from jet lag, but her body craved more coke. Miserable and feeling sick, she was in no shape to be driving. She curled up in the back seat of the limo and restlessly slept for the duration of the trip.

Lethargic when she arrived home, she climbed from the limo and lumbered up the sidewalk to the front door. Unlocking the door, she stepped inside. No one expected her for another five hours, since she had caught such an early flight.

Elizabeth was relieved to find that no one appeared to be home. She went to her room, fell into bed with her clothes on, and cried herself to sleep once more. She did not wake until early the next morning.

* * * *

"Hey sleepyhead," her mother addressed Elizabeth as she padded into the kitchen to get some coffee. "Congratulations! Your dad and I watched the awards ceremony. You got home early yesterday, didn't you?"

Elizabeth looked over into her mom's smiling face. Even though she had dark circles under her eyes, she sounded cheery. Entirely *too* cheery; she grated on Elizabeth's frayed nerves. She guessed her dad was still asleep, and she wished her mom was as well. "Yeah. I got home about 2:30," she curtly answered. Pouring a cup of the coffee her mom had already brewed, she sat down at the table.

"You still look tired," her mom remarked. "Are you okay?" She took a seat at the table beside her.

"For sure. I'm fine," Elizabeth lied, sipping her coffee. "Jet lag…you know. You look a little tired too."

"I had a radiation treatment yesterday," she revealed. "But I'm okay," she quickly added. Changing the subject, she asked, "So where was Alan? I didn't see him on television. Would they not let the two of you sit together for some reason?"

"He didn't get to take me to the ceremony," Elizabeth revealed, taking another sip of coffee and looking down at the table. Her heart ached at the mention of his name. "His dad was taken to the hospital in Lexington. So Alan had to fly home," she partially lied.

"Oh…I'm sorry to hear that. Is his dad alright?"

"I don't know. I need to find out. I haven't heard from Alan. I'm going to get some coffee down, go take a shower, and go over to Alan's apartment to see if he's home yet."

"That sounds like a good idea," her mother agreed. "Do you want me to fix you some breakfast?"

"No," Elizabeth replied. "My stomach is still a little woozy. A little air sickness I guess," she lied. What she wanted was a hit of cocaine, but Elizabeth would not allow herself the pleasure.

"Want some Pepto-Bismol?" her mother helpfully asked.

"No. I'll be fine. I'll eat later," Elizabeth promised, finishing the rest of her coffee.

She stood up from the table, went over to the sink, rinsed her cup out, and left it in the sink. She did not want her mom to 'mother' her right now. Her mind was preoccupied with thoughts of Alan and her craving for a certain drug. "I need to motor."

"Okay. It's good to have you home. Congratulations again!" her mother said.

"Thanks," Elizabeth said with a forced smile. She walked over and gave her mom a hug. "It's good to be home."

She headed out of the room to take her shower and get to Alan's. She had to talk to him at least one more time and try and reason with him. She loved him too much to give up without a fight.

* * * *

Slowly pulling her car into Alan's apartment complex parking lot, she parked close to his unit, beside his car. *He's home!* she concluded with a mixture of anxiety and excitement. Her heart beat rapidly as she vacated the car and made her way into the building. Her stomach knotted and her hand shook as she rang the bell and knocked on the door to his apartment.

She held her breath and painfully waited. It seemed to take forever before she heard the 'click' of the deadbolt being released. *Alan is about to open the door*. Elizabeth's heart beat in her mouth.

Suddenly he stood before her in the doorway. His blond hair was still wet and tousled, and he wore no shirt. Elizabeth picked up the fresh scent of Dial soap. *He must have just gotten out of the shower*, she ascertained.

A familiar yearning stirred her body. The warm feeling was quickly extinguished as Elizabeth looked up and noted Alan's cold, hard eyes glaring at her and heard his voice sharply demand, "What do you want?"

"I want to talk," she told him.

228

"We don't have anything else to say to one another," he maintained.

"Alan, please don't, like, shut me out," Elizabeth pleaded.

"I think you've got that a little backwards," he argued. "I think you shut *me* out when you decided to do drugs, drink and sleep with another man."

"That's what I want to talk about...how it all began. It wasn't something I chose."

"It wasn't...something...you...chose?" he slowly repeated, a skeptical look on his face. "What...did the drugs...and alcohol...and Jameson all just mysteriously land in your body without your consent?" he acerbically questioned.

"Can I, like, come in, so I can explain?" she asked.

"You know...I don't really want you in my apartment," Alan stung her by declaring. "What you don't seem to understand is nothing you have to say can possibly change anything. It's too damn late! I don't trust you anymore. And if I don't trust you, then I can't be with you. That's all there is to it! If that breaks your heart, then so be it. Maybe that will make us even!"

If Alan had wielded a knife and slashed her with it, Elizabeth's pain could not have been any greater. "Ow! You're right. You *are* totally breaking my heart," Elizabeth honestly admitted, tears springing to her eyes. "I...I never meant...meant...to hurt you. I love you. Believe that, even if you don't believe another word I have said. I am so ashamed of myself."

Her shoulders began to shake as the tears splashed down her cheeks and her body began to convulse with sobs. Alan knew he could not just shut the door in her face and send her on her way in this state, even though the angry part of him wanted to. "Shit!" he cursed. "Come on in. I can't have you blubbering in the hallway like this."

Elizabeth rushed forward into his apartment. She collapsed on his sofa, dropped her head into her hands and allowed her emotions to get the best of her. After several minutes, she had finally weathered the worse of her emotional breakdown.

She raised her head to find Alan standing across the room from her, leaning against the kitchen counter. "Are you through?" he asked very coldly.

"The question is more like, 'are *we* through'?" she mustered the courage to ask.

"I think I've already answered that," he responded, crossing his arms.

"You can't possibly have stopped loving me overnight. I know I've hurt you terribly and you're very angry, but somewhere under all that, you must, like, still care about me," Elizabeth argued, wiping away fresh tears.

"You're right," Alan hesitantly admitted. "I can't stop loving you just like that," he snapped his fingers. "Believe me, I wish I could. But love and trust are intertwined. Yesterday, when I found you in bed with Jameson...when you admitted to using drugs...I lost all sense of trust in you. So regardless of any feelings still lingering, it's over between us. My feelings are just sad remnants of something past. I'm sure I can put them behind me eventually."

"But can't you learn to trust me again? Won't you at least say you'll try?" Elizabeth pleaded, folding her hands in front of her. "I know I've screwed up all around. But I want to believe that you love me enough to give me another chance. To give *us* another chance."

"Do you plan to keep on acting?" Alan unexpectedly asked.

"Acting?" she questioned. "I...guess. Why?" she asked in bewilderment. "Is that what you are saying it will take for you to give us another chance? Do I need to totally quit acting?"

Elizabeth secretly wondered if she was strong enough to make this sacrifice. Her acting career had become very important to her. If it had not been so important, she never would have gotten involved with drugs in the first place.

"Are you saying that you would give up acting if I asked you to?" Alan tested her.

Elizabeth hesitated for a second. Then she replied, "If that's what it takes to have you in my life again, then I'll give it all up. You're what I want most."

Alan gave her a very hard stare before he shook his head and somberly declared, "You know, you almost had me believing you, but then again, I always did say you were an excellent actress, didn't I…?"

"Alan, I'm not putting on an act." Elizabeth rebutted his unfair criticism.

"Maybe you are and maybe you aren't," he said. "It really doesn't matter. The fact is even if you love me, you love acting just as much, if not more. If you did give it up, I can picture how unhappy you would be. If I really wanted to get even with you for all the pain you've given me, I would snatch it all away from you. But, I'm also smart enough to know that you would succeed in making my life miserable too. And, quite frankly, I've had enough misery from you. I'm not interested in prolonging the agony!"

Elizabeth was shocked anew by Alan's irate, pain-filled words. She had mistakenly thought she was beginning to get through to him. She had allowed herself a weak moment of hope that there might still be a chance for them, but he had swiftly squelched all likelihood for this occurrence.

Elizabeth's eyes automatically welled with tears once more. "I'll always love you," she stated as she stood.

"Yeah…well…sometimes love isn't enough," he tersely replied.

Elizabeth nodded her head, as she started walking for the door. She was unable to speak, because she was too overcome by her emotions again. She had single-handedly destroyed their entire future with a series of mindless acts. Elizabeth had never felt so helpless or forlorn in her entire life. Her heart literally ached with relentless pain. She did not know how she was going to be able to make it without Alan in her life.

She opened the door, walked out into the hallway, and shut it behind her. She quickly made her way to the parking lot and to the sanctuary of her car. She sat in her car and cried and sobbed again for several moments, letting it all sink in once and for all. There truly was nothing else left to say. She had lost the crucial battle, even though she had vigilantly fought for the two of them.

Elizabeth ruefully realized now that she should have been battling for their relationship all along, but it was too late to do anything about it now. The only thing which made her intense hurt even remotely bearable was hoping that, by removing herself from Alan's life, as he seemed to want, Alan would find some measure of peace again. The last thing she wanted to do was hurt him anymore than she already had.

Elizabeth started her car, put it in reverse, pulled out onto the highway and drove away, not only driving back to her house but also out of Alan Michael's life.

Chapter 23
Downward Spiral

Compounding evils is not a way to resolve troubles. But this fallacy is only uncovered with experience.

~ Sissy Marlyn ~

lizabeth drove around for a while getting all of her emotions under control before she went home. She could not bear a barrage of questions from her mother right now. She wanted to escape to the solitude of her room and not come back out for a very long time.

To her relief, when she got home, her mother told her she had received a call from her agent. Elizabeth went directly to her room and called Christopher. She needed to hear something good to take her mind off of the trauma of breaking up with Alan.

"Elizabeth, I have very good news for you," Christopher told her, a happy inflection to his voice.

"Awesome. What's up?" Elizabeth questioned, rubbing her throbbing forehead and swollen eyes.

"Arthur Goldbloom would like to team you and Jameson Thornton for another movie he is producing. Since the public fell in love so much with the two of you as a couple the first time around, he wants to go for round two. I've made arrangements for you to fly to Los Angeles tomorrow morning. They're not wasting any time on this one. They want to get started filming right away."

"And they are filming in LA?" Elizabeth questioned, suddenly more alert.

"Yes. There have been provisions made for proper lodging while you're here. We'll discuss all of the details, including your ample salary, tomorrow when you get into town."

So tomorrow she would be going far away from Bowling Green, Kentucky. Right now, this arrangement sounded like a welcome relief to Elizabeth, even though she would be working with Jameson again. She wanted to be far away from any reminders of Alan Michaels, and the reminders were everywhere here at home. "When will the limo be here to pick me up?" she asked. Tomorrow could not come soon enough.

* * * *

Elizabeth was taken straight to her agent's office as soon as she arrived in LA. They discussed all the details of her contract and where she would be staying. Elizabeth gasped when Christopher said, "You'll be paid $500,000 dollars, plus three percent of gross."

"Wow! That is so totally rad!" she exclaimed. A dull ache filled her heart as she realized she wanted to share this happy news with Alan. "So when do I start filming, and how long will I be in LA?" she fired questions, trying to put her thoughts of Alan back aside.

"You'll start filming day after tomorrow," he told her, adding, "I told you they were not wasting any time with this one. You'll be in the LA area about six months. You'll be living in a secured penthouse just on the outskirts of Marina Del Rey."

"I'm so stoked!" she bellowed. She could not sign the contract fast enough. Needless to say, Christopher Nelson was 'stoked' too, since he would be paid twenty percent of her salary and gross.

* * * *

Taken to her penthouse, her new home for six months, Elizabeth called her parents and told them of the new arrangement. Her mom sounded a bit downtrodden, "Six months is a very long time," she commented.

"For sure. But $500,000 is a lot of money," Elizabeth revealed.

"Did...did you say $500,000?" her mother asked in disbelief.

"Yeah, mom. Needless to say, I'm totally stoked."

"You should be," her mother agreed. "I hope you can come visit some during the time. Because we will sure miss you."

"I don't know," Elizabeth honestly told her. About that time, there was a knock on her door. "Someone's at my door. I need to go," Elizabeth said.

"Okay. Call again soon," her mother said.

"I will," Elizabeth agreed.

She hung up the phone and started to the door as someone knocked a second time, a little harder. Elizabeth looked out the peephole and saw Jameson Thornton standing in the foyer. She unlocked her door and opened it. *I might as well go ahead and face him, because tomorrow we'll be working together again.*

"Hello, Liz," Jameson said in a quiet voice. He seemed a bit uncomfortable.

"Hi, James," she said. "What brings you to my penthouse, and how did you know where I was staying?"

"I called your agent. He had no problem telling me where you were staying. Security had no problem letting me in," he informed her. Then he gingerly asked, "How are you? You left before we could talk the other day. How are things with Alan?"

"Come on in, and we'll, like, talk," Elizabeth said, stepping back a little.

Jameson strolled into the penthouse and Elizabeth shut the door. She led him over to the wine-colored sofa. Two dark wood chairs with wine-colored cushions sat at a right angle at each end of the sofa. A cherry desk sat against the room across the wall. A welcoming Jacuzzi also resided in the room. Various paintings of the ocean and seaside decorated the beige walls. Track lighting and table lamps provided a relaxing glow to the room.

"Nice digs they are putting you up in," Jameson commented, as he moved a cushy, golden pillow out of his way and had a seat on the couch.

"Yeah. For sure, it's nice," Elizabeth agreed. She sat down in one of the chairs. She felt a bit awkward. She knew they needed to talk about what had happened between them but she was not looking forward to this conversation.

"So what did Alan say to you?"

"Not much," Elizabeth admitted. "And he didn't give me much chance to try and explain either. He just walked out. He was so hurt. I can't believe I did something so horrible to him." She paused for a second. Then looking at him with troubled eyes, she inquired, "James, just tell me one thing. What happened the other night? I can't remember anything. I only know I woke up naked in bed with you, and there were signs we had sex."

"Well…neither one of us was feeling any pain," he said. "I guess, between the drugs, alcohol, and the excitement of the day's events, we just got caught up in the moment. I'm sorry, Liz, I should have had more control over the situation. I feel awful about Alan finding us like that."

"Alan's very hurt," Elizabeth confessed, biting her lower lip to keep her emotions in check.

She felt like crying every time she thought of Alan. But she was tired of crying. It served no purpose. "Alan made it totally clear he considers 'us' a lost cause. I totally blew it. There's, like, no going back now."

"I'm so sorry, Liz," James empathized. "Is there anything I can do to help?"

"I'm so sure. Thanks, James," Elizabeth responded, her eyes reflecting her gratitude for his caring companionship. "But there is absolutely nothing that can be done now. It's totally over."

"Well…I think Alan has got to be a major fool not to give you another chance," Jameson stated.

"I guess some things are totally unforgivable," Elizabeth sadly uttered, her voice instantly choking up. "It's impossible for me to imagine what my life is going to be like without him in it. I feel like I've been ripped in half."

"Come here," James directly in a soft voice, opening his arms wide.

Without resistance, Elizabeth stood and moved into his soothing embrace. Jameson tightly hugged her, squeezing her against his robust chest. "I just want you to remember that you aren't alone. I want to help fill in the painful gaps you are feeling right now. You just tell me what I can do to make it better for you, and you can consider it done."

After Elizabeth allowed Jameson to silently hold her for several more moments, she slowly pulled back to look into his compassionate eyes. She surprised him by asking, "You don't...like... have any coke with you, do you?"

"Are you telling me you think that might help?" he asked.

"I don't know if anything would truly help right now, James," she confessed in agony, but quickly added, "But coke might at least totally kill some of the pain. Anything is bound to be better than what I'm, like, feeling right now. I feel half dead, and the part of me that's still alive is totally sliced wide open and raw."

"Well...I'll be glad to share some coke with you again then," he said.

"Awesome," Elizabeth eagerly agreed, sitting down beside Jameson. She was already yearningly looking forward to the high cocaine would undoubtedly provide.

Elizabeth would have struggled to give the drug up if Alan had given her another chance. But he had not wanted her anymore. Now, the only sure joy she had left in her life was coke.

Cocaine would have to fill the gap where Alan's love had been. Or at least provide the illusion of happiness, which was currently so visibly absent from her life. Jameson's supportive friendship and coke's extreme highs were her only viable hope for survival now.

Jameson pulled a vial of the drug from his pant's pocket, and the two instantly got high together. "Thanks, James," Elizabeth happily gasped, as her miracle drug began to instantaneously numb and camouflage some of her unbearable heartbreak.

"I'll always be here for you, Liz," Jameson promised, allowing an arm to drop affectionately around her shoulders and pulling their bodies close together.

Elizabeth turned her head. Jameson's face rested within inches of hers. She could feel his hot, rapid breath and see a glimpse of fire in his eyes. His cologne pleased her nostrils.

Without restraint, Jameson raised a hand to one of her cheeks and caressed her soft skin. When Elizabeth did not pull away, he slowly allowed his hands to travel downward, warmly massaging her shoulders. Elizabeth could tell that Jameson badly wanted to kiss her, and she thought fleetingly about resisting him. However, since Alan no longer wanted her, she could find no logical reason for Jameson not to be allowed to kiss her.

Jameson's needy lips initially made brief contact with hers, but when Elizabeth did not resist, he engulfed her entire mouth. "Liz, let me make you feel whole again," Jameson yearningly pleaded in a hoarse voice.

He vigorously rubbed her shoulders and down the tops of her arms and huskily kissed her, under one earlobe and along the side of her tempting, exposed neck. He seductively added, "I'm not asking for any kind of commitment from you. I just want to bring you comfort. Let me be here for you. I can make you happy again, or at least try my darnedest. I can tell by the way you just responded to my kisses that you want me. Don't fight your impulses, Liz. I can promise you, you won't be sorry."

"James," she hoarsely gasped.

Jameson instantly responded by covering her responsive, wanting lips with his for several more moments. Standing, he requested, "Say my name again, Liz,"

"James," she seductively purred in a low, husky voice.

Jameson reached to scoop her into his arms. Kissing her over and over, making her dizzy with passion and drug-induced euphoria, he carried her down the hallway to the awaiting bedroom.

* * * *

Spent, Jameson warmly held Elizabeth and gazed into her eyes. He reached to affectionately brush away strands of fallen hair that concealed part of Elizabeth's lovely face. "How do you feel?" he asked.

Elizabeth did not know how she felt. A terrible confusion settled upon her. Always believing sex without love morally wrong, Elizabeth had tried to live her life accordingly. However, her steamy copulation with James just now, as well as a few days ago, had absolutely nothing to do with love.

Their physical exchange far from love, Elizabeth had only allowed Jameson's lovemaking as yet another form of mind alteration. She used sex, in addition to drugs, to chase away her overbearing misery over losing Alan.

"You okay, Liz?" Jameson asked, uneasily noting her extended silence.

"I'm fine, James," she finally answered, with a strained smirk. In actuality, she was far from 'fine'. Her mind was hopelessly muddled, but she did not wish to share this reality with Jameson.

"Good," he replied with a pleased smile. "I care about you a lot, Liz. I'm not saying this to pressure you. I know your heart still belongs to Alan. But I'm planning to see to it that you are happier than you've ever been in your life."

Elizabeth seriously doubted Jameson's words. It was not that she believed she could never fall in love with Jameson and be happy. Given sufficient time to get over Alan, she thought this might certainly be possible.

But what Elizabeth could not fathom was being happier with Jameson than she had been with Alan. There had been times when Alan had so perfectly filled Elizabeth's heart that her heart had felt like it was overflowing with happiness and contentment. The illusionary world of cocaine was the only other thing in her life that had come as close.

"Are you hungry?" Jameson's intrusive voice asked.

Elizabeth was not hungry, but she nodded her head anyway. She wanted to get out of bed. Lying here naked with Jameson only served to make her feel more and more guilty, and make her think of the intimacy she had never gotten to share with Alan.

"Do you want to go out someplace and grab a bite to eat, or would you rather I ordered something in?" Jameson asked, affectionately touching her face. His loving touch proceeded to make Elizabeth even more uncomfortable.

"Um...maybe we should go out," she replied.

"Okay," he agreed with a grin. "You jump in the shower. I'm going to go call and make us a reservation at a great restaurant I know of."

"Don't make it too fancy," Elizabeth said. "I don't have many dress clothes with me."

"I only have the clothes that are on the floor over there, and not only are they casual, but also a little wrinkled now. So don't worry about dressing up," he said, bending to give her another kiss.

He slid out from beneath the cushy, maroon comforter then, and unabashedly walked across the room to stoop and pick up his clothes. Even though Elizabeth had been intimate with him for the second time, she almost felt as if she should shield her eyes from his nudity. The bravado from the cocaine was wearing off quickly.

Elizabeth was relieved when Jameson slid his boxer shorts on. Glancing back over his shoulder, he said with a grin, "See you shortly", and to Elizabeth's utmost relief, he made his way out the door.

She quickly vacated the bed and rushed into the large, beige, marble-lined, adjoining bathroom. She turned the lock on the gold handle, walked past the Jacuzzi tub, and opened the door to the glass, octagon-shaped, stand-up shower. Her fingers twisted the ivory handles, sending a spray of warm water down on her – and washing away her sins once more.

* * * *

After dinner, Elizabeth allowed Jameson to spend the night at her penthouse. She simply did not want to be alone. She feared, if she was left alone, her thoughts would turn to Alan again and profound feelings of grief would return.

Before they left for the Culver City Studios the next morning, Elizabeth and Jameson got high together. *Another benefit of letting him spend the night*, Elizabeth concluded with only slight remorse. She started her new job, filming her new movie, with renewed confidence, compliments once again to a boost from her good buddy – cocaine.

* * * *

Before she and Jameson left Culver City that day – twenty-eight acres of back-lot sets and soundstages – Elizabeth walked up to him and whispered in his ear, "How about one for the road?" Her only valid complaint about coke was that its exhilarating effects wore off much too soon. She hardily craved another hit.

Jameson gave her a smile and led her to his dressing room, inside one of the on-site trailers. She climbed the three, metal steps, shut the slim, white door behind her, and locked it. The trailer actually a mobile home, it had a kitchen, living room, bedroom, and even a bathroom onboard.

Jameson took her hand and began leading her toward the back, where the bedroom was. "Where are you taking me?" Elizabeth asked, fighting aggravation.

"You asked for *one* for the road, didn't you?" he mischievously teased.

"That's not what I was talking about?" Elizabeth protested with a staged giggle. She pulled her hand loose and lightly swatted his hand.

"Now…what else could you possibly mean?" He played dumb, pulling her into an embrace and bestowing a long kiss. "Sure you don't want to join me in the bedroom. I can give you a high that way too," he promised, lust in his eyes.

Am I going to have to sleep with him to get more coke? Elizabeth briefly wondered, feeling a mixture of disgust and slight panic. She wanted the cocaine bad enough that she considered Jameson's proposition to get some.

"It's a little late in the day for some coke, isn't it?" he questioned.

"Why?" Elizabeth said, giving him another enticing kiss. "You know it, like, totally frees all of my inhibitions."

"That it does," Jameson agreed with a gleeful chuckle. "Okay. But you can't make a habit of using coke this late in the day. It will keep you from sleeping. Then you'll have to take something different to come down. That will make you groggy in the morning, so you'll need more coke. It can get to be a vicious cycle. One I don't want either one of us to fall into. Okay?"

"For sure. Okay," Elizabeth quickly agreed. "What if I just…like…did one line instead of two, since it's so late?" she diplomatically compromised, taking note of the serious, concerned expression on Jameson's face.

"That sounds like a plan," Jameson eagerly acquiesced, his lips arching into a smile again. "Then after, I'll help you work the extra energy off," he lewdly suggested.

Elizabeth nodded. She would agree to anything right now to get another dose of her favorite mood enhancer.

* * * *

Jameson practically moved into the penthouse with Elizabeth. Staying busy, high, and sexually active slowly mended her broken heart.

Elizabeth eventually planned to cut back on her cocaine use, but right now, it enabled her to not only survive but flourish.

Elizabeth got high at least three times a day now. And sometimes she found excuses to use even more – an excessively bad day, or to celebrate an excessively good day. Jameson expressed his growing concern over her stepped up drug use, but Elizabeth assured him she did not have a problem. She promised Jameson that, very soon, she would curtail her increased usage of cocaine.

If Jameson seemed too concerned and did not seem to want to share the drug, Elizabeth persuaded him otherwise by using sex as the lure. The perfect tradeoff, Jameson enjoyed more and more of Elizabeth's body, and Elizabeth enjoyed more and more cocaine. In Elizabeth's eyes, life was good, even though a severe emptiness engulfed her when she was not high.

* * * *

Three months passed. News of Elizabeth and Jameson's 'hot' romance plastered the front of all the tabloids. This information drew concern from her mother. She called Elizabeth one evening to share her worries.

"What's going on, Elizabeth? You never did say why you and Alan broke up. I know you adored him. Now, it appears you are living in sin with your co-star. You were *not* raised this way."

"Mom…everything is awesome," Elizabeth assured her. She was glad Jameson was not there right now. He had gone out to buy them some more coke.

"How is everything awesome?" she questioned. "I know being a famous actress has got to be a dream come true for you. But you are giving up your morals to be where you are. The newspapers even alluded to you and Jameson abusing drugs. I don't know whether this is true or not, because I know they make up lies. But the last interview I saw you in, you looked kind of out of it."

"Gee…thanks mom," Elizabeth chuckled.

"I'm not trying to criticize you, honey. I just need to know that you are okay."

"I am totally okay, mom," Elizabeth lied. She did not like this conversation. Her mom was laying a guilt trip on her. "Look…I'm sorry…I'd like to talk longer, but I have to be on the set at 5:00 a.m., and I have lines to learn. Just don't believe everything you read, okay?"

"So you aren't living with your co-star? And…you aren't doing drugs?" her mother dared to ask.

"No," Elizabeth lied to her.

Technically, she and Jameson were *not* living together. He had not moved in. He just stayed there a lot. As to the other, Elizabeth was not about to admit her drug use to her mother. There were some things that were better left unsaid. Her use of cocaine was *not* a problem, so there was no need for her mother to know about it.

"I really totally gotta go, mom. I love you," Elizabeth said.

"Your dad and I love you too, Elizabeth. If you are doing anything that you aren't proud of, or goes against your moral upbringing, you can always change your life," her mother quickly added.

"I know, mom. Thanks. Bye," she said. She barely waited for her mom to say bye before she hung up the phone.

Thankfully, Elizabeth looked up to see Jameson come through the door. "Treat time!" he said with a smile, holding up a brown bag.

"Oh yeah. It's totally time for that," Elizabeth agreed, hopping up off the couch. She could not wait to ingest some more of the drug and put aside the guilt her mother had bestowed.

Chapter 24
Quicksand

*What's it mean to be at the point of no return?
Desperation? Back against the Wall? At this point, it's either
sink or swim — swim upstream to find new, clearer water.*

~ Sissy Marlyn ~

About a month later, Elizabeth's too-frequent drug use interfered for the first time with her acting career. She had just greedily sucked a few lines of the wondrous powder up her nostrils, and was in the process of filming a heated love scene with Jameson, when her nose began to bleed.

Naturally, taping had to be suspended until they could stop the eruption of blood. It took some time to get Elizabeth's nostrils to stop profusely bleeding. While Elizabeth squeezed the bridge of her nose, Jameson held a makeshift icepack — ice cubes folded in the middle of a rag — under her nose.

After what seemed an eternity — actually seven minutes — Elizabeth breathed a sigh of relief as the defiant blood finally ceased flowing. Ryan Axman was again the director for this new movie. Elizabeth certainly was not prepared for his insensitive, ensuing wrath.

"Well, I hope you are happy, Elizabeth!" he barked. "We certainly can't film with you looking like that. Go to your dressing room and clean yourself up! And I mean in more ways than one. I told you before that Arthur will *not* tolerate drug use on his set. That *especially* goes for coke heads. Do you understand?"

"Lay off, Ryan!" Jameson growled, stepping in front of Elizabeth.

"I will if she will!" he said, pointing an accusing finger in Elizabeth's direction. "I suggest you take Elizabeth back to her dressing room and have a very long talk with her, Jameson. Or I'll have a lengthy, revealing conversation with Arthur. You catch my drift?"

"Loud and clear," Jameson replied, giving him a perturbed grimace. Then he turned toward Elizabeth and said, "Come on, Liz."

He carefully helped Elizabeth to her feet and wrapped an arm around her as he swiftly led her away. "James, am I, like, in trouble?" Elizabeth timidly asked. She stared up at him in wide-eyed fear, overcome by all that had just transpired.

"We'll discuss it behind closed doors," Jameson answered in a quiet voice. He nervously swept her farther away.

Once inside Elizabeth's trailer, Jameson finally broke his silence, saying, "Liz, we have a problem here. We need to talk about your coke use…"

"What about my coke use?" she snapped, on the defensive. "Anyone can have a nosebleed," she pointed out, sounding a bit angry now. "Ryan can't prove I'm using coke or any other drug."

"Liz, as we've discussed before, Ryan has been in this business for a while. You're not the first cocaine snorter he's seen. Do you have any idea why you had the nosebleed today?"

"How should I know?" she asked, a tinge of anger present in her voice now. She did not like the direction this conversation was taking.

"Your nose bled because coke eats away the membrane inside the nose. This is a sure sign you are using way too much. You've been promising for some time to cut back. Now is the time. You can't afford to have another episode like you did today," Jameson explained.

"But, James, even if I, like, cut my drug use, if I've damaged my nose, how can I be sure I won't totally have another nosebleed?" she questioned.

"Good point," Jameson said with a slight frown on his face. "I have somewhat of a solution."

"What?" she asked, a slight panic building. She feared he would say give up coke altogether. Elizabeth was not prepared to cross this bridge.

"I'll...I'll teach you to freebase," he reluctantly offered. "But smoking coke is much more addictive than sucking it up your nose. You get a more intense high, even though it doesn't last as long. You have to promise to cut your coke use by at least half. Can you agree to that?"

Elizabeth did not want to agree to Jameson's terms. She could not imagine cutting her coke use in half. But since she had thought he was going to ask her to give it up altogether, she was relieved.

"For sure. Okay," she agreed. "You're totally right, James. It's time I curtailed my coke use. Will you show me tonight how to freebase?"

"Yeah," he grudgingly consented. "And I'll give you what I feel should be enough cocaine for the rest of the week. Once that's gone, I won't give you anymore until next week. Is that understood?"

"James, you're talking to me like I'm some sort of lame, drug addict. I can use less coke anytime I want," she argued, seeming offended.

I sure hope that's true, Jameson mused. "Okay," he said. "You need to get out of those bloodstained clothes and get on with the business of acting."

"Aye aye, sir," Elizabeth replied rather sarcastically, giving him a mocking salute.

Jameson hesitantly left her trailer. He went to summon one of the wardrobe and makeup people. He wanted Elizabeth to get back to the set as soon as possible. Time was money in this business.

For the first time since he had happily shared cocaine with Elizabeth, Jameson regretted introducing her to the drug. He would see to it that Elizabeth's coke use did not destroy either Elizabeth's career or her life. He resolved himself to accomplishing this important goal. He hurried off to find Tammy and get Elizabeth a change of clothes.

* * * *

By Wednesday of that week, Elizabeth shuddered to find that her supply of cocaine had grown dangerously low. However, she tried to convince herself this shortage was not really her fault. *I'm just not used to freebasing. That's all*, she concluded.

The highs from freebasing indeed greater than snorting, they did not last near as long and they made Elizabeth crave the drug even more. *That's why I* accidentally *used more than I should have*, she argued.

Elizabeth meticulously divvied up what remained of her stash. She set aside a fixed allocation for each of the remaining days of the week. However, even with sacrifice, trying to use the drug only three times a day again, Elizabeth came up short.

Having completely depleted her supply by Friday morning, she thought in sickened panic, *How can this be?* She frantically searched the paper bag her stash had been in, turning it inside out.

She searched hiding places in her trailer, but also came up blank. All of the cocaine was definitely gone. She plopped down on the sofa, lowered her head, closed her eyes, and put her hands on top of her head.

I can't believe I used it all, she thought in agony. *I have to have at least enough to make it through the day*, she concluded. Arguing in her mind, *I have to be sharp on the set. I can't be preoccupied with unfulfilled cravings. Jameson will understand this.*

However, as she mulled over the fact that Jameson might turn down her request, a wave of incomprehensible fear seized her. She almost felt as if she could not catch her breath. *I can't go almost two days without any cocaine*, she accepted, knowing Jameson was not supposed to give her more until Sunday. *It's not that I'm addicted to coke*, she still tried to convince herself. *It's just that coke is too overpowering to stop taking all at once. James will realize this. He'll help me. He won't let me suffer*, she attempted to convince herself and ward off the panic attack gaining momentum.

Leaving her trailer, she sought out Jameson. She learned he was filming a scene, one she was not in. She went to the soundstage, stood off to the side, and impatiently waited for the filming to wrap up.

When Jameson came off the soundstage, Elizabeth rushed to his side. "Are you, like, headed to your dressing room? I so totally need to talk to you," she told him.

Jameson could tell something was wrong. Elizabeth's voice had a hint of panic in it and she seemed very agitated. "What's up?" he asked, heading toward the exit doors.

"Can we talk in your dressing room?" she asked, not wishing for their conversation to be overheard.

"O…kay," he said, wondering what the secrecy was all about.

They stepped out into the bright California sunshine and headed to Jameson's trailer, a few yards away. Relieved when they arrived there and stepped inside, Elizabeth locked the door behind them, as if she expected someone to barge in on them unexpected.

She took a seat at the small, built-in, kitchen table. "You want something to drink?" Jameson asked, pulling two glasses from some overhead cabinets.

"No," Elizabeth replied.

"Okay," he said, leaving the glass he had retrieved for her on the counter.

He opened up the small refrigerator, pulled out a carton of orange juice, and poured some of the beverage in his glass. Then he came over to the table and sat down across from Elizabeth. "So what can I do for you?" he asked, knowing Elizabeth wanted something.

"Um…" she hesitated. "I…like…I used all of the cocaine you gave me. I need a little bit more to tide me over until Sunday."

Jameson took a large swig of his juice. Swallowing he said, "I gave you a very generous supply. I expected you to have some left over. Not come up short. You're supposed to be cutting back; remember?"

"I have been cutting back," Elizabeth argued, rubbing her arms as a chill ran through her. "Freebasing is different; that's all. The high doesn't last as long, so I used more than what I should have."

"And you craved it more," Jameson also pointed out, turning his glass up again.

"Okay. It does for sure make you crave it more. I can't go through the next few days without any coke. I'll go through withdrawal," she pointed out, fear in her eyes.

"I'm not so sure that would be such a bad thing," Jameson pointed out, downing the rest of the juice and sitting his empty glass on the table with a clatter.

"Come on, James. This isn't funny. I need your help," Elizabeth half-pleaded, rocking a bit in her seat.

"Believe me, Liz. I'm not laughing," Jameson said, eyeballing her with a hard stare. "I can't help you right now. I have absolutely no coke on hand."

"None?" Elizabeth questioned with doubtful eyes.

"None," Jameson repeated with emphasis. He could tell that Elizabeth did not believe him. "I gave you all I had. As I said, I thought it would be plenty."

"Well…when can you get some more?" Elizabeth asked, feeling as if the oxygen in the room suddenly depleted.

"Not until after work today. I can go down on Sunset Strip and get some from my buddy there."

"You'll get some," Elizabeth verified, biting her lower lip. She contemplated the fact that she would have to go through the rest of the day without any coke. *But at least I'll have more tonight*, she thought with a slight measure of relief. Later today was better than none until Sunday.

"Yeah. I'll get some," he agreed, his lips a hard, disapproving line. "But next week you've got to make what I give you last. You've got to start cutting back. I know freebasing gives an incredible high, but you can't start using more and more. The stuff will kill you eventually. Look at John Belushi."

"I promise I'll cut back," Elizabeth assured him again.

At this point, she would promise Jameson anything to get more coke. She knew today was going to be hard, but she would struggle through. She could not wait for the day to end and Jameson to get her more of her wonder drug.

Chapter 25
The Turning Point

Life is a cycle from birth to death. And sometimes it's a choice between life and death.

~ Sissy Marlyn ~

*E*lizabeth managed to successfully struggle through a complete week of drastically reduced coke use. However, Friday, she awoke nauseated and weak. She naturally assumed her body was retaliating because she radically withheld the drug it so loved. Almost as if proving her point, her stomach somewhat settled when she finally allowed herself to freebase later that day.

Saturday morning, she awoke nauseated, dizzy and weak again. Now, Elizabeth wondered if she might be coming down with some bug. She sent Jameson to a nearby pharmacy for some Pepto-Bismol. This remedy helped a bit, although she still felt a bit ill.

As soon as Elizabeth awakened Sunday morning, she ran to the bathroom and hurled. Jameson stood in the doorway to the bathroom and shared his concern, "Liz, you might need to see a doctor."

"I'll be fine, James," she assured him with more confidence than she felt. The whole room seemed to be spinning. She held a cold washrag to her forehead and lumbered back to the bed. She laid flat on her back and tried not to move. "Just get me some more Pepto-Bismol; okay?" she half begged.

Jameson left the room to go and get the pink bottle. It had helped yesterday, so maybe it would today as well. Jameson knew Elizabeth was still freebasing, and she had not stopped taking coke cold turkey. He was surprised she was so ill. *Maybe she is right. Maybe she just has some type of bug.*

He hurried into the kitchen, scooped the bottle of Pepto-Bismol off a shelf in the refrigerator, and hurried back to the bedroom. He wanted to help Elizabeth feel better. He did not like that she was sick.

* * * *

Monday morning, Elizabeth woke feeling somewhat better. *It must have been one of those twenty-four hour things*, she told herself again.

About an hour into filming, however, all at once, the room began to spin violently, and before Elizabeth knew it, she lie flat on her back staring up into the concerned faces of Jameson and Ryan. *Damn! I fainted*, she concluded. She had freebased only a short while ago, so Elizabeth was even more surprised by her odd circumstances.

"Liz, are you okay?" Jameson asked, slowly helping her to sit.

Elizabeth managed a meager nod, but even this small movement made her woozy all over again.

"She's been sick all weekend," Jameson explained to Ryan.

"Well, then perhaps she needs to see a doctor," Ryan strongly suggested.

"I think that might be a good idea," Jameson agreed.

"N...no," Elizabeth started to disagree. However, the small energy it took for her to talk and move her head again caused her to swoon once more.

"Liz," she heard Jameson calling. However, he sounded very far away, and she could not make herself answer him. Darkness came at her from all directions, as she slipped back into a state of unconsciousness.

* * * *

When Elizabeth finally awakened again, an unfamiliar, older man with bifocals slowly came into focus. As she gained further control of her senses, she sluggishly realized she was lying completely on her back in a strange room.

251

"Well, welcome back, young lady," the stranger greeted, very slowly helping her sit up.

He made sure her back was fully supported by the wall behind her before releasing her. He still hovered very close, however, just in case she should unexpectedly faint once more. "I'm Doctor Phillips. Jameson Thornton wisely brought you to my office. He informed me that you passed out more than once earlier. Are you still feeling faint?"

"Um...a little...I guess," she stuttered in bewilderment, still trying to shake the prevalent fog from her brain.

Elizabeth studied the man's white coat, stethoscope, and her surroundings for a few moments. There was a sink, some counters with cotton swabs and other medical items, and health information charts on the walls. She realized now that she sat on an examining table in a doctor's office.

"When's the last time you ate, young lady?" the physician began his standard questions, his eyes studying Elizabeth's pale face intensely.

"Uh...breakfast," Elizabeth answered. It had not been much – some toast and an orange – but Elizabeth had eaten this morning.

Cocaine suppressed her appetite. But, Elizabeth always made sure she ate something at least three times a day. Actually, she believed she chose rather healthy meals, even if they were not large. Elizabeth ate a lot of salads and fruits.

"Okay. What exactly did you eat for breakfast?" Doctor Philips continued his thorough interrogation.

"About the same thing I have every morning for breakfast, but I don't usually faint afterward," Elizabeth responded rather evasively and with some aggravation.

She certainly did not believe that her food intake had anything to do with her fainting spells. Elizabeth quickly added her own diagnosis, "I think the problem is I've had some sort of virus the last couple of days. I've been sick at my stomach each morning. It has made me weak, so I fainted. I don't think it's any big deal. James shouldn't have brought me in here to waste your time."

"Now why don't you let me decide if you're wasting my time or not," the doctor suggested, patting her arm and giving her a small grin. He promptly continued his insightful line of questioning. "Now regarding this virus you think you have, have you been sick all day or just in the morning?"

"It's just been in the morning. I usually feel much better later in the day," Elizabeth answered.

There was slight hostility in her voice. She was actually angry at Jameson for having brought her to this doctor. Elizabeth truly believed that her mysterious illness tied exclusively to her drastic cutback of her coke use. However, she certainly did not intend to share this theory with Doctor Phillips. Elizabeth just wanted to somehow convince him there was nothing he could do for her, so she could leave his office.

"Uh huh," she heard the doctor respond. Then he followed up with yet *another* question, "So when was the last time you had your period?"

Elizabeth wondered why in the world he would ask her such a bizarre question. *What does my monthly cycle have to do with anything?* "I guess it was about a week ago," Elizabeth grudgingly answered, growing more frustrated by the minute.

"And how many days did it last? Was it a regular, heavy or scarce flow?" Doctor Phillips continued to Elizabeth further dismay.

"If you want to know the truth, the last few months, I haven't really had a normal period. I've just spotted a little for a few days, and that was it," Elizabeth replied rather snappishly.

She figured her messed up monthly cycles were also directly related to both her increased and decreased drug use. The strange irregularities had not especially bothered her. Elizabeth figured that once she finally ended her drug use altogether, her periods would no doubt return to normal.

"And you are on the pill?"

"Y...e...s," she answered rather sassily, blowing out her mouth in aggravation. "What's all this got to do with anything?" she challenged.

"Maybe nothing. Maybe everything," the doctor vaguely commented. "I think we definitely need to run a pregnancy test."

Elizabeth's mouth dropped open and she instantly exclaimed, "Wh...what?! No, doctor. I don't think so. I said I'm on the pill. I can't be pregnant!" She argued, half chuckling at the absurdness of his diagnosis.

"Miss Warren, I'm sorry to tell you that the pill is not always 100 percent preventative. And if you happened to miss a dose somewhere along the way, then the chances of a rare pregnancy increase even more. However, we won't really know anything for sure until I get the results of a pregnancy test," the doctor staunchly maintained.

"This is ridiculous! I told you I had my period the last few months. You can't have a period and be pregnant," Elizabeth contested.

"What you told me, Miss Warren, was that you spotted for a few days each month. That is not really all that rare for a lot of women in their first trimester of pregnancy," Doctor Phillips informed her. "But…there is no reason to get all upset. I'll send Nurse Williams in, and she will draw some blood. Then we'll know for sure."

The doctor turned, walked across the room, and opened the door. "The nurse will be right in," he told Elizabeth. He walked out of the room, softly closing the door behind him.

Elizabeth stared at the closed door. She brought her hand up to her open mouth and rested it there. *It couldn't possibly be true, could it?* Her stomach turned again now, but it churned from anxiety. She *had* on occasion missed a birth control pill here and there. Her focus had been on using cocaine, not on keeping up with pills.

The door opened and a chubby woman in nurse's scrubs with Peanuts' characters on them came into the room. With a smile, she approached Elizabeth and said, "I'm here to draw a little blood, honey."

As Elizabeth watched the nurse prepare her arm, she could not believe this scenario was unfolding. As the air in the room seemed to grow thin, she sucked in a deep breath and tried to console herself. *It's okay. I'm sure I'm not pregnant. What else would the doctor think? He's just grasping at the first logical, normal explanation for my symptoms. He doesn't know about my drug use. That's probably what has my cycle whacked out too. As to the fainting and upset stomach, I'm sure it's just a bug. It has to be. When the test comes back negative, the doctor will diagnose me with a virus. Then I can finally get out of here. And I'm not coming back!*

With this agenda in mind, Elizabeth irritably allowed the nurse to draw some blood. After the nurse left the room, she waited impatiently for Doctor Phillips to return with the results on her blood test. She wished she had some cocaine with her to settle her nerves. *Another reason I'll be glad when I can leave here.* She looked at a clock on the wall and nervously counted each *long* minute.

* * * *

Doctor Phillips had graciously allowed Jameson to wait in his private office while he examined Elizabeth. He realized if Jameson waited in the regular waiting room, he would be constantly mobbed by curious admirers and fans. The doctor kindly walked Elizabeth there after her examination was complete.

As soon as Jameson heard the doorknob turn, he anxiously swiveled his head and watched as Elizabeth and the doctor came into the room. Doctor Phillips led Elizabeth to the chair beside Jameson. He watched as she had a seat. Then he walked around and sat down behind his desk.

"Well…what's the diagnosis?" Jameson asked the doctor.

"I'd like to know that myself," Elizabeth added.

Jameson noted that Elizabeth was still very pale, although he was relieved to see that some of her color had returned.

"I'm assuming the two of you are a couple…as is reported in the papers and on television," Doctor Phillips stated, making a steeple out of his index fingers.

"We are," Jameson replied. "What does that have to do with anything?" he questioned, confusion etched all over his scrunched face.

"Well…it seems Miss Warren's problem is….she's pregnant," the doctor relayed, tapping his pointed fingers against his bottom lip.

"P…pregnant?" Jameson repeated. His eyes became quarter size and darted from the doctor's face to Elizabeth's. Her mouth had dropped open, and the color was fading from her face once again. "Liz, are you okay?" he asked, squeezing her hand.

"I…how can I be pregnant?" she asked in a small voice.

"I'd kind of like to know that too," Jameson agreed. "She…she's on the pill," he told the doctor, as if his diagnosis could not possibly be correct.

"So she told me," the doctor said. "The pill is not 100 percent, Mr. Thornton. Or perhaps Miss Warren missed a dose. Regardless, she

255

is expecting. I'd like to set her up an appointment with an OBGYN ASAP."

"Yeah," Jameson agreed, sounding very distracted. He noted Elizabeth's hand was shaking. "Could you please give us a moment alone?" he asked Doctor Phillips.

"Of course," he said. He stood and started walking toward the door. "Take all the time you need. I'll have my nurse schedule an appointment for Elizabeth with an OBGYN. She'll leave the card for you at the desk. Just pick it up on your way out."

"Okay," Jameson mumbled, only half listening. He was relieved when the doctor left the room. "Liz, it's going to be okay," Jameson said as soon as they were alone.

"How can it be okay?" she questioned.

It suddenly felt as if a freight train were running through her head. Elizabeth desperately wished she had some cocaine to smoke right now to calm her nerves. She dropped her head and gasped for air, as the panicked thought occurred to her, *How can I take cocaine if I'm pregnant?*

"Look...I'm here for you, Liz. This is my responsibility too," Jameson reassured her, rubbing her shoulders. "I'm sure Doctor Phillips can recommend a good abortion clinic. You probably will only have to miss a day or so of work."

Elizabeth's head snapped back up. She stared at Jameson's face in disbelief. He talked about abortion as if Elizabeth would just be alleviating some minor annoyance. Unfortunately, in strong contrast to Jameson, being pregnant to Elizabeth meant she was now carrying a living being.

"I...I can't have an abortion, James," Elizabeth muttered, protectively dropping her hands over her abdomen."

"Sure you can," he encouraged, giving her a persuasive squeeze. "You just haven't thought all this through yet. I know it's a big shock. It is for me too. But you really have no other choice if you consider everything. After all, you are filming a movie. Arthur and Ryan won't be happy if you are noticeably pregnant. And if that isn't enough, would you really want to bring a child into this world who was retarded or deformed, or maybe both? You know you've been using cocaine. That's bound to do a number on an unborn child. So you see, abortion is best for everyone."

Elizabeth could not believe how competent Jameson's arguments for abortion sounded. *God, what if I* have *damaged this baby because of my drug use? What then?* However, the thought of disposing of a child severely disturbed Elizabeth. She had done some pretty horrible things since getting mixed up with cocaine. *Could I possibly add* killing *to the list?*

"Liz, why don't I go and talk to the doctor for *us*?" Jameson suggested, breaking the long, pensive silence.

"No," she slowly replied. Bashfully glancing at Jameson's serious face and then back at her abdomen, she said, "I...I totally need some time to think. It's just too overwhelming right now."

"I know," Jameson agreed, squeezing her shoulder. "But you'll have time to think, Liz. It's not like they are going to do the abortion today. This isn't even an abortion clinic. I'm just going to get all the arrangements made. You won't have to worry about anything."

Jameson's persistent, carefree attitude toward the impending, merciless murder of their child made Elizabeth's blood run cold. In direct response, her body shook. "James, I just for sure want to get out of here. Can we please just leave?" Elizabeth pleaded.

"Okay...sure," he reluctantly agreed. He rose to his feet and offered her a hand. Pulling her to her feet, he placed a staunch arm around her back. "I'll take you home. We can always make plans tomorrow."

"Yeah...tomorrow," Elizabeth deceptively agreed.

Jameson opened the door and they stepped out into the hall. Nurses smiled at them, and stepped out of their way, as they made their way down the hallway. Jameson led Elizabeth to a back doorway out of the building, hidden from nosey eyes.

Elizabeth felt a flicker of relief. She realized this feeling was to be short-lived. She needed to make a decision about this baby, and she needed to make it quickly. Outside, she collapsed in the back of the limo, her mind tangled in agonizing turmoil. *Acting or the baby. Jameson or the baby. Cocaine or the baby.* These thoughts all swirled in her head. She shut her eyes and lay her head back against the seat, trying unsuccessfully to block everything out. She had never been so confused or torn in her life.

* * * *

When they walked into the penthouse, Jameson noticed they had a message on the answering machine. It was Elizabeth's father. He sounded upset.

Elizabeth called home at once, even though she did not really want to talk to anyone. Her father answered the phone, "Daddy, what's wrong?" Elizabeth asked him.

"It's your mother, Elizabeth. Th...things aren't good."

"What do you mean by that?" she asked, her attention suddenly riveted to the phone and her dad's voice.

"She...she's in the hospital, Elizabeth. It...it's only a matter of time. How soon can you get a flight home?"

"My God!" Elizabeth gasped. She lowered the phone for a minute and grasped her head. *When it rains, it pours!*

"What?" Jameson asked, coming over beside her.

Without answering him, Elizabeth put the phone back up to her ear. "I'm sorry, daddy," she said, choking back a sob. "I'll get a flight as soon as I can."

"I'll see you soon, sweetie," her dad said.

Elizabeth hung up the phone and collapsed into Jameson's arms, bawling like a baby.

"What?" he asked again.

"My...my mom. Sh...she's dying. I need to fly to Bowling Green," Elizabeth explained.

"Your...mom? What happened to her?" Jameson asked.

He did not even know Elizabeth's mother had cancer. She had never told him. They talked very little about their personal lives. Their relationship was mostly physical in nature. Their conversations had to do with their careers.

"My mom has cancer," Elizabeth revealed now.

"So you are going to fly home?" Jameson asked.

"Yeah. No duh," she replied, giving him a look of incredulousness.

She could not believe Jameson would ask this question. But then again, she could not believe how nonchalant he had been about suggesting she have an abortion either.

"O...okay," he agreed. "I'll let Ryan know what's going on. I can get a private jet chartered for you," he offered, being helpful once more.

"I...I'd appreciate that," she said.

"Okay. I'll do that," Jameson said. "You go sit. I'll arrange everything."

Elizabeth did not argue. She was beginning to feel absolutely awful. Her body craved coke in the worst way. *But I'm pregnant*, she reminded herself. *I can't do that.*

She wearily took a seat on the couch. Jameson made all the arrangements for her to fly home, and also true to his word, he called Ryan and let him know Elizabeth had a family emergency.

Elizabeth went into the bedroom and threw a few items in a small suitcase. She actually still had clothes at home she could wear. Jameson rode in the limo with her to the airport. "Do you want me to come with you," he half-heartedly offered.

"No," she replied.

She really did not want him with her. Jameson's biggest form of support to Elizabeth was providing her with coke, and she did not want this support from him right now. She fought not to think of the drug, but she found it virtually impossible not to. *No more though*, she told herself again. *I can't do that to this poor baby.*

"I'll see you soon, Liz," Jameson said, giving her a kiss before she hopped on the chartered jet. "Call me if you change your mind about me being there with you, and I'll fly to Kentucky."

"I'll be fine," she said, even though she had no confidence in her statement. *I want some coke*, her mind screamed. "Bye, James," she said, and boarded the plane. *Goodbye coke. I don't have any with me. So I can't take any.*

As the plane taxied down the runway, Elizabeth was seized by a crushing panic. *I can't believe I don't have any coke with me. How will I be able to stand it?* Once again, as in the limo earlier, she closed her eyes and leaned her head back against the seat, trying to shut out the voices in her head and the rest of the world at large.

* * * *

A few short hours later, Elizabeth arrived at Greenview Regional Hospital in Bowling Green. Elizabeth began to suffer the first, undeniable effects of withdrawal. Her body ached from head to toe, and she shook with chills.

"Sweetie, are you okay?" her dad asked as he approached her in the hospital corridor.

"I'm fine, daddy," she lied. "I'm tired from jet lag, that's all," she excused.

"You're pale," he pointed out.

"Am I?" she asked. "I'll duck in the bathroom and put on a little blush." If her dad was concerned, Elizabeth knew her mother would be as well. And causing her mother concern was the last thing she wanted to do.

Elizabeth darted into the closest bathroom. As she approached a sink, she held on to the counter and noted her white completion and the dark circles under her eyes in the mirror. She pulled forth a cosmetic bag from her purse and attempted to disguise her fatigue. Her hands shook as she applied the makeup. She located a small container of Ibuprofen and washed down two pills with some water cupped in her hands.

A few moments later, she vacated the bathroom and joined her dad in the hospital corridor again. "Let's go see mom," she requested. She tried to ignore the antiseptic smell. It turned her stomach.

"She's been wanting to see you," her dad told her, leading her on down the hall. They passed busy doctors, nurses, and orderlies. "I wanted to call a few days ago, but she wouldn't let me. Then this morning, she took a turn for the worst. Her doctor says she could go anytime now," he shared, tears coming to his eyes.

They stopped shy of an open doorway, and her father pointed to the name on the wall: Gladys Warren. It was her mom's room. "I'll let you have some time alone with her," her dad said. "I'll be right here if you need me."

"Okay," Elizabeth agreed a little unsurely.

She took a deep breath and tried to settle her crawling nerves. She wished to high heavens she could go and get high now. She always could face anything when cocaine accompanied her. *You can't have any more!* she determinedly reminded herself.

Elizabeth forced her legs to walk through the open doorway and into her mother's room. Her mother lay in a hospital bed with an IV stuck in her arm. Her eyes were closed and her mouth was open as she seemed to fight for air. Tears came to Elizabeth's eyes. She could tell that what her father and the doctors had said was true – her mother was slipping away.

Elizabeth quickly approached the bed and carefully slipped her mother's hand into hers. Her mother stirred and opened her eyes. Her lips curved into a smile. "Elizabeth," she uttered in a small, weak voice.

"Yeah, mom. I'm here," she said, giving her hand a gentle squeeze.

"It's so good to see you. But...you look tired, honey. I...I need to talk to you," she muttered.

"Okay," Elizabeth agreed.

She released her mom's hand and used both hands to pull a chair up to the bed. Then she sat down. Her legs had felt weak. When she reached for her mom's hand again, her hand shook.

"Are you nervous? Your hand is shaking," Elizabeth's mom noted, giving her daughter's hand a weak squeeze this time.

"I'm...it's the jet lag, mom." She used the same lie she had told her dad. "Don't worry about me. I'm fine."

"But I do worry about you, Elizabeth," her mother uttered. "That's what I want to talk about."

"I don't want to talk about me," Elizabeth argued.

"Elizabeth...I have no strength to argue. Okay?" her mother said, her glazed eyes staring into Elizabeth's tired ones.

"I don't want to argue," Elizabeth agreed.

"Good," her mom said. She took a labored breath and said, "Please just let me talk...and...and listen. Okay?"

"For sure. Okay," Elizabeth concurred.

"I'm worried about your lifestyle." She paused and took another deep breath. With a grimace of pain, she continued. "I love you, Elizabeth."

"I love you too, mom," she said, squeezing her hand and fighting tears.

"I...know," she said. "So will you do something for me then?"

"Anything," Elizabeth promised, some tears escaping and rolling down her cheeks.

"I want you to...to be happy."

"I am happy," Elizabeth tried to assure her.

"No...you're...not," her mother argued. "You love acting, and you have that. But what have you given up for it? The man you love, your morality. True happiness doesn't...come...from...from things, Elizabeth. It comes from loving yourself and loving others. I want you to find yourself again...and...find true love. Can you do that for me?"

Elizabeth's shoulders began to shake and she began to sob. She stood from the chair, wrapped her arms around her mother and hugged her. Her heart was breaking. Her mother's dying wish was for her to get her life straightened out. She needed to do this, both for her mother and for the unborn grandchild her mother would never know.

"I promise you, mom," Elizabeth pledged, giving her a fleeting kiss on her cold lips. "I'm going to seek true happiness. My life is going to change. This I promise you."

"Good," her mother said, another smile coming to her mouth. "Now, can you call your father in here too?"

"For sure," she said.

She released her mom and she walked over to the door. Sticking her head out, she called to her dad, who leaned against the wall in the corridor. Her dad came forward into the room.

A half hour later, Elizabeth's mother passed away. Elizabeth and her father held one another and shared tears. Elizabeth heard her promise to her mother ringing in her head. Her brain countered, screaming for more cocaine. Her body aches and weariness also shouted for more of the drug. But Elizabeth resigned herself, *No! It's time to change. For mom and for this baby. And...for me.*

Chapter 26
Rehab

Life is about making choices.
Some of them are tough, but they can change our lives.

~ Sissy Marlyn ~

After Elizabeth helped her dad make funeral arrangements, she went back to the hospital. This time she went to the psychiatric unit. The clip-clop of her sandals on the white, polished floor echoed in her head as she approached a middle-aged woman sitting behind a desk in the center of the floor. A blond in a white coat, with pallid floors and walls all around her, this woman looked ill herself. *Can I really do this?* Elizabeth questioned.

"Can I help you," the woman asked, studying her with icy blue eyes.

"I...I hope so," Elizabeth said, her heart beating in her mouth as she closed the rest of the distance. Standing right in front of this creepy stranger, Elizabeth mumbled, "I...I think...I think...I might...I might be addicted to...to cocaine."

She heard the words tumble out of her mouth, and a feeling of immense relief washed over her. But at the same time, Elizabeth wondered, *Did I really say that?* Like a near death experience, she felt removed from her own body, hovering near and watching.

"Okay," the woman said in a calm voice, reaching for something under the counter. "We do offer excellent treatment programs for drug addiction here. We offer both inpatient and outpatient care. The first step is you being evaluated by one of our psychiatrists. I need for you to fill out these information sheets, sign the consent form, and we'll have someone see you."

"Alright," Elizabeth murmured, taking a clipboard from the woman's outstretched hand.

The woman pointed to a few empty chairs by the wall. Elizabeth walked over to the chairs, sat down in one, and began filling out the paperwork. She found it very hard to be honest on the questionnaire, but she was truthful anyway. She admitted to freebasing and to doing cocaine several times a day. She also admitted to an intense craving for the drug at this very moment.

When she finished filling out the questionnaire, she stared at the blank signature line for several long moments. Breaking out in a sweat and feeling nauseated, she released the pen from the clip and signed her name, consenting to be evaluated by a psychiatrist and possibly hospitalized.

She stood and took the clipboard back over to the lady at the desk. "Thanks," the woman said with a slight smile as she took the clipboard back from Elizabeth. "You can have a seat again. I'll process your paperwork, and we'll get you in with a doctor as soon as possible."

Elizabeth unsurely glanced at the empty chair behind her. Then she briefly glanced up the hallway in the direction she had come. *It's still not too late to change my mind and leave*, she mulled over.

Struggling with herself, she forced herself to turn, walk back over to the chairs, and sit back down. As she waited for a doctor to see her, she tapped her legs, squirmed in the chair, and watched a clock on the wall, counting the minutes and even seconds. She listened to the fluorescent lights annoyingly buzzing overhead, staring up at them occasionally as if her stare could quiet them. Debating leaving over and over, she mused, *Maybe I'm doing the wrong thing*. However, Elizabeth once again remembered her dying promise to her mother, and she also stroked her abdomen, reminding herself of the innocent life she now needed to protect.

"Miss Warren," the woman finally called, breaking her pensiveness and causing her to jump. "The doctor will see you now."

She stood, followed the young lady through some double doors, down another colorless, antiseptic-smelling hallway, and into an office. When the woman vacated the room and pulled the door closed behind her, Elizabeth shuddered and fought for air. The room suddenly seemed much too small.

"Elizabeth Warren," a baldheaded man with a gray mustache, wearing a suit and tie, said with a smile.

He sat behind a large desk with his hands folded over his abdomen. Sunlight streamed through partially opened mini-blinds across the room. It seemed to spotlight a framed Psychiatry degree that hung on the wall above this man's head. "I'm Doctor Wallace Cleaver. I'm a huge fan of yours. I'm looking forward to your next movie," he told Elizabeth with an admiring grin.

"Thanks," she said, looking down at her feet in embarrassment. *Everyone knows who I am.* She wondered in shame, *Will the lady who led me here jump on the phone and tell all her friends that she met the movie actress, Elizabeth Warren, and that she is addicted to cocaine?*

"Would you like to have a seat? I think the two of us need to have a chat," the doctor directed.

Elizabeth skittishly looked back up at him and hesitantly walked toward his desk. She took a seat in one of the chairs in front.

"So I take it you got caught up in some of the Hollywood drug fair," the doctor commented.

"Yeah. For sure," she admitted, looking him in the eye. She did not plan to hold anything back. She wanted to conquer her drug habit, and conquer it now. She was ready to turn her life around and take control of it again. She wanted all the ugliness gone. "There...there's something else you should know, doctor," she said, sheepishly lowered her eyes again. "I...I'm pregnant." This statement really sounded funny on her lips, but it was true. As hard as it was for Elizabeth to accept, she *was* going to have a baby. There would be no abortion. She had made up her mind about this as well.

"Oh...I see," the doctor stated.

"So...that brings up a question," Elizabeth admitted, biting her lower lip.

"Okay. Ask away," he invited, throwing his open palms out.

"Will...will this...my...my baby... Man, this is hard. I need to know if my baby will be born retarded or deformed because of my drug use."

"It's a good question," he stated, his lips pursed. "Unfortunately, I can't answer that for you. Using drugs while pregnant obviously does affect the fetus. A lot depends on how far along you are. Do you have any idea?"

"I don't," Elizabeth confessed, exhaling with frustration. "I only found out about being...being pregnant earlier today."

"Well...here are the facts," he stated, rolling a pencil between his hands. "In the early stages of pregnancy, the chances aren't as great of the baby being damaged by your drug use. In fact, if you stop now, I would say there is a good chance you might be able to deliver a healthy baby. Only time will tell. But you can't continue to use cocaine."

"That I know," she agreed, nodding her head and ringing her hands with anxiety. "It's why I'm here."

"So you are admitting you are addicted to cocaine?" the doctor inquired, pointing the lead of the pencil in her direction.

"Y...yeah," Elizabeth agreed. "If you had some coke available right now, I would for sure have a horrible time not taking it," she confessed. "I need help."

"You've made the first step. You've admitted you have a problem, and you are asking for help. I'd like to help you," he said, dropping the pencil back in a holder on the desk. It settled with a clunk.

"What do I need to do?" Elizabeth asked.

"You are probably not going to like the answer to that question," he replied, pushing back in his desk chair and sitting up straight.

"Why? What is it?" she asked, giving him an apprehensive stare.

"I think you need inpatient care. That means you check into the hospital and stay for several weeks, or maybe even a month or so. I don't know how that jives with your Hollywood schedule, but this is the treatment I am suggesting. You need to be completely isolated from cocaine for a while. And you won't be in Hollywood. Am I wrong?"

"No...you aren't wrong," Elizabeth admitted. "Cocaine is available everywhere there." She looked down at her lap again and told him in a quiet voice. "There's just one thing.... My...my mom died today."

"Oh...I'm sorry," he extended his sympathies.

"I'd like to be there for her visitation and funeral. Can I check myself in afterwards? I don't have any cocaine with me. I left it all behind in California."

"The next few days are going to be hard. Death is depressing to deal with anyway, and your withdrawal from cocaine will make you even more depressed," the doctor pointed out. "Not to mention you will be experiencing painful physical symptoms to the withdrawal. How will you handle the depression and pain without having more cocaine?"

"How will I handle it here?" she asked. "I can't take anymore. I need to stop for the baby's sake. I feel like crap right now, if you want to know the truth. And I'd kill for a hit of coke. But I'm not going to do it."

The doctor scratched his chin. "You sound like a very determined young lady," he stated. "However, I still think the best advice I can give you is to admit yourself *now*. Don't take the chance of letting the addiction win. The craving for coke will eat at you, and as you feel worse and worse, it will get harder and harder to not seek some more out. No matter how resigned you are now."

Elizabeth quietly studied the beige, weaved carpet at her feet for a few moments. This psychiatrist was the expert. She did fear her craving for coke. It was very strong right now, and he was saying it would get worse. "O...okay," she agreed. "I need to call my father and let him know what's going on."

Doctor Cleaver pushed his phone across the desk toward Elizabeth. "Be my guest," he said. "You're making the right decision, young lady."

I hope so, she contemplated, picking up the receiver and dialing her dad's number.

* * * *

As soon as Elizabeth's agent found out about her drug addiction and subsequent hospitalization, he released an official, albeit completely bogus, media release. The media was informed that Elizabeth was being treated for an addiction to painkillers. She supposedly developed this addiction following a very painful, wisdom tooth extraction and infection.

Elizabeth's agent's tireless goal was to obtain pity for Elizabeth from her many fans, instead of disdain for having thoughtlessly dawdled in the nefarious world of cocaine. Elizabeth hated that her agent was lying. But she also prayed that his persistent damage control would keep her from being fired from her new movie. Elizabeth genuinely believed she would need her job more than ever. After all, she would soon have a child to support.

And it seemed Elizabeth would be raising her child alone. She had heard nothing at all from Jameson. He obviously was distancing himself from her, and Elizabeth was actually fine with that. She suffered alone in the hospital, tirelessly fighting her overwhelming addiction.

She went through bouts of severe depression. She had angry outbursts. She was overcome with intense cravings. Her body ached relentlessly, and she had bouts of sleeplessness.

Elizabeth was amazed that she did not miscarry the baby. She had found out that she was three months pregnant. She realized, by the time she was ready to leave, she would likely be showing.

Arthur could fire her for being pregnant. A pregnancy clause resided in her contract, and she had agreed *not* to get pregnant. Elizabeth tried to put these fears aside. If Arthur fired her, then she would just have to accept his dismissal. Right now, her primary focus was on completely overcoming her addiction and taking control of her life once again.

* * * *

Elizabeth opened the door to Dr. Cleaver's office. She had a private therapy session. She stepped into his office and stopped in pure, unadulterated shock. Alan sat on the sofa, less than five feet away.

Their eyes met and held. Alan's expression completely neutral, he neither smiled nor grimaced, so Elizabeth could not tell if he was happy to see her again or not. *What on earth is he doing here?* she pondered, her stomach nervously tumbling.

It had been a very long time since Elizabeth could remember being so terribly self-conscious or miserably anxious. However, she sadly recognized that she had not allowed herself the liberty. Cocaine had always been close at hand, and she had used it plentifully at the first sign of discomfort.

"H...Hi, Alan," she finally stuttered, managing to break her stunned silence.

"Hi, Elizabeth," he returned her greeting.

Alan's familiar, pleasant, deep baritone voice; his handsome face; and his sparkling blue eyes caused pleasurable stirrings within Elizabeth. She wanted to ask him what he was doing at the hospital. However, instead of engaging Alan in intelligent conversation, she silently gaped at him, helplessly unable to snap out of her dazed stupor.

"Elizabeth, are you okay?" Alan inquired, after several more minutes of strained silence.

"I'm sorry, Alan," Elizabeth managed to utter in a quiet voice. "It's just...it's totally a shock seeing you again. Especially in...like...this place. What are you doing here?"

"I...um...your father...he asked me to come. He said it was important for your recovery for you to talk with me again. So...here I am," Alan confessed. He seemed a bit unsure of his actions now.

"My dad shouldn't have pulled you into the middle of this mess," Elizabeth stated.

She was a little upset with her father now. She had discussed with him that her psychiatrist had said he thought she needed to talk with Alan and deal with her feelings head-on about their breakup. Evidently, her father had now shared this information with Alan.

"Elizabeth, your dad is concerned about you. So am I," Alan pointed out in a calm, convincing voice. "We just want to do everything in our power to see that you kick your addiction. You're all your dad has left now. He was pretty broken up at the funeral home."

"You were there?" Elizabeth asked in surprise.

Alan merely nodded.

"I wish I could have been there with my dad," Elizabeth stated, looking down at her shoes.

Alan was sorry he had mentioned the funeral home. Something had made him go there when he had read about Elizabeth's mother's death in the paper. He had expected to see Elizabeth there. Her father had shared that she was in the hospital overcoming an addiction to drugs. Alan had been happy to hear that Elizabeth was finally facing her problem. Part of him still deeply cared about her, even though he had tried to deny this fact. Face to face with her again, the feelings flooded back. Alan did not know whether to stand and bolt, or embrace Elizabeth.

"So what exactly does my father hope your visit will accomplish?" Elizabeth boldly asked.

"Your total recovery," he answered with assurance.

"Or does he hope for the two of us to…like…get back together?" she dared to ask.

She held her breath as she waited for his answer. Her heart hammered against her ribcage. She suddenly wanted to run out of the room without waiting for Alan's response. She feared the rejection that was sure to come.

"I'm quite certain that was the furthest thing from his mind," Alan replied with confidence. Then in a quiet voice with down-turned eyes, he stated, "He also told me that you and Jameson are expecting a baby." He absently glanced at Elizabeth's abdomen before meeting her eyes again. "I guess the two of you are closer than ever. Will there be a wedding on the heels of you leaving this place?"

"I don't really think Jameson cares what I do anymore," Elizabeth angrily admitted, watching the pained expression turn to puzzlement on Alan's face. "The last time I saw, or talked to, Jameson, he was trying to convince me to have an abortion. I figure he's angry and disappointed in me both for checking into the hospital and for not aborting the baby. But, you know, I can't focus on Jameson right now. I'm fully focused on myself and my recovery."

"That's good," Alan said, sounding a bit distracted. "That's the way it should be."

He was still digesting that Jameson had asked Elizabeth to have an abortion. He could not imagine him doing such a thing. *How can a man want to kill his own child? What a bastard!* "I'm sorry about Jameson, Elizabeth," Alan found himself saying.

Before she could reply, Doctor Cleaver opened the door behind her and walked into the room. "What's going on here, doc?" Elizabeth turned her head and asked him.

He shut the door and instructed, "Why don't you have a seat beside Mr. Michaels. I feel we all need to talk."

"I was planning on sitting down and talking with *you*," Elizabeth said. "But what I want to know is why Alan is here and why it is so crucial to my recovery?"

The doctor walked over to his desk and had a seat. He pointed to the couch. Elizabeth reluctantly walked over and sat down beside Alan. His pleasant, familiar smell caused long forgotten yearning in Elizabeth. She stared at Doctor Cleaver and tried to ignore that Alan sat beside her.

"I strongly feel the two of you still have some serious, unresolved issues. I'd like to see if we could perhaps begin to deal with those today," Dr. Cleaver revealed, leaning back in his chair, grasping the padded arms, and tapping his fingers on the end.

"Do you really want to talk about things now, Alan?" Elizabeth asked, daring to look him in the eye. "Because the last time I saw you, you said we had nothing further to say to one another. I got the impression you never wanted to see me again. I'm still shocked to see you here."

Alan looked down at the sofa and picked at a loose button for a few moments before he looked back up at Elizabeth and revealed, "You're right. I would not be here today if your father hadn't practically begged me to come."

"So you're, like, only here out of pity?" Elizabeth inquired with a sad frown.

"Yes...and no," he replied. "If I didn't still care, I wouldn't have come. Regardless of whether I felt sorry for your dad or you. So...it's more than just pity."

His confession of feelings caused Elizabeth's heart to ache. "I still care about you too, Alan," Elizabeth admitted. "I'm sorry I hurt you," she apologized again, vividly remembering his crushed expression the morning he had found her with Jameson.

"Elizabeth, why don't you tell Alan exactly how you've dealt with your pain over your breakup with him?" the doctor suggested.

Elizabeth gave him an aggravated stare. "What are you trying to get me to say, Doctor Cleaver?" she asked. "If you are trying to get me to tell Alan that I became a cocaine addict because of our breakup, that is so totally *not* true," she disagreed, looking at Alan and shaking her head. "The truth is Alan and I broke up because I *was* a drug addict...or already on my way to becoming one. I did things I never would have if it hadn't been for my coke use. Things like...like sleeping with Jameson," Elizabeth stated, lowering her eyes in shame.

"Uh-huh," Dr. Cleaver agreed, steepling his fingers and touching them to his chin, a familiar mannerism. "And your relationship came to a screeching, heartrending close because of your drug addiction. But there never was any real closure on your part. You treated your tattered emotions to a drug-masked haze. Am I right?"

"Yeah. For sure. I've already admitted to this," Elizabeth pointed out.

"Here's where the problem lies...you used cocaine as a crutch. Now you no longer have that crutch, so the buried pain will erupt. In fact, I'd say some of it is coming to the surface just in seeing Alan today. So you will now have to deal with this underlying pain. If you don't, your suppressed pain will weigh you down, ultimately overwhelming you. Consequently, you will be very tempted to abuse drugs again. This is what you need to understand, and why you need to face that pain head-on once and for all," Doctor Cleaver explained.

"So do you want to talk about all this, Alan?" Elizabeth asked, looking at him for the first time in several moments.

"If it will help you deal with the pain...then yes," he said. He sat nervously on the edge of the sofa, rubbing his hands together.

"You'd do that for me...even after what I put you through?" Elizabeth asked. She was so touched, tears sprang to her eyes.

"Yes, I will," Alan said, unable to resist reaching to touch her hand.

His supportive touch moved Elizabeth even more. She began to cry; her shoulders quivered. Without hesitation, Alan enfolded her in his strong arms. His simple, tender gesture warmly stirred Elizabeth's very soul. She had forgotten how wonderful it felt to have his reassuring arms wrapped around her.

It dawned on Elizabeth that she had never felt as secure in Jameson's arms, nor had his mere touch so thoroughly aroused her. Elizabeth wished she could remain in Alan's uplifting arms forever. Her heart thumped steadily against his robust chest, and she thought she could feel his heart beating steadily as well.

"Very good," Doctor Cleaver's voice interrupted their private interlude. "Now let's talk."

So began an extended series of stringent, soul-searching therapy sessions between Elizabeth and Alan. Eventually, after both openly and honestly shared their deepest hurts, they formed a friendship. Elizabeth was grateful for her father's meddling, and she soon held Dr. Wallace Cleaver in high esteem, supremely grateful for all of his wisdom and careful guidance.

Chapter 27
Leaving on a Jet Plane

Sadness always precedes a loved one leaving. Especially hard is a father letting go of his daughter.

~ Sissy Marlyn ~

A month after Elizabeth voluntarily checked into the hospital, Dr. Cleaver and Elizabeth's support group unanimously concluded she was healthy enough to leave the safety of the rehab center. The evening before her release, Alan came to visit one last time. They sat at a table in the corner of the recreation room. Others in the room played cards, watched television, and visited with other visitors.

"So are you nervous about leaving?" Alan asked.

"For sure," Elizabeth honestly relayed.

Already four months pregnant and beginning to show, Elizabeth was supposed to be flying back to California the next day. Filming for her new movie would begin again immediately. MGM wanted to finish filming before it was time for her to deliver. Elizabeth was more than a little anxious about going back.

Alan looked down at the Formica table top and drummed his fingers for a few seconds. Then he looked Elizabeth in the eye and said, "I've been thinking…I don't like you going back to California alone."

"I for sure don't like it either," she confessed, an apprehensive expression on her face. "But what else can I do?" She shrugged her shoulders and continued, "I'm under contract to finish the movie, and they, like, want me back ASAP. And if there is one thing I've totally learned since being in here, I have to face up to my fears. Going back is one of them."

"Yeah...but I don't think you should have to face your fears alone..."

"What other option do I have?" Elizabeth asked with confusion.

"I...I could go with you," he gingerly suggested, biting on his thumbnail.

"You...you could do what?" Elizabeth questioned, eyeballing him in disbelief.

"I've got a couple of weeks vacation coming. I could fly out to California with you. I probably can't be on the soundstage with you. That you would have to handle alone. But I could be there for you all the other time."

"You...you'd do that?" Elizabeth asked, still shocked.

"We're friends now, right?" Alan questioned. "Aren't friends supposed to be there for one another?"

"Yeah...but...that's a little over the top...for 'just friends'."

"Why? I'll just make sure you settle in okay. Then you'll be on your own. Or...maybe you won't be on your own..."

"If you are referring to Jameson when you say that, the answer is I *will* be *on my own*. Jameson and I have to work together to finish the movie. But that's all we will be is co-stars. Nothing else," Elizabeth staunchly maintained.

I hope that's all you'll be, Alan was thinking. Whether he and Elizabeth were romantically involved or not, he did not want to see her end up back with Jameson. He thought he was scum. "So how about it? Can I escort you back to California then?" Alan asked.

"I...I don't know, Alan," Elizabeth unsurely responded. "I don't want to use you as a crutch. That's what cocaine was. I need to start standing on my own two feet."

"I agree," Alan said. "But can it really hurt to have a soft place to fall? Just for a short time?"

"You are mighty convincing," Elizabeth said with a smile and a nervous chuckle, reaching to squeeze his hand in gratitude.

"Then go with your gut, and say yes," Alan prodded.

Elizabeth looked into his caring eyes. She could use some support in getting started out again, and he would only be there a short time. "Okay," she agreed.

"It's nice to have you back, Elizabeth," he stated with a bittersweet smile.

"What do you mean?" she asked, puzzled. *What was he suggesting?*

"I lost you to the drugs. I didn't much like the other woman. I liked the one I originally met and the one who is back now," he clarified, giving her a brief hug.

"Thanks. It's good to be back," she declared with a proud grin.

Alan released her then. "I better be going. Can I pick you up tomorrow? We can ride to the airport together. Are you leaving out of Louisville?"

"Yes. But...dad was supposed to pick me up. How about you meet us at the house? I'd like a little time alone with him before I leave."

"Sure. I understand," Alan said. "I'll see you tomorrow at the house then. What time?"

"I get out of here at 10:00 a.m."

"See you at about 10:15 then, okay?"

"Okay. For sure. See ya," Elizabeth said, giving him another smile.

It felt strange to be making plans with Alan again. Yet, it also felt oh-so-right. Elizabeth suddenly looked forward to leaving the hospital, instead of dreading it as she had been. It was good to have Alan back in her life again, even if he was just a friend – and even if her heart did still ache a little because they could no longer be more to one another.

* * * *

Elizabeth's stomach tumbled as she left the hospital walls. Carol, her sponsor, and Dr. Wallace, both gave her hugs and words of encouragement to boost her morale. Her dad took her hand, as if she were a child, and led her down the bland hallway to an elevator, and out the front doors of the hospital, with a smile on his face. "I'm proud of you, Elizabeth," he said, as they stepped outside into bright sunshine.

"Thanks, daddy," she said, taking a deep breath and walking with him to the car in the parking lot.

The birds sung in the trees and the sun warmed her face. *I'm on my own again.* The thought scared her to death right now. *One day at a time*, she reminded herself, taking one last glance at the hospital – a six-story, brick building and…her sanctuary.

Elizabeth climbed into her dad's Mercury. As her dad started the car and headed out, he glanced at Elizabeth and told her, "I'm going to miss you, sweetie. The house is really empty with…with…your mom gone."

"I'm sure," she said, reaching to pat his hand. "I miss mom too, dad. There was a time when I never would have for sure thought I would have said that. But we totally got a lot closer after I found out she was dying. I hate that I've…like…let her down."

"Let her down? How so?" he asked, his brow puckering. He looked away, out the windshield, as he pulled out onto the highway.

"By getting involved with drugs. And…by doing the very thing she always feared…getting pregnant. She'd be heartbroken if she were still alive, wouldn't she?"

Her dad stopped at a traffic light, he turned his head to look Elizabeth in the eye. "Her heart would have ached for what you've been through…yes," he admitted. "But you haven't let her down. You faced your problem and conquered it. I think she is looking down and is proud of you. And I know she would have liked to have known her…her grandchild."

He turned his head to look back out the windshield as the light turned green and he moved the car forward again. Elizabeth noticed his eyes looked misty. "I wish she could still be here to get to know her grandchild too," she told him, squeezing his hand.

Her dad reached and turned on the radio. Elizabeth almost wished that he had *not*, because he listened to AM radio. But she knew he was trying to gain control of his emotions, so it was grin-and-bear the talk radio for the rest of the drive home.

* * * *

Alan's car was parked in front of the house. Her dad pulled the Mercury up in front of the garage and shifted into park. "Looks like your ride is already here," he commented. His lips straight-lined and his eyes relayed sadness.

"Yeah. For sure," Elizabeth uttered. "My flight leaves in a few hours. And an hour and a half of that will, like, be spent driving to Louisville."

Elizabeth's father pulled the key out of the ignition and opened his door. Elizabeth also vacated the car. Alan walked up the driveway toward them. His teeth, eyes and hair all shined in the sunlight.

"It's good to see you on the outside again," he commented, approaching Elizabeth, placing his arm around her waist and giving her a slight squeeze.

Elizabeth automatically wrapped her arm around him and squeezed him back. "Thanks. It's nice to be on the outside," she said, feeling this way for the first time.

"Yeah. I just wish she could be *here* for a little bit longer," her dad chipped in, leaning on the back of the car.

"I do too, daddy," Elizabeth said, moving out of Alan's loose embrace and coming to stand beside her dad. "I totally dread going back to California."

"Then why don't you tell them to stick their movie, and stay here," her dad encouraged.

"I can't, daddy," she said, her eyes remorseful. "I have a contract with them. And...I'll need the money. I'm going to be a single mother."

"You know that you and the baby are welcome right here with me," he said, pointing to the house.

"I know, daddy. And I for sure appreciate that," Elizabeth said, kissing him on the cheek. "Right now, though...I've got to go inside and get my stuff. Alan and I really need to motor."

"Okay," he begrudgingly agreed.

As they started toward the house, he looked back over his shoulder at Alan. "Thank you for offering to look out for Elizabeth, Alan. I've been worried about her going back to California on her own. You're a fine young man. I would have been proud to have had you for a son-in-law."

"Daddy!" Elizabeth chastised, looking back at him, a mortified expression on her face.

"It's okay, Elizabeth," Alan said with a chuckle, patting her dad's upper arm. "I wouldn't have minded having you as a father-in-law either," he said.

Elizabeth quickly opened the door. This conversation was getting way too weird for her. *It's time to gather my stuff and get the heck out of here*, she concluded. She headed down the hall to her bedroom. There was not much stuff to pack. She had brought very little from California, and her dad had brought some of her things up to her at the hospital.

She took a few seconds to throw what few items still remained into a small travel case. Then she rushed back up the hall. Alan and her father still stood in the doorway. They laughed and seemed to be very comfortable with one another. Elizabeth's heart twisted as she realized she wished Alan *could* have been her husband.

She quickly chased away this sad thought, plastered on a smile, and announced, "I'm ready to go."

Alan reached to take the travel case from her. "I'll go put this in the car and give you and your dad a few more minutes alone," he said.

"Thanks, Alan," Both Elizabeth and her dad said in unison.

Alan opened the front door and stepped outside, closing it behind him.

"I guess this is it," her dad said, rocking on his heels.

"I guess so," Elizabeth concurred. "I'll call you when I get to the penthouse. And I'll keep in touch. It won't be like we are totally cut off from one another."

"It better not be," he pretended to chastise.

He opened his arms and Elizabeth collapsed into a tight bear hug. "I love you, daddy. Call anytime," she said.

"I love you too, sweetie. You can come home anytime. Damn the money or some contract."

"Thanks, daddy," Elizabeth said again, giving him a peck on the lips. "I *really* have to go."

He nodded and released her from his arms. He watched as she opened the door. Elizabeth blew him one final kiss before she shut the door. It was hard leaving him. She hated that he would be all alone. *I'll call as often as I can*, she vowed.

Alan waited by the passenger side of the car. He swung the door open as Elizabeth approached. A melancholy pain touched her heart again. *He's such a gentleman, and he always treated me so well. How could I have hurt him so?*

"You okay?" he asked, noticing her pinched face.

"Yeah..." she answered. Then she added, "It's hard. It's hard leaving dad all alone. And...well...I...like...miss what we had. I hate that I blew it." Tears suddenly stood in her eyes.

"Hey," Alan said, pulling her into an embrace. "No negative stuff. We weren't even talking and now we're friends again. The girl I met..." He stopped then because he almost said, 'and fell in love with'. *No, don't go there*, he told himself. He started again with, "As I said before...you're back, Elizabeth. Let's celebrate. Not mourn the past. Okay?" he asked, tipping up her chin.

Their eyes met and Elizabeth was seized by a strong urge to kiss Alan. *No! We're only friends!* she had to remind herself, looking away from his alluring eyes. "You're right," she agreed, reaching to wipe away a few tears that had escaped. "Let's get out of here. We need to get on with the future now, and put the past behind."

"Now that's the spirit!" Alan said.

Elizabeth climbed into the car, and he hurried around to his side, so they could be on their way.

Chapter 28

Reconciliation

A hug and a kiss from a friend is nice, but
a hug and a kiss from someone you love is tops!

~ Sissy Marlyn ~

When Elizabeth and Alan arrived at the penthouse, Elizabeth stood before the door fidgeting with her key. She dreaded going inside. This place held a lot of bad memories for her.

"This is a nice entranceway," Alan teased, noticing her uneasiness. He looked up at the crown molding around the ceiling and back at the gold-plated, private elevator behind him. "I'd sure like to see the inside of the place though."

Elizabeth sucked in a deep breath. Then she stuck the key in the lock and turned it. She listened to the click, took another renewing breath, and pushed open the door. Looking inside, she felt only sadness.

Alan took a gentle hold on her upper arm and urged her forward. He shut and locked the door behind them. Walking up beside Elizabeth, he surveyed his surroundings, taking in the cushy furniture, hot tub, wet bar, perfect color scheme, and expensive looking paintings on the wall. Everything was in its place – obviously the maid service was tops. The place nice, it did not have a homey feel to Alan.

"So we've made it inside," he commented, noting Elizabeth seemed to be frozen in place. "Are you going to show me around?"

"I hate being here," Elizabeth stated in a gruff voice, cringing.

"Bad memories, huh?" Alan asked.

"Yeah…for sure…that is, the memories I have. The rest is totally a drug-hazed blur. I stayed high most of the time. In fact…I don't think there is any left…but we probably should for sure be on the alert for packages of cocaine. I totally don't want them in sight or within reach."

"I understand," Alan said. "I'm glad I'm here with you. I wouldn't have wanted you to face this alone."

"I'm glad you are here too," Elizabeth said, giving him a slight smile and breathing a sigh of relief. "Come on. I'll show you around," she finally offered, taking his hand.

* * * *

When the alarm went off at 4:00 a.m. the next morning, Elizabeth, with a groan, snapped the button to shut it off. She had not been up this early in a very long time, and it had been an even longer time since she had gotten up this early without waking up with a dose of coke. She sat up on the side of the bed, stretching and trying to shake sleep from her brain.

Standing, she made her way over to a switch on the wall by the door. Upon flipping the switch, light from a ceiling lamp doused the room. Elizabeth's eyes squinted in retaliation, but she left the offensive light on. She made her way over to the dresser to extract some underwear from a drawer. Then she went into the connecting bathroom to revitalize herself with a shower. *I can do this*, she told herself.

* * * *

Alan was still asleep when Elizabeth left the penthouse. She left him a note, thanking him again for being in California with her and telling him to have a great day. In the limo, on the way to the set, Elizabeth's head began to throb, her stomach to twirl, and she broke out in a cold sweat.

She wanted to bang on the partition between the limo driver and her and ask him to pull over and let her out. The air in the car felt too thin. *You're just used to your nerves being calmed by coke*, she accepted. She felt an all too familiar yearning. She rubbed her forehead and temples, and she silently prayed for strength. *I can do this*, she told herself again. *One day at a time. Or right now…one minute at a time.*

* * * *

The limo stopped, and Elizabeth heard the driver's door slam. *Shit! We're here!* she concluded.

A few seconds later, her door opened and the chauffeur looked in at her. Elizabeth slowly emerged from the limousine. The driver shut her door behind her and wished her a good day. He made his way back around to the driver's side, got in, and drove away.

Elizabeth's feet felt like lead as she propelled them in the direction of the soundstage door. She could feel her heart beating at her temples as she pulled open the door and walked inside.

Looking across the way, by the lighted set, she spied Jameson and Ryan. Ryan started in her direction. "Welcome back, Elizabeth," he said, giving her a forced smile.

The first thing that took her by surprise was that Ryan had cut his shoulder length hair short. Next, she noticed he did not have on his glasses. "Ryan, I almost didn't recognize you," Elizabeth stated. "Less hair, and no glasses."

"Well...I was pulling out my hair trying to keep on schedule without one of my main stars being here," he declared. He waited a second for Elizabeth's response. When she said nothing, he continued, "My girlfriend talked me into contact lenses, so here's the new, improved me. I'm assuming I am talking to the new and improved *you*. No longer getting wasted and about to become a mom in a few months," he stated rather sarcastically.

"That's right," Elizabeth stated, trying to sound confident.

"Okay. Here's the deal. We've filmed everything we could without you. These next several weeks, we are going to be on a very tight schedule. We will film everything we need to on this soundstage. Then we'll move to the next and film all we need to on that one. And so on. As to your pregnancy, we are going to film around that. We will film you from the waist up. Anything else we need, we'll use a stand-in. Have you got all that? Are you up to the challenge?"

"Yeah. For sure," Elizabeth answered both questions at once. She noticed she was wringing her hands, so she dropped her arms to her sides. "When do we start," she challenged. It was almost as if Ryan was being confrontational and trying to make her nervous, and Elizabeth was determined not to let him get the better of her.

"ASAP," he answered. "You make your way off to *Makeup and Wardrobe*. Here's the script for the first scene."

Elizabeth took the pages from his hands. Ryan gave her a hard stare. Then he turned and walked away.

Elizabeth looked back toward the lighted set before she made her way off. Jameson still stood there, glaring at her. He had made no attempt to start in her direction. Elizabeth averted her eyes and started off to *Makeup and Wardrobe*.

* * * *

Later that day, after successfully filming several scenes, Elizabeth was in her trailer quickly studying her lines for the next one. There was a knock at the door. When she opened the door, she found Jameson standing there. They had not filmed a scene together yet. The next one would be their first.

"Hello, Liz," Jameson said, eyeballing her with a serious expression on his face.

"Hello, Jameson," she said, no sign of a happy, welcoming smile on her face. "I'd prefer you call me Elizabeth."

"O…kay," he stated in a mocking voice. "Do you mind if I come in? I think we need to talk."

Elizabeth felt her heart race. *What if he comes inside and tries to get me to do cocaine again?* She stepped out of the trailer and shut the door behind her. "Actually, I'd rather *talk* out here."

"Why are you so uncomfortable around me?" Jameson asked, staring holes through her.

"Well…the last time we were together you were, like, giving me coke right and left and trying to convince me to have an abortion. That might have something to do with it," she stated, crossing her arms across her chest.

"Hey…don't make it sound like I pushed cocaine on you. You were begging for it. I only gave it to you in the first place because you were already hooked on speed. So don't go dumping your cocaine addiction in my lap," he growled, sinking his hands in his pockets.

"What are you like here for Jameson?" she asked, becoming impatient. She had lines to study and no time to argue with him. As far as she was concerned, they were merely co-stars now.

"I think we have some unresolved issues," he acknowledged, bouncing on his toes.

"What unresolved issues?" Elizabeth questioned, separating her arms and placing her hands on her hips.

"How about the fact that you are carrying my kid, E...liz...abeth?" he snapped, sliding a hand out of his pocket to point at her swollen abdomen.

"Oh...so now it's a *kid*?" she sarcastically inquired, folding her hands over her belly. "The last I heard from you it was just some *thing* to be gotten rid of."

"It may still be a *thing*, if it's born retarded or deformed," Jameson hostilely pointed out.

"To you maybe," she said with an ugly grimace on her face. "To me it will still be a child. And I'll love him or her regardless."

"And what do you expect from me?" Jameson asked, raking a hand through his hair.

"Absolutely nothing," Elizabeth answered with conviction. "I for sure don't want anything from you, Jameson. Not even friendship. I just want to finish this movie, and then we'll go our separate ways. Sound like a plan?"

"Sounds like a plan, Liz. We were never friends anyway. Did you really think we were?" Jameson questioned. "We both used one another. I used you for sex and you used me for drugs. You were green as grass when you first started. I used that to my advantage, and you fell right into my hands. In fact...do you want to know a little secret?"

"I doubt it," she stated. "I really need to get back to studying my script." She had turned and was reaching for the doorknob to her trailer.

"I'll tell you anyway," Jameson said, grabbing her arm. "You and I might never have been together to make that bastard if I hadn't gotten you so wasted that night at Arthur's after the People's Choice Awards."

"Why is that a secret?" Elizabeth asked, pulling her arm free. "I know I did a lot of stupid stuff due to using cocaine."

"That's just it," Jameson laughed. "You did *not*."

"What are you going on about, Jameson?" she questioned in exasperation.

He drew in very close to her ear and said, "You passed out that night, Liz. You never knew we were having sex. I hadn't planned on Alan walking in and catching us, but that couldn't have happened any better if I had planned it. From there on out, you were mine...all mine. I always get what I want, and I wanted you. I don't want this kid you are carrying though."

"Did you...did you just say you...you r...raped me?" Elizabeth asked. Her mouth had dropped open and gone dry all at once. She stared at Jameson with large, rounded eyes.

"Rape is when a woman says no, Liz. You weren't saying anything," Jameson stated with a sinister smile all across his face.

"You bastard!" Elizabeth exclaimed, balling her fists and striking his shoulders.

Jameson took a tight grip on her arms and pushed her away. "No...that's the kid you are carrying," he declared. "I'll see you on the set, Liz. The sooner we finish filming this movie the better."

Elizabeth watched him walk away. She felt sick to her stomach. The morning after the first night they had spent together played through her head again. She never had been able to remember what happened. Now, Jameson had filled in the blanks. He had raped her. She and Alan had broken up because Jameson had raped her.

Shaking, Elizabeth opened the door, went back inside her trailer, and collapsed on the couch. *How am I going to continue working with that monster?* she wondered in agony. She had harbored disdain for Jameson because he had wanted her to have an abortion and had not contacted her since she had been gone. But now, she considered him absolutely evil. *What am I going to do?* she questioned, rubbing her head.

She wanted to leave the soundstage and not return. She wanted to go to the police and press charges against Jameson. *But how can I do that? It's his word against mine, and I was drunk and stoned that night. I have no real proof of anything. Oh, God! I'm carrying this monster's child.*

She fisted her hand and punched the pillows on the couch. Then she laid back and cried. She had thought her life was taking a turn for the better, but now she was not sure. Elizabeth was lost in a haze of misery and confusion.

* * * *

Alan was watching a rented movie on the large screen television in the recreation room at the penthouse when he thought he heard a door slam. He hit the pause button on the VCR and turned down the volume on the television.

He got up off the couch and headed up the short hall toward the living room. He was surprised to see Elizabeth sitting on the sofa in this room. "You're home awfully early, aren't you?" he asked with a smile.

His voice startled her and she jumped.

"I'm sorry. I didn't mean to scare you," he said. As he started toward her, he noticed she had been crying. "What happened? Didn't it go well today?" he asked. "You should have woke me up this morning. I would have gone to the soundstage with you. If they would let me."

She looked up at Alan's caring face, and Elizabeth burst into tears. Alan took a bouncing seat on the couch beside her and pulled her into his arms. "What did they do?" he asked again.

"Th...*they* didn't do anything," Elizabeth revealed. "It...It's Jameson..."

"What did that SOB do?" Alan asked, bristling.

Elizabeth wanted to tell Alan exactly what Jameson had done, but she feared his reaction. If he did something stupid and went after Jameson, he would be arrested. She did not want to see Alan get into trouble. Her stupid actions had already caused him enough pain.

"I...I just can't work with Jameson anymore, Alan," Elizabeth professed in despair. "He...he called the b...baby a bastard."

"He's the bastard!" Alan exclaimed, holding Elizabeth and stroking her back.

It felt marvelous to Elizabeth being held in his arms again. She never anticipated what happened next. She never intentionally meant to kiss Alan, but it happened nonetheless. The comforting familiarity of his touch and his highly desirable, masculine smell drew her to him like a strong magnet.

First, she gently touched her grateful lips to the side of his balmy neck. However, when Alan stirred in response, drawing his head back a short distance, Elizabeth allowed her responsive mouth to greedily make contact with his. Despite himself, Alan heartily reciprocated.

They kissed for several moments before Alan broke contract, pushing Elizabeth away and exclaiming, "Whoa!"

"I'm sorry, Alan," Elizabeth began to apologize. "I know you don't want anything romantic with me anymore. I just..." She lowered her head down in her hands, shaking it. *One mistake after another. Where does it all end?* "Please don't be mad," she pleaded when she raised her head again.

"I...I'm not mad," he told her. "I just...I'm confused, that's all," he confessed.

"Confused?" she questioned with puzzled eyes.

"I...it's time I was honest with you, Elizabeth," he said, placing an arm along the top of the couch. "I...I still love you..."

"Oh my God, Alan!" she exclaimed, tears springing to her eyes again. "I still love you too. I never stopped..."

"But..."

"But?"

"I...I don't know...where do we go from here?" he asked, sounding a bit exasperated.

"I don't know either," she replied. "But whatever we do...we'll be doing it from Bowling Green. I quit the movie today."

"You...you did what?" he asked in surprise. "Are you sure that's what you want to do?"

"No," she confessed. "But I have no other choice. I can't work with Jameson. They said I will be held in contempt of contract. I won't be paid the rest of the $500,000 they promised me..."

"F...*five*...hundred thousand? For real? I had no idea you were being paid that much. Wow!"

"Yeah. But it's not worth it. I love acting, but not all of the *evils* that come with it. This isn't my world, Alan. And I don't want to raise my...my baby here."

Her heart ached as she thought of the child she was carrying. Once again, her mind screamed, 'The child of a man who raped me'. Elizabeth reached to rub her temples. "My life's a wreck. So I understand if you don't want to get involved with me again," she told Alan, peeking up at him. She had her elbow resting on the sofa arm and her head propped up on her hand.

As if her baby knew that it was being thought about and worried over, at that very instant, the child moved. "Oh!" Elizabeth declared with a slight, delighted giggle, raising her head and dropping both hands down on her tummy.

"What's going on?" Alan asked in bewilderment, intently watching Elizabeth laugh and clutch her stomach a little tighter.

"The baby's moving!" she proudly shared, still chuckling in response.

"No kidding? Can I feel?" Alan enthusiastically asked with utmost curiosity.

"For sure!" Elizabeth happily agreed without hesitation.

She swiftly took one of Alan's hands and placed it prominently in the center of her swollen abdomen. A wide smile spread across his face as soon as he felt the baby's determined movement under his hand. "Wow! That is really neat! It feels a little like you have popcorn popping in there. Does he or she move around like that often?!" he inquired with apparent excitement.

"It's only every so often," Elizabeth disclosed.

She was touched that Alan had referred to the baby as *he* or *she* instead of *it*. Elizabeth's heart was both warmed and a little saddened. Glad to be able to share the joy of her child's movement with Alan, at the same time, Elizabeth was a bit sad because Alan was not the child's father. *How different everything would be if that were the case.*

"You okay?" he asked, noticing her silence.

"Yeah. Just wishing things could be different," she confessed, a bittersweet smirk on her face.

"Me too," Alan admitted. His emotions were very mixed as well at the moment.

A phone ring interrupted their private moment together. Alan got up and walked over to the desk to answer it. "It's your agent. Christopher, right?" he asked Elizabeth, holding out the phone.

Elizabeth halfheartedly got up from the sofa and walked over to the desk, taking the phone from Alan's outstretched hand.

"Elizabeth," Christopher addressed, "Arthur Goldbloom called me. Why'd you walk off the set today? He said Ryan told him you said you were quitting."

"I am," she replied in a somber voice.

"Why?" he asked.

"I can't work with Jameson Thornton," Elizabeth responded. "He said some pretty nasty things to me today, and I refuse to work with him. They can sue me or whatever."

"Whew!" Christopher blew into the phone. He could tell his young star was determined. "Okay. What if we can do this…what if you don't have to film any other scenes with Jameson? Will you stay and finish the movie then?"

"How can that be possible?" she asked, her forehead furrowing.

"You let me handle that. If I can arrange that and promise you that you won't have to work with Jameson Thornton anymore, will you stay?" he probed.

"If Jameson is taken out of the picture, then yes…I will stay," Elizabeth answered. She really did not want to let Arthur down.

"Let me work my magic then," Christopher said. "I'll talk to you a little later. You just hang tight."

"Okay," Elizabeth agreed. She hung up the phone then.

"So are we staying or leaving?" Alan asked.

"I guess we are staying…for now," Elizabeth replied. "Look, Alan, I for sure don't want you getting hurt again. So if you think I'm jerking you around, then maybe you should just go home."

Alan closed the small distance between them. He placed his arms around Elizabeth's neck. "I don't want to go anywhere," he said and drew in for a kiss.

Elizabeth kissed him back. They stood kissing for several moments again then. Elizabeth thought she had died and gone to heaven. "Wow!" she gasped when they finally separated. "That felt so totally right."

"Didn't it though? I'm where I should be…right here with you," Alan professed with a blissful smile, giving her another kiss. "We'll find a way to work all this out, Elizabeth. I lost you once. I don't intend to again."

"I love you so much, Alan!" she uttered, the tears starting again.

"I love you too, Elizabeth," he said, pulling her into an assuring embrace.

Chapter 29
The Proposal

What's that old song? Love and Marriage...Love and Marriage...They go together like the horse and carriage.

~ Sissy Marlyn ~

The next day, Elizabeth went back to the Culver City soundstage to begin filming again. Even though they were not happy about it, MGM agreed to film all of Elizabeth's scenes without Jameson. It would mean a lot of unnecessary work on their part, splicing together two separate scenes to make it appear Jameson and Elizabeth were together. But the alternative, scrapping what they had already filmed and starting from scratch with a new actress, would have been disastrous to their movie budget. The drawback was Elizabeth's name would be mud in the industry from now on.

Elizabeth did not care about getting a black mark on her professional reputation at this point. She merely wanted to fulfill her contract with MGM, finish the movie, collect the rest of her salary, and go home to Bowling Green. She wanted to be left alone to raise her child and to spend time with the one man she loved and would always love – Alan.

* * * *

Elizabeth arrived back at the penthouse that evening at 6:00 p.m. She was tired and hungry, but at least she had a sense of fulfillment.

Ryan had worked her hard from 5:00 a.m. until 5:00 p.m., barely giving her time to study lines in between scenes and to eat, but she believed everything had gone well that day.

When Elizabeth opened the door to the penthouse, she gasped. A candelabrum filled with burning candles sat on every table. Around the base of each one resided a wreath of beautiful flowers. Alan was sitting on the sofa, smiling at her.

"Alan, what is all this?" Elizabeth called, returning his smile.

"Just a little surprise," he said, standing. He walked over to her and held out his hand. Elizabeth took it. "You must be hungry. Why don't we go into the dining room?"

As they approached the dining room, also lit by a candelabrum that sat in the middle of the dining room table, Elizabeth could smell a delightful aroma coming from the kitchen. "You cooked too?" she asked.

"No, not...exactly," he replied with a chuckle. He released her hand, pulled a chair back from the table and directed Elizabeth to have a seat. Then he pushed her chair back up to the table. "Sit tight. I'll be right back."

Elizabeth stared at the dancing candlelight on the white china plate in front of her and in the glass of the china cabinet against the wall. Alan disappeared through the wooden hinged doors leading into the kitchen. A second later, he reappeared. He pulled out a chair across from her and took a seat.

The hinged door opened again, and a man in a chef's uniform came into the room with a platter of food. "Alan, what is all this?" Elizabeth asked with a delighted giggle.

"It...it's dinner," he said with a snicker and a shrug.

"Almond butter chicken with orange sauce to be exact," the man in the chef's hat announced. "May I place some on your plate, madam?"

"It sounds wonderful. Please do," Elizabeth told this stranger.

He carefully proceeded to use thongs to place some of the delectable entrée on both Elizabeth and Alan's plate. Then he sat the platter on the table between the two of them. Reaching under his arm, he pulled forth a peppermill. "Fresh ground pepper?" he asked Elizabeth.

"A little…yes," she answered, smiling at Alan as she watched the chef turn the peppermill and distribute a small bit of pepper across her meal.

The man spread some fresh pepper over Alan's portion as well. Then he left the room for a second. He came back with a crystal stemmed glass of milk for Elizabeth and a crystal stemmed glass of iced tea for Alan. "Enjoy! I'll be back to check on your drinks, and of course, to serve dessert when you are finished with the main entrée," he said as he turned and left the room again.

"I can't believe you did all this," Elizabeth told Alan, her eyes sparkling in the candlelight.

"Oh…you haven't seen anything yet," he replied with a knowing smile.

Elizabeth's heart was warmed by Alan's visual display of love for her. Her emotions on the edge because of her pregnancy, she almost felt like crying. Instead, she put some food in her mouth and concentrated on eating.

"Yum," she moaned. "This is good!"

"It is isn't it?" Alan agreed, placing a piece of chicken in his mouth as well. "So how was your day?"

Elizabeth and Alan settled into conversation about her busy day at the set then. Occasionally the chef would pop back in to fill their glasses, and as promised he brought them a luscious chocolate mousse dessert when they had finished their main entrée. He left after that, wishing them a good night.

"Thank you for all this, Alan," Elizabeth said, giving him a lingering kiss, as they both stood from the table after finishing dessert. "You treat me like a queen. You always have," she stated, tears of gratitude standing in her eyes.

"The night is young, Elizabeth," he said, taking her hand and leading her into the living room.

Alan led her over to the couch. Then he walked over to the stereo by the wet bar, placed a cassette in the player, and pushed play. Settling on the sofa with Elizabeth and placing his arm around her, he directed, "Close your eyes. Lay your head on my shoulder and listen very carefully to the words of this song. This is exactly how I feel. How I've always felt."

The song playing was Alabama's *When We Make Love*. Elizabeth did as Alan asked and laid her head on his shoulder, shut her eyes, and concentrated on the words of the song. She knew the song fairly well and had always liked it, but tonight, it took on a whole new meaning for her.

From this moment, it would always be her and Alan's song, and the words would always have a very special meaning for her.

> There's a light, in your eyes tonight.
> You know I know that look anywhere.
> You got plans, and I'm one lucky man.
> Before we get so carried away,
> There's just something I've been wanting to say.
>
> When we make love,
> It's more to me than just an affair.
> I want you to know how much I care.
> When we make love,
> Oh it's such a precious time.
> We share our hearts, our souls, and our minds,
> When we make love.

"Alan, if you are trying to seduce me, you are doing a wonderful job," Elizabeth purred, giving him a kiss packed with heat.

"Elizabeth, I love you very much," Alan said in a husky voice when the kiss ended.

"I love you too, Alan. From the bottom of my heart," Elizabeth proclaimed, taking his hand and placing it over her racing heart. "I want you to make love to me."

"And I will," he told her. "But I want tonight to seem as if you and I were on our honeymoon," he explained.

Elizabeth intently watched as he stood, reached in his pocket, pulled out a ring box, and swiftly knelt down on one knee in front of her. Gazing lovingly into her eyes and snapping the ring box open, he asked, "Elizabeth, will you put this ring on your finger and tell me you'll marry me? As soon as you say yes, and wear my ring, I want you to know, in my heart, I'll already consider you my wife. Even if we can't actually finalize things with a wedding until we get back to Bowling Green. I love you, and this has been too long coming."

Tears clouded Elizabeth's eyes as she looked at the ring. The large round diamond sparkled in the candlelight. She could barely catch her breath, and she was rendered completely speechless for a few seconds. Finally, she managed to take the box from Alan's hand. Her hand shook as she pulled forth the ring and slid it on her finger. It was a tight fit because her fingers were swollen because of her pregnancy. "I...I want...I want nothing more...than...than to be your wife," she muttered, forcing her useless tongue to begin to work.

Alan immediately sprang up and enfolded her in his arms, kissing away the tears that had escaped and were coursing down her cheeks. "This has been a long time coming. In fact...I had another ring I had bought for you. I was going to propose the...the night of the People's Choice Awards. I took that ring back," he confessed a little sadly, breaking eye contact with her for a moment.

"Alan...are you sure you want to marry me?" Elizabeth questioned. "I...I come with a lot of extra baggage," she said, looking down and placing her hand on her tummy.

Alan took his hand and placed it on top of hers. "When you let me feel the baby move yesterday, I...I came to a decision. This baby is a part of *you*. And I love *you*. So I'll love this little boy or girl too. We'll raise this child together. I'll love it like it was my own. We can't change the past, Elizabeth. But we can make a wonderful future together. Let's focus on the future, okay? Now...do you still want to be my wife?"

"I always have," she professed, throwing her arms around his neck again and smothering him with kisses. "Make love to me, Alan."

"That's exactly what I'm going to do," he told her.

He stood and scooped her into his arms and carried her off to the bedroom.

* * * *

The rest of Alan and Elizabeth's time in Marina Del Rey at her penthouse was unquestionably wonderful. Like newlyweds, they insatiably made love every evening. Elizabeth enjoyed waking up with

Alan beside her each morning. It all felt so right. They happily basked in their deep love for one another and their special time spent solely as a couple.

At the end of two weeks, when Alan had to go home, Elizabeth was very sad. They lay in bed and he held Elizabeth in his arms, stroking her hair. His flight left in three hours.

"I don't want to leave," he told her, kissing her temple.

"I don't want you go," she said, raising up and kissing him on the lips.

"You're only here another five weeks, but it'll seem like eternity," he told her, pushing the hair back from her face and kissing her again.

"I know," she agreed, her eyes relaying remorse. "But when I get home, we'll have a nice deposit for a bank account and a baby due in a few months. So you'll for sure need to keep your day job," she said with a bittersweet smile.

"Yep," he agreed. "I guess I better go take a shower and get dressed. I need to get to the airport early for my flight."

"I need to take a shower too. Because I'm going to the airport to see you off," she told him.

"Hmm...so are you thinking what I'm thinking then?" he asked with a devilish grin.

"If what you are thinking is that we should shower together, then our thoughts are totally in sync," she said, her eyes twinkling.

They both scrambled from the bed and eagerly headed off to the bathroom, arm in arm.

* * * *

Elizabeth was lonely without Alan. He called her each day and they talked and talked on the phone, but it was not the same as being face to face. She counted the days until filming would be complete, and she could go home to Bowling Green and her future with Alan.

The last week of filming, Jameson Thornton showed up at the soundstage. Elizabeth was unsettled to see him. She went to Ryan and complained. "He won't be filming scenes with you, Elizabeth," he assured her, his face strained. "He is here to film the scenes of the two of you that we are going to splice together. We're on a budget here, and since it will take extra time to work with these pieces of film, then

Jameson needs to be here filming *now*. There should be no reason the two of you have to talk or interact," he tried to reassure her.

Elizabeth did not like the fact that Jameson was there, but since Ryan assured her she would not have to work with him, she fell into a false sense of security. Jameson waylaid her one afternoon on the way to her trailer. He stood at the entranceway.

Elizabeth stopped dead in her tracks several feet away, considering her options. *Should I go back to the soundstage?* She did not want to run to Ryan like some schoolgirl tattling on a classmate. *What's the worst that can happen if I talk to Jameson? He makes my skin crawl, and I think he's a skank, but I can't let him think he has the upper hand.*

She started walking in his direction again. "Can I help you with something?" she asked as she drew near. There was an angry set to her face, and she had her arms crossed.

"Can you help *me*?" he asked, his voice laced with sarcasm. "You're helping me alright. You've trashed this movie. Keeping us from working together and having them splice scenes together. And even filming you from the waist up, you look like a fat cow. This movie's going to be a farce. I don't care if you throw your own career away, but it pisses me off that you have messed with mine."

"You should have thought about that before you *raped* me," Elizabeth spat, shuddering as the word ripped from her lips.

"You came back for lots more after that first night," Jameson reminded her, taking another step closer. Elizabeth backed away a few steps. "That sack of shit in your stomach is living proof of that."

"You're the sack of shit!" Elizabeth cursed, trying to stop her body from shaking. She was shaking both out of anger and because she was upset. "Get away from me Jameson, and stay away. Or I swear I'll place charges of rape against you. What do you think that would do to your precious image? I've already trashed mine, so I have nothing to lose. Right?"

"You're finished in this business, Elizabeth. You mark my words!" Jameson threatened, kicking the asphalt with his shoe. "Go back to Bowling Green and raise that bastard with your grease monkey boyfriend. It's where you belong. Down on the farm. A real nothing. Just like you were when you first started out on *Bardstown*. Just like you would have stayed if I hadn't come along and helped you. You would have been fired and sent home. You owe me."

"I owe you a slap across the face," she spurted, balling her fists. "And if you don't leave me alone, I might just give you exactly what you are owed."

"Ew...I'm real scared," he stated, laughing and holding his hands in front of him and shaking them. "I'm done with you. I've had my say. I'll be more than happy to steer clear of you. We are *done*, and so are you."

He turned and walked away in a huff. Elizabeth watched him go. When he was out of sight, she opened the door to her trailer, rushed inside, locked the door behind her, and collapsed on the nearby bench seat. She broke down and cried.

She was crying out of relief. She had held her own. It was over. She did not care if her Hollywood career was finished. She loved acting but not the atrocities that came along with it. She would finish out her days on the set and wash her hands of Hollywood and being a star. She would concentrate on being a loving wife to Alan and a good mom to her son or daughter.

Chapter 30

Home

Home is where the heart is.
It is also a refuge from the evils of the world.

~ Sissy Marlyn ~

Elizabeth and Alan married a month after she returned home. The priest in Elizabeth's parish allowed them to marry in haste due to the impending birth of her child – a child he believed to be Alan's.

Two months later, November 5, 1985, Elizabeth gave birth to a seven-pound baby girl. She was born with a full head of curly, jet black hair – just like her father's. Elizabeth tried not to think about the resemblance. She wanted to pretend Jameson Thornton was never a part of her life.

Alan was sitting in a chair, at the side of Elizabeth's hospital bed, coddling their newborn child. "Alan," Elizabeth called.

"Huh," he replied, looking up at Elizabeth.

He had been mesmerized by looking at the baby. He had been in the delivery room when Elizabeth had given birth and had been awed by it all. Now, he was awed by this tiny, soft child he held – *his* daughter.

"I've been thinking about what I'd like to name her," she said, pointing to the baby.

"What do you have in mind?" Alan asked. "She's cute as a button. Yes, you are," he said, looking down and talking to the baby. "We could always call her Buttons," he said, looking back up at Elizabeth with a playful smile on his face.

"I'd rather name her after you," Elizabeth said, gazing at him with love in her eyes.

"After me? We're going to call her Alan?" he asked. "Or my middle name is Paul. That's even worse…"

"No," Elizabeth chuckled. "I want to name her Alana. Alan with an A added to the end. Alana Gladys. If you don't mind using my mom's name for her middle name. I wish my mom could be here to see the baby," she stated, a sad expression appearing on her face.

"Alana Gladys Michaels," Alan said, smiling. "I like it. What do you think, Alana? Do you like being named after your dad…and your grandma?"

Just then it looked as if the baby smiled. "Hey! She likes it. She's smiling!" Alan exclaimed, holding her out to Elizabeth.

"Alan, I think her smile was gas. I don't think babies can smile when they are this young," Elizabeth said with a laugh.

"Bull! Where'd you hear that? Mommy is crazy, Alana. Do you know that?" he said, kissing the baby on her tiny forehead. Looking up and giving Elizabeth an ear-to-ear smile, he said, "I love you, Elizabeth." He was touched she had named the baby after him.

"I love you too, Alan," she said, returning his smile. *We're going to have a good life*, she thought with contentment. It felt good to be home again and to accept what was truly important in life – her love for her husband and her baby. Elizabeth would have a happy life in Bowling Green. *Acting be damned!*

Continue the Journey. . .

You have just completed the first novel in my *"B" Series*. Since you now
love the characters and would like to see what happens with
Elizabeth, Alan and young Alana,
check the **Sissy Marlyn** website
www.sissymarlyn.com
or
Bearhead Publishing:
www.bearheadpublishing.com
for release date on the next novel in the trilogy: *Bowling Green*.

Also on the horizon, for you mystery readers: the second installment of
the *Jury Pool* murder series – *A Killer's Mind* – due out
before Christmas 2006.

Keep reading. Remember: *Readers are Happy People!*

Thanks!

Sissy Marlyn

Printed in the United States
83093LV00005B/5/A